THE DAUGHTER'S DEFIANCE

Part 7
of
The Windsor Street Family Saga

By
VL McBeath

The Daughter's Defiance
By VL McBeath

Editing services provided by Susan Cunningham at Perfect Prose Services
Cover design by Books Covered

ISBNs: 978-1-913838-28-7 (Ebook Edition)
978-1-913838-29-4 (Paperback)

Main category - FICTION / Historical
Other category - FICTION / Sagas

Legal Notices

Explanatory Notes

Meal Times

In the United Kingdom, meal times are referred to by a variety of names. Based on traditional working-class practices in northern England in the nineteenth century, the following terms have been used:

Dinner: The meal eaten around midday. This may be a hot or cold meal depending on the day of the week and a person's occupation

Tea: Not to be confused with afternoon tea or the beverage of the same name, tea was the meal eaten at the end of the working day, typically around five or six o'clock. This could either be a hot or cold meal.

Afternoon tea: Taken at around four o'clock, this would typically consist of sandwiches, cakes, and a pot of tea.

Money

In the nineteenth century, the currency in the United Kingdom was Pounds, Shillings and Pence.

- There were twenty shillings to each pound and twelve pence to a shilling.
- A crown and half crown were five shillings and two shillings and sixpence, respectively.

For further information on Victorian-era England visit:
https://vlmcbeath.com/victorian-era

Previously in
The Windsor Street Family Saga

Set in Liverpool (UK), *The Windsor Street Family Saga* was inspired by a true story and it is **recommended that the books are read in order.**

For further information visit my website at:

https://valmcbeath.com/windsor-street/

Please note: This series is written in UK English

CHAPTER ONE

Liverpool, March 1895

The gates to Princes Park glistened in the early spring sunlight, but even the crocus, flowering along the edge of the grass, couldn't put a smile on the lips of Mrs Nell Marsh. Her husband, Thomas, strolled beside her, resting a hand on the pram she pushed ahead of her.

"Cheer up."

She sighed. "I will once the doctor sorts Maria out."

"At least she agreed to him calling. It's a start."

"It is, but to be honest, it's unsettled me. She wouldn't have seen him if she didn't think it was serious. I shouldn't have come out and left her..."

"Don't be silly. It's not as if she's on her own. Alice is with her. And Elenor and Leah. You said yourself it was better for us to take the children out for half an hour."

"I know, but..." She looked down at her great-nephew

Freddie, who slept in the pram, and his older brother Georgie, who bounced along by her side.

"May I go running now we're here, Aunty Nell?"

"Only if you don't go far. We can't stay out for long."

"I won't." He raced down the path.

"I hope he burns off some energy. Poor Alice is worn out with him."

"She's not the only one. I'll be glad to be back at work for the afternoon."

She tutted. "You can tell you're not used to children. You hardly see anything of him."

"I see enough. It will only get worse when this little fellow starts walking."

Nell gazed down at Freddie. "We've another few months yet, and the weather should be nicer by then, so we can bring them here more often."

"I'll leave that to you. As long as we can still take walks by ourselves on Sundays."

"That depends on how things are."

They reached the path that led to the lake and Nell called after Georgie as he raced towards the ducks. "We need to go now."

He stamped his foot. "I don't want to."

Mr Marsh marched after him and took hold of his shoulder. "You'll do as you're told."

"But I've not even seen the ducks."

"Don't answer back."

Georgie stumbled towards Nell as Mr Marsh pushed his shoulder.

"Don't be rough with him. I don't want to take him home with grazed knees."

"No, well... He needs to learn how to behave."

"Not like that." She pulled Georgie away from her husband. "We'll ask Mam if we can come out again later."

"All right." Georgie pouted as they walked to the gate, kicking his feet into the gravel of the footpath.

Mr Marsh clipped his ear. "Pick your feet up or your father will hear about this. He won't buy you new shoes before he has to."

Nell bit her lip. *Remind me not to bring them out together again.* "They'll polish up. It's only a bit of dust..."

"Yes..." Georgie cowered as Mr Marsh glared at him. "I-I'm not doing it any more."

"Well, make sure you don't." He checked his pocket watch. "We'd better get a move on. I need to be back at work soon."

"You go on ahead. Georgie can't walk as fast as you."

"I don't like leaving you."

"I'll be fine. I've walked home on my own enough times."

He sucked air through his teeth. "Very well. I'll see you later."

Nell paused for breath as he headed towards the gate, but Georgie distracted her.

"May we stay in the park now?"

An image of her sister Maria's drawn face flashed into her mind. "Not now. Let's go home and find out how Granny is first."

"She's poorly."

"She is, but the doctor will make her better."

"That's good." He let go of her hand and raced along the path before he ran back. "I don't want to catch Uncle Thomas up."

She chuckled. "I don't think you will. He's got longer legs than you."

He raced off again but stopped and pointed towards a bench near the exit. "There's Aunty Elenor."

"So it is." *What's she doing here? With Ruth Pearse, too.*

Georgie made her flinch as he shouted to them. "Aunty Elenor..."

Elenor opened her arms to catch him, but the smile froze on her lips when she spotted Nell. "Mam."

"Good afternoon. I wasn't expecting the two of you to be here."

"No." Elenor's eyes flicked to Ruth. "I didn't know I was coming."

"It was my fault, Mrs Marsh. I called on the off chance that Elenor would like to take a walk."

"I see." She glanced around as a couple of young men sauntered past. *Did the tall one just wink at them?* "What's going on?"

Elenor's face turned scarlet. "Nothing."

"It doesn't look like nothing. Do you know them?"

"No!" Elenor's voice was a pitch higher than usual.

"What about you, Ruth?"

"No. Not me."

Nell stared after them. "I don't want you here while they're walking around. You can come home with me."

"Maaam!"

"Mam, nothing."

Elenor tutted as she stood up. "We're not children any more."

"I'm well aware of that, and so, it would appear, are those young men." She indicated for them to start walking. "All I

4

can say is, it's a good job I didn't have Uncle Thomas with me. He's only just gone back to work."

Elenor gulped. "We don't know them..."

"I'm glad to hear it, but even so, you have a knack of upsetting him. I wish you'd behave yourself while he's around."

"Then he should stop pretending to be my dad. What I do has nothing to do with him."

Nell glared at her daughter. "It has everything to do with him. He's been very good to us since we were married."

"Maybe to you..."

Nell groaned. "I'm not arguing, but I'd like to point out that we wouldn't all be living together if he hadn't offered to put in the extra money to get us a bigger house."

"We could have had two houses."

"You know full well Alice didn't want to be on her own when she moved back to Liverpool. Why are you being so awkward?"

"I'm not."

"You could have fooled me. Now, hurry up. I want to see how Aunty Maria is."

The walk to their three-storey terraced house on Upper Hill Street took them less than quarter of an hour, and Nell helped Georgie inside before she manoeuvred the pram through the door. She stepped back into the street when Elenor failed to follow her.

"Aren't you coming in?"

"Ruth called to see me..."

"She's seen you."

"Not for long. Please, Mam, let me stay out a little longer. We won't go back to the park. I promise."

"Where will you go?"

Ruth interrupted. "Mam asked me to nip to the shop for her."

Nell's eyes flicked between them. "As long as that's all you do. Don't be late home..."

A smile brightened Elenor's face. "I won't."

Nell sighed as her daughter left. *She'd better behave herself.* She went back inside but stopped when Alice met her in the hall.

"Will you take a walk with me?"

"I've just brought Freddie in..."

Alice glanced at her son, who was still asleep. "He'll be fine where he is."

"Will your mam see to him?"

"She's taking a lie down, but Leah's in there with Georgie." Alice reached for her cloak. "I need to talk to you."

"Is everything all right?"

Alice said nothing as she stepped outside, and they'd walked to the corner of Windsor Street before she spoke. "The doctor gave Mam some pills for her indigestion."

"That's good. Hopefully, they'll help."

"He gave her some laudanum, too, for when she's in pain."

Nell cocked her head to one side. "Will she need that once the indigestion passes?"

Tears spilled from Alice's eyes as she paused at the side of the alehouse and took a deep breath. "He said she won't get better."

"Not..." Nell reached for the wall. "You don't mean..."

Alice nodded. "I'm sorry. I wasn't going to tell you until we were sitting down, but..." She fumbled for her handkerchief. "What will we do? She can't leave us."

Nell pinched the bridge of her nose as she squeezed back her tears. "You're sure that's what he meant? What exactly did he say?"

"That her heart has got no better, but he thinks there's a growth in her stomach. That's why she can't eat very much."

"She's eaten more since she's been cutting her food up small."

"He said it won't last."

Nell wiped her eyes. "Did you tell her?"

"No. I didn't want to say anything until Dad comes home. The doctor wants him to call so he can talk to him."

"So, we need to keep it to ourselves?"

Alice sighed. "That's the idea, but how can we? Harry will know something's wrong, and he's bound to ask when he comes up to bed."

Harry. As nice as he is, he does like to talk. "Would he keep it to himself if you told him?"

"I think so, but it doesn't seem right, him knowing before Dad, Billy and Vernon. Not to mention James. It will be months before he finds out."

Nell thought of her nephew, who had settled in Brazil. "We can't worry about him now. We'll have to write and hope he gets home in time. Did the doctor say how quickly she'll deteriorate?"

Alice shook her head. "I didn't think to ask, but he gave me a letter to give to Dad."

"All right, I'll tell you what, why don't you wait up with me tonight and we'll tell them all together when they come in from the alehouse? If your dad needs any more information, he can speak to Dr Randall tomorrow."

Alice nodded. "We need to make sure Vernon comes with them. I'll ask Harry to hurry them all up, too. I don't want to be up for half the night."

CHAPTER TWO

Maria was sitting by the fire when they got home, but her eyes were closed as Georgie played with a toy train by her feet. Leah joined them from the kitchen.

"Here you are. Where've you been? No sooner had Georgie run in than you both disappeared."

Alice gave her a weak smile. "It was my fault. I wanted a quick word with your mam."

"Quick? You've been over an hour."

"We walked to the park and lost track of time. Have the boys been all right?"

"Fine. I gave Freddie some milk and Georgie had a biscuit."

Alice glanced at Maria, who hadn't moved since they'd arrived. "Did she take some of her medicine?"

"I think so. She said she had stomach ache."

Nell wandered into the kitchen. "We'd better get the tea on then. Has Elenor been home?"

"I've not seen her since dinnertime. Ruth Pearse called for her, but they didn't say where they were going."

Nell stepped back into the living room. "I saw them together in the park. How long have they been friends again? They weren't speaking to each other the last I heard."

Leah shrugged. "I don't know. They seem to like falling out and making up again."

"Well, I wish they wouldn't bother with the making up. I can't help thinking the girl's trouble."

Leah laughed. "Don't you start. Aunty Maria worries enough for everyone, and it's not done her much good."

Nell stared at her. "What do you mean?"

"All this worrying. It must have upset her stomach over the years, which is probably why she's ill now." She paused when Maria's eyes flicked open.

"Oh, my. I must have fallen asleep. When did you get in?"

"Only five minutes ago." Alice crouched down by the chair. "How are you feeling?"

"Better, now you ask. The stomach ache's gone."

Nell smiled. "Alice said you'd had some pills from the doctor."

"He said to take one before each meal." She pushed herself up from her chair. "I'll be as right as rain in no time."

Nell put up a hand as Maria started towards the kitchen. "You sit down. I'll do the tea."

"I need something to do. If I sit here for much longer, I won't sleep tonight."

Nell glanced at Alice. "All right. But don't overdo it."

Maria tutted. "I can hardly do that when it's only a bit of fish."

"Very well, but let me put the kettle on." Nell checked the clock as she headed to the kitchen. "Edith and the men won't be home for a while yet, but Elenor shouldn't be long. I told her not to be late."

Maria appeared from the pantry with a handful of potatoes. "Where's she gone?"

"To the shop..."

"She's been a long time."

She has. "She was with Ruth Pearse. I imagine they're talking."

"It's nice to see them getting along again."

Hmm. Nell flinched as the front door slammed. "That will be her." She stepped into the hall, pulling the door closed behind her. "Where've you been?"

Elenor turned away to hang up her cloak. "We told you we were going to the shop."

"Which one? You could have gone to Liverpool in the time you've been out."

"We had to take the shopping to Mrs Pearse, so I stayed for a cup of tea."

"So you won't want one now, then?"

"I can always have another. Is Aunty Maria better?"

"Don't change the subject. I've told you I don't like you going round to the Pearses' house."

"Why not?"

"Because the woman's evil."

"She's changed. Since you married Uncle Thomas, she's not said a word against you." She pushed past Nell and sat at the table with Leah.

"Then why do you keep falling out with Ruth? Isn't that because of her mam?"

"No! We just have disagreements. Everyone does."

"I don't." Leah didn't look up as she passed Georgie his train.

"You don't have any friends, that's why."

"Yes, I do."

"Why don't you ever see them, then?"

"I do."

"That's enough." Nell put her hands on her hips. "She's considerate enough to help me around the house before she goes out, that's why. It would be nice if you did the same. I don't want you out with Ruth Pearse every afternoon now the weather's improving."

"You don't stay in all the time..."

"I won't have you answering me back, either. When you run your own house, you can make the rules, but while you live here..."

Elenor stood up from the table. "I know, I have to do as you say." She stomped up the stairs and slammed a door on the top floor.

Maria glanced at Nell as she went back to the kitchen. "It's time Mr Marsh dealt with her for the way she talks to you. A good hiding never did the rest of us any harm."

Nell sighed. "That's not the way to deal with her. I'll speak to her when she calms down."

"And how many times have you done that? I tell you, she needs a good hiding."

"Well, I'd thank you not to say anything to Thomas. He doesn't need another excuse to be angry with her."

The evening game of cards was still in progress when Maria tossed her hand into the middle of the table.

"I can't keep my eyes open. I'm going to bed."

Alice's forehead creased. "Are you all right?"

"Better than I've been, but the tablets must be making me drowsy." She pushed herself to her feet. "Good night."

Edith watched her go. "She still looks ill to me."

"It will take a few days for the pills to work properly." Nell sighed as Elenor set down her own cards.

"It doesn't stop her being cross with me."

"You annoy her, that's why." Leah drew the cards towards her.

"And you're a goody two-shoes."

Nell groaned. "She doesn't answer everyone back, if that's what you mean."

Edith studied Elenor. "Why don't you get a job like me?"

"Work!"

Nell tutted. "Don't sound so disgusted. You could at least consider it..."

"Are you trying to get rid of me?"

"No, but it might give you something to do, other than skulking around here. You'd earn some money, too. It's nice having some of your own."

"I don't want to work. That's what husbands are for."

Nell banged the table. "For goodness' sake, you're only sixteen."

"I could get married if I wanted to."

"Not without permission, you couldn't. Now, it's time you were going to bed. All of you."

Edith and Leah stood up, but Elenor stayed where she was. "It's not nine o'clock yet."

"If you're going to argue every time I open my mouth, I'd rather you were upstairs."

"I could always go out."

Nell gasped and turned to Alice. "Will you talk to her, please, because if she carries on like this, I'll have no choice but to ask Uncle Thomas to get involved."

"You wouldn't..."

"Then stop trying my patience. Until you have a husband and a house of your own, you do as I say. I'm sick of having an argument with every conversation. Now go."

As soon as they were alone, Nell slumped into a chair by the fire. Alice took the seat opposite.

"What do I do with her?"

"Give her time. It's only a phase."

"Is it though? She's always been wilful. I don't remember you being like that at her age."

"Mam reckons she's got a lot of her dad about her."

Nell raised an eyebrow. "She said that?"

"One day, when Elenor had argued about going out, she said Jack had been a law unto himself."

"He was, but not in a bad way."

"Elenor has the look of him, too, with those blue eyes."

"She doesn't have his dark hair, though." A smile flitted across Nell's lips. "Jack's was always tousled, as unruly as he was."

"So don't blame Elenor if she's like him. I'm sure she'll settle down."

Nell nodded. "I had hoped she'd do that when you came back from Wales, but it didn't make much difference. Thomas isn't happy that the extra year he paid for her to go to school didn't calm her down, either."

"I don't think it was ever likely to. She hated school when she had to go. Forcing her to stay for another year was never going to work. Still, he wouldn't have known."

"He's still no idea how to treat her."

"It can't be easy for him. He's never had a family of his own."

Nell snorted. "I used that excuse for long enough when we were first married, but it will be five years this year. He should be used to them by now."

"I suppose so..."

Nell studied her niece. "I'm glad you didn't stay in Wales."

"So am I. Moving away sounded like such an adventure when Harry suggested it, but I missed you all too much. I'm glad I'm here now Mam's as she is, too." Alice stopped at the sound of the front door. "This will be them. Shall I do the talking?"

"Only if you want to."

"I'll try." Alice took a deep breath as Billy joined them. "Are you on your own?"

"No, the others are here. Even Vernon."

"Oh, good." She went to the door and waited for them all to join them.

"What's going on?" George's voice was gruff as Alice shut the door.

"I-I ... we ... want to talk to you all, and this was the only way we could think of without everyone else being here."

Nell stood up and gestured to the chairs. "Come and sit down."

George took the seat Nell had vacated. "Is this about your mam?"

"It is." Alice pursed her lips. "I think you all know she finally agreed to see the doctor today."

George grunted. "She seemed all right at teatime,"

"She was, but Dr Randall said it's not likely to last." Alice handed him a letter. "He wants you to call tomorrow."

George looked up at her. "We paid good money for him to make her better."

"And he's given her some pills, which is why she was well enough earlier, but ... she's going to get worse." Alice stifled a sob as Mr Wood put an arm around her shoulders, his rough Irish accent filling the room.

"Why didn't you tell us earlier?"

"Because Mam was here, and she doesn't know. I wanted to check with Dad whether we should tell her or not. That's why we waited up."

George studied the letter. "Is she dying?"

Alice nodded and buried her head in Mr Wood's chest.

"Then we say nothing. I'll visit Dr Randall tomorrow, but until I say the word, I don't want any of this repeating. Not even to Jane or Rebecca." He stared at Nell. "Do you hear?"

"They've a right to know."

"And we'll tell them once I've spoken to the doctor. We keep this between ourselves for now."

Nell pursed her lips. "Please may I tell Rebecca? I'm seeing her tomorrow and I won't be able to keep it to myself."

George studied her. "Very well. But it goes no further. I don't want Maria finding out."

Mr Marsh stepped to Nell's side as Mr Wood led Alice upstairs and Billy saw Vernon to the front door.

"I thought you were acting strangely earlier."

"It was rather a shock."

He wrapped his arms around her. "And there was me thinking you'd argued with Elenor again."

"Why would you think that?" Nell couldn't keep the squeak from her voice.

"You looked as if you weren't talking to each other when I came home. It's as well I don't jump to conclusions as quickly as I used to. I was ready to take my belt to her."

"Don't do that! Please, it was my fault. I'm upset about Maria, that's all." She took a breath. "Let me deal with Elenor. All the girls will need support over the next few months and shouting at them won't help."

CHAPTER THREE

The centre point of Sefton Park, the place Nell always met Rebecca, was roughly at one end of the lake, and her sister was waiting on their usual bench when she arrived.

"Am I late?"

"No, I was early. No boys today?"

"Alice and Leah have taken them to visit Betty."

Rebecca smiled. "It makes a change for it to be just the two of us."

"It does. I'm not sorry, though. I've something to tell you."

Rebecca's face dropped. "About Maria?"

Nell nodded. "Dr Randall called yesterday and said the reason she's not been well is because there's a growth in her stomach."

"What sort of growth?"

"I don't know for sure. George is going to visit him on his way home to find out more."

Rebecca's face paled. "Will we lose her?"

"It looks like it." Nell pinched the bridge of her nose. "Dr

Randall gave her some pills for the indigestion, which helped last night, but other than that, he can't do anything for her."

Rebecca rubbed her hands over her face. "First Tom, and now this. How old is she now?"

Nell cocked her head to one side. "I was thinking about it earlier and decided she'll be sixty at her next birthday."

"It's a decent age, but it's still too soon. Who else knows?"

"Everyone in our house except the children. George doesn't want Maria finding out, so he's told us to keep it to ourselves."

"Do I have to pretend I don't know?"

"No. I told him I was seeing you today."

"Thank you. I've as much right to know as anyone. More so than Mr Marsh and Mr Wood. What about Jane? Will Alice tell Betty?"

"I doubt it. She won't want to anger George. He'll call and tell Jane when he's ready."

"I hope I don't bump into her then. I wouldn't be able to stay quiet."

"There's not much chance of that. She's at Betty's more than ever since the latest baby was born, and with you being where you are, you couldn't be further apart."

"I know. It doesn't matter how much I plead with Hugh to move back..." Rebecca paused at the sound of laughter. "Someone sounds like they're having a good time. To be young again... The things I'd do differently..."

A group of youngsters rounded the corner and Nell jumped to her feet as Elenor leapt away from a young man whose arm she'd been linking.

"W-what's going on?" Nell stared at Elenor as Isobel and Ruth moved to either side of her.

"I-I didn't know you'd be here."

"I don't doubt that…"

Rebecca grasped her daughter Isobel by the shoulders. "You said you were visiting a friend's house. What are you doing here?"

"S-she was out…"

"And you happened to bump into Elenor?"

"Y-yes."

Ruth interrupted. "It's our fault, Mrs Grayson. We saw her while we were walking. Me and Elenor … through the railings … and we shouted to her."

Nell's eyes bored into each of them. "Did you shout to these young men, too? Or are they the reason you're here?" Nell glared at her daughter. "If I'm not mistaken, these are the ones who were in Princes Park yesterday. The ones you said you didn't know."

"W-we didn't know them then…"

"It's not what you think, Mrs Marsh." Ruth raised her voice. "We met them again at the shop and they started talking to us."

Nell turned to the one who had linked Elenor's arm. "Do you make a habit of speaking to unchaperoned girls without an introduction?"

"We were introduced…"

"…by the shopkeeper." Ruth spoke over the young man and Nell's eyes narrowed as she studied her.

"Since when was a shopkeeper in a position to determine whether a man is worthy of a young girl's company?"

The man who was still nameless bowed to Nell. "My apologies. Life on board ship can be lonely, and we often forget formalities…"

"You're a sailor?"

"William Massey. Will to my friends. An engineer on a cargo ship."

Elenor hesitated. "I thought it would be all right ... with Dad being a sailor."

"Dad was a master mariner."

"But he started as an ordinary sailor..."

Nell took a breath. "Are you walking out together?"

Mr Massey grinned at Nell. "I'd hardly call it that. I go back to sea tomorrow." He indicated to his friend. "We both do."

"But you were linking arms..."

"Mam, please. We've not done anything wrong." Elenor's face was crimson. "I'm old enough to walk out with someone, and I'm with my friends. What harm is there?"

"You should have told me what you were up to and introduced Mr Massey to Uncle Thomas before you accepted his arm."

Elenor lowered her head. "You won't tell him, will you?"

Not if I don't have to. "We'll see. If Mr Massey's leaving in the morning, you can come home with me now and we'll pretend this didn't happen." She studied Mr Massey, noting his muscular frame and fair hair. "How long are you away for?"

"A couple of months."

"Very well." She turned back to Elenor. "If the two of you want to walk out together next time Mr Massey's home, I expect you to introduce him to Uncle Thomas first."

Rebecca looked at the other man in the group. "What about you? I hope you don't have your eye on Isobel."

"Mam!" Isobel's cheeks coloured.

"Mam, nothing. If your dad finds out about this, there'll be trouble."

The man bowed. "As lovely as your daughter is, I can confirm my role here is as chaperone not as someone in search of *company*."

It was Rebecca's turn to flush. "Right. Well ... good. Either way, it's time I took Isobel home. Good day to you." She turned to Nell. "I'll see you next week."

The men smirked at each other as Rebecca grabbed Isobel's arm and ushered her away, but Nell glowered at them. "This isn't a laughing matter." *Thomas will go mad.*

"No. We're sorry." Mr Massey pursed his lips. "May I walk Elenor home? We won't be far behind you."

"Please, Mam. Ruth and Mr Young will stay with us." Elenor's eyes pleaded with Ruth.

"Yes, that's right. We'd have walked home together, anyway."

Nell studied the four of them, "Very well, but I don't want Mr Massey coming to the house. The top of the road will be far enough." She took out her watch. "It's nearly three o'clock. Be home in half an hour." They all nodded. "And have a good voyage, both of you."

Her heart was pounding as she strolled away. *I hope I've done the right thing.* She turned to check Elenor was still with Ruth. *I might not like her, but I'd rather she was there than not, and at least he goes away tomorrow.*

Maria was dozing by the fire when she got home, but she opened her eyes when Nell picked up the teapot.

"You weren't out long."

"Rebecca had things to do."

"That's not like her."

"It was something to do with Isobel. Shall I put the kettle on?"

"That would be nice. I could manage a small piece of cake, too. I didn't eat much at dinner."

Nell smiled as she came back from the kitchen. "That's a good sign. The pills must be working."

"I think they are, although I'm still tired. Hopefully, I'll get a few decent nights' sleep now I'm more comfortable."

"Let's hope so. Do you want me to make a start on the tea when we've had this?"

"No, I can manage. I need something to do." She glanced towards the table. "Did Leah go out?"

"She went with Alice. Don't you remember?"

Maria's eyes narrowed. "I don't remember Alice going out, either. Have they gone far?"

"They walked up to see Betty. You must have fallen asleep before they left."

"Yes, that must be it."

Nell scurried to the kitchen. *Don't get upset. She only fell asleep.*

She was pouring the tea when the front door opened, but she stopped and hurried to the hall. "You're here."

Elenor hung up her cloak. "You told me to be."

"I know, but thank you." Nell held out an arm to stop her going into the living room. "I don't want anyone knowing about this afternoon."

"I won't tell them."

"No, I don't suppose you will. Have you arranged to see Mr Massey again?"

23

"He said he'd write when he gets back to Liverpool."

"Are you keen on him?"

"He's nice enough, but I told you, I've not known him long."

"Would you like to see him again?"

Elenor shrugged. "If he wants to see me."

"Well, if he writes, will you tell me? You're only sixteen and we need to handle the situation carefully with Uncle Thomas."

"He can't stop me from seeing him."

"Whether he can or not, it would be easier for all of us if he was happy about you walking out with someone. I'm only trying to help."

Elenor moved Nell's arm out of the way. "Are you sure?"

Nell took a deep breath as she followed her daughter into the room, and Maria smiled as they joined her.

"You're home early."

"I wanted to sit with you while everyone else is out."

"You're a good girl, but I was about to make tea."

"Perhaps she could help you." Nell cocked her head to one side. "She needs to improve her cooking. I'd planned on writing to James while I have time."

"Ask him when he's coming home again. It's been nearly two years."

"I will." *And I'll tell him he'd better be here as soon as possible.*

Once Maria's teacup was empty, she took Elenor's arm as she stood up. "I'm glad you'd like to cook. It may be too soon for you to be interested in finding a husband, but you need to be prepared in case anyone sweeps you off your feet. You're not much younger than I was when I married your Uncle George."

"Really? How old were you when you started walking out with him?"

"Sixteen. Dad wasn't happy, of course, he said I was far too young, but it's as well I talked him into liking Uncle George. Dad died two years later and if I hadn't been married, we'd have all been homeless."

Elenor smirked at Nell as she ushered Maria into the kitchen. "You'll have to tell me more."

CHAPTER FOUR

Sunday dinner was over, and the tidying up finished, when Nell allowed Mr Marsh to wrap her cloak around her shoulders.

"Let me tell Maria we're going."

Mr Marsh peered back into the living room. "I'd say she's asleep already."

"Let me check."

When Maria didn't stir, Nell returned to the hall where Mr Marsh held open the front door.

"She seems peaceful enough and Leah and Edith are with her."

"It's times like this, having a large family is useful." He took a deep breath. "It's been too long since we walked out together, just the two of us. I would say that spring is finally on its way."

"I hope so. Where shall we go?"

"Sefton Park would be nice. There's a chance we could bump into Mr and Mrs Grayson, too. I mentioned we may walk in their direction."

Nell smiled. "It sounds like you have it all planned."

"Not really. It was only a suggestion. I'd like to spend some time with you. I hadn't realised how little we'd see of each other once we were married."

"It's only to be expected now we've been together for nearly five years. It's a pity I can't come to the alehouse with you. You see more of George and Billy than you do of me."

His mouth fell open, but he closed it when Nell grinned. "I thought you were being serious for a moment."

"As if. Imagine a woman walking into a place like that. Not that I'd want to."

"I'm relieved to hear it."

"It's a shame the tea rooms aren't open of an evening. I miss our trips for afternoon tea."

Mr Marsh nodded. "I often think about them. I don't regret not going to sea any more, but I do miss my days off in the week. Nowadays, everywhere's shut when I'm not at work." He paused until they passed through the gates of Sefton Park. "I know where we could go. The Adelphi. They may even be open on a Sunday."

"It would be more expensive."

He gazed at her. "It would be worth it. We'd better not mention it to everyone else, though. I couldn't afford to take all of us."

Nell's chuckle froze on her lips. "Actually, would you make an exception? There is someone I'd like to invite. Just once."

He stared at her. "Please don't say Elenor. You should let me punish her for the way she treats you, not bribe her to behave herself."

She shuddered. "Gracious, no, I meant Maria. I

remember when I told her we were going there for our wedding night, she said she'd love someone to take her, even if it was only for afternoon tea. Could we treat her before it's too late?"

"That's a lovely thought. Will she be able to eat anything, though?"

"She won't mind whether she can or not. To sit in the restaurant and look out over St George's Hall will be enough for her. If she can manage a bit of cake, so much the better."

"Then consider it booked. I'll call in one dinnertime and make the arrangements. How about next Saturday for afternoon tea?"

"That's Easter weekend. You'd better make it the week after."

"Of course. Should we invite Mr Atkin?"

Nell shook her head. "He wouldn't thank you for it."

"You're probably right."

A cool breeze swept across the expanse of grass as they approached the lake and Nell pulled her cloak tight. "The weather's trying to remind us that winter isn't over yet."

"It will be, soon enough." Mr Marsh raised a hand in a wave. "There's Mr and Mrs Grayson. I had a feeling we'd see them."

Rebecca smiled as she walked towards her. "Fancy seeing you here."

"I think it was arranged." Nell smirked as the men shook hands. "Have you been here long?"

"Half an hour or so. How's Maria today?"

"Not too bad. She ate some dinner, but she'd dozed off by the time we left."

"At least she's still eating."

"I was talking to Thomas about the afternoon teas we used to take, and we've decided to invite her to the Adelphi for one while she's still able."

"Could she eat that much?"

"I doubt it, but she'd like the experience. It must be strange to know a place so well, but never go inside."

"It is. I've never been in myself."

Nell grinned. "Something for you to work on with Mr Grayson, then."

"There's no chance he'll spend that sort of money..."

Mr Marsh interrupted them. "Shall we carry on walking? Together, of course."

Nell linked Rebecca's arm. "We should do this more often."

"It certainly breaks up a dull afternoon of being spoken at."

Nell peered behind her to check the men were out of earshot. "What happened with Isobel the other day?"

"Don't ask." Rebecca kept her voice low. "I'm sure she's lying about what they were up to, but she won't have any of it. I've told her she's not allowed out any more without Florrie."

"Are they out now?"

"No. She said she didn't want to be chaperoned by her little sister and that she'd rather stay at home. What about Elenor?"

"She said she's only just met Mr Massey, the man she was with. He said they're not walking out together because he's often away at sea. Thank goodness."

"Is she out with him now?"

"No. He went to sea the day after we saw them, so she's

at Ruth's for the afternoon. I don't know what to do when he gets back to Liverpool, though."

"Do you trust her not to see him?"

"No."

"You'll have to accompany her whenever she goes out."

"That won't go down well. She'll say she's with Ruth."

"Do you trust Ruth?"

"Not at all, although I may be doing her a disservice. It's her mother I don't like."

"If it means Elenor has a chaperone..."

"Exactly. She's better than nothing." Nell gazed at the wide, open spaces. "I've been wondering if I'm being too hard on her. I mean, what harm can it do walking around the park with friends? They can hardly get up to anything out here. Especially not if the weather's bad."

"You have a point, although I walked out with Hugh over a winter. It's amazing what you do when you're young."

"It probably stopped you getting into trouble, though."

Rebecca checked over her shoulder again. "Hugh wouldn't have done anything even in the middle of summer."

"I'm not sure I'd have the same confidence in Mr Massey. Did you see him? He's a few years older than Elenor."

"He's rather handsome, too."

"Exactly. So what do I do? I can't tell Thomas."

"Perhaps we should encourage her and Isobel to always walk around the park together. They could come with us, then do their own thing until we're all ready to go home. That way, even if Mr Massey's in Liverpool, she won't be on her own with him and we'll be here as well."

Nell nodded. "That could work. She'll want to involve Ruth, too, but I need to stop worrying about that."

Rebecca sighed. "They're growing up. It was so much easier when they were younger."

"If Betty's anything to go by, it could get harder, too. I hope none of them have the problems she's had. Or worse, go the way Grace did."

Rebecca shuddered at the mention of their nephew's late wife. "Don't get ahead of yourself."

"I'm sorry, it's just that Sarah called to see Maria yesterday, and she had the grandchildren with her."

"Poor mites. The little boy won't even remember his mam."

"I know, but apparently Sam's met someone new, and he's getting married again."

"Really! What's the new woman like?"

"I've not met her, but Sarah says she's nice enough, and at least the kiddies will have a mam again."

Rebecca sighed. "I'd like the chance to be a granny, but I don't know if I could stand the heartache of getting there. If either of them died, like Grace did…"

"You can't worry yourself unnecessarily. Surely as a family we can't be so unlucky for it to happen twice."

"You'd hope not…."

"Oh, my goodness!"

"What's the matter?" Rebecca followed Nell's gaze. "Oh, my…"

Nell stopped to catch her breath. *What's he doing here?* She flinched when Mr Marsh and Mr Grayson caught them up. "Is everything all right?"

Nell gulped. "Yes. Fine. I-I … erm … I've just remembered, I didn't post the letter to James…"

"That's because I did when I went to work on Friday."

Mr Marsh smirked at Mr Grayson. "You're getting very forgetful..."

Nell's heart pounded against her chest. "Yes, you're right, I'd completely forgotten." She linked Rebecca's arm and hurried her away, keeping her voice low. "What do I do now?"

"You need to confront her."

"She might not know."

"But she might."

"I don't want to argue with her. Not with Maria as she is."

"Stop making excuses." Rebecca spoke through gritted teeth. "You need to find out if she knows Mr Massey is still in Liverpool, and if she does, why they lied. At the very least, you should stop her going out of the house."

"What if he isn't really a sailor, and it was all a ruse?"

"Why would he say such a thing?"

A shiver ran down Nell's spine. "There must be a perfectly logical explanation. Perhaps his ship's been delayed."

"Well, unless you ask, you'll never find out."

Nell pursed her lips. *I'm not sure I want to know.*

CHAPTER FIVE

The following Friday, George and Mr Marsh sat on opposite sides of the fire, their legs outstretched, as Nell and Alice tidied up the table after breakfast. Nell paused as Billy took the chair near his dad.

"The first holiday of the year. Do you have any plans for today?"

George turned to Billy as they both shrugged. "Go to the alehouse?"

Maria huffed as she came in. "Don't you see enough of that place?"

"What else is there to do?"

Mr Marsh looked across at Nell. "I was hoping we could take a walk this afternoon."

"It's Easter! We've food to prepare for Sunday and Maria can't do it on her own."

His smile dropped. "What about everyone else?"

"We're all doing it. There'll be twelve of us, plus children, for Sunday dinner, and another seven in the evening. It takes time."

Mr Marsh's shoulders sagged. "I may as well go to the alehouse, then. I thought having a day off in the week would be different."

"Not Good Friday." Nell put a hand on his shoulder. "The holiday in June will be different. There'll be no family gatherings, so we can suit ourselves."

He grunted as he stood up. "I may as well buy myself a newspaper. I've nothing better to do this morning."

Nell rolled her eyes as he left. "He's still not used to family life. He was a bachelor for too long."

"Not long enough." Elenor's voice was barely a whisper, but Nell glared at her.

"Stop that."

"What's going on?" Maria was breathless when she spoke.

"Nothing. We just need to divide up the chores."

Elenor frowned. "What chores?"

"Didn't you hear me? We have all the food to prepare for Sunday."

"I've arranged to go out."

Nell spun around. "Who with?"

"Ruth."

"On Good Friday?"

"Why not?"

"I've told you why not. If Ruth calls here, you can tell her you're busy."

"I-I said I'd go there."

"Then she'll be disappointed." Nell picked up the last of the cups. "For a start, you can dry the dishes while I wash up. Aunty Maria will lift out the baking things."

Elenor huffed. "Ruth will be mad with me if I don't turn up."

"I'm sure she'll come here if she's wondering where you are. Here..." She passed Elenor the tea towel.

"Can't I help with the baking instead?"

"Once you've helped me. The faster you work, the quicker you'll be."

Elenor pouted as she followed Nell to the kitchen. "Why can't Leah do this?"

Nell glanced over her shoulder and lowered her voice. "Because I want a word with you."

"What have I done now?"

"That's what I'd like to find out." Nell turned on the tap and poured some boiling water from the kettle into the sink. "Is it really Ruth you've arranged to meet, or is it Mr Massey?"

Elenor flinched. "No. How could it be...?"

Nell held her daughter's gaze. "I saw him on Sunday, in the park. Three days after he was supposed to go back to sea. Did you know he was still here?"

"I-I..."

"You did, didn't you?"

"H-he told me he was going away."

"I don't believe you. Did you see him on Sunday?"

Elenor remained silent as she stared at the floor.

"I'll take that as a yes."

"We only went to the park..."

"Alone?"

Elenor's cheeks flushed.

"So you're using Ruth as an excuse to walk out with him. Does she know?"

"Yes." Her voice was a whisper.

"Has it crossed your mind that I'll be the one who gets into trouble for allowing you to walk out with him?"

"It's nothing to do with you."

"It's everything to do with me." Nell spoke through gritted teeth. "You're my daughter and you're only sixteen. How long have you been walking out with him? And the truth this time."

"I told you, not long."

"But longer than a day? You lied when you said you didn't know him. Is he even a sailor?"

"Yes! He goes away tomorrow. There was a delay."

"That was convenient. Are you sure it's not another figment of your imagination?"

"No. It's the truth. I promise."

Maria disturbed them as she headed to the pantry. "I thought you were washing up. I could have had it washed, dried and put away in the time you've been in here." She reached over to the tap. "The water will be overflowing in a minute."

Nell glared at Elenor. "We're doing it now. It won't take long. Will it?"

"No."

Nell waited for Maria to disappear again. "If I find out you're still lying, you won't set foot outside this house for six months, do you hear?"

"You can't keep me in."

"It's either that or Uncle Thomas hears about it. It's your choice."

Elenor huffed as Nell passed her a plate. "We only want to see each other, and I thought you'd stop us."

Nell sighed. "Listen. I know you're growing up, I was young once too, but you need a chaperone. Have you any idea how people will talk if you walk out with a man on your own? A man older than you."

Elenor averted her eyes as she placed the plate on the worktop. "May I see him before he goes away?"

"Not on your own."

"Please, Mam."

"No. I'd come with you myself, but Uncle Thomas will want to know why I'll take a walk with you and not him..."

"He can't come..." Elenor's eyes were wide.

"I'm not that daft." Nell glanced into the living room. "Why don't you ask Edith to accompany you? She doesn't get many days off, and she'd probably enjoy a walk."

"Then Leah will want to join us..."

Nell sighed. "You can't be choosy. You either go with the two of them or not at all..."

"Can't you tell Leah you need her here?"

"How would you feel if I said that to you?"

"She won't mind. Please, Mam. Can we ask?"

Edith was kneading the dough for some hot cross buns as Nell wiped her hands and joined her at the table.

"I'd say you've done that before."

"I used to do them for Mam when she couldn't do them any more."

"I've not talked to you much about her. Did she teach you to cook?"

Edith nodded. "I can do most things if I need to, but I'm thankful I haven't needed to since I've been here. It was hard having to cook for Dad and my brothers when I'd done a full day at work..."

Nell glanced at Elenor. "Did you hear that? You don't know how fortunate you are."

"I can teach Elenor if you like. We could make tea together on Saturday to start with."

"That's a good idea..." Nell paused at the scowl on Elenor's face. "Don't be like that. You'll need to do it if you ever get married."

"Could I take Edith to the park later and we can talk about it?"

"Why not? As long as Edith doesn't mind ... and Leah's happy to stay here and help me."

Leah didn't look up from rolling out some pastry. "I don't mind."

"I'd like that." Edith smiled at Elenor. "I don't go out often enough. If you want to shape these buns with me, we can go before dinner."

Elenor was finally smiling when Mr Marsh returned with his paper.

"You were a long time. Did you go for a walk?"

"No, a few of the regulars from the alehouse were outside the shop, so I joined them." He unfolded the paper and opened it to the centre pages. "They were talking about this. What do you think?"

Nell scanned the mass of words. "What am I looking at?"

"The advert at the top of the second page. In the middle. About booking a train to Blackpool."

Her eyes narrowed. "Why were they talking about that?"

"Because one of them has booked a trip. I thought you might like it."

"For the day?"

He nodded. "It only takes a couple of hours to get there, and there'd be time for dinner and a walk along the pier before we came back."

Nell grimaced. "It sounds very extravagant."

"Nonsense. It's what people do nowadays, and the prices really aren't that expensive. Not that we'd go third class, obviously."

"Obviously." Nell glanced around her. "Would we all go?"

"I wasn't planning on it, but if we enjoy it, there's no reason we couldn't go again next year. Anyone who's behaved themselves could come with us then."

Nell wiped the palms of her hands on her skirt. "Yes, well, we could. I've never been to the seaside, and it would be nice, if they have a tea room."

"My thoughts exactly. I'll have to wait until next week to book, but leave it with me. I'm looking forward to it already."

CHAPTER SIX

M aria had settled by the fire for what had become her
usual afternoon nap when the letterbox rattled, and
Nell walked to the hall to retrieve the letter. Alice glanced up
from her place at the table when she returned.

"Is it anything exciting?"

"It's from Mrs Robertson."

"I thought she was away."

"She must be back." Nell sliced open the envelope and
took the seat opposite Alice. "Let's see. Oh, goodness..." A
smile spread across her face. "They're getting themselves
another house in Liverpool."

"Why would they do that?"

Nell scanned the rest of the letter. "Violet's had all the
schooling she needs, so they don't need a governess any
more."

Alice's forehead creased. "How old is she? Not eleven?"

"Twelve!" Nell gasped. "I find that hard to believe."

"What's it got to do with them getting a house?"

"They only lived on the ship because they couldn't afford

to keep a house *and* hire a governess, but now Violet doesn't need any more education, they've decided it's time they settled down. For part of the year at least."

"Where will they move to?"

"I've not got to that." Nell turned to the last page. "Ah, they've not decided. I'll have to give her some suggestions."

Alice laughed. "Why not? She doesn't know Toxteth Park very well. Will you visit her this week if she's in Liverpool?"

Nell sighed. "Not this time. They sail again on Thursday, but they should be onshore for longer next month. I'll ask Uncle Thomas if we can walk round some of the smarter streets in the area and see if I can find anything."

"I hope he doesn't think it's for the two of you. He'd move out tomorrow if he could."

Nell shook her head. "He knows better than to even suggest it." She glanced at the clock. "I may as well write to her now. If I get the letter in the post, she'll have it before she leaves again."

The letter was written and posted, and the tea made before Mr Marsh arrived home for the evening. He had a broad grin on his face as he lay a newspaper on the table.

"You're cheerful."

"I've booked our trip to Blackpool, for the June bank holiday, that's why."

"That's nice."

"It's more than nice. I've arranged for two seats in a first-class carriage on the seven o'clock train out of Liverpool. It should get us to Blackpool before ten, and we don't need to leave again until six in the evening."

"First class!"

"Only the best for you, my dear."

Edith and Leah giggled as Elenor rolled her eyes.

"What's up with you three?"

Leah sat up straight at the table as Mr Marsh glared down at them. "Nothing. Sorry, Uncle Thomas."

He nodded. "Then get on with what you're doing." His eyes narrowed. "What *are* you doing?"

Edith looked up. "Deciding what we're cooking for tea on Saturday. I'm teaching Elenor and Leah..."

"Oh, you needn't do that." He beamed at them. "I'm taking your mam and Aunty Maria out for afternoon tea."

Elenor stared at Nell. "Why didn't you say?"

"It was meant to be a surprise..."

Alice's brow furrowed. "You know she won't be able to eat much?"

"We know that..."

Maria appeared at the kitchen door. "Did someone mention me?"

"We did." Nell smiled at her. "Do you remember when I married Thomas, we went to the Adelphi for the night? You said you'd love to go there one day, even if it was only for afternoon tea."

"Did I? That would have been nice."

"It still can be. We've arranged a table for Saturday and we'd like you to join us."

"Me?" Incomprehension covered Maria's face. "To the Adelphi?"

"It's perfectly all right. They let people like us in, as long as we have the money."

"But what will I wear?"

"Your Sunday dress and new hat."

"Are you sure?"

"Of course I am. We thought it was right that you had a treat for all you do."

"Well, that's lovely. Thank you. What time will we go?"

Mr Marsh smiled. "I've arranged for a carriage to pick us up at half past three, and we'll have afternoon tea at four, so don't fill yourself up at dinnertime."

Maria tittered. "As if. I'll start making room for it now."

Mr Marsh stood on the footpath and offered a hand, first to Maria and then to Nell, as they climbed down from the carriage. Maria gazed up at the light-coloured stone facade of the Adelphi.

"Are we really going inside?"

Nell took her arm. "We are. I hate seeing you ill, and so now you're feeling better, we thought you'd enjoy it."

"I certainly will." She flicked a hand over her cloak. "Am I all right?"

"You're very smart. Shall we go?" Nell watched her husband as he took Maria's arm and led them up the steps into the expansive reception area.

"My. Look at this." Maria gazed up at the chandeliers as Mr Marsh strode towards one of the staff. "Aren't they're wonderful?"

Nell chuckled. "Whenever I see them, I imagine having to clean them."

"They must have enough people working here to do that."

"They will have, but still..." Nell paused when Mr Marsh returned with a waiter.

"There's a restaurant area downstairs in the central atrium, if we'd like to sit there. It may be preferable to Mrs Atkin climbing the stairs."

Maria peered into the space beyond the welcome desk. "That's very thoughtful, and it's lovely in there. Have you seen the size of those plants around the tables?"

"They could hardly have small ones in a room that big." Nell took Maria's arm as the waiter escorted them to a table on the far wall.

"You should be comfortable here." He bowed to Mr Marsh. "Would you like me to serve now, sir?"

"Yes, please."

Maria took her seat, a grin on her face as she surveyed the room. "I feel like the Queen sitting here. If her palace is fancier than this, then it's completely unnecessary."

Nell laughed. "I doubt she'd need anywhere so enormous."

"Not even if all her children and their families lived with her." Maria continued to study the surroundings as a waiter brought a large pot of tea. "George would never bring me to a place like this."

Mr Marsh straightened his napkin. "I did ask if he'd like to join us, but he declined."

"He'd hate all this splendour." She cocked her head to

one side as she studied Nell. "Is this what it's like on the ships?"

"They're not so grand, or as big, and they don't have the chandeliers, but yes, they're similar."

"I can understand why you liked it, then. And James. Why would he leave somewhere like this for a house in the middle of a jungle?"

"He must have had his reasons. You should ask him next time he's home."

"It would be nice to see him again." She sighed. "Since I've been ill, I want to be at peace with everyone. After what happened to Tom..."

"Don't say that." An image of their brother on his deathbed flashed into Nell's mind. "Tom had been ill for years."

"He was younger than me, and we can't ignore these things at our age. I can only hope I'm still around to see Vernon and Lydia's next baby."

Nell's eyes widened. "I should hope so, it's due in a couple of months. You need to stop worrying like this and concentrate on getting better." Nell sat up straight as the waiter brought a stand laden with sandwiches and cakes. "That looks nice."

"It does." Maria licked her lips. "Not that I'll eat much."

Mr Marsh smiled at her. "You have what you like. I'm sure we can manage the rest."

Maria's eyes were moist. "You will take care of Nell and the girls when I'm not here?"

Nell tutted. "Come on, what's brought this on? We're supposed to be having a pleasant afternoon out, not getting all morbid."

"I'm sorry, I can't help it." She helped herself to a small square of egg sandwich. "You'll keep an eye out for George, too...?"

"We'll all be fine. And that means you, too. Now, shall I pour this tea and we'll talk about something more cheerful?"

CHAPTER SEVEN

The walk to Betty's hadn't got any more enjoyable, but Nell was relieved the sun had some warmth, and Leah made a pleasant companion.

"Elenor said you told her to get a job, but she doesn't want one. Do you think I should get one?"

Nell shrugged. "I don't see why not. You've not much else to do and it's nice having your own money."

"It would mean I'd never be at home, though. Edith's out for as long as the men and I wouldn't like that."

"You could always give it a try. You won't be able to do anything once you're married."

She studied Nell. "Would you have gone to sea if Dad hadn't died?"

"Of course not. Not as a stewardess, anyway. I'd always hoped to travel with him like Mrs Robertson does with her husband, but we couldn't have taken you and Elenor."

"You must have been very sad after the accident."

"I was at the time, but you have to get on with things. At least I had Aunty Maria. I'd have been lost without her."

"I wonder if me and Elenor will be friendly like that when we get older."

"It would be nice if you were."

"She's not nice to me now. Do you think she'll change?"

Nell sighed. "Who knows? I had hoped she'd settle down once she left school, but there's still time."

They turned the corner into Betty's road as a gust of wind caught the bottom of their skirts.

"Ah." Nell pulled her cloak around her. "That's to remind us it isn't summer yet."

Leah laughed as she clasped a hand to her head. "It's my hat I'm more worried about."

They hurried to Betty's front door and, after a brief knock, let themselves in. Betty smiled as she saw them.

"That was well-timed. The kettle's just boiled."

"The time we arrive shouldn't surprise you now we walk the first part of the journey with Thomas. He's nothing if not punctual."

Leah hung up her cloak. "Is Charlie in bed?"

"He is. He had me up half the night, so he's been cranky this morning."

Nell studied her niece. "Is he all right?"

"Don't worry. He's teething. He's some back teeth coming through."

"Did you give him any laudanum?"

"That's how I got him to sleep, but not before he'd been awake for a couple of hours."

"Bless him. Mr Crane mustn't have been happy."

"He didn't notice. I brought Charlie down here until he was asleep and then carried him back upstairs. Not that I'll be doing that for much longer."

"What do you mean? Are you in the family way again?"

Betty nodded. "Either that, or I've put on weight. My skirts are tight."

"You've not seen the doctor?"

"There's no point. I've been through it so many times, I know what to expect. It's not quickened yet, so I'm guessing it will be due about October."

"It's as well the other two are old enough to look after themselves."

Leah took a seat at the table. "I'm not sure I want a baby."

Nell frowned. "Why not?"

"It sounds too hard. When I was still at school, one of the girls said you might even *die*. Is that what happened to Grace?"

Nell glanced at Betty before sitting beside her daughter. "You can't worry about things like that. You don't want to spend your life as a spinster."

"I wouldn't mind having a husband..."

Nell patted her hand. "I'm afraid that if you have one, you get the other. You'll be glad of it, too, when the time comes. No woman wants to be childless. What would I do without you and Elenor?"

"You'd still be at sea."

"I wouldn't have been there forever. What would I have done when I was too old to work? That's why it's a good idea to take a job now, to get it out of your system."

Leah studied Betty as she poured the tea. "Did you work when you were younger?"

"Erm ... no. Aunty Jane wasn't as broad-minded as your mam back then."

"I don't know what I'd do if I wanted a job. Not sewing like Edith. She's always tired."

Betty pushed a cup of tea to Leah. "How about domestic service?"

"Urgh. No, thank you."

"I've an idea." Nell sat up straight. "Why don't you see if any of the tea rooms in town need a waitress? They don't work long hours."

"Would I need to bake?"

"I don't think so. They want girls to take the orders, serve the tea and cakes, and then tidy up. You could do that."

"How much would I get paid?"

"I've no idea. I could get Uncle Thomas to take me to one and I'll find out."

"May I come? I've never even been inside one, so how do I know whether I'd like it?"

Nell grimaced. "You know what he's like. He always wants to spend time on his own with me when he's not working. He says the rest of you see enough of me in the week."

Leah huffed. "Could we go by ourselves when he's not around, then?"

"I'd have to ask for some money."

Betty's forehead creased. "You must have your own. I thought our Matthew and John were paying you back the money you lent them for their apprenticeships."

"They are, but Thomas puts it into the Friendly Society for me, and I need his permission to take it out."

Betty sighed. "That's annoying. If I want anything for myself, I save it in a tin in the wardrobe so Bert can't find it."

"I should do that, but I've had an account at the Friendly

Society since I was at sea and had more money than I needed. When I got married, Thomas took it over. I know it was foolish, but he was insistent, and as a new wife, I didn't think I should refuse." She turned to Leah. "Let that be a lesson to you. Always keep some money to yourself. Wherever it comes from."

"I need to earn some first."

Alice was at the table with Elenor and the boys when they got home, and Leah flopped down beside her.

"Have you had a nice afternoon?"

"Yes." Leah grinned at her sister. "Mam says we should both get jobs."

"I didn't say that. I said it wouldn't be a bad idea."

Elenor pouted. "I don't want one."

"I do. Mam said I could work in a tea room."

"You've never even been in one."

"That doesn't matter. I can still serve the tables."

"That's enough." Nell took a deep breath. "If you don't want a job, Elenor, then that's fine, but don't criticise Leah if she wants to earn her own money."

"She always has to do as she's told."

"It would be nice if you did, too. Where's Aunty Maria?"

Alice frowned. "She went to visit Aunty Sarah, but now you mention it, she should be home by now."

"You let her walk by herself?"

Alice gave a feeble smile. "She said she'd be all right."

Nell jumped up. "I hope nothing's happened to her. I'd better go and see where she's got to. Which way does she usually walk? Down Sussex Street or Windsor Street?"

Alice rolled her eyes. "Windsor Street, of course. She won't go near Sussex Street with all those Catholics."

Of course. Nell grabbed her cloak but didn't wait to put it on before she stepped outside.

When she got to the corner of Windsor Street, she paused and peered down the road. It was filling up as mothers made their way to school to pick up their children, but there was no sign of Maria. *That's strange.* She hurried past the dawdling groups but stopped when she reached the junction with Sussex Street and studied the backs of the women walking away from her. *No, she's not there.*

She turned the corner and carried on to Sarah's, not stopping to knock when she arrived. "It's only me."

Sarah met her at the door to the living room. "You took your time."

"What do you mean? Is Maria still here?"

"Yes, I'm here." Maria sounded breathless and Nell dashed into the room to join her. "I'm sorry, but I was worn out by the time I got here and couldn't face walking home on my own. We knew someone would come looking for me."

Sarah stood with her arms folded. "We were expecting you half an hour ago."

"I've not long been back from Betty's." She crouched by Maria's chair. "Are you all right?"

"Much better, but I was well enough when I left home. That's why I didn't want to risk going back on my own in case I came over faint again."

Nell scowled at Sarah as she stood up. "Why didn't you or one of the girls walk with her instead of waiting for me?"

Sarah pointed to the table behind her, where two of her daughters were sewing. "In case you haven't noticed, Ada and Mabel are busy, and I don't have the energy to walk to Upper Hill Street and back, either. We're not as young as you."

"All right." She turned to Maria. "Are you ready to go?"

"I think so." Maria pushed herself up and walked to the door where Nell helped her on with her cloak. "I'll see you soon, Sarah, but perhaps you should come to me next time."

Once the front door closed behind them, Nell linked Maria's arm as they headed towards Windsor Street.

"What was up with her?"

"What do you mean? She's been fine with me. She told me about Sam's new lady, Margaret. She's rather taken with her."

"That's fortunate."

"It is. They've announced a date for the wedding, too. Boxing Day of this year."

Nell screwed up her face. "That's a strange day."

"Sam said it's a holiday, so he won't need to take any time off work."

Before Nell could answer, Maria sucked air through her teeth and held her side.

"What's the matter?"

"I've a pain under my ribs. We must be walking too quickly."

Nell glanced around. *We're hardly moving.* "All right, let's take it more gradually. If you need to stop, let me know."

"Let's see if we can make it to Windsor Street and stop for a rest on the corner."

"Take my arm then." *I hope Alice thinks to do the tea. George will be home before us at this rate.*

CHAPTER EIGHT

Mr Marsh came home from work and rubbed his hands together, a broad grin on his face.

"Now for two days' holiday and a trip to Blackpool. I'm really looking forward to it."

"You're home early, too, even for a Saturday." Nell returned his smile as she handed him a cup of tea. "Have you been to Blackpool before? It's near where you grew up, isn't it?"

"No, it's miles away. Blackpool's closer to Liverpool than where I'm from."

"How will we know where to go when we get there?"

Mr Marsh chuckled. "We follow everyone else. There'll be plenty who've been before, and if not, we can ask. I'm sure people will point us in the right direction."

"I hope the weather's nice. I'd like to wear my new hat."

"I'm taking my umbrella just in case. We can't be too careful."

Alice rested her chin on her clenched hands. "I wish we

were coming with you. It would be lovely to see the sea without all the docks in the way. And some sand."

Nell took a seat at the table. "There's another holiday in August. If we enjoy it, we could all go."

"I'd like that. If Harry gives himself any time off, that is. He might be forced to give his workers a day off, but he's not so keen on stopping himself."

Mr Marsh sipped his tea. "If there's the chance of a day trip, I'm sure he'd be interested. What would you do with the children?"

"We'd take them with us."

"Really?"

"Of course. The boys would love it."

He sniffed and placed his cup on its saucer. "I suppose it wouldn't cost too much if you travel third class."

Nell rolled her eyes. "Don't be like that. I'm sure Mr Wood could take them first class if he wanted to."

"I only meant you wouldn't expect children in first class, that's all." He glanced at the clock. "Shall we take a walk when we've finished this?"

"We can do. We may meet the girls if we go to Princes Park. They've taken Georgie and Freddie to feed the ducks."

He groaned. "Perhaps we'll go to Sefton Park, then."

"They won't bite."

"I'm aware of that but I don't relax the same when they're with us."

"What about Alice? Is she allowed to join us?"

Alice held up her hand. "Thank you anyway, but before you answer, I'd better stay with Mam. I don't want her waking up to an empty house. Besides, I need to be here when the girls come home, to make tea."

"They shouldn't need much supervision. I thought your mam would object when Edith suggested it, but she seems happy to let her take charge."

Alice sighed. "It gives her a break, that's why. She might insist on cooking during the week, but it wears her out. I'm sure she thinks that if she carries on as if nothing's happened, it will all go away."

"If only it was that simple. Still, she may prove the doctors wrong yet." Nell picked up her cup but put it down again when the letterbox rattled. "What's that?" She went to the hall and retrieved two letters from the doormat. "I don't have a letter for weeks and then two at once. This is from Mrs Robertson and this..." she turned the envelope over "...is from James!"

Alice grinned. "About time, too. What does he say?"

Nell put the letter from Mrs Robertson behind the clock and sliced the envelope of James's letter before returning to the table.

"Not a lot." Nell scanned the single sheet of writing paper. "He got my letter about your mam and said he's leaving Brazil in July so should be with us about mid-August."

Alice's face paled. "Why's he leaving it so long?"

"He says he can't get away any sooner." Nell sighed. "I tried not to alarm him with the letter I wrote, but perhaps I overdid it and he didn't understand how serious it was."

"What did you say?"

"That she was ill, there was nothing more the doctor could do for her and that he should come home as soon as possible."

Alice shook her head. "He's not stupid. He should have realised what that meant."

"Then I don't know. There's not much we can do about it, anyway. If I write again, the letter will only arrive a week or two before he's due to leave."

Mr Marsh joined them and put his cup and saucer on the table. "Talking about leaving, are you ready to go?"

"Give me a minute to finish this tea. I'll read Mrs Robertson's letter when we get back."

The park was busy when they arrived, but there were more people leaving than arriving and Nell nodded to several neighbours as they passed on the footpaths.

"We came at a good time. Everyone's on their way home."

"I suppose it's a benefit of the girls cooking the tea. At least having a big family means you can usually get away when you want to."

"It's easier when it's you who wants to take me out. Maria won't argue with you, but if I decide to go out on my own, it's a different matter."

"I've not seen her like that recently. Perhaps she's accepted you're a married woman and as long as I'm happy for you to do something, then so is she."

"I'm afraid it's more likely to be because she's not well. She's lost a lot of her fire lately. On one hand, it's nice, but on the other..."

"Come on, cheer up." Mr Marsh pointed to a seat near one of the smaller lakes. "Shall we enjoy the view?"

"That would be nice." Nell stretched her legs out in front

of her. "I love the blossom at this time of year. It's a shame it can't stay like this."

"You wouldn't appreciate it if it did."

"I'm sure I would."

He shook his head. "You'd stop noticing. It's only when we miss something that we appreciate the things we have..."

His words faded from her consciousness as she gazed at the two men walking towards her. *Mr Massey. How long's he been in Liverpool? And where's Elenor?*

He smirked at her as they approached but looked away when Mr Marsh glared at him.

"Do you know those men?"

"What men? Oh, them. No. Why would I?"

"Why did he smile at you?"

"How do I know? He must have seen me here with Rebecca and recognised me."

"Are you sure that's all it is?"

Nell's voice squeaked. "What else would it be?"

"I hope you've not forgotten we don't keep secrets from each other."

"Of course not."

"Then why are you so flustered?"

"I-I'm not used to strange men smiling at me. And I don't like you questioning me. All I was doing was sitting here minding my own business."

"Yes, well." He settled back beside her. "I must admit, he was a little on the young side."

"What does that mean?"

"It means I'm confident he's not your type."

"I should hope you know that I don't take an interest in other men, whatever their age."

He patted her hand. "Calm down. I didn't mean to upset you."

You could have fooled me. She slumped in her chair. *What do I do now? I can't let Elenor walk out with him unchaperoned.*

Mr Marsh nudged her. "You're not sulking, are you?"

"You need to watch what you say. You should remember we've argued about things like that in the past and it never turns out to be my fault."

"All right, I'm sorry." He reached for her hand. "I don't want an argument to spoil Monday. You do realise we'll have to be up early?"

"Monday?"

"We're going to Blackpool." He gasped. "Don't tell me you've forgotten."

Her heart rate quickened. *I can't leave Elenor on her own all day.*

"I've arranged for a carriage to pick us up at half past six in the morning. I didn't think you'd want to walk at that hour."

"No..." *I don't want to go to the railway station at any time on Monday.* "That was thoughtful."

"You're not very excited."

"Oh, I am, but ... I don't know what to expect. That's all. I'm sure I'll be fine once we get there."

He took out his pocket watch. "We should be heading back. It's nearly half past four."

Nell nodded. *Elenor had better be home. I'll kill her if she isn't.*

. . .

Maria and Alice were at the table when they arrived and once Mr Marsh disappeared into the backyard, Nell popped her head into the kitchen where Edith and Leah were peeling potatoes.

"Where's Elenor?"

Leah spoke without looking up. "She went to see Ruth."

Nell's stomach churned. "She's supposed to be learning how to make tea. When did she go?"

Edith stopped what she was doing. "She'd gone by the time I arrived at the lake."

"She left Leah on her own with Georgie and Freddie?"

"I didn't mind. She was being a nuisance, telling me not to get a job."

"That's beside the point. How long were you on your own?"

Leah creased her forehead. "I didn't notice. The boys were still feeding the ducks when she left, so probably about half past two."

"And I expect it was turned three when Edith arrived." Nell took a deep breath when Edith nodded. *Don't overreact. She wasn't with Mr Massey when I saw him.*

Edith lowered her voice. "Don't look so worried. She said she'd be home for five."

She'd better be. "Would you like me to help with anything?"

"No, it's all under control. You sit down."

Nell wandered to the fireplace and picked up Mrs Robertson's letter, but dropped it back behind the clock, and hurried to the hall, when the front door opened. "Oh. It's you."

Billy grinned at her. "That's a fine welcome."

"I didn't mean it like that. I thought it might be Elenor."

"She's on her way. I saw her walking down Upper Hill Street."

She bit her lip. "Was she on her own?"

"I think so, why?"

"Leah said she'd gone to see her friend, and I wondered if they were still together."

"No. She's all yours."

Maria smiled at Billy as he joined them. "Are you on your own?"

"Dad won't be long, but I walked with Vernon and he needed to be home."

"He shouldn't even be in the alehouse with the baby nearly ready to arrive."

"He's not worried. It is the fifth time he's done it."

"That doesn't make it any easier on Lydia."

Billy shrugged. "Take it up with him, not me."

Maria was about to respond when the front door opened again and Nell slipped into the hall, pulling the door closed behind her.

"Where've you been?"

Elenor kept her head down. "Out."

"I know very well out, but where in particular? You had no right to leave Leah on her own with the boys."

"They weren't causing any trouble."

"I don't care. What I care about is you disappearing off to see Mr Massey without even a word that he's back in Liverpool."

Elenor's head shot up, her eyes wide. "How did you know?"

"Because I saw him. When I was with Uncle Thomas,

too. If you don't start telling me what's going on, you're going to end up in a great deal of trouble."

"He only arrived yesterday..."

"That's convenient. Is he about to leave tomorrow as well?"

Elenor lowered her eyes. "No. Not for another ten days."

"Well, if you think you're going out as and when you like, you've another think coming. I thought we'd talked about this, but it clearly didn't sink in."

"But I want to see him."

"I asked you to introduce him to Uncle Thomas first and make it official. You'll get yourself a reputation if you walk out with him on your own. Don't you care?"

"It wouldn't be that bad."

Nell snorted. "Do you want to be the talk of the street, with everyone pointing their fingers every time you go outside? Trust me, it's not very nice. Now, get in there and help Edith with the tea. We'll talk about this later."

CHAPTER NINE

E lenor was the first out of the house the following
morning, but Nell pulled her back inside as the rest of
the family left.

"Not so fast. I want a word with you."

"We're going to church."

"I'm aware of that, but you can walk with me and tell me
what's going on. Let everyone else get ahead of us first."

Elenor pouted. "We're not walking with Uncle Thomas,
are we?"

"No. I've told him I want to speak to you about your
behaviour."

She gasped. "What did you do that for? You know how
angry he gets."

"Then you'd better start behaving yourself. I've asked
him to let me sort you out, so you'd better cooperate. I don't
want to be in trouble any more than you do."

Elenor stamped her foot. "All I want to do is walk around
the park with Will. Why is that so wrong?"

"It's the way you're making such a secret of it. People

only do that if they've something to hide." Nell glanced at the clock. "We need to go."

Elenor said nothing as she stepped outside and waited for Nell to join her.

"What are your plans for the next ten days?"

"To see each other in the afternoons."

"And who's chaperoning you?"

"Ruth."

Nell stared at her. "That magical person Ruth who has a habit of disappearing and leaving you on your own? You must think I'm daft."

"I don't want her listening to our conversations."

"Why not? You shouldn't be talking about anything that needs hiding."

"We're not, but it doesn't feel right..."

"Where are you meeting him this afternoon?"

"Sefton Park."

"Then I'll be there, too. It's time we introduced him to Uncle Thomas..."

"No!" Elenor's face paled. "You can't do that. Please, Mam. You know he'll try to stop us."

"He won't if it's all in the open."

"He'll find a reason."

Nell sighed. "Do you have a better idea?"

Elenor gave her a sideways glance. "May I tell Alice? She often takes the boys to the park."

"What about Mr Wood? He'll be with her this afternoon."

"I'd rather he knows than Uncle Thomas."

"All right. Speak to them as soon as you can and tell me what they say."

"I'll ask Alice first." Elenor hesitated. "I want to be sure Mr Wood won't tell Uncle Thomas. I don't want him to find out about Will until he has to."

"Very well."

They turned into the churchyard as Maria struggled up the path on Alice's arm.

"Let me help Aunty Maria to her seat and I'll tell Alice you want to speak to her. Wait for me after church so we can walk home together."

"What if she says no?"

"We'll need to think of something else. I won't have you going out with Mr Massey on your own."

The sun broke through the clouds as Nell left church at the end of the service, and she blinked several times as she scanned the graveyard. Elenor stood away from the door but acknowledged her as she approached.

"I spoke to Alice."

"Will she chaperone you?"

"She will, and she said not to worry about Mr Wood. He won't say anything, but she suggested we don't link arms so he won't think too much of it."

"And are you happy to do that?"

Elenor nodded. "It will only be for today, while Mr Wood's with her, and at least we'll be able to talk to each other."

"That's all I want you doing every other day, as well. You need to tell me where you're going, too, so I don't accidentally take Uncle Thomas there at the same time."

"He'll be at work ... and you're going on your trip tomorrow."

"That's beside the point. You don't realise the risk I'm taking by doing this. Aunty Maria wouldn't have let Alice out of the house at your age if she'd known she was seeing anyone. She wasn't happy when she was twenty-one."

"Aunty Maria was only sixteen when she started walking out with Uncle George..."

"I don't care. With her, it was all perfectly above board. There was no sneaking out and lying. There'll be trouble if you bring any disgrace on the family..."

"I won't. I promise."

Nell nodded. "Good. Now, let's get home so we can have dinner ready for when Aunty Maria arrives."

They walked at a good pace and caught up with Edith and Leah as they turned into Upper Hill Street.

Edith turned round as they approached. "Isn't Uncle Thomas with you? He's usually stuck to your side on a Sunday."

Nell chuckled. "I told him we need to do the dinner, so it would be better if we went ahead."

Edith smirked. "It won't take four of us to drain the cabbage and make some gravy.

"He needn't know that."

Leah linked Nell's arm. "Who's walking with Aunty Maria?"

"Uncle George. Alice reckons he feels guilty about everyone else helping when he's not."

Edith shook her head. "He must want something. That's usually the reason men are nice to us."

"He's not that bad."

Edith sighed. "Maybe not, but I remember what my dad and brothers were like. Not to mention their friends."

"Well, Uncle George is different. He's probably in a good mood because he doesn't have to go to work tomorrow but he'll still get paid."

"We all are. We don't get many days off." Edith pushed open the front door and walked straight into the living room. "What's everyone doing this afternoon?"

"I'm walking to the park with Uncle Thomas. What about you?"

"I don't know." She looked at Elenor and Leah. "What are you both doing?"

Leah shrugged. "We could go to the park, too?"

"I-I'm seeing Ruth." Elenor said no more before she slipped out of the back door, leaving Leah staring after her.

"She sees more of Ruth than she does of us."

"Hopefully, they'll fall out again soon. Why don't you come to Princes Park with me and Uncle Thomas? He shouldn't mind, given we're going out together tomorrow."

"I'd like that." Edith walked to the kitchen and took the meat from the range. "I hardly see you when I'm at work all week, and then he keeps you to himself on a Sunday."

"Well, we'll have to fix that. Let me speak to him."

The dinner was ready by the time George escorted Maria into the house, but she paused to catch her breath. "My. I need to practise my walking. I was never this bad."

Alice unfastened her cloak. "You've not been well."

"I should be getting better, but I feel as if I'm getting worse."

"You're doing fine." Nell helped her into a seat by the fireplace. "Sit there a minute and get your breath back, then you can come to the table. We're almost ready."

"It might take more than a minute. Serve everyone else, first. I don't want much."

Nell ushered everyone to the table, and once they had their plates, Nell helped her sister to the seat next to Elenor.

"There you go. A slice of beef, one potato and a few carrots. You should be able to manage that."

"I hope so."

Everyone's plates were long empty by the time Maria laid down her knife and fork, and Mr Wood waited for her to settle back in her chair before he banged a teaspoon on the side of his cup.

"I hope you don't mind waiting a minute longer for pudding, but I've an announcement. It's mainly for Mr and Mrs Marsh, but I thought you'd all like to hear it."

Maria's eyes were bright. "Go on."

He grinned. "Alice was so envious of you going to Blackpool that I've arranged for us to join you."

Alice clapped her hands together. "How wonderful. Are the boys coming, too?"

"No. Just the two of us. I thought the girls could look after them." He looked at Mr Marsh. "I hope you don't mind."

"Mind ... n-no, of course not..." His face reddened as Nell fought to stop her dinner coming back up.

What do I do with Elenor now? She risked a glance across the table where Elenor struggled to hide her smile. *I'm not leaving her on her own.*

Leah folded her arms and banged them on the table. "Why can't we all go?"

Nell hadn't realised she'd been holding her breath and coughed as she tried to speak. "I-I told you, we'll all go in August."

"Well, don't book any tickets without me." Billy glanced round the table. "It would have been nice to be asked, if I'm honest."

Mr Wood grimaced. "I'm sorry. I didn't realise everyone else wanted to go. There should be tickets left if anyone wants to join us."

Nell stole a glance at her husband as he sat in silence. "It would be nice for us all to go, but we can't leave your mam."

"Oh." Alice's cheeks flushed as her eyes flicked first to Elenor and then to Maria. "I'm sorry. I wasn't thinking..."

"Don't worry about me. You go and enjoy your day out. The girls will be here for me." Maria patted Elenor's hand. "Won't you?"

"I ... erm..."

Nell glared at her. "Of course they will. We'll sort something out so no one's on their own."

Mr Marsh was tight-lipped as he and Nell followed Edith and Leah around Princes Park. Nell studied them as they laughed together.

"They get on so well. It's a shame they can't come with us tomorrow."

"You'd like that, wouldn't you? The more the merrier."

She shook her head. "I'd like it because they'd enjoy it."

"I should be thankful they need to stay with Mrs Atkin then."

"Don't be like that." Nell's stomach cramped, and she took a deep breath. "There's no harm in other people joining us."

"I wanted a day out together. Just the two of us."

"And we still can. It's only Alice and Mr Wood coming and we needn't stay with them."

"They'll follow us around like sheep..."

Nell sighed. "Are you going to let it ruin our day? We may as well not go if you are."

"Of course we'll still go. You're not getting out of it that easily."

"I'm not trying to get out of it, but if you're going to be in this sort of mood..."

"I'm not in a mood."

"You could have fooled me." Her stomach cramped again, and she bent forward to relieve the pain.

"What's the matter?"

"I've got stomach ache. May we sit down?"

His petulance changed to concern as he ushered her to the nearest seat. "What's brought this on?"

"I-I don't know." She grimaced again. "Maybe I ate too much dinner."

"You didn't finish your pudding."

"I didn't feel like it."

"Are you sure you're all right?"

"Give me a minute. Will you go after the girls and tell them we've stopped? They can carry on walking if they want and we'll catch them up."

"Can I leave you on your own?"

"Yes, I'll be fine." *I'll be even better when you go to Blackpool...*

He returned less than a minute later, but Edith and Leah were with him.

"What's the matter?" Leah squeezed onto the seat beside her. "Uncle Thomas says you've got stomach ache."

"Not again." Edith studied her. "You've not had that for ages."

Nell swallowed hard as she avoided Mr Marsh's gaze. "I-I'm worried about your Aunty Maria. She's been like a mam to me and I hate to see her ill."

Leah linked her arm into Nell's. "There's no point making yourself ill over it. She'll be better soon enough, and we don't want you ending up the same way."

"I won't, I promise, but I can't help worrying."

"I was like that when my mam was ill." Edith's tone was steady as she stood in front of Nell. "Is she going to die?"

"Erm..."

Mr Marsh cut Nell off. "Not yet. Now can we stop being so morbid?" He looked between Edith and Leah. "You two carry on and we'll catch you up."

Reluctantly, they left and Nell watched them with tears in her eyes. "Don't be hard on them..."

"They shouldn't know too much about Mrs Atkin. It will only upset them, and you don't want her finding out."

"You're right." Her stomach twinged again. "I don't think sitting down is helping. Let's go to the lake and see if I can shake it off."

CHAPTER TEN

Despite the early hour, the day was bright as Mr Marsh shook Nell's shoulder to wake her.

"Come along, sleepy. Time to get up. The carriage will be here in half an hour."

She pulled her knees to her chest as her stomach spasmed. "I can't go..." Her face was twisted as Mr Marsh gazed down at her.

"What do you mean? We've been looking forward to this for weeks."

"I-I'm sorry, but I'd be no company. I've hardly slept, and the pain is worse than yesterday..."

She avoided his gaze as he perched on the edge of the bed.

"Will you be all right?"

"I'll be fine. Why don't you ask Billy to go with you? He's bound to be awake with all the noise downstairs and he's miserable about being left behind." She grimaced. "We can book again for August..."

"And you don't know what's brought this on?"

"No. I'm sorry. Really, I am. I know you've been excited about going, but I'd only spoil it."

"Only because I'd be with you. It won't be the same strolling down the pier with Billy..."

"Please go, both of you, and have a good day. I'll stay in bed for another hour and see how I feel."

Mr Marsh hesitated as she doubled up again. "As long as you don't mind."

"Of course I don't. The girls are here..."

He leaned forward to kiss her forehead. "Very well."

Nell watched him leave, his shoulders rounded, but didn't relax until he'd gone upstairs to speak to Billy and then returned, taking the second flight down to the living room. *Billy must have said yes.*

Her stomach continued to churn until she heard her nephew tearing down the stairs five minutes later, shouting for a cup of tea. *If anyone was still asleep, they won't be now.*

As soon as the front door closed and the carriage pulled away, she drifted back to sleep, only waking when Edith and Leah barged downstairs with Georgie and Freddie.

Leah's voice travelled across the landing. "I'm going to tell Mam about Elenor..."

"Leave her to me. I'll speak to her."

"She won't listen..."

Nell groaned as they disappeared into the living room. *What's she done now?*

A second later, Elenor followed them. "Mam knows, anyway..."

Time to get up. She grabbed her dressing gown but didn't wait to fasten it as she headed downstairs. Leah had her hands on her hips when she arrived.

"...we saw Ruth in Princes Park yesterday, but she wasn't with you..."

"That's enough."

Three sets of eyes turned towards Nell as she stood in the doorway.

"Mam!" Elenor's face went white. "I thought..."

"You thought I'd gone out?"

"Y-yes."

"And that with me *and* Alice out of the way, you could sneak off with Mr Massey?"

Leah gasped. "You're walking out with someone...?"

Edith looked at Leah. "That explains a lot."

"I wasn't going to leave them for the whole day."

"Yes, you were."

Nell glared at Elenor. "Well?"

Elenor said nothing as she dropped onto a chair by the fire. "I didn't think you'd mind..."

"And in which world was that likely? I've been telling you for months you weren't to see him without a chaperone. Did you really think I was going to leave you here without any supervision?"

Edith studied Nell. "Is that why you had stomach ache yesterday? Because you were worried about Elenor?"

"I've been ill all night worrying about what she'd get up to, with me and Alice missing, and I was right to be."

Elenor wiped her eyes with the back of her hand. "When did you decide to stay at home?"

"As soon as I found out Alice wouldn't be here to walk to the park with you."

"Why didn't you say...?"

"I wasn't going to announce it in front of Uncle Thomas.

I had to let him see I was ill to get out of going today. Have you any idea how upset he was? If he finds out why I didn't go, there'll be trouble."

"So he doesn't know you were pretending?"

"I was doing nothing of the sort. I've been sick to my stomach all night. I can only hope that now they've gone, I'll relax."

Leah flapped her arms by her sides. "So what do we do now?"

"First, someone needs to take Aunty Maria a cup of tea. She'll be wondering what's going on." Nell stepped to the table but stopped when she saw a note by the teapot written in Mr Marsh's elegant script. "What's this?

'Mr Atkin has joined us for the day.

I'll miss you.

Thomas.'

Nell turned the paper over in her hand. "That's short and sweet."

Edith peered over her shoulder. "Does he mean Uncle George?"

"I expect so. He'd never call Billy Mr Atkin. At least that gets them all out of the way. Right, someone pour the tea, then after breakfast, you and Leah can tidy up while Elenor comes to the shop with me."

Elenor gasped. "The shop?"

"Yes. And if you've got any sense, you won't argue."

Elenor stared at the footpath as she waited outside the house for Nell to manoeuvre Freddie's pram from the hall. Once the door was closed and Georgie was holding the side of the handle, she turned the pram towards Windsor Street.

"Where are you meeting him?"

"What?" Elenor's eyes were wide.

"Mr Massey. Where are you meeting him? And what time?"

Elenor huffed. "In Sefton Park. At eleven o'clock."

"We've time to go to the shop first then."

"What do you mean?"

Nell started towards Windsor Street. "If you think I'm leaving you to spend the day with him, you're very much mistaken. We'll go to the shop and then the park. You won't listen to a word I say, so maybe I can talk some sense into him."

"You can't do that!"

"I can, and I will. If you want to walk out with someone, I want to know who they are. Did he introduce himself to Alice yesterday?"

"They waved to each other."

"What about Mr Wood?"

"He didn't seem interested."

"Well, I am, and Uncle Thomas will be too, so we'll take a walk together while he tells me the truth about himself."

"He's already told you..."

"Not enough, he hasn't."

"What about Aunty Maria? She'll wonder where we are..."

"I told Edith we might be a while. You're not getting out of it that easily."

Elenor waited outside the shop with the pram and once Nell rejoined her, they took the long way round to the park.

"We'll be late going this way."

"It's not much further, but we can't go back past the house in case anyone's in the front room. You should be thankful I think of things like that. Does Mr Massey ever bring his friend with him? What's his name? Mr Young."

Elenor nodded. "Sometimes."

"Was he bringing him today?"

"He didn't say."

"We'll find out then, shall we?"

Mr Massey was waiting near the lake when they arrived, but his smile faded when he saw Nell.

"Mrs Marsh."

"Mr Massey. Shall we carry on walking?" Nell indicated to the footpath. "No Mr Young today?"

"Erm, no."

"It must be unfortunate that I've turned up and spoiled your day together."

Georgie had been quiet by the pram but he pointed at Mr Massey. "I saw him yesterday." He sniggered to himself. "He gave Aunty Elenor a kiss."

Nell gaped at her nephew. "A kiss?"

Nell turned to Elenor, but Mr Massey stood between them before she could speak.

"It's not what you think."

"What is it then?"

He looked down at his feet as Nell rounded on him. "Well, it was a kiss, but only on her hand. When she was leaving."

"So that makes it all right?" She left the pram and stood

in front of Elenor. "Do you think I'm stupid? People don't kiss each other in public. Especially when they're not even married. Many a woman would blush at the suggestion of linking arms with a man, let alone anything else. What's wrong with you?" She spun to Mr Massey. "How old are you?"

"Twenty-one."

"Did you hear that?" She shook Elenor's arm, but she pulled it away.

"Stop it. I'm not doing anything you haven't done."

"What?" Nell took a step backwards. "You can't compare me and Uncle Thomas with the two of you."

"I'm not. I saw you with another man. Years ago."

"What man?" Nell's heart pounded.

"The one who came asking after you. You ran to the end of the street to meet him and he kissed your hand. Twice. He even looked as if he was going to kiss you properly. In the street..." Elenor's words faded into the background.

Ollie. They were watching us?

"...so if it's all right for you..."

Nell flinched. "It wasn't the same at all. He was a friend who'd come to say farewell. I haven't seen him since."

"Does Uncle Thomas know about him?" Elenor's smirk changed to a gasp as Nell slapped her across the face.

"You ungrateful madam. After everything I've done for you."

Elenor's eyes were defiant as she touched the red mark on her face. "So he doesn't."

"Yes, he does. Not that it's any of your business, but he was the reason Uncle Thomas disappeared for three years."

"Oh." Elenor's shoulders sagged.

"I'm sorry you're disappointed, but that doesn't come close to how I feel about you right now." Nell thought her heart would burst through her chest. "Were you planning to ruin my life so you could get your own way? Well, good luck to you. If you want to leave home and elope together, don't let me stop you, but don't come crying to me when it all goes wrong."

Nell grabbed the pram and set off along the path, not waiting to see if Georgie was with her, but Mr Massey caught her arm.

"Mrs Marsh, I'm sorry. We wouldn't have said anything."

"You may not have..." She glared at Elenor, who had tears in her eyes.

"I wouldn't either. I just wanted you to understand."

"I understand perfectly well. What you don't seem to realise is that you're still a child."

"I'm not!"

Nell gasped. "I'm not explaining it to you now and certainly not in front of Mr Massey, but you've a lot of growing up to do. If you want to live at home, you do as you're told and realise that I know a lot more about life than you do."

"Please, Mrs Marsh, don't be angry." Mr Massey suddenly seemed younger than his twenty-one years. "I promise you can trust us from now on. We won't walk out together without a chaperone. You can join us, if you like. I'm fond of Elenor, but..."

"You'll be going away soon, and don't want the burden of a wife. Is that it?"

He kicked a stone across the path. "We've not known each other long enough."

"I'm glad one of you has some sense." She pulled out her pocket watch then looked at Elenor. "We need to get home for dinner, then, assuming you don't plan on eloping this afternoon, I suggest you meet Mr Massey here at two o'clock."

Elenor glanced at Mr Massey, who nodded.

"I'll send Edith and Leah to chaperone you. I can't expect them to stay in all day, and I trust them to keep an eye on you." She pushed Elenor ahead of her. "Good day, Mr Massey."

CHAPTER ELEVEN

Georgie ran beside the pram as Nell stormed towards the entrance to the park.

"Slow down, Aunty Nell."

"I need to get home for dinner." She paused for breath, glaring at Elenor. "I hope you're happy."

When Elenor didn't respond, she bent down to Georgie. "Shall we sit you in the pram with Freddie?"

He stepped away from her.

"Don't be frightened. I'm not cross with you." She wrapped an arm around him and kissed his forehead. "Let me lift you up."

"Is Aunty Elenor naughty?"

"It's all sorted out now." She settled him at the end of the pram with his back to her, but Elenor kept her head down as they carried on walking.

"I didn't mean to cause any trouble."

"Well, next time, stop and think. You've a lot to learn, and I can see I'll need to teach you myself. Not that it should concern you at your age."

"What do you mean?"

"I mean, young ladies shouldn't be interested in men when they're only sixteen. I was twenty-four when I married your dad."

"How long had you known him before that?"

"A couple of years."

"I'd like to get to know Will better, and we've not even spoken of marriage."

"That's beside the point. The thing is..." *How do I say this?* "Your body's changing..."

"I know." Elenor clasped her arms across her chest.

"Not just that. You're getting to an age where..." Nell's cheeks flushed. "Let's say that, if you get too close to a man, you'll end up in the family way..."

Elenor gasped. "Have a baby? But I'm too young."

"Exactly. That's why you need to be careful."

"Is that why you're worried?"

Nell nodded. "Can you imagine telling your Aunty Maria...? Or Uncle Thomas...?"

Elenor shuddered. "Why haven't you told me this before?"

"Because you're too young and you wouldn't tell me what you were doing."

"So I can't go near him?"

"Walking is fine. But no more than that. Not even a kiss." *It can lead to much more...*

Elenor fell silent.

"That's why you don't see men and women close until they're married. Women can't be having children before a wedding band. They'd bring shame on the family."

"How would you know if you'd been too close?"

"You just would."

Edith had dinner made by the time they got home, and once it was over, the girls disappeared, leaving Nell to tidy up. Maria watched as she cleared the table.

"Are you feeling better?"

"I am, thank you. Going for a walk this morning did me the world of good." She grinned. "Who'd have thought that George would want to go to Blackpool?"

"Certainly not me. I'm glad he has, though. It's better than him being in the alehouse all day, which was his only other alternative."

"I expect they'll still call in on their way home." Nell gave the table a final wipe. "What would you like to do this afternoon?"

"I thought we could take a walk around the block, to get my lungs working again."

"We can, if you like. Which block were you thinking of? I doubt you'd make it as far as Princes Road."

Maria's shoulders slumped. "You're probably right."

"We could do the square around Windsor Street and Sussex Street."

"I'm not going there."

Nell sighed. "It's a perfectly normal street."

"The street may be normal, the people aren't. The Catholics should have stayed in Ireland."

Nell shook her head. "All right, calm down. How about we walk down Windsor Street to Upper Warwick Street and back again?"

"Yes, that will be enough. I won't do it as quickly as you

would on your own."

The sun was warm when they stepped onto the footpath, and Maria clung to Nell's arm as they set off.

"Why did you take a walk with Elenor this morning?"

Nell shrugged. "We don't spend a lot of time together, and the way she's been answering me back lately, I thought it was a good way of talking to her."

"And was it?"

"I hope so. She's growing up now, changing, and it's not always easy."

"You indulge her too much. In my day, and yours, you had to get on with it, and none of us were any the worse for it."

Nell paused when they turned into Windsor Street. "Would you say I set her a bad example?"

"By going away, you mean?"

"By seeing Thomas on and off for so many years."

"Has she said something?"

"Not as such."

"It's your guilty conscience, I shouldn't wonder. Leah doesn't seem troubled by it."

"She takes things much more in her stride."

"As long as she knows who's in charge, that should be enough."

Nell sighed. "Do you think that should be me or Thomas?"

"Well, that's a question." Maria's breathing had become laboured. "If she was a boy, I'd definitely say Mr Marsh, but maybe it should be you. I get the impression he doesn't know how to handle them."

"He doesn't. He'd be happiest if he could take me away

and the two of us lived somewhere else."

"He'd better not. He'll have me to answer to if he does."

Nell grimaced. "And me. I couldn't think of anything worse."

The walk that would usually take less than ten minutes had taken over half an hour, and Maria collapsed into her chair as Nell hung up their cloaks.

"You sit there and I'll put the kettle on." She stopped by the fireplace. "I'd forgotten about that letter."

"That's not like you. Who's it from?"

"Mrs Robertson. It came on Saturday, but there's been so much going on, it went clean out of my head. Still, we've an hour or so until the girls come back, so I'll read it in a minute."

Maria was asleep by the time she'd made the tea, and Nell put a cup on the table beside her before she retrieved the letter. *Let's see what she has to say.*

Dear Mrs Marsh

We arrived back in Liverpool on Wednesday, but you may be pleased to hear I won't be going away again this month. We're disembarking over the weekend and moving to a small house near you, on Hill Street, until we find a more permanent home.

I passed your list of suggestions to my husband for consideration, so I may have more news when you visit. Any day next week is agreeable, if it's convenient for you.

Warmest regards

Mrs Robertson

Hill Street. That's no more than five minutes' walk. She couldn't keep the smile from her face. *That's the best news I've had for a while, although I don't know how she'll manage in such a small place.*

Maria stirred as Nell leaned forward for her cup. "Did I doze off again?"

"Not for long. Your tea will still be warm."

Maria sat up straight. "I'll have this and then get the tea cooking for tonight. It will seem strange with only five of us."

"You'll do no such thing. I'll do it."

"You can help, but I'm not ready to sit down and die just yet."

Maria and the girls had gone to bed, and Nell was sitting by the fire when the front door opened. *Here we go.* Mr Marsh was the first into the living room and she stood up to greet him.

"Did you have a nice time?"

"Very nice, thank you, but how are you?"

"Better, thank you. Are you on your own?"

"No, we're here." Alice joined them with Mr Wood. "It's such a shame you weren't with us. We had a lovely time."

Mr Wood smirked. "Billy was glad you couldn't make it. He really enjoyed himself."

"And there were no problems with George joining you?"

"There was a queue for tickets, but he got one with five minutes to spare. It's a good job we were there early."

"At least it all worked out. Shall I put the kettle on?"

"Please." Alice took a seat at the table. "I'm worn out after everything we've done. I didn't realise the piers went out so far over the sea. We ended up walking along two of them."

"Goodness. Give me a minute." Nell disappeared to the kitchen. *He's too quiet.* She took her time putting the cups and saucers on a tray before she carried it to the table. "Did you have anything to eat?"

Mr Wood grinned. "We found someone selling fish and chips. They wrapped it in old newspaper and we sat on the beach eating it."

"Was it nice?"

"Delicious!"

"Well, I'm glad you enjoyed yourselves. Perhaps we can go again in August." She didn't wait for Mr Marsh to respond and slipped back into the kitchen. "The tea won't be a minute."

Once it was poured, Mr Marsh joined her at the table. "You've made a good recovery."

"Yes." *I'm being too cheerful.* "I went back to sleep after you'd gone and felt a little better when I woke up."

"What have you done since?"

She coughed to clear the squeak from her voice. "Nothing much. Elenor helped me with the shopping this morning and then I was well enough this afternoon to take a short walk with Maria. When we came back, I wrote to Mrs Robertson. She'll be in Liverpool for the next month, so I'll visit her later in the week."

"Unless you're ill again."

"Well ... yes, but I should be over it soon." She walked to the door. "If you'll excuse me, I need to go to bed. I didn't sleep very well last night and my stomach still isn't right. See you in the morning."

CHAPTER TWELVE

N ell dabbed her napkin against her lips and sat back in her chair as Leah finished the last of the cakes.

"Did you like that?"

Her daughter cleared her mouth. "It was wonderful, thank you. I understand now why you enjoy coming here so much. Did Uncle Thomas give you the money in the end?"

"No, after our last discussion, I kept some for myself rather than hand it over to him."

"Didn't he mind?"

"He raised an eyebrow, but it's my money and I told him so."

Leah grinned. "I need to do that if I ever have any money of my own."

Nell glanced around. "Could you imagine yourself working in a place like this?"

"Oh, yes. Especially if they let us have a few sandwiches and cakes while we're here."

"I'm not sure they would, but I wouldn't ask until you get

the job. Do you want to go to the counter and ask about the vacancy?"

Leah hesitated. "Would you do it? I don't know what to say."

"You can't be shy when you're working."

"It will be easier when people expect you to speak to them. This is different."

"All right, but you can come with me."

They approached a stern-looking woman in a navy dress suit, who peered at them as they reached the counter. "Is there a problem?"

"Oh, no, everything was lovely. So much so..." Nell pulled Leah closer to her "...my daughter's interested in the job advertised in the window. Is it still available?"

"It is. What makes you think she's suitable?"

"She's very helpful at home. She serves the family, and she's keen to learn."

"Has she worked in a tea room before?"

"No, but that's why we came for afternoon tea today, so she could see what's involved."

The woman flicked her hand. "There's a lot more to it than waiting tables, I can assure you. Is she numerate and literate?"

"Erm ... yes. I think so. She's been to school if that's what you mean. She even did an extra year to round off her education."

"It wasn't because she failed at school?"

"Oh, no. She has a school certificate to show she's competent in reading, writing and arithmetic."

The woman studied Leah. "How old are you?"

"Fifteen."

The woman scowled. "Fifteen, madam."

"Oh, I'm sorry. Madam."

"We address all our customers as sir or madam. Without exception."

Nell smiled at her daughter. "It quickly becomes habit."

The woman raised an eyebrow. "You've done this sort of work yourself?"

"Not exactly. I worked as a stewardess on a couple of transatlantic ships, so I'm familiar with waiting on tables, as well as many other things that go on behind the scenes."

"Would you like a job, too?"

"Oh, gracious no. I've since remarried, but I thought working here might be something Leah would be good at."

The woman ran her eyes over Leah once more. "Very well. We've not had any other suitable applicants. Be here for nine o'clock tomorrow and I'll give you a trial day. I'll assess you and you can decide if you like the work."

Leah nodded. "Thank you. I'll be here."

Leah couldn't keep the grin off her face as they walked home. "To think I'll be working by this time tomorrow."

"Don't build up your hopes. That woman looked a bit of a stickler; you have to hope she likes you first."

"I will. Wait until Elenor hears. Do you think she'll be jealous?"

"Who knows? Since Mr Massey went back to sea, she's not interested in anything."

Leah cocked her head to one side. "Is she in love?"

"Love! I doubt it. Where did you get that idea from?"

"My friends were talking about it the other day, but we

weren't sure what it is. Have you been in love?"

A smile flicked across Nell's lips. "I loved your dad."

"But not Uncle Thomas?"

"Oh, yes, but that's a different sort of love. One where you care for someone very much."

"So how's that different to how you felt about Dad?"

Nell flushed. "It's difficult to say. It could be because we were young, or because it was the first time."

"But what does it feel like?"

"You'll know."

Leah huffed. "That's not much of an answer. How will I know when I'm in love, if I don't know what to expect?"

Nell studied her. "You're not walking out with anyone, are you?"

"No! I'm just curious ... and want to be able to tell my friends."

"Well, I suppose one way of describing it is if your heart rate quickens or even skips a beat when he walks into the room. Or you get butterflies in your stomach every time you see him. You can't help it. It just happens."

Leah's eyes narrowed. "What if they don't love you back?"

"Then it's not meant to be."

"I don't like the sound of that."

"There's not much you can do about it. You may break someone's heart for the same reason. They fall in love with you, but you don't return it."

"So, it's not straightforward, then?"

Ollie's image crept into her mind as she glanced at her daughter. "I'm afraid not."

"Is that why Uncle Billy and Uncle James never got

married. Because they didn't find anyone to love."

"I expect so."

"It seems strange that Uncle Vernon did."

"Why do you say that?"

Leah giggled. "He doesn't seem the type. He's more like Uncle George. I can't imagine his heart skipping a beat when he sees Aunty Maria."

"That's because they've been married for so long. Those first feelings don't last forever."

Leah's forehead creased. "Why do married people keep having children then? Shouldn't a man and woman be in love to have them?"

"Well ... I ... erm ... I didn't say they didn't love each other, but their hearts settle down."

Leah nodded. "So Uncle Vernon and Aunty Lydia still love each other?"

"I imagine so."

"Which is why she's having another baby. Do you think she's had it yet?"

"I hope so. Uncle Vernon will be around tonight if she has."

Maria and Alice were knitting when they got home, and Alice looked up at them.

"How did you get on?"

Leah grinned. "I'm going for a trial tomorrow to see what they think of me."

"Well done. Did you enjoy your afternoon tea?"

"I did. I know why Mam likes it so much. I hope I like the work. It seems like an easy way to earn money."

Maria's brow was furrowed as she counted the stitches on her needles. "Nothing's ever easy. If they pay a decent wage, they'll expect their pound of flesh."

"At least I'll finish at five, so I'll be home in time for tea."

"Well, I hope they like you." Alice folded up the jacket she was making. "I'd better get a move on. I promised Lydia I'd pick the children up from school. I won't be long."

Nell took the seat next to Maria. "Any news of the baby yet?"

"Not yet, but hopefully Alice will come home with some. I've been on tenterhooks all day."

"I'm sure she'll be fine. They say it gets easier with each one."

"Vernon's desperate for another boy. He's worrying about his old age."

Nell rolled her eyes. "Trust him."

"You can't blame him. They already have two girls, and if it's another one, they'll only have Henry to take care of them in their old age."

"I'm sure they'll love it, whatever it is." Nell turned as the front door opened and Elenor joined them. "You've been out a long time, where've you been?"

"To the park." She took the seat next to Leah.

"All afternoon?" Nell's eyes narrowed.

"I'd arranged to meet Isobel, and she brought one of her friends."

Maria studied her. "You don't look happy."

"I'm just tired. I didn't sleep very well last night."

"What have you got to keep you awake?"

Elenor fidgeted with her fingers. "Nothing."

"She'll be thinking of..." Leah stopped as Nell glared at

her. *Not now...*

"She'll be sad that I've got a job, and she hasn't."

Elenor stared at her. "You've not got a job."

"I have. Me and Mam went for afternoon tea at a place looking for a waitress. I start tomorrow..."

Nell interrupted. "You've a trial day tomorrow."

"That's only to check I like it."

"And they like you."

Elenor pouted. "You took her for afternoon tea? Why didn't you take me?"

"Because you weren't here."

Leah grinned. "You can visit me when I'm at work."

Nell tutted as she stood up and headed for the kitchen. "You haven't started yet. Now, get this table ready while I start the tea. Everyone will be here soon."

Nell was carrying the bread to the table when Alice arrived home.

"Any news on the baby?"

"Yes, another girl."

Maria huffed. "What a shame."

"Don't be like that." Nell gawped at her. "As long as the baby and Lydia are healthy, you should be happy."

"I am, but ... Vernon..."

"Don't you want to visit her?"

"Of course I do, although I don't know how I'll get there."

Nell grimaced. "You won't be able to walk that far. I'll tell you what, if you cheer up, I'll check if we have any spare housekeeping money for a carriage."

"Would you? That would be such a relief. I can't not see the little thing."

"I should hope not. Leave it with me."

CHAPTER THIRTEEN

The midsummer crowds thronged around Princes Park lake as Nell and Jane sat watching Betty and Alice help Georgie and Freddie feed the ducks. Nell smiled at Rebecca as she joined them.

"Is there room for a small one?"

Nell moved closer to Jane. "Are you on your own?"

"I walked here with Isobel and Florrie, but they're meeting some friends. How's Maria?"

Nell sighed. "Not so good. She's no energy, and she's lost a lot of weight."

"Is she all right being left on her own?"

"Not for any length of time. Elenor's with her for now, but I'd better not stay out long."

Jane gazed out over the lake. "Do you think the end is near?"

"I do. She's hardly eating anything and the little she is, we're mashing up for her."

Rebecca patted Nell's hand. "You've done your best."

"I've tried ... and Alice is very good with her." Nell wiped away a tear. "It will happen to all of us at some point."

"Come on, cheer up. She's not gone yet. I'll have to start meeting you at your house so I can see more of her."

"She'd like that..."

Jane finally turned to face them. "I'll walk home with you when we leave here. We get on better now than we have for years, but I don't want there to be any arguments between us at the end."

Nell gasped. "You can't tell her..."

"She must have guessed."

"Maybe she has, but George won't let us say anything to her. You will be discreet?"

Jane rolled her eyes. "I'm not all bad. I can be considerate."

"When the mood takes you." Nell smirked at her sister, but Rebecca interrupted.

"How's Leah getting on with her job?"

"She's enjoying it. I wasn't sure how she'd get on with the woman in charge, but apparently, she's less stern than she was when we first met her."

Jane tutted. "What is it about you and your family that the women want to work?"

"We want to be able to support ourselves, if the need arises. Well, some of us do. Elenor's showing no inclination to follow Leah's example."

"She's got some sense then."

"I wouldn't say that."

Concern crossed Rebecca's face. "Are you still having trouble with her?"

"Not at the moment, but I can only pray it stays that way."

Jane leaned forward. "What have I missed?"

Nell sighed. "She met a young man a few months ago and started walking out with him without telling me."

"How did you find out?"

"We saw them in Sefton Park. Thankfully, Elenor was with Isobel and her other friend Ruth, but there was no doubt they were together."

Jane's eyes brightened. "What's he like? Is he handsome?"

Nell gasped. "You are the limit. It doesn't matter what he looks like. The fact is, she's only sixteen and doesn't want a chaperone. We wouldn't have done that when we were courting."

Jane sniggered. "You speak for yourself. Did you never wonder where I sneaked off to when Maria was busy?"

Nell shook her head. "Why doesn't that surprise me?"

"I was fine, and she will be, too. She's a bright enough girl. Does Maria know?"

"I daren't tell her." Nell shuddered. "Not in the state she's in."

Rebecca studied her. "If you're having no trouble at the moment, is that because he's away?"

"He is." She turned to Jane. "He's an engineer on a ship. He left about a month ago and won't be back until the end of July. The problem is, he's twenty-one and I can't relax when he's here."

"You sound like Maria was with Alice."

"Don't think it hasn't crossed my mind, but I realise now why she was concerned. I feel so helpless."

"Why don't you stop her going out, then? I'm sure Mr Marsh would help if you didn't want to do it yourself."

"I don't want to tell him, either. He'll only blame me for giving her ideas."

Jane frowned. "Why would he do that?"

"Oh ... because he doesn't think I've brought her up properly."

Rebecca sat up indignantly. "You've done very well. He should try bringing up two daughters on his own."

"He wouldn't see it as his job." Nell gazed out over the lake. "It's funny. When Betty and Alice were Elenor's age they both confided in me and I tried my best to help, yet Elenor won't speak to me."

"Does she have anyone else she can talk to?"

"Ruth Pearse, most likely, but she's the one I blame for all this."

"Are you sure?"

"Not for certain, but it's strange how all these things happen when she's around. I could crown her."

Rebecca indicated towards their nieces. "What about Alice? She'd talk to her."

"She's been chaperoning them, but Elenor doesn't confide in her." A wry smile crossed Nell's face as she spoke to Jane. "Do you remember, all those years ago, when you were having problems with Betty, you asked how I'd feel if Elenor or Leah got themselves into trouble? At the time, I thought I'd take it in my stride, but now I'm not so sure."

Jane gasped. "You don't think she's ... you know?"

"Oh, no, I don't mean that, although whether it's because Mr Massey's a gentleman or because she's only just maturing ... if you get my meaning..."

Rebecca blew out her cheeks. "At least that's something, but you can't rely on that forever. She's growing up."

"Which is why I'm dreading him coming back."

She turned to Jane. "To answer your earlier question. Yes, he's good-looking. So much so, I'd guess he could have a woman in every port if he wanted."

"Ah."

"Exactly."

"Would you like Betty to say something to her? You know, to tell her why she needs to be careful."

"I couldn't do that. When I first met Mrs Robertson, she asked me to explain the intricacies of giving birth and I was mortified. It's not the sort of thing you talk about."

"Betty's been through so much, she talks more freely than we do. It might be worth a try. Go and ask her now. She won't mind that Alice is there."

"Very well." Nell stood up and straightened her skirt before she approached Alice.

"Are you ready to go?"

"No, we're probably all right for another half an hour. I wanted a word with you both."

"Has Mam sent you?" Betty looked towards the bench where Jane and Rebecca were watching.

"She may have." The smile on Nell's face was short-lived. "It's about Elenor."

"What about her?" Betty glanced at Alice.

"I'm concerned about her friendship with Mr Massey. She's very fond of him, but I worry, with him being that much older than her, that, well, you know..."

Alice's eyes narrowed. "He seems nice enough to me. I've not got the impression he'd do anything he shouldn't."

"I'm worried she won't talk to me about him. Has she spoken to you about what they talk about?"

"No, she's always rather vague."

"Which is why I worry. Why would she keep things to herself unless they were up to no good?"

Betty sighed. "I hope they're not. You don't realise the trouble 'keeping a man happy' causes until it's too late. Would you like me to talk to her?"

"Would you? I've tried to explain that if they get too close, she could end up in the family way, but I'm not convinced she realises how serious it would be."

"Would Mr Massey marry her if she did?"

"Well, that's the thing. He could clear off to sea and disappear, if he was that way inclined."

Betty studied her. "If she really likes him, the fact she may not see him again could be the best deterrent."

"I hadn't thought of that." Nell cocked her head to one side. "I saw Mrs Robertson last week, and she said that even if he did go to sea, the company he works for could find him. As long as he doesn't change company."

"Which he may do if he suspects you'll chase after him."

Nell nodded. "Your mam said she was going to come to our house to visit Aunty Maria on her way home. Might you have time to join us and speak to Elenor?"

"I've arranged for a neighbour to pick Betsy up from school, so I'm in no hurry. I'll see what I can do."

Betty positioned the pram alongside the wall and lifted out her son as they reached Upper Hill Street. "Come on, birthday boy. Let's go and see Aunty Maria."

Nell stroked his hand as Betty rested him on her hip. "I can't believe it was a year ago we were all so worried about you."

"Thankfully, it's all forgotten, for now." She ran a hand over her already swollen belly. "I hope this one is easier."

"How've you been feeling this time?"

"Remarkably well. I must be used to it by now."

"You're looking well, which is more than I can say for your Aunty Maria."

Jane was in the living room when Nell and Betty arrived, and Nell slipped into the kitchen to put the kettle on as Jane reached for Charlie. "Here you are, my latest grandson. Aunty Maria's not seen much of you." Jane took the seat on the other side of the fireplace. "I heard Lydia had another girl."

"She did. She's a lovely little thing. They've called her Maria after me."

"That's nice. I don't have a granddaughter named after me yet." She glared at Betty.

"Perhaps next time." Maria smirked. "Lydia usually calls on a Tuesday afternoon. You should visit when she's here."

"I will."

Nell rejoined them and put the tea tray on the table. "Has Elenor gone out?"

"Only into the backyard with Alice and the boys. They won't be long."

Nell glanced at Betty, who was still standing up. "Would you mind seeing what she's up to and tell them we're here?"

"Not at all." Betty glanced at the cake on the table. "You start without us."

CHAPTER FOURTEEN

M r Marsh's back was straight, and he held his head
high, as he escorted Nell around Princes Park.

"Days like today remind me of when we were courting.
Life seemed less complicated, then."

Nell raised an eyebrow. "Really?"

"Well, we had our differences, but we had plenty of
good times, and spent a lot of time on our own. I miss
that."

"We don't do so badly."

"No. And this time next week, we'll be ready for our trip
to Blackpool. I'm so looking forward to showing you
everything we did last time."

Nell smiled. "I'm looking forward to it myself. I hope
Maria will be all right with me not here."

"She'll have Alice with her. And Elenor."

But how do I deal with Elenor if Alice can't leave Maria?
"I still worry."

"About Mrs Atkin?"

Nell nodded. "She's gone downhill a lot these last few

weeks, and the fact she didn't even attempt to go to church this morning isn't a good sign."

He patted her hand. "I can't argue with you, but you know I'll be here."

"And I still have Jane and Rebecca."

Mr Marsh stared straight ahead. "I had hoped Mrs Atkin's illness might have put an end to Elenor's sullenness, but sadly it hasn't. Have you spoken to her lately?"

"I've tried, but since her birthday, she's become more withdrawn than usual. Even Edith's struggling with her."

"What about this friend of hers? Ruth Pearse."

"What about her?"

"She must talk to her. Could you speak to her and find out why she's so moody?"

Nell studied Princes Park mansions as they strolled past. "She's not a girl I like, to be honest with you."

"But Elenor's your daughter and it's high time you were firmer with her. Children shouldn't talk to their parents the way she speaks to you."

"All right, I'll speak to her when we get home."

"The way she's carrying on, you'd think she had a suitor who'd jilted her."

Nell gulped. "Don't be silly. She's only recently turned seventeen."

"That's as maybe, but you should still speak to Miss Pearse. If Elenor's interested in men at such a young age, she needs stopping."

Nell sighed. *You don't know the half of it...* "How do I do that? I can't be with her every hour of the day."

"Well, I suggest someone is. There's something going on, and I don't like it."

. . .

Elenor was in the backyard with Georgie and Freddie when they got home, and Nell joined them while Alice made the tea.

"Have you been out this afternoon?"

"Only to Ruth's. We didn't go far."

"That's a shame, it's been a lovely day." When Elenor didn't reply, Nell continued. "Mr Massey must be due back soon."

"Tomorrow."

"I'd have thought you'd be happy to see him."

"I will be."

But? "You should be happy now. I was always excited for at least a week before your dad came home."

"Ruth's having some problems, that's all."

"Why's that making you so miserable?"

Elenor tutted. "She's my friend."

"Betty told me she spoke to you."

"Only because you told her to."

"Because I'm worried about you. I thought that if you won't talk to me, you might talk to her."

"So she could report back?"

"Not at all. Being able to speak to someone closer to your age can sometimes help."

"Well, it didn't."

"I wish you could be a bit more cheerful. Aunty Maria doesn't like to see you like this."

"What's it got to do with her?"

"She cares for you, that's why." Nell pursed her lips.

"You know she's ill? Well, the doctor can't do any more for her and she's not likely to be with us for much longer."

"Oh." Elenor's face fell. "How much longer does she have?"

"We're not sure, but it would be nice if she could see you happy."

"I'll try..."

Nell studied her but Elenor turned away.

"Don't look at me like that. I'm fine. I just want Will back safely."

I can understand that. "You won't want to hear this, but if you plan to spend the rest of your life with him, that fear never leaves you."

"So why did you marry Uncle Thomas? He was always going away."

"Because he said he'd get a job in Liverpool when we were married. Would Mr Massey do that?"

Elenor shrugged. "I haven't asked. It's too soon."

"If it's too soon to ask, it's too soon to worry about him. Why won't you tell me what's really the matter?"

"Because it's none of your business." Elenor threw the ball she'd been playing with to Georgie and stomped to the back door.

"You are my business..." Nell didn't finish her sentence as the door slammed and Georgie bounced the ball to her.

"Play with me, Aunty Nell."

She glanced after Elenor. "Later. Shall we go inside and get a biscuit?"

There was a spring in Elenor's step when she came downstairs the following morning, and Maria looked up as she sat down.

"It's nice to see you with a smile on your face. Are you doing something special today?"

"I'm walking into town with Ruth. We decided it would cheer us both up."

"That's nice." Alice handed Georgie a slice of bread as Nell poured four cups of tea.

"What time are you leaving?"

"Soon."

"That's good. I'm walking that way myself, so I'll go with you."

Elenor glared at her. "I'm going with Ruth."

"Then I'll walk with her as well. It's about time I met her properly."

"We wanted to go around the market."

Nell kept the smile on her face. "So do I. Is Ruth coming here or are you walking there?"

Elenor stared at the table. "I'm going there."

"I'll have to hope her mam doesn't answer the door then. The last thing I want is to see her."

"You needn't come."

Nell ignored her. "Perhaps I'll wait on the corner until Ruth comes out and then we can carry on together."

Elenor left the crusts of her bread on the plate, and as soon as she stood up from the table, Nell went to the hall to fetch her summer cape.

"It's going to be warm today."

Elenor said nothing as she fixed her best hat in front of the mirror, something Maria didn't miss.

"You're looking very smart for a Wednesday."

"I want to make an effort. It's not often I go into Liverpool." Elenor was out of the front door before Nell could fix her own hat, but she pushed in the hatpin and hurried after her.

"Wait there, one minute."

Elenor stamped her foot as she turned towards her. "Why can't you let me go on my own?"

"You know jolly well why, because I don't believe a word about you going into Liverpool other than to the docks to meet Mr Massey. It would explain your best clothes, too. Are you even meeting Ruth on the way or was that another lie?"

Elenor's face coloured as she set off down the road leaving Nell to chase after her.

"Didn't you listen to anything Betty said to you?"

"Yes, I did, and I won't do anything I shouldn't, but I want to see him on my own."

"You won't mind if I walk behind you then."

Elenor huffed. "As long as you keep your distance. We've not seen each other for two months so we'd like some time to ourselves. To talk."

Nell nodded. "I can manage that. Where are you meeting him?"

"At the Albert Dock, but we need to be quick. His ship should be here by now and he doesn't know I'll be there."

"Then why are you going?"

"To surprise him."

"Are you sure that's a good idea?"

"Yes!" Elenor bit her lip. "Please, Mam. If you insist on coming with me, hurry up."

. . .

Crowds surrounded the landing stage when they arrived and Elenor stood on her toes as she searched the faces of those leaving the ships that were docked. "I can't see him."

"Perhaps he's disembarked already."

"I'm hoping he's still on board."

"Well, you can't go and ask. This is no place for a young woman as it is. You'll have to wait here."

For once Elenor took her advice without argument, and the two of them stood by the entrance to the dock while they waited.

"He could be hours if he needs to unload the cargo."

"Uncle James usually comes straight home."

"Because he only has to disembark passengers, who can walk off themselves."

Elenor's shoulders slumped. "I hadn't thought of that. How long will it take?"

"I've no idea. It depends what they're carrying."

Elenor studied the large, black-hulled ship in the far corner of the dock. "There are still men on board. I'll find somewhere to sit while I wait. You don't have to stay if you don't want to."

Nell took a deep breath. "Of course I'm staying. If I leave, you're leaving with me. We need to be home for dinnertime, too."

"What if he's not appeared by then?"

"Then you'll need to wait for him to contact you."

Elenor walked to the nearest wall and perched on the edge. "I hope he's quick." Her eyes didn't leave the ship as men lifted numerous barrels and crates onto the side, before they were moved into the left-hand wing of the red-bricked warehouse. As the clock turned half past eleven, Nell stood up.

"We're going to have to go."

"Please, may I stay? They've nearly finished."

"You said that an hour ago. They'll probably move on to the next hold. We must have seen the whole ship's crew, but not one was Mr Massey. Is that definitely his ship?"

"Yes!"

"Well, I'm sorry, but we've been here too long as it is. Several men have given us strange looks as they've walked past."

Elenor huffed and raised herself onto her toes one more time, but suddenly pointed. "Over there. He's getting off."

Nell watched as Mr Massey waved to a couple of men on the quayside. "It looks as if he has other people waiting for him. You can't disturb him with his friends."

"But we've waited all morning..."

"After all the work they've done, I imagine all he wants is a pint of ale. Leave him be until later."

Nell wandered back to the entrance of the dock, but as Elenor bounced on the spot beside her, Mr Massey walked straight past, his eyes fixed on a woman in a turquoise dress, with elaborately styled fair hair. She approached him with a smile.

"Will! No!" A train passing on the line overhead drowned out Elenor's shout, and she watched as Mr Massey wrapped an arm around the woman's shoulders and led her across the road.

Elenor's eyes were wide as she stared at Nell, but no words came from her lips, despite her mouth moving.

"I'm so sorry." Nell took her arm. "Let's get you home. There'll be time to talk about it later."

CHAPTER FIFTEEN

Elenor didn't say a word as they walked back from the dock, and as Nell cleared the table after dinner, her food remained untouched in front of her.

At least Maria didn't sit with us.

Once Nell had collected up her plate, she nudged Elenor to move from her seat.

"Why don't we take a walk? You look like you could do with some fresh air."

Maria studied her from her chair by the fire. "Is she all right? Did something happen in Liverpool?"

"She had an argument with Ruth, that's all. She'll be fine when we get back." Nell directed Elenor into the hall and helped her with her cloak as Alice followed them. She pulled the door closed behind her.

"I don't know what's wrong, but I hope you feel better soon. I'll speak to you later."

Elenor stared at the floor. "There's nothing to say."

"I'm sure we'll find something. Why don't you talk to your mam? She'll be able to help."

Elenor shook her head. "She won't."

Nell held her tongue until they arrived in Princes Park, and once there, she ushered Elenor to a secluded bench near the entrance.

"I'm sorry about what happened."

"You're not, though, are you? You must be thrilled."

"I don't like you being upset. That's why I've been trying to help."

"Help! You've done your best to keep us apart."

"That's not true. If I'd wanted to do that, I'd have had Uncle Thomas lock you in your bedroom. As it is, you've met Mr Massey whenever you wanted. The only stipulation was that you had a chaperone."

"Well, he didn't need one today, did he? Did you see that woman?"

Nell closed her eyes as she nodded. "I did." *The strumpet.*

"It's all your fault." Elenor spat out her words.

"My fault?" Nell's eyes shot open. "Why?"

"Because you insist on Alice walking with us."

Nell's heart raced. "I thought Alice let you walk on your own, she just followed..."

"That wasn't enough. He wanted to be on his own with me."

"W-what do you mean?"

Elenor's defiance faded. "He said I was the prettiest girl he'd ever met."

"Did he...?" Nell gulped. "Did he say that to get *close* to you?"

Tears ran down Elenor's cheeks. "He said he loved me,

but because we couldn't be alone, he's obviously found someone else."

The blood drained from Nell's face. "When did he tell you that?"

"When we first met."

"When precisely? Which month?"

When Elenor didn't respond, Nell shook her arm. "You need to be honest with me."

"In March."

Five months ago. A bitter taste rose to the back of Nell's throat, and she rubbed a hand over her face. *Don't let her be in the family way.*

"I've not done anything wrong."

"He told you that too, did he?" Nell struggled to breathe as she held Elenor's gaze. "I hope you've not fallen for the oldest trick in the book. Did he...?" She wiped her eyes. "Did he *touch* you?"

"He said he wanted to spend the rest of his life with me..."

"So he did! Oh, Elenor. That's what all men like him say." She stood up and stepped away, her heart thumping. "That would explain why he's moved on to someone else."

"It wasn't like that. He contacted me every time he came back. He's always wanted to see me. Until today."

"If you hadn't gone to the dock, you'd have been none the wiser. He may have been seeing her every time he's been in Liverpool."

Elenor sobbed into her handkerchief, but Nell glared at her.

"Are you with child? Is that why you've been so fractious

and why you were so keen to meet him alone today?" She held her breath as she waited for a reply.

"Ruth said I might be ... but how would I know?"

Nell gripped her stomach as she stumbled back to the bench. "Why did you tell Ruth and not me? I should have known..."

"She's my friend and my skirts were tight, so she helped tighten my corset."

"And what about the ... bleeding. Have you had any more since that first time?"

"Bleeding?" Her forehead creased. "No, that stopped again."

Oh, dear Lord. She caught her breath. "Have you any idea what you've done?"

"No." She sobbed as she grabbed Nell's hands. "I'm frightened, Mam. Please, tell me I'm not having a baby."

"I wish I could. Why on earth didn't you tell me you were seeing him when you first met?"

"I didn't know this would happen."

An icy shiver ran down Nell's back. *I'll need to tell Thomas. And Maria. Not to mention George. And it will all be my fault. Oh, God, why've you done this to us?*

"Mam. Talk to me." Elenor shook her shoulders. "What am I going to do?"

She took a deep breath. *Stay calm.* "Mr Massey needs to be told and he should do the honourable thing and marry you."

"I can't see him again. You saw him with that *woman*."

"What would you rather do? Speak to him or live your life in shame? No respectable man will come near you if they know you have a baby."

"I could find someone who wanted it..."

"After what happened with Edith?" Nell pressed her hands into her stomach as the cramping started again. "Whatever you choose, you can't be seen in public until after it's born."

"What about Aunty Maria? And Uncle Thomas? They can't find out."

"We have no choice. The only way to hide it would be to send you away, but we'd have to explain why you were going."

Elenor buried her head in her hands. "Why isn't Alice still in Wales? I could have gone to stay with her."

Nell gazed at the bushes opposite. "Betty may be able to help."

"Betty? You can't tell anyone."

"I don't know what else to do." Nell pressed her fingers into her temples. "She won't tell a soul. Trust me."

"What if she can't help?"

"Then you'd better start praying."

Perspiration covered Nell's brow as she approached Betty's house the next day and she wafted her face with her fan before she let herself in.

"Anyone home?"

Betty appeared from the kitchen. "Aunty Nell. I wasn't expecting you today."

"No, I wanted a word..." She froze as Jane followed Betty into the living room. "What are you doing here?"

"I could say the same about you. You're looking rather warm."

"So would you be if you'd walked here in this heat."

"That's why I arrive early. What can we do for you?"

"Oh, nothing..."

"You said you wanted a word."

"I-it was nothing important. I-I'm just concerned about Maria. Would you have time to visit her on Monday? I told you, most of us are going to Blackpool for the day, and I don't like to leave her."

Betty frowned. "Isn't Alice staying with her?"

"Oh, yes, but she may like a break."

"What about Elenor? Is she going with you now?"

"No, but ... erm ... she's not much company at the moment."

Jane shrugged. "I'm not doing anything on Monday, so I'll call. Betty doesn't need me here with Mr Crane at home."

"Thank you. Maria's gone downhill since you last visited, so don't be surprised when you see her."

Betty rested a hand on Nell's shoulder. "I'm sorry. Let me put the kettle on. You look like you could do with a cup of tea."

Jane studied Nell as Betty disappeared. "Why did you walk all the way here to ask me to visit Maria? Why not call on me at home?"

"I-I did. But you were out, so I guessed you'd be here."

"Then why were you surprised to see me? Are you hiding something?"

"No, not at all." Nell coughed to keep the squeak from her voice.

"You've not had the doctor out to Maria again?"

"Not since last week. He gave her some more pills..."

Jane sank onto the nearest chair. "It's such a terrible thing. How's George bearing up? The poor man."

"He's out most of the time. It's his way of coping."

"Is he going to Blackpool with you?"

"He is. He enjoyed himself last time, they all did. That's why we're going again."

"It's a shame I didn't know. I'd have come with you."

CHAPTER SIXTEEN

E lenor was waiting on the corner of Windsor Street and Upper Hill Street as Nell walked home from Betty's the following Saturday.

"Did you speak to her?"

"I did, but she had no more ideas than I've already suggested. She asked if the baby's started moving yet?"

"How would I know?"

"You'd feel it. In your belly."

"I've had butterflies in my stomach since we spoke about it, but I thought it was because I was frightened."

"Let's hope it is and there's still a chance you may lose it."

Elenor's eyes brightened. "Might that happen?"

"It's not likely, but Betty's gone through it more times than she'd care to remember, so she's always wary."

"Would I know if I did?"

"Oh, yes. You'd be in a lot of pain, for one thing. And you'd start bleeding. It isn't very nice, but under the circumstances it would be a blessing."

"Did she say anything else?"

"Only that the best option would be to marry the father. I don't suppose you've heard from him."

"I had a letter from him shortly after you'd gone out. He wrote it yesterday, but said he'd only just got back."

"It's not the first time he's lied about the dates of his voyages."

"No." Elenor studied the floor. "He wants to meet me in Sefton Park tomorrow. Alone."

"Then you must go and tell him about the baby." *There's no point sending a chaperone now.* "If he's any decency, he'll offer to marry you there and then."

"I'm not sure I want to marry him."

Nell gasped. "You don't have a lot of choice."

"But what about that woman? Do you think he's been close to her?"

Nell sighed. *Probably.* "I've no idea, but you need to talk to him. I've already told you, the other alternatives would be worse."

Mr Marsh was sitting by the fire when they arrived home and he put down his newspaper as Nell joined him.

"Here you are. Have you been out together?"

"We met on the corner of Windsor Street." Nell peered into the kitchen. "Where's Maria?"

"She nipped outside. She won't be long."

"On her own?"

Elenor headed to the back door. "I'll go and check."

He swivelled in his chair as she walked past. "There's no need. Alice is with her."

The door had closed before he finished his sentence. "Well, she has the two of them now."

Nell smiled. "I'm glad Elenor's concerned about her. Have you had a good day?"

"Only because I left work at three. Shall we go for a walk?"

"Would you mind if I have a cup of tea? I've just come back from Betty's."

"On a Saturday?"

"I ... erm ... I'd promised to visit her this week, but Jane's been there the last few days, so I decided to go today. At least I'm home earlier than usual." She stood up. "Is that a letter for me?" She peered behind the clock on the mantlepiece. "It's from Mrs Robertson. Hopefully, that means she's in Liverpool again."

Nell sliced open the top of the envelope. "Yes, she is. She said I can visit any time next week. That's good." She refolded the letter. "Let me put the kettle on. We may have time for a quick walk after that."

He rested his head on the back of the chair as she disappeared. "We need to plan our day for Monday. You'll love walking down the pier, but I want to take you onto the sand to see the donkeys, too. There were dozens of them giving rides to the children."

"I'm looking forward to the fish and chips."

He laughed. "Then we'll do that as well."

Nell had returned to the living room as the back door opened and Maria joined them. "You're home."

"I am. I've put the kettle on..."

Maria tutted as she retook her seat. "I feel like such a slouch making you and Alice do everything."

"Don't be silly. You're not well."

"I'm not getting any better, either. I asked the doctor if I'd recover when he called earlier."

Nell's mouth fell open. "What did he say?"

"He didn't really, but he suggested we pray for me to get my strength back."

"We've been doing that for months."

"Not specifically for my strength. Or at least, I haven't. Anyway, I'll try it tonight. Will you ask the vicar to pray for me in church tomorrow?"

"Of course I will."

Once Sunday dinner was over, and the dishes washed, Nell took the last of the plates from Alice and set them on the dresser while Mr Marsh sat with Billy.

"I'll be ready to go out in a couple of minutes."

"Splendid. I was feeling left out, now everyone else has gone." He looked at Billy. "Will you join us?"

"No. Thanks anyway, but I said I'd follow Dad to the alehouse. Will we see you in there later?"

Mr Marsh cocked his head to one side. "I may, depending on what time we get back from Sefton Park."

"Oh, actually–" Nell gulped "–I-I thought we could go to Princes Park today. For a change."

"But we always go to Sefton Park."

"Does it matter if we don't?"

"Well, no, probably not, although it won't take so long to walk around Princes Park."

As long as we don't bump into Elenor and Mr Massey, I

don't care. "You can meet Billy in the alehouse if we're back early."

He studied her. "Are you up to something?"

"Not at all, but I could do with being here a bit earlier so Alice can go out. Maria won't stay asleep for long and I'd rather not walk too far today, with us going to Blackpool tomorrow. I walked to Everton and back yesterday, don't forget."

"Yes, of course." He smiled at Billy. "I'll probably see you later, then."

Billy stood up and bid them farewell as Nell fixed her hat. Once they were ready to leave, she linked an arm through Mr Marsh's.

"It makes a pleasant change to be going to Princes Park. To think I was there so often when I was with Miss Ellis, yet I hardly go there now."

"It's likely to be busy today with it being the holiday weekend."

"Well, we won't be out for long. I feel guilty enough about leaving Maria tomorrow, so I should spend some time with her today."

He gave her a sideways glance. "You are looking forward to tomorrow?"

"I've already told you I am. I was quite envious after you came home with your tales in June. It's a shame Alice and Mr Wood can't join us."

"And Mrs Atkin."

"Well, yes. That would be nice, although I doubt she'll ever make the journey."

"She'll be a big loss to us all when the time comes."

"Don't talk like that. Not yet."

"I'm sorry. Have you heard when your nephew's due home from Brazil? It's to be hoped he's here soon."

"It is. I'm cross with him for leaving it so long after getting my letter, but he said he'd be here around the middle of the month. Billy keeps an eye on the timetables, so you'll have to ask him."

"I will." He smiled at her. "I'm glad to see you and Elenor talking to each other again, even if she is still miserable with the rest of us. As a reward, would you like to ask her to join us tomorrow? Edith and Leah will be with us anyway, and it might do her good to spend the day with them. It may even cheer her up."

Nell kept her head down as she grimaced. "I'll ask, although whether she'll come is another matter."

Mr Marsh had a skip in his step as he walked. "It's not possible to be miserable in Blackpool. It may be what she needs."

After a short walk, Mr Marsh escorted Nell home, before heading to the alehouse. By the time he arrived home with Billy and George the tea was laid out on the table. Nell checked the clock. *Where's Elenor?*

Edith disturbed her thoughts. "May we sit down?"

"Erm ... yes, I suppose so. I don't know where Elenor's got to. Did you see her in the park?"

When she and Leah shook their heads, Nell marched to the front door to check the street. *No sign of her. I hope this means that she's made up with Mr Massey and he's going to marry her. What if she wants to bring him home for tea?* She checked her watch again. *Who am I kidding? She won't bring him here unannounced.*

She went back into the living room. "We may as well sit down. She must have lost track of time."

Maria's eyes narrowed. "Where was she going?"

"To the park with Ruth. She must have gone back to her house."

"Surely Ruth's mam will have tea laid out by now. That should remind her of the time."

"Unless they invited her to stay."

"Without telling you?"

"It was only a thought." Nell sighed as she put a small triangular sandwich, filled with meat paste, onto a plate and handed it to Maria, who sat by the fire. "See how you get on with that."

Maria stared at it. "Would you cut it in half? I don't like wasting any if it's too much."

Without arguing, Nell returned to the table. "I hope you're not all going to stay out late tonight. We have to be up early in the morning."

George took a bite out of his sandwich, bigger than the piece Nell had cut for Maria. "It might be early for you, I'm up at that time every day."

"You can wake us all up, then. And make a pot of tea." She stepped back as he glared at her. "I was only joking."

"I should think so, although Thomas could do that, with him being a steward."

Mr Marsh smiled. "If it gets us all into the carriages on time, then I'm more than happy to. I ordered two with there being six of us going. Or maybe seven if Elenor comes."

Alice raised an eyebrow. "You've invited her?"

"Not yet. I suggested it this afternoon to cheer her up, but we haven't seen her since to ask."

Nell glanced at the clock again. "I'm sure she'll be here soon."

The girls had gone to bed and Alice had settled Maria on the settee in the front room when Nell finally joined her by the fire with a cup of hot milk.

"I'm getting worried now."

"As you should be. It's turned nine o'clock. Why did you let her go out unchaperoned?"

Nell groaned. "It seemed like a good idea at the time, and she promised she'd behave herself."

"And you believed her after everything that's happened these last few months?"

"What else could I do? There was no one free to chaperone her, and I knew the park would be crowded this afternoon."

"How do you know she went to the park?"

"She told me that's where she was meeting him."

"But they needn't have stayed there."

Nell closed her eyes. "I didn't think of that. I was so pleased she was talking to me again, I took her at her word." She stood up and headed for the hall. "She'd better be home before Uncle Thomas gets back or there'll be trouble." She opened the front door and peered into the darkness. *Should I go looking for her? I could be at Ruth's in five minutes.*

She nodded to herself and grabbed her cape before popping her head into the living room. "I'm going to walk round to Ruth's to see if she's there."

"You can't go on your own. It's dark."

"What else can I do?"

"Wait for Uncle Thomas."

"No!" Nell shuddered. "I'd rather he wasn't involved."

"Then I'll come with you." Alice stood up. "We'll be safer together and no one will miss us for ten minutes."

CHAPTER SEVENTEEN

Lights were on in the bedroom when Nell and Alice arrived at the Pearses' house, and Nell peered through the letterbox before knocking on the door.

"I hope they're not in bed."

Alice shivered beside her. "I doubt they will be if Elenor's here."

"You're right, so why haven't they answered?" She knocked again. "I don't believe there's no one home."

She stepped backwards to study the upstairs windows but jumped when a scream pierced the air.

"Was that from inside?"

Alice's face paled. "It sounded like it."

Nell hammered on the door, louder than before, not stopping until Ruth pulled it open, tears in her eyes.

"What's going on?"

"There's been an accident." Ruth was breathless as Nell pushed past her, but she froze as Elenor lay at the bottom of the stairs, blood running from the corner of her head.

"What happened?" She knelt down beside her daughter and slapped her face. "Elenor, can you hear me?"

"What are you doing here?" Mrs Pearse joined them in the hall.

"I've come for my daughter. What have you done to her?"

"Me! Nothing."

Nell glared up at Ruth. "Well?"

Ruth was trembling on the other side of Elenor. "She fell downstairs."

"That must have been what we heard." Nell put her face close to her daughter's before shaking her shoulders. "She's still breathing. Elenor, speak to me." She looked up at Mrs Pearse. "Do you have any smelling salts?"

"Y-yes. In the bathroom. I-I'll get them." She stepped over Elenor's legs and clung to the handrail as she disappeared onto the landing. Nell leaned forward again. "Has she been drinking?"

Ruth yelped. "Please don't ask while Mam's here. If you wait until we're alone, I'll tell you everything."

Nell turned to Alice, who stood behind her. "We need to get her into the front room."

"Should we move her as she is...?"

Mrs Pearse swayed as she returned with the smelling salts and Nell grabbed them from her before thrusting them under Elenor's nose. "Elenor, wake up."

She coughed as she inhaled the vapours, her eyes flickering as everyone stared down at her. "W-what happened?"

"That's what you're going to tell me." Nell looked up at Mrs Pearse. "May we take her into the front room?"

"Y-yes. I suppose so. You'll need a cloth for her head, first. Let me get you one."

As soon as Mrs Pearse left them, Nell helped Elenor sit up. "Will you be able to stand up?"

"I-I don't know. My leg hurts. And my arm. And my head."

Nell pulled Elenor's hair away from the cut. "I don't think it's too bad."

"I-it's inside my head that hurts."

"We'd better get the doctor."

"No!" Elenor tried to scramble to her feet but crumpled back to the floor when her ankle refused to hold her weight. "No doctor."

"All right, calm down. We'll get you to a chair and once Mrs Pearse has left us, you're going to tell me what happened."

Elenor gripped Nell's shoulders as Alice helped her to her feet, and by the time Mrs Pearse arrived with a bowl of water and a towel she was on an immaculate velvet settee. Mrs Pearse immediately slid a crocheted mat beneath her head as Nell soaked a corner of the towel in the water and wiped the cut.

"It's not deep, just badly grazed, but we need to stop the bleeding."

Mrs Pearse twisted her fingers. "I didn't know Elenor was here."

"You didn't know?" Nell moved Elenor's hand to hold the towel as she glared at Ruth. "I'd assumed she'd stayed for tea."

"I met her in the park and we were talking, so she came

here but I left her upstairs and sneaked a couple of sandwiches up to her once I'd finished tea."

Mrs Pearse stood with her hands on her hips. "Why didn't you tell me? She could have joined us at the table."

"She ... she wasn't feeling very well." Ruth's voice was a whisper. "I'm sorry."

"It's a good job your father's out..."

Nell stood up and walked to the door. "I think we can say that about all the men, but they'll be home soon. Thank you, Mrs Pearse."

"Oh." She hesitated. "You want me to leave?"

"I'd like to speak to my daughter, and I know how you like to gossip. Perhaps my niece Mrs Wood can join you in the other room. I'd hate for you to accidentally overhear anything."

"I'd do no such thing..."

Nell raised an eyebrow but said nothing as Alice led Mrs Pearse from the room. Ruth watched, her mouth open.

"She won't like that."

"No, well, I don't like a lot of what she's done in the past, so we'll call it quits." Nell stood over the settee. "Why didn't you come home?"

Elenor lay back on the settee, an arm over her face to hide her tears.

"Did you meet Mr Massey?"

"Yes."

"And?"

"He said the baby couldn't be his."

"Who else's could it be?" Nell's voice squeaked.

"No one's. I promise. I haven't even spoken to another man, except his friend when he's been with us."

130

Ruth took over as Elenor sobbed. "He said he couldn't be with her if she was carrying someone else's child."

"It's not anyone else's." Elenor's voice squealed. "He only said that..."

Nell's tone softened. "Did he leave you in the park?"

"Don't be cross with him. He'd been so nice until then. Telling me how he loved me and had missed me. I didn't think he'd mind about the baby ... it was a shock..."

"Did you tell him you'd seen him at the Albert Dock with that woman?"

"No..."

Nell looked at Ruth. "Were you with them?"

"I was with his friend, Mr Young. You won't tell Mam, will you?"

"It's to be hoped you don't have to do that yourself, if he's anything like Mr Massey."

Ruth's cheeks turned crimson as Nell continued.

"Did you see Mr Massey leave?"

Ruth nodded. "They were in the bushes..."

"Stop!" Nell closed her eyes. *I don't need to know this.* "So Elenor found you and you brought her here?"

"Yes."

"Then what happened?" She turned back to Elenor. "Why didn't you come home?"

"I was too upset. I don't want a baby..."

"You should have thought of that."

Ruth bit her lip. "Mr Massey told her she needed to get rid of it."

"Get rid..." Nell gasped. "You mean give it to someone to adopt?"

She shook her head. "He said that if she drank a bottle of gin, it would go away."

Nell caught her breath as she looked from one to the other. "She's been drinking gin?"

"Mam likes to have some in, so I took a bottle upstairs."

"She's drunk a bottle of the stuff?" *I'm not surprised she has a sore head.* "That would explain why she fell."

"Not exactly." Ruth glanced at Elenor. "She couldn't drink all of it, but his friend said that if the gin didn't work, falling down the stairs would."

Elenor buried her head in the back of the chair. "I guessed it was you at the front door and I panicked. I knew I wouldn't do it if you found me first..."

Nell sat in the nearest armchair, staring at the ceiling. "I don't know what to say."

"Please, Mrs Marsh, don't think badly of them, they were trying to help..."

"Help!" Nell sat bolt upright. "She could have killed herself. I can't believe you'd do such a thing."

"I had no choice..."

"You could have spoken to me!" Nell dived towards the settee and pulled at Elenor's skirt. *Nothing.* "It hasn't even worked."

Elenor's sobbing increased. "What will happen now?"

I've no idea. "First of all, we'll see if you can walk and get you home. The bad head will be as much to do with the gin as the fall, so you'll have to get on with that." She put a hand to her mouth as she turned to Ruth.

"The gin! Your mam will notice it's missing." *I'll never live it down if she finds out.*

"I doubt she will. She has quite a few..."

"She drinks it regularly?"

Ruth twisted her fingers together. "Please don't tell her I told you."

Nell raised her eyebrows. *Can tonight get any stranger?*

It was after half past ten when Nell left the Pearses', and Elenor walked between her and Alice, her arms around their necks, as she limped home.

Nell's heart was racing. "What will we say if the men are back from the alehouse?"

"You can't tell them."

"We'll have no choice. They'll be wondering where we are, and I'll have to explain to Uncle Thomas why I won't be going to Blackpool tomorrow."

"You can still go."

Nell spluttered. "I don't think so..."

"But he mustn't find out. He'll beat me..."

Alice stopped, pulling Elenor back as she did. "I get the impression you're not telling me the truth." She held Elenor's shoulders. "Are you in the family way?"

Elenor sobbed onto Alice's shoulder. "Don't be cross with me."

Alice looked at Nell. "Did you know?"

She sighed. "I'm sorry I didn't say anything, but I found out the other day, when we took a walk. She was seeing Mr Massey this afternoon, and I'd hoped that when she told him, he'd offer to marry her."

"But he didn't?"

"No." Elenor's sobs echoed around the street. "He was really angry and told me I couldn't keep it."

Alice gasped. "Is that what happened?"

Nell nodded. "How do we explain that to everyone else?"

"You can't tell Mam. It will kill her."

"I'm aware of that, but she's not the one I'm most worried about."

"Tell Uncle Thomas what you told me. That she had an accident and you can't leave her."

"He'll be furious."

"Maybe he will, but accidents can't be helped. We'll stay with you, if it helps."

Nell gulped. "It will, thank you."

Alice attempted a smile. "Once they're all out tomorrow, we'll talk about it properly."

CHAPTER EIGHTEEN

Nell's heart hammered on her chest as she opened the front door and helped Elenor up the step. Alice hadn't shut it behind them before Mr Marsh appeared from the living room.

"Where on earth have you been? We've been worried sick about you."

Nell sighed. "I'm sorry. Elenor had an accident, and we had to go to the Pearses' house to get her."

Mr Marsh's face softened. "What sort of accident?"

"I-I fell down the stairs and hurt my arm and leg ... and head." Elenor pulled back her hair to reveal the bloodied skin.

"Is that why you didn't come home for tea?"

She nodded. "I meant to, but I couldn't walk. We thought it would ease, but it got worse."

Mr Marsh moved out of the way as Nell helped Elenor into the living room.

"Has she seen a doctor?"

"We wanted to get her home first." Nell sat her in a chair

at the table. "Sit there for a minute and then we'll help you up the stairs." Nell took a deep breath as she stood up. "You do realise this means I won't be going to Blackpool with you tomorrow? I'm sorry."

"Not go!" The redness that had faded from his face immediately returned. "Why should you stay at home because of something she's done?"

"Because she's my daughter and I can't leave her to fend for herself."

"Mrs Wood will be here."

Mr Wood jumped to Alice's side. "She's here to be with her mam, and the boys. She can't take care of an invalid as well."

"He's right." Nell put a hand on Elenor's shoulder. "We can't expect Alice to do everything."

"But we've been looking forward to it ... and it's the last holiday of the year." He glared at Elenor, whose cheeks flushed.

"I'm sorry. I didn't do it on purpose." She winced as she tried to stand. "I'd like to go to bed."

Nell ignored Mr Marsh's gaze as she took Elenor's arm, but her weight was heavy as they struggled to the stairs. Mr Wood followed them into the hall.

"May I?" He swept Elenor up and carried her up both flights of stairs without pausing. "I'll leave you here." He left her by the bedroom door and stepped to one side as Nell joined them. "See you in the morning."

Nell waited for him to go back downstairs. "Will you be able to get yourself into bed? I don't want to wake the others."

Elenor gave Nell a faint smile. "I'll be fine. Thank you. I hope you're not in too much trouble with Uncle Thomas."

Nell sighed. "So do I."

Mr Marsh was already in their bedroom when she returned to the first floor, and he stood by the window as she joined him.

"How did you even know to fetch her? You shouldn't be going out on your own after dark."

Nell was too weary to argue as she slipped off her dress. "We didn't have a lot of choice when Ruth came to tell us. Besides, I wasn't on my own. I had Alice with me."

"Two women is no better than one."

She turned to glare at him. "It was all we had, and I used to manage perfectly well before I met you." She fastened her nightdress and climbed into bed. "I'm not arguing. Good night."

Nell was awake the following morning when Mr Marsh got out of bed, but she remained still and kept her eyes closed while he dressed, and he left without a word. Seconds later, Edith and Leah bounced down the stairs, presumably waking anyone who was still asleep, but she stayed where she was. I don't need an argument at this time of day.

Once she was sure they'd gone, she slipped on her dressing gown and went upstairs. Elenor was lying in bed, staring at the ceiling.

"How are you feeling?"

Elenor didn't move. "I'm not. It's as if I'm in a bad dream."

"I take it you were all right overnight."

"You mean other than everything hurting?"

"There was no bleeding?"

Elenor squeezed her eyes shut. "It didn't work, did it?"

"There's still time, but these things rarely do."

"Then why did Will suggest it? How did he even know...?" Her eyes widened. "Do you think it's because it's not the first time...?"

Nell sighed. "He may have heard it from someone else."

"I hope so. I'd hate it if he's done anything like this before." Tears fell onto her pillow. "He's so nice, so charming, so good-looking..."

The sort of man women love...

"I wish I'd done more than hurt my leg last night." Her voice squealed as she buried her face in the pillow. "I should have killed myself..."

Nell gasped. "Don't even think that. We'll sort something out. Let me see your head." She turned her over and pushed back her hair to reveal a large scab with bruising around the edges. "It will be sore for a few days, but it should mend itself. Do you have a headache?"

Elenor nodded.

"Let's get you out of bed, then. Some fresh air may do you good." She pulled back the bedcovers, but stopped when she saw the bulge under her nightdress. "Oh, my. It's bigger than I expected."

"I've been wearing a corset..."

"Hasn't Edith noticed?"

She shook her head. "I always get changed in the dark, or once they're downstairs."

"You won't be able to hide it for much longer."

"But I have to..." She returned to the pillow to bury her sobbing.

Nell wiped her own eyes as she stroked Elenor's hair. "How are your arm and leg this morning?"

"I don't know."

"Let's see." She rolled up the left sleeve of Elenor's nightdress to reveal shades of black and purple radiating from her elbow. "That looks sore. Can you move it?"

She bent it backwards and forwards several times. "It hurts a bit, but it's not too bad."

"That's something. Let's hope your ankle's as good." She helped Elenor to her feet, and she steadied herself with a wince.

"I'll have to hobble, but it's not too bad. I made out it was worse than it was last night so Uncle Thomas wouldn't be so cross with me."

"Even when me and Alice were struggling to get you home?"

"I wasn't lying. It was sore ... and swollen..."

Nell scowled as she reached for Elenor's dress. "Let's get this on and you can give your face a wash before we go for breakfast. You must be hungry if you didn't eat last night."

"I've not been hungry for weeks."

"Well, you need to eat. The last thing you want is a sickly baby."

"I don't want a baby at all."

"That's as maybe, but as that's no longer an option, having a healthy one seems preferable."

Mr Wood was at the table with Alice and the boys when they arrived downstairs and he smiled as Elenor took her seat.

"You should have told me you were awake. I'd have come to get you."

"Thank you, but my ankle doesn't feel so bad this morning. The swelling's gone down a bit."

"That's good to hear. You'd still better sit with your foot up today."

"I will. Where's Aunty Maria?"

Alice pushed the bread towards her. "In the front room. I took her a cup of tea, but she didn't want anything to eat."

Nell wandered into the hall. "I'll pop in and see her before I sit down."

Maria was propped up on the settee that had become her makeshift bed.

"How are you this morning?"

"I've been worse. Mr Marsh woke me up, last night, though. Why was he shouting?"

Nell sighed. "Because I couldn't go to Blackpool."

"I'd forgotten that was today." Her forehead creased. "Why haven't you gone?"

"It's nothing to worry about, but Elenor had an accident yesterday evening. She was at Ruth's house and fell down the stairs. That's why she wasn't home for tea."

Maria pushed herself up. "Is she all right?"

"She hurt her arm and leg and banged her head. I couldn't leave her today, in case there was a problem, but Thomas wasn't very understanding."

"He's never had children of his own, that's why. Or it could be because he's a man. Possibly both."

Nell smirked. "You're probably right. Let me get my breakfast and I'll be back." She stood up to leave as the letterbox clanged. "Who's writing to us?" She walked to the hall. "It's from James."

Maria's face lit up. "Is he coming home?"

"Let's see." She tore open the top of the envelope and pulled out a single sheet of paper. "Next Friday!"

"Thank goodness." Maria put a hand to her chest. "I've been holding on to see him, but I won't last much longer."

Nell's head shot up. "What do you mean?"

"What I say."

"Nonsense. You shouldn't talk like that. He'll be here for a couple of weeks, so you need to be well enough for that."

"I'll try my best."

"I should hope so. Now, I'll bring you some bread and butter. You need to build up your strength."

Nell passed Alice the letter as she returned to the table. "It's from James. He'll be here next week."

"Finally. Does he say why he's left it so late?"

"No. He doesn't say much."

Alice's forehead creased as she read it. "That's not like him. I hope he's all right."

"He won't know what the situation's like here. For all he knows, your mam may have ... you know ... and he wouldn't want to say anything, just in case."

"I suppose so."

Nell took the bread to Maria but went straight back to the table, looking at Mr Wood as she sat down. "Do you have any plans for today?"

"Not really. I'm meeting some blokes from work at the alehouse at dinnertime, but that's about it."

Alice tutted. "It's more than we can do."

Nell stirred a spoon of sugar into her tea. "Perhaps those

with nothing else to do can have a picnic in the backyard. You know, sandwiches and things, so we don't feel left out. I'm sure the boys would enjoy it."

"I would." Georgie rubbed his tummy.

"Then that's what we'll do. You could teach Freddie to play ball, too, and pretend we're on the beach."

He nodded. "May I go and practise?"

Alice lifted him down from his chair and opened the back door. "Off you go."

The sun was bright at midday as they sat down for their picnic, but there was enough shade behind the house for four chairs and several small tables.

Maria smiled as she watched everyone help themselves to the selection of sandwiches and pieces of pie. "This is nice. It's not often the four of us are here on our own."

Nell offered her a corned beef sandwich. "You need to eat something."

"And I will. Give me a minute to catch my breath." She patted Elenor on the knee. "How's your head?"

"A little better, thank you. It's my ankle that's still throbbing."

"Put it on here, then." She pulled up a stool. "That's it. You need to watch what you're doing in future."

"I will. I'm not looking forward to seeing Uncle Thomas again. He wasn't very pleased that I stopped Mam going to Blackpool."

"She'll be able to go again, and it's nice to see you more cheerful than you have been, even if you are injured. You've put on a bit of weight, too, which suits you."

Nell's heart skipped a beat. *If she's noticed...* She gulped as Maria continued.

"A day like today may be what you need."

"It will be no good if you don't eat something." Nell thrust a plate at her. "Come on, no more excuses."

Maria's shoulders slumped. "Is this you getting back at me for all the times I told you to do things?"

"Not at all, I just don't want you giving up. Now, take a bite."

By the time she'd eaten half the sandwich, Maria put a hand on her swollen belly. "That's enough. I get full so quickly."

Nell's smile dropped. "Would you like another cup of tea to wash it down?"

"I couldn't manage anything else. Would one of you mind walking me to the front room? I'm ready for a sleep."

Alice stood up. "Let me. I need to put Freddie down for his nap soon, too."

Once Alice and Maria had disappeared, Nell stood up and looked at Elenor. "You stay here while I tidy up. As soon as Alice gets back, we need to talk."

CHAPTER NINETEEN

Nell hadn't finished drying the dishes when Elenor hopped into the kitchen.

"What are you doing in here?"

"I didn't want to sit on my own."

"We won't be a minute. Let me help you to the other room, I don't want you hurting that leg any more than it is."

"It will be fine. That's not the bit that's worrying me."

Once she'd helped Elenor to a seat Nell wiped around the sink, and by the time she'd finished, Alice had joined them.

"That was well-timed. Shall we stay in here, or go outside?"

Alice glanced into the hall. "We'd better go outside. We don't want to be overheard."

Elenor grimaced. "What about the neighbours?"

Alice smiled. "If we sit in the corner near the window, and keep our voices down, we should be fine. I saw the woman from next door going out with a friend."

Nell helped Elenor from her chair. "That was very

obliging of her. Who's this?" She stopped as the front door opened and a moment later Jane joined them.

"Nell! I thought you'd gone to Blackpool."

"Oh, I'm sorry. There's been so much going on, I didn't think to tell you I wasn't able to go."

"What have I missed? Is Maria all right?"

"She's as fine as expected. It's Elenor. She had an accident last night, and I didn't want to leave her."

Jane studied her niece. "Are you hurt?"

"I'm a bit bruised..."

Nell nodded. "We were about to sit in the yard so she can have some fresh air."

Jane flicked a hand. "Don't let me disturb you. I'll sit with Maria for an hour, if you like."

"Would you? That would be a great help." Alice walked to the hall. "She's in the front room. Let me see if she's awake then I'll get you a cup of tea."

As soon as they were alone, Elenor bent down to pick up the newspaper Mr Marsh had left on a side table.

"What do you want that for?"

"I was reading it while I was waiting for you. I want to show you something."

"Let's do it outside." Nell took Elenor's arm and helped her into a seat in the yard. "What is it?"

Elenor pointed to a small advertisement halfway down the page. "This."

Nell read it out loud. "Chemist, druggist and surgeon dentist..."

"Not that bit. Here." She moved her finger to the text several rows beneath the heading.

"Banner's patent female pills. One shilling, one and a

half pence. Reliable to bring about all that is required." Nell gazed up at her. "You mean to stop the baby?"

"Ruth told me about them and said they'd make me normal again, but we had no money." Elenor's eyes pleaded with her. "Will you buy some for me? Please."

Nell stared at the newspaper. "To get rid of the baby..." *It would be so easy and Thomas would never find out. Or Maria ... or anyone else. It would solve all our problems.* She was about to reply when Alice interrupted.

"What are you doing?"

She dropped the newspaper by the side of the chair. "Oh ... nothing. Elenor brought this out in case we left her on her own. Was your mam awake?"

"She was once Aunty Jane had taken a seat." Alice smiled at Elenor. "Are you going to tell me what's going on?"

"There's not much more to tell."

"But you spoke to Mr Massey?"

"I did, but as soon as I told him about the baby, he disappeared."

"He may have been in shock yesterday. Now he's had time to sleep on it, he may realise he should marry you."

Elenor shook her head. "He's going to sea again on Thursday and said he didn't want to see me again unless..." She pointed at her abdomen.

Nell sighed. "He told her to get rid of it..."

"No!" Alice gasped. "Does that mean he'd want to see you if you weren't in the family way?"

Elenor nodded as she turned to Nell. "I love him, Mam, and I want his children one day. Just not yet."

Alice studied her. "I hope you're not thinking of trying last night's trick again. Stand up." She helped Elenor to her feet and placed a hand on her abdomen. "You'll kill yourself before you lose that. I'm surprised it's not quickened."

Tears welled in Elenor's eyes. "I've got to try something."

Alice huffed. "If he says he wants to be with you, why not tell him you lost the baby but you'd like to be married quickly so you can be *close* again?"

Elenor's forehead creased. "You mean, lie to him?"

"He's hardly treated you fairly."

"But he'll know. Even Aunty Maria's noticed I've put weight on."

"We'll tighten your corset for you."

Elenor sighed. "What do you think, Mam?"

Nell stood up and wandered to the bottom of the yard. "I think he should marry you, but even if you were married next week, there's no way you'd avoid the scandal." She looked at Elenor. "Do you know where to find Mr Massey?"

"He's in a room on Windsor Street."

Nell raised an eyebrow. "You've been?"

"I have an address."

"Then we need to pay him a visit."

"But my ankle..."

Nell groaned. "I'll put some strapping on it. We can't let him think he's got away with this."

It was turned four o'clock by the time Nell knocked on the door of the boarding house, and a buxom woman with braided buns pinned to either side of her head opened the door.

Nell cleared her throat. "We'd like to see Mr Massey. Is he here?"

She stepped backwards. "He's having a cup of tea. Come in."

Mr Massey gave a casual glance at the door as they walked in, but as soon as he saw Elenor, he jumped to his feet, spilling tea into the saucer.

"What are you doing here?" His eyes darted to Nell. "Mrs Marsh."

Nell's heart was racing. "Is there anywhere we can talk in private?"

The landlady studied them. "Use the front room if you like, but don't be long."

Mr Massey nodded and led the way down the hall. "I-in here."

Nell didn't take the seat he offered. "I expect you know why we're here."

He blinked furiously but remained silent.

"Very well." Nell took a deep breath. "I believe Elenor told you she's in the family way..."

"It wasn't me..."

Nell glared at him. "Exactly what sort of a girl do you think my daughter is? She's not one of these women you pick up on the docks..."

"Oh, no, I didn't suggest..."

"Then what are you implying? For your information, you're the only one she's been close to, although I wish I could say the same about you and the company you keep."

"What...?" His brow creased.

"We saw you at the Albert Dock on the day you arrived in Liverpool, two days before you contacted Elenor."

His mouth hung open as he searched Elenor's face but Nell continued.

"She was so excited about seeing you, she wanted to surprise you, but you had other ideas."

"I-I went to the alehouse..."

"I don't doubt it, but you didn't go on your own. And not all the company was male. Is that how you knew to recommend the gin, because you've had cause to suggest it before?"

"No! I don't know what you're talking about, but..." He suddenly quietened. "You must have seen me with my sister."

Nell snorted. "Please give me credit for having some sense."

"No. Really, she is. The one in the blue-green dress?"

The pitch of Nell's voice rose. "A man who remembers what his sister wears? That's impressive."

"She is, honestly." He turned to Elenor. "You believe me, don't you?"

"I don't know." Elenor's gaze was cold, and she reached for Nell's arm. "I did what you asked."

He cocked his head to one side. "What did I ask?"

"You told me to get rid of our baby..."

Nell took over as tears filled Elenor's eyes. "I found her at the bottom of a flight of stairs after she'd drunk a considerable amount of gin."

He stared at Elenor. "You did that?"

"Didn't you notice me hobbling? Or this." She pulled back the ringlets around her face to reveal her cut.

"I-I'm sorry." His concerned expression couldn't hide the smile in his eyes. "Did it work?"

"No..."

"Yes..."

He looked between the two of them. "Now who's lying?"

Nell's cheeks burned as Elenor spoke.

"Mam and my cousin wanted me to tell you it did, so you'd want to be with me again, but I won't lie to you."

He took a step backwards. "So why are you here?"

Nell recovered her composure. "Because you need to do your duty and marry her. She wouldn't be in this mess if it wasn't for you."

"She was happy enough at the time..."

Nell stepped forward, following him as he continued to retreat. "Don't you dare blame her. She had no idea what was going on, or even that ending up with a baby was a possibility."

"She must have..."

"How? Maybe the strumpets who hang around the docks know what they're letting themselves in for, but young girls like Elenor don't. It's not the sort of thing decent people talk about outside marriage."

He said nothing as he studied the rug by the hearth.

"Are you going to do the honourable thing and give this child a father?" Nell held her breath as he slowly raised his head.

"I go away again on Thursday..."

"Then cancel it..."

"I-I can't..."

"You could if you wanted to. Elenor's dad was a sailor on a cargo ship and he had men not turning up all the time."

"Th-things have changed."

"Not that much they haven't. Now, you'll need to speak to the vicar about setting a date. We can't keep this baby hidden for much longer..."

Elenor stepped closer to him. "Please."

His eyes flicked to the door, but eventually he nodded. "Very well. I'll speak to him tomorrow and let you know the date."

Nell kept her eyes on him. "Which church?"

"Well ... erm ... there must be one locally..."

"There are several, and they'll expect you to go together."

"Oh. I-I didn't realise. Right." He took a deep breath. "Shall we meet at our usual place in Sefton Park, tomorrow, then you can show me which church?"

"Two o'clock?" Elenor nodded. "I'll be there."

Nell held his gaze. "So will I."

CHAPTER TWENTY

Elenor's limp was noticeably improved when Nell helped her to the familiar bench in Sefton Park the following afternoon, and she glanced around before taking a seat.

"He's not here."

Nell checked her watch. "We're a few minutes early. Let's not panic."

"What if he doesn't come?"

"Then we'll go and find him."

"Where? If he's changed his mind, he's not likely to be at the boarding house."

"Calm down."

"How can I?" Elenor wiped her eyes. "The baby's going to be showing soon."

"Which is why we have to get you up that aisle while you can still wear your corset."

"What about those pills in the newspaper? You didn't say anything when I showed you the advertisement."

"Let's wait and see if Mr Massey arrives, shall we?" Nell

kept her watch in her hand and sighed as the big hand reached the five. *It doesn't look like he's coming.* "Is he ever late?"

Elenor shook her head. "He's usually early."

Nell patted her hand. "Come on. Let's take a walk to Windsor Street."

The landlady opened the door in the same manner as the previous afternoon, but her forehead creased when she saw them.

"Are you here to see Mr Massey?"

Nell nodded. "If we may."

"I'm afraid he left this morning and didn't say when he'd be back."

"Oh." Nell hesitated. "Did his friend Mr Young go with him?"

"He did."

Nell sighed. "Very well, thank you."

Elenor sobbed into her handkerchief as Nell led her down the steps. "I knew he wouldn't marry me."

Nell bit her lip as she stared along Windsor Street towards Upper Parliament Street. "Can you take yourself home while I walk to the Albert Dock?"

Elenor's eyes widened. "You can't go on the ship."

"I won't go aboard, I just want to see if it's still there."

"Why?"

Nell's shoulders drooped as she exhaled. "He didn't listen to me, but he may take notice of Uncle Thomas."

"No!" Elenor's shriek caused Nell to step back. "You can't tell him. He'll send me away."

"Well, if he does, I'll go with you. He won't like that."

"You'd do that?"

"Listen. I'm not proud of what you've done, and I'm furious that you kept everything secret, but I won't let him send you away. I know how easy it is to be seduced..."

"You do?"

"Not in the way you were, but I'm well aware that men can be persuasive, and it's unfair for you to take all the blame." Nell's cheeks burned as Elenor's mouth fell open.

"I didn't know what he was doing. He said he wanted to show how much he loved me."

Nell gritted her teeth. "Many men can't tell the difference between love and lust. It would appear Mr Massey is one of them."

Elenor wrapped her arms around Nell. "For years I thought you didn't care..."

"Of course I cared. Everything I've done was as much for you and Leah as it was for me. Now, wipe your eyes and get yourself home. I'll be as quick as I can."

Mr Marsh was standing in front of the fire, his hands behind his back, when Nell walked into the living room.

"You've decided to join us."

"Am I late? I'm sorry. I wasn't expecting you yet."

"Clearly."

She ignored the sneer on his face and smiled at Maria, who sat in the chair beside him. "How are you feeling?"

"A little stronger than yesterday. I'm so looking forward to James being here."

"Only three days to wait now. Has Alice done the tea?"

"She has. She's outside with Elenor and the boys."

"I'll see if she wants me to do anything." Nell darted towards the door before Mr Marsh could stop her but she jumped when Georgie threw the ball to her.

He laughed when she failed to see it. "You're supposed to catch."

Nell tutted as she tossed it back to him. "You'll have to try again then."

She caught the ball three more times, before she passed it to Freddie. "Do you want to throw?"

Once the boys were playing, she joined Alice and Elenor. Elenor looked as if she'd been crying. "Is the ship there?"

"It is. He probably thought we wouldn't be able to find him if he went aboard."

"What do we do now?"

Nell sighed. "Short of going on board and dragging him off, I don't think there's much we can do."

"I don't want to marry him if he doesn't want me."

"You don't have that luxury."

Alice picked up a stray ball that hit her leg and threw it to Georgie. "Do you know how long he'll be away for his next voyage?"

"Months. I'll probably have had the baby by the time he comes back."

Nell clenched her jaw. "Then we need to do something now. We can't stand by and have the family name disgraced."

"No, we can't."

Nell spun round and took a step backwards as Mr Marsh joined them. "H-how long have you been there?"

"Long enough to gather that she's in the family way." His

dark eyes were cold as they flicked between her and Elenor. "How could you?"

"I-I'm sorry..."

Nell stared at the ground as Alice ushered the boys into the house, but he stepped closer to her.

"How long have you known?"

"Not long."

"But long enough, and you let her carry on living here as if nothing's happened?" His voice hissed as he spoke. "I want her out of here by this evening."

"No." Nell's head shot up. "She needs help, not punishment."

"If I had my way, I'd take a strap to her. She's a disgrace. I've said for years you're too lenient with them, and now it's time for her comeuppance. Get out." He pointed to the back door as Elenor clung to Nell's shoulders.

"I've nowhere to go."

"There's a workhouse down the road...."

Nell extended her arms to shield Elenor. "She's not going to the workhouse, or anywhere else for that matter."

Mr Marsh's face was puce. "Those of us who pay the bills will decide who's welcome here, and fallen women most certainly are not. Mr Atkin will hear about this when he comes in."

Nell grabbed his arm. "Please don't let Maria find out. It will kill her."

"All the more reason for *her* to move out then."

"And how would we explain that? I'm sorry, but if you force Elenor out of the house, then I'm going with her."

"You'll do no such thing. You're my wife."

"And she's my daughter. She was tricked into it, and

while everyone's ready to punish her, he's going to get away scot-free with what he's done."

"Men don't behave like that without encouragement."

Nell stepped forward, her eyes fixed on him. "Oh, yes, they do. Men have been forcing themselves on women for years, and because we can't fight back, we have our lives ruined. Well, I won't let that happen to my daughter. Either she stays here and we support her, or I leave with her."

He snorted. "And what will you live on?"

"I'll sort something out. It's not as if I haven't worked before."

His expression hardened. "For the sake of Mrs Atkin, I won't say anything tonight, but I don't want her near me. Do you hear?"

He stormed back into the kitchen as Nell leaned against the side wall of the yard and sank to the floor, her heart threatening to burst through her chest. She hadn't had time to catch her breath when Elenor fell to her knees and threw her arms around her.

"Thank you. I didn't deserve that..."

Nell clung to her. "We'll sort something out. I need to let my heart calm down first." She patted the ground, inviting Elenor to sit beside her. "I hope the neighbours didn't hear that."

"They will have. You can't keep anything secret around here."

Nell reached into her apron pocket. "Here."

Elenor took the packet from her. "The pills?"

"The chemist said that the longer you've been having *problems*, the less likely they are to work, but I decided it was worth a try."

Elenor turned them over in her hands. "Should I take one now?"

"No. We need the men out at work. He said there could be complications taking them so late."

Elenor's brow creased. "What did he mean?"

"You'll be in a lot of pain and could lose a lot of blood. We need to be ready."

"Will I die?"

Nell sighed. "It's not likely, but there's a chance. It has to be your choice."

She stared at the packet in her hand. "Would you take them, if you were me?"

Nell thought back to the time before she was married. *Would I have risked my own life?* She puffed out her cheeks. "Probably." *The shame would have been too much.*

"Even if it killed you?"

"It's hard to be sure until you're in the situation, but when you're desperate, you'll do anything."

"I don't want to live if I have to have this baby." She continued to stare at the pills. "I'll take one in the morning, and then another if it doesn't work..." She flinched and stuffed them behind her back as Mr Marsh strode into the yard, his nostrils flared.

"Who's the father?"

Nell looked at Elenor before answering. "Why?"

"He has to take responsibility for this."

"He's a sailor, and he's going on a voyage on Thursday."

"Does he know?"

Elenor nodded. "He won't marry me."

"We'll see about that. Where's he staying?"

Nell answered. "He's from one of the cargo ships at the

Albert Dock. We think he went aboard when we confronted him..."

"So, this has all been going on behind my back?"

Nell fidgeted with her fingers. "I knew how you'd react, and I wanted it sorted out before we told you."

A vein bulged in Mr Marsh's neck. "What's his name?"

"William Massey."

Mr Marsh turned on his heel. "Right, Mr Massey, let's see what you've got to say for yourself."

CHAPTER TWENTY-ONE

There was no sign of Mr Marsh when Alice called them in for tea, and George nodded at the empty chair as he picked up his knife and fork.

"Where is he?"

Nell gulped. "He ... erm ... he wanted to see someone."

"Was it so important he had to miss tea?"

"H-he didn't say."

George shook his head. "He's a strange fellow."

You're not wrong. Despite it being her favourite tea of liver with mashed potato, Nell pushed her food around her plate. *I hope he doesn't bring him back here and cause a scene.* She glanced at Elenor, who'd eaten less than her. *She's probably thinking the same.*

"What's the matter with you two?" Edith looked between them. "You've hardly eaten a thing."

Elenor pushed her plate away. "I'm not hungry."

George pointed his knife at her. "You can still get it eaten. We don't waste food in this house."

Nell sliced a piece of liver. "I'm concerned about Thomas. I thought he'd be home by now."

Elenor retrieved her plate. "I'm worried about that, too."

Leah choked on her food. "You are?"

"I-I don't like to see Mam upset."

Leah snorted. "When did that ever bother you? You never think of Mam, or Uncle Thomas. Or anyone else."

Nell put a hand on Leah's arm. "That's enough."

"But she doesn't."

Alice dropped the fork she was using to feed Freddie, and with George distracted, Edith reached across to Elenor's plate and took the liver she'd pushed to one side. Elenor gave a grateful smile and scooped up a portion of potato, ready to share as George looked back at his plate.

Leah watched as the exchange took place but Nell nudged her before she could speak.

"How was work today? Were you busy?"

"Yes. I've decided I need a rich husband so I can go out for afternoon tea myself. So many groups of women come in unescorted, and the bills get sent to their husbands."

Edith cleared her plate. "We won't find anyone like that. We'll be scrimping and saving for the rest of our lives."

Nell forced down a piece a liver. "You never know, you might."

"Don't give them ideas above their station." George stood up from the table. "If they want afternoon tea, they'll have to make it here and be done with it." He reached for his cap as Billy joined him.

"We'll see you later."

Elenor relaxed back into her chair as they left and pushed her plate to Edith.

"Are you sure you don't want it?"

"Quite sure. I need to nip outside."

Maria watched her leave from her chair by the fire. "What's up with her? I thought she'd cheered up the other day."

Nell bit her lip. *I hope she won't mind me saying this.* "If you must know, she's seen a boy she likes, but he's signed up to go to sea."

Maria straightened herself in the chair. "What's she doing looking at boys at her age?"

"I ... erm ... he's a friend of Ruth's family and she met him there."

"Well, I'm jolly glad he's going away. It's the best place for him."

"I don't think she'd agree with you, especially since you told her you were married when you were her age."

"That was different."

"It may have been, but if you could be careful what you say to her." Nell shot Leah a glance. "And you..."

"I always am. She's the one who argues."

"Even so, don't mention anything. Please." She stood up to take Maria's plate from her. "Would you like a piece of cake?"

Maria shook her head. "No, I'm done for tonight. When you're ready, I'll go back to my room. I'm tired again."

Nell carried the plates to the kitchen. "I'll take you now." She turned to the girls. "Would you tidy the table, and I'll have a cup of tea and some cake once Aunty Maria's settled."

Alice stood up and took Freddie from his seat. "I'll have the same. Let me get these two in bed and I'll be back."

Nell hadn't got Maria on her feet when Mr Marsh burst

through the door. He kept hold of the doorknob as he scanned the room. "Where is she?"

Nell froze as she let Maria drop back into the chair.

"Who are you looking for, dear?"

Mr Marsh softened his expression as Maria cocked her head to one side. "Elenor. Has she been in for tea?"

"Oh, yes. Not that she ate much. She's in the yard."

"Thank you." He glared at Nell then disappeared down the hall. As soon as he'd gone, she darted to the back door. "Will someone see to Aunty Maria for me?"

Elenor was in the privy when Nell arrived, but before she could knock on the door, Mr Marsh joined them with Mr Massey in tow. Nell's mouth fell open as she glanced between them.

"I believe you two know each other. What in God's name were you thinking, letting your daughter walk out with–" he pointed at Mr Massey, struggling for words. "–with *him*?"

"I-I didn't know. Not to start with."

"But you've known him for months. That's why he recognised you when we were in the park. If I remember rightly, you said he must have seen you with Mrs Grayson, but that was a lie. You were well aware he was carrying on with your daughter. What sort of mother does that make you?" His face was red as he hammered on the privy door. "Get out here, now."

The door opened slowly, but Mr Marsh yanked it back and pulled a sobbing Elenor into the yard.

"Is this him?"

Mr Massey pushed his shoulder. "Leave her alone. She's done nothing wrong."

"Nothing wrong!" Mr Marsh glowered at him. "Nothing

wrong! You have the nerve to stand there in front of me and say that. Her mother may have no morals, but I'm afraid I have, and the two of you have brought shame on this family."

Elenor shrieked as Mr Marsh's hold tightened on the top of her arm, but he ignored her.

"You're going to marry her if I have to drag you to the church myself."

"I'll do what I want, not what you tell me..."

"Get off me." Elenor screamed as she struggled to free herself, but when Mr Marsh's grip held firm, Mr Massey grabbed his wrist and prised his hand away, pulling Elenor towards him.

"You brute. You're worse than me. I may have done wrong by her, but I acted out of love.

"Love! You don't know the meaning of the word."

"At least I won't beat her up."

"I've not laid a finger on her."

"But you'd like to, wouldn't you? Well, you'll have to thrash someone else because Elenor's not staying here." Mr Massey moved Elenor further down the alleyway. "Go, now. I'll see you outside."

Nell reached out after her. "You can't leave me with him."

"You're going nowhere." Mr Marsh grabbed the neck of her dress, but she spun round, popping several buttons from the back.

"I'm not staying here if you're going to take your anger out on me."

"Leave her alone." Elenor glared at Mr Marsh but ducked when he raised a hand to her and swung it towards her head. Mr Massey stepped in front of him and grabbed his wrist.

"You lay a finger on her and you'll regret it. The same goes for Mrs Marsh." He shoved him backwards. "I'll be round with my friends if I have to. Men like you disgust me."

Nell fought back her tears as Mr Massey led Elenor away.

"I'm sorry, Mam. I'll call when he's not here."

May God help me now. She flinched as Mr Marsh made a grab for her, pulling her arm from his reach. "Stay away from me." She edged towards the door. "I don't want to see you right now. You're not the man I married." She turned to go into the kitchen, but Edith and Leah stood in the doorway, their mouths open. After a second, Leah pulled her inside as Edith shut the door in Mr Marsh's face.

"You did the right thing, Mam."

Nell gasped. "You heard?"

Edith plumped up the cushions of Nell's favourite chair as Leah guided her to it. "I expect half the street did. Is it right that she's in the family way?"

Nell nodded as she wrapped her arms around herself. "And it's all my fault."

Leah crouched down beside her. "How can it be your fault? She didn't tell anyone about Mr Massey when she first met him."

"But I should have stopped her from seeing him when I found out. She was only sixteen." The tears she'd tried so hard to hold back suddenly ran down her face. "I must be a terrible mam."

"You're not, you're the best." Leah wrapped an arm around her. "You can't listen to Uncle Thomas."

Edith smiled as she sat in the chair opposite. "Leah's right. I wish you'd been my mam when I was growing up."

Nell buried her face in her hands as her sobs became uncontrollable. *Twist the knife, why don't you.* She didn't look up when Alice joined them.

"What's going on?"

"Didn't you hear the argument?" There was excitement in Edith's voice.

"I heard some shouting, but I couldn't make out what it was about."

"It was Aunty Nell and Uncle Thomas arguing about Elenor. Mr Massey was here, too."

"Mr Massey?"

Nell rummaged for her handkerchief and wiped her face. "Uncle Thomas went to find him. That's why we were both on tenterhooks over tea. We were worried he'd arrive with him."

"Where are they now?"

Nell shrugged. "Uncle Thomas was so angry, Mr Massey thought he would beat Elenor, so he took her away."

"She's gone with him? Just the two of them?"

Nell snorted. "That's the least of my worries. The damage has already been done. She said she'd call tomorrow when Uncle Thomas is at work."

"Where is he?"

"I neither know nor care, as long as he isn't near me. I knew he'd be angry, but I've never seen him like that before. It was terrifying."

Alice wandered to the dresser and pulled out a bottle of sherry. "Would you like one of these to calm your nerves?"

"Please. Although it may take most of the bottle. I hope

Elenor's all right. For the first time in my life, I felt like I'd built an understanding with her..."

Alice handed her the glass. "She won't forget it. Will she marry Mr Massey now?"

Nell huffed. "Who knows? He did seem concerned for her when Uncle Thomas had hold of her, so..."

Edith cocked her head to one side. "Is that why Uncle Thomas went looking for him? Because he wants them to be married."

"If she's going to walk away from this with any dignity, it's the only option."

"What about Aunty Maria? Does she know?"

Nell's head shot up. "No, and she mustn't find out, at least not until they're married. The shock would be too much for her."

"But she'll notice her clothes are tighter. I did."

"You did?"

Edith nodded. "A few weeks ago. It makes sense now. I remember my mam always had tight skirts before my brothers arrived."

Leah's eyebrows drew together. "Who knows about it?"

"Only us. And Uncle Thomas." *And Betty.*

Edith chortled. "And probably most of the street by now."

Nell's face hardened. "That's all his fault. If it forces Elenor to move away, I'll never forgive him."

CHAPTER TWENTY-TWO

A fresh pot of tea was brewing when Nell helped Maria into the living room at ten o'clock the following morning. She settled her into a chair before Alice carried a cup over to her.

"Would you like anything with that? You didn't eat any breakfast this morning."

Maria looked over to the table. "Do we have any scones? I might manage a mouthful."

Alice nodded. "I was going to make some this afternoon for James coming home, but there are a few left from the other day."

Nell carried her own tea to the chair opposite. "How are you feeling today?"

"Not too bad, which is more than I can say about you. Have you been crying?"

"It was nothing."

Maria shook her head. "How many times must I tell you? I know when something's wrong."

"I had an argument with Thomas last night, that's all. It's over now."

"Are you sure?"

Other than not knowing where he's gone or when he'll be back. "Yes, I'm sure."

Maria glanced around her. "Where's Elenor? I've not seen her this morning."

"She ... erm ... she had to nip out. She won't be long." *I hope.*

Maria rested her head back on the chair. "It's strange how she doesn't want to work like the other two."

"Why do you say that?"

"No reason. I've been thinking about them, that's all."

Alice handed Maria a piece of buttered scone with a scraping of raspberry jam across the top. "See if you can manage that. You need to be in good health for tomorrow."

Maria smiled. "It will be so nice to see James. I don't suppose I'll be here next time he visits."

"Don't say that."

"I'm not a fool. I know I won't get better, but I'd like to see him one last time and then I can go..."

"No..." Alice's eyes filled with tears, but she turned as the door opened behind her. "Elenor."

"You're here." Nell jumped up but took a step back as Maria watched them.

"Why wouldn't she be?"

"Oh, no reason." She turned to Elenor. "Would you like a cup of tea?"

"Please, and one of those scones, if I may. I've not eaten this morning."

Maria scowled at her. "You went out without breakfast?"

"Y-yes. I needed to see Ruth..."

Nell pulled a chair from under the table. "Sit yourself down."

"Actually, I need to nip outside. I won't be long."

I need an excuse to go with her. "Oh ... I was about to check on Georgie and Freddie. They've been out there for a while." She followed Elenor into the yard and ushered the boys indoors before pulling Elenor away from the windows. "Where've you been?"

"Mr Massey rented a room."

Nell's eyes widened. "For the two of you? Did anyone see you?"

"Nobody who'd recognise us." She pulled a cheap band from her pocket and slipped it over her third finger. "We were Mr and Mrs Massey."

"But..." Nell struggled to speak.

"Don't worry. We sat and talked for most of the night. What happened with Uncle Thomas made him realise he really does care." A smile spread across her lips. "He asked me to marry him."

Nell exhaled. "That's wonderful. I take it you said yes?"

She nodded. "I did. We've been to see the vicar this morning."

"You've set the date?"

"The sixteenth of September."

Nell's forehead creased. "Couldn't you have made it sooner?"

She shook her head. "He needs to be in Liverpool for another couple of weeks before we have the banns read. Besides, I want time to take the pills."

Nell gasped. "But ... why? You don't need to now."

"I can't help thinking I've forced him into marrying me, so if the pills make things go back to normal, then we can start courting properly and see what happens."

"Does he know?"

"Does he need to?"

"Probably not, but I told you these pills aren't without problems. Especially not when you're so late."

"But I may die in childbirth anyway..."

"That would be an act of God, not deliberate." *It would be easier to explain, too.* Nell's shoulders dropped as she studied Elenor. "If you love him, I'd suggest you marry him now."

"But I don't want a baby."

"Once you're married, you'll be in the family way soon enough, so I don't think it's worth the risk of taking the pills if he's prepared to make an honest woman of you."

"So, you wouldn't take them?"

"Not now, although I wish you could get married earlier. To those of us who know, you're already showing."

"Who else knows?"

"Edith and Leah heard the argument."

Elenor groaned. "That's all I need. Leah won't be able to hide her glee."

"She's not that bad, and I've told her to watch what she says."

"She won't listen. She never does."

"I think she will. Now I'd better go back inside. Aunty Maria will wonder what's going on. Let me have those pills so you're not tempted."

"They're here." Elenor passed her the packet. "I was about to take one."

Nell pushed them into her apron pocket. "Let something good come out of this, shall we? We'll love the baby when it's born and pray you have a safe delivery."

Elenor sighed. "You're right. How were you with Uncle Thomas once we'd gone?"

"I didn't hang around to find out. I went inside and I've not seen him since."

"He's gone?"

Nell nodded. "I suspect he was so angry he didn't trust himself not to do anything stupid."

"I'm sorry."

"Don't be. He'll never mean as much to me as you and Leah do. I don't think he realised that until last night."

The dinner dishes had been tidied up and Nell was helping Maria to her room when she spotted a letter on the doormat. *I didn't hear the postman.* She settled Maria onto her settee and picked it up on the way out.

Thomas. For me. There's no stamp. Has he been here? She opened the front door and peered down the street. *He must have been and gone.* She went back inside and sat on the stairs as she prised it open.

Dear Elenor

I'm writing to tell you I won't be home for the foreseeable future.

I'm not proud of the way I behaved last night, but equally, I'm furious at the shame Elenor has brought on the family. So much so that I can't be in the same house as her.

If you need to explain my absence to Mrs Atkin, please

*tell her I'm working from the office in London and you
don't know when I'll be back. At least you won't be lying
on one count.*

    Sincerely

    Thomas

Oh, my. She blew out her cheeks. *What do I do now?* She
stared at the paper, not moving until Elenor joined her.

"What are you doing here?"

She handed Elenor the letter.

"Oh, Mam. I'm sorry. Do you want me to go so he'll come
home?"

"No." She rubbed her hands over her face. "He has to
accept the situation for what it is."

"How will you manage without his wage?"

Nell's eyes narrowed as she gazed down the hall. "We'll
get by, and if we can't, we'll move to a smaller house. We
won't need a house this big soon."

"What do you mean?"

"I presume you'll move out when you're married, so with
him gone, I can have your bed in Edith and Leah's room.
Aunty Maria isn't likely to be with us much longer either..."

"Oh, Mam." Elenor squeezed onto the stairs beside her.
"Don't you think he'll come back even when I'm married?"

"I've no idea."

Elenor paused. "Mr Massey didn't want me to stay here
with Uncle Thomas and said he'll stay in Liverpool and rent
a room. It might be for the best if I move in with him now.
Then Uncle Thomas may come home."

Nell grimaced. "He'd go apoplectic if he knew you were
living together."

"It can't be worse than it is now."

"Maybe not, but what would I say to Aunty Maria and Uncle George?"

Elenor sighed. "That's more difficult."

"I don't want you leaving if you don't have to." Nell pushed herself up. "I need to go. I said I'd see Mrs Robertson this afternoon and I'm already late. Will you sit with Aunty Maria for a while?"

"I was going to, anyway." Elenor caught hold of her arm as she reached for her cloak. "Do you think Uncle Thomas will calm down?"

It took him three years to get over Ollie, and even then he needed a nudge to come back. "I'm afraid he's very good at bearing a grudge, but the fact you're getting married may help."

"How will you tell him? There was no address on the top of the letter."

Nell shrugged. "It will be up to him, then. There's nothing I can do."

Mrs Robertson's new house was on the other side of Upper Parliament Street, and less than five minutes after she'd left home, Nell knocked on the front door. The housekeeper showed her into the first-floor living room, but Mrs Robertson's smile disappeared as Nell entered the brightly decorated room.

"You look dreadful. Is everything all right?"

Nell sighed. "I'm sorry I'm late, but you wouldn't want my life at the moment."

"Oh, goodness, take a seat. What is it?"

"Where do I start?" Nell paused as she sat down. "Would you mind if I wait until the maid's brought in the tea? Once I start, I won't stop."

"That sounds serious."

"Oh, it is, but before that, how are you?"

"I'm fine. We're ready to go to South Africa on Saturday, which makes a change, and hopefully it shouldn't get so cold."

"I wish I could come with you."

Mrs Robertson's face straightened. "Oh, I think my husband has a full crew, but..."

Nell held up a hand. "I wasn't being serious. I may want to join you, but I wouldn't be able to..." She stopped as the maid arrived with the tea. "How long will you be away?"

"Two months."

"Ah, a lot will have happened by the time you're back. I'll start with Maria..."

Mrs Robertson's eyes were wide as Nell finished with Mr Marsh. "So, he's gone?"

Nell raised her shoulders. "You know what he's like."

"Might he have gone back to stewarding?"

"Who knows, although now you ask, it wouldn't surprise me if he's on his way to Australia as we speak. He always liked to get as far away as possible."

"But without a word?"

"He'll think the letter was enough."

Mrs Robertson tutted. "And you can't even contact him. Why don't you go to the White Star office and ask after him?

If he wanted a job quickly, he's most likely to try a company he's worked for before."

Nell sighed. "To be honest, I don't feel like chasing him. If I mean so little to him, that he'd take off for this, then perhaps we're better off apart."

"But the money..."

"We'll manage. I'll get a job with Leah in the tea room if I need to."

"Aren't you even curious?"

"I am, but I won't beg him to come back."

Mrs Robertson studied her. "What about your sister?"

"Maria?"

"No, Rebecca."

Nell's forehead creased. "What about her?"

"Isn't Mr Marsh friendly with her husband? She may have heard something."

"I doubt it. I've not seen her this week, with one thing and another, but if she knew even half of what's been going on, she'd have been around."

"He might know something, though. Why don't you pay her a visit? Better still, tell her that Elenor's getting married. It's the sort of thing she won't keep to herself ... and news travels."

Nell nodded cautiously. "You have a point, although I doubt Thomas would talk about Elenor. He's so ashamed of her."

"But if it gets word to him..."

"I will, but James will be home tomorrow, so it will have to wait." *I'll let him stew in his own juice for a while, first.*

CHAPTER TWENTY-THREE

Alice cleared away the last of the breakfast dishes as Nell helped Maria into a dining chair and pulled the pins from her hair. The once dark brown hair, now heavily flecked with silver, was so much finer than it had been even a year ago. Nell dragged the brush along its length and divided it with a centre parting.

"Do you want the braided buns?"

"Yes, please. It should help to fill out my face. I don't know why it's getting thinner, when my belly's getting bigger."

"Don't worry. We'll get you looking your best." Nell's fingers moved swiftly as she plaited each side of the hair and twisted them into position. Once finished, she reached for a royal blue hat that matched Maria's dress and secured it in position before handing her a mirror. "How's that?"

She straightened the hat. "A lot better."

Nell took the mirror from her and helped her to her usual chair by the fire. "We're in good time, too. James should be here in the next half an hour, and we want smiles, not grumbling."

"I won't grumble. Not this time. I don't want to frighten him off."

"He'll be pleased to hear it."

Once the plates were back in the dresser, Alice banged on the window and waved for Elenor to bring in the boys. "I want to get them smartened up. I can't believe this is the first time James has met Freddie."

Maria sighed. "It's only the second time he's seen Georgie."

"I know."

Elenor ushered the boys straight through the living room and joined Alice as she took them upstairs. Maria watched them go.

"It's a shame Mr Marsh had to go away when he did. Was that what you argued about?"

"Erm ... yes. I was disappointed he wouldn't be here."

"I suppose he couldn't help it. He'd been looking forward to seeing James."

Nell raised an eyebrow. "Had he?"

"He kept asking after him."

Only to check up on me, I shouldn't wonder. "Never mind. He may get back before James leaves."

"That would be nice. I hope George can be civil, too. I've asked him..."

"Stop worrying, it will all be fine." Nell paused as the front door closed and she dashed to the hall. "You're here!"

He laughed as she threw her arms around him. "Just about. I nearly went to the old house!"

"That goes to show you don't visit often enough. We've been here nearly three years."

"I'd say it's worth being away for a while, if I get such a warm welcome."

She lowered her voice. "It's because we've been worried you wouldn't get here in time."

"In time?"

Nell paused as Alice appeared at the top of the stairs.

"I'll be down in a minute."

"There's no rush, I'm not going anywhere for a while." He turned back to Nell. "What do you mean?"

"Your mam's not well. You'd better be prepared for a shock..."

Maria's voice cut her off. "What's happening out there? If that's James, don't keep him to yourself."

Nell stepped back. "After you. She's been looking forward to this for months."

James ran a finger round his collar as he stepped to the door. "Mam!"

She held out her arms. "Come and give me a hug. I've missed you."

Confusion clouded his face as he crouched beside the chair. "It's good to be back. How are you doing?"

"I'm as well as I've been for weeks. It's such a tonic having you here. How long are you staying?"

"Ten days this time. Has the doctor said what the problem is?"

"There's something growing in my stomach, but he can't do anything about it."

"A growth?" He turned to Nell. "Why didn't you tell me? I'd have come home sooner."

"You said you couldn't get away."

"Well, no, not easily, but..."

Maria patted his hand. "We didn't want to worry you. Now, pull up a chair and sit with me."

He did as he was told as Nell headed to the kitchen.

"Let me brew the tea while we wait for Alice. You've a new nephew to meet."

"He's a new nephew *and* niece, don't forget."

James smiled. "Vernon and Lydia had another girl, you mean?"

"I do. They named her Maria after me! Lydia said she'd bring her round later with the other girls."

"We've quite a family now. I'm looking forward to meeting them all."

"Well, you can start with Freddie." Alice carried her youngest son, while Georgie followed, hiding behind her skirt. "Don't you remember Uncle James?"

The child shook his head.

"Well, I remember you." He stood up but did a double-take when Elenor joined them. "My! I remember you too, but you're not the little girl you were."

Elenor's face coloured, and she wrapped her arms over her abdomen. "I-I'm seventeen now."

James tutted. "Time must work differently in Brazil. I'd swear I was only away a few months..."

Nell rolled her eyes as she returned with the tea tray. "It's been over two years."

"Perhaps I should have come bearing gifts then." He took a couple of sweets from his pocket and offered them to the boys. "Will this do for now?"

Georgie's eyes twinkled as he snatched one, but Alice scowled at him.

"What do you say?"

"Thank you."

"That's better." She accepted the sweet for Freddie and took the wrapper from it. "How was your journey?"

James retook his seat "Fairly uneventful. Have I missed anything while I've been travelling?"

Only my life falling to pieces, but that will have to wait. "You always ask that, and I never remember what you already know. When did you get our last letter?"

"A couple of days before I left, so the news was at least two months old."

"That would explain why you hadn't heard about baby Maria. She was born at the end of June. Did you hear Sam has met a new lady and will be married on Boxing Day?"

James paused. "Yes, I think you mentioned it."

"That's about it then."

"How's everyone else? I've not heard much about Billy."

Maria smiled. "He's the same as ever. I just wish he'd find a nice young lady, so he's not on his own when me and his dad are gone..."

"Come on, what sort of talk is that?"

"I'm being honest. I'd like the same for you, too. Have you met anyone?"

James gritted his teeth. "I've told you. All the eligible women in Brazil are spoken for. I won't ever be on my own, though. Not as long as I stay where I am."

"So, you won't come back?"

"I doubt it. Not while I'm able to work."

· · ·

Alice had taken Maria into the front room for her afternoon nap while Nell and Elenor tidied up after dinner. James watched them from the kitchen door.

"Does Mam go for a lie-down every afternoon?"

Nell placed a dry plate on the side. "She does. She spends more time in there than she does with us now."

"How's Dad with her?"

"He tries his best, but you know what he's like. He's happy to let the rest of us see to her."

"I'm glad you're all here. I can't help feeling I've let her down."

"You have your job to do."

He studied her. "Are you able to go for a walk this afternoon, or do you need to stay with her?"

Elenor finished at the sink and reached for a towel. "You go if you like. I'll stay until you're back. I said I'd see Ruth later, if you don't mind."

Ruth or Mr Massey? Nell nodded. "Very well. We won't be gone for long." She wandered to the hall to collect her cape and popped her head into the front room. Alice was on a chair beside Maria's makeshift bed.

"We're going out for an hour, but Elenor said she'll stay until we're back if you want to go out."

Alice's face was pained. "She had hoped James would sit with her."

"Ah ... yes..." James's face flushed. "I will. When we get back. She's asleep now, so there's no point being here when she wouldn't know."

Nell raised an eyebrow to Alice. "I'll make sure we're not out long."

CHAPTER TWENTY-FOUR

The sky was overcast, but the air was warm as they arrived in Princes Park, and Nell gazed up at James.

"Are you glad to be back?"

"You mean at home or being in the park?"

"Both, I suppose. Does it matter?"

"You tell me. The park's as nice as ever, but I sense something's not right at home, and it's not just Mam."

"What makes you say that?"

"You, for one thing. You don't look happy."

"How can I be when I know your mam won't be with us for much longer? She's been as much a mam to me as she has to you. Maybe more so with you being away for as long as you have."

"You're right. I wasn't thinking."

"I know we complain about her, but she's done so much for us. It's going to be hard when she's gone."

James stared into the distance. "She seems different today."

"Are you surprised? She wants things to be right with

you before the end, which is why it would be nice if you could spend some time with her. Just the two of you."

"What do I say?"

"What do you think? Tell her what you're doing in Brazil or reminisce about things you remember from growing up. She won't care as long as you're with her."

"It would have been better if she'd shown some interest years ago."

Nell sighed. "Don't be like that. I doubt it would have made any difference to you staying in Brazil."

"If she'd been less critical, I may have visited more often. Even now, all she seems interested in is me settling down. Why can't she give it a rest?"

"She worries about you, that's all. You should be glad she cares."

When he said nothing, Nell continued.

"She's really picked up these last few days, knowing you'd be here. I've a horrible feeling she'll go downhill quickly once you've gone."

"So, it will be the end of an era when I leave. She won't be here next time I'm back."

Nell studied him. "Didn't you realise that from my letter?"

"I thought you'd only said she was ill to make me come home."

"So, you could have been here earlier if you'd wanted to?"

He sighed. "One of the men I'm particularly friendly with in Brazil was making the journey, so I waited to travel with him. It's a long voyage when you're on your own."

Nell's head dropped. "I didn't say more in the letter

because I didn't want to worry you. Perhaps I should have done."

They walked in silence until they reached the lake, and James indicated to a bench.

"Shall we?"

Nell sat in the familiar spot and gazed out over the water. "It's a long time since I sat here."

James's brow furrowed. "Why?"

"Oh ... we go to Sefton Park more often now, since Aunty Rebecca moved house. It's a good place to meet."

"There's still no sign of her moving back?"

"She's trying to persuade Mr Grayson, but he's not ready."

"Isn't Mr Marsh still friendly with him? She should ask him to help out, like he did when they moved away."

Nell caught her breath. "He's ... erm ... he's working away at the moment."

"Away? Has he gone back on the ships?"

Who knows? "He's gone to the office in London. There was something that needed doing down there..."

"That's annoying. When will he be back?"

"He didn't know last time I heard from him."

"Is that another reason you're sad?"

"Not at all. We've been married for long enough now, and it's not like when your Uncle Jack went to sea for years at a time. He's only been gone for a few days."

James studied her. "You're sure?"

"Yes. I'm not a lovestruck young girl any more." *And I'm not ready to tell you why he's gone.*

The pause lingered for a little too long before James spoke. "How's Dad? Is he keeping well?"

"He has his aches and pains, but he's still working, which can only be a good thing."

"It's typical Mam has to go first."

"That's not very nice. You may not see eye to eye with your dad, but he's a good man and the rest of us need his wage."

He fidgeted with his fingers. "I feel like a foreigner coming home after all this time. I've forgotten the day-to-day struggles."

"Don't they have any in Brazil?"

"Not really. All the plantation owners and managers have more than enough money, and those of us working are all single men. We don't have families relying on us."

"So, none of you are married?"

"Not among my friends." He cocked his head to one side. "There are a couple of married chaps, now I think about it, but we don't mix with them. They brought their wives with them from their own countries."

"That must be hard on those they left behind."

James shrugged. "They have their reasons. Most of us do."

Nell pulled her watch from inside her cape. "We'd better be going. Elenor wants to go out and we can't leave Alice on her own."

He stood up and offered her an arm. "Elenor's so different from when I last saw her."

"She's growing up."

"More than I expected. I don't remember Alice being so mature at her age."

A lump settled in Nell's stomach. "We're all different."

"Is Leah the same?"

"Not at all. Not that you'd expect her to be. She's still only fifteen." *And hopefully won't be in the family way by the time she's seventeen.*

Voices travelled down the hall as Nell arrived home and she acknowledged Rebecca as she went into the back room.

"I wasn't expecting you to call today."

"I wanted to see Maria, and knowing James was home, I was feeling left out. Have you been to the park?"

James embraced his aunt. "Only Princes Park. I believe Aunty Nell doesn't go there any more."

Nell tutted. "I didn't say I don't go, just that I'm not there as often as I used to be. Has Elenor gone out?"

"She left about half an hour ago. There was no point her staying in with Rebecca here."

"I've not seen her for a few weeks, but I thought she looked well."

Not you, too. "Yes, she's happy enough." She disappeared into the kitchen with the teapot. *She won't be able to keep things hidden for much longer.* She paused by the sink, trying to recall what she was supposed to be doing. *The kettle!* She turned to the range as Rebecca joined her.

"How are you doing?"

"Me? I'm fine. I'll get this on, then I'll be with you."

Rebecca lowered her voice. "I need to speak to you."

"Now?"

"Before I leave."

Nell nodded. "I'll come out with you when you go."

James was sitting beside Maria when Nell carried the refilled teapot to the table. His face was stern.

"I can't promise…"

"Please. I'd hate to think that this is the last time you'll see him."

Nell raised an eyebrow. "What are you talking about?"

"I'd like James to promise he'll visit his dad when I'm gone."

Nell tutted. "Will you stop saying that?"

"No, I won't. I know you want to keep it from me, but I'm not stupid. I want to make sure you all stay in touch when I'm not here."

"And why wouldn't we? James will want to visit us." When he failed to reply, Nell nudged his shoulder. "Won't you?"

"Yes … of course … but I don't know if it will be as often as it is now."

Nell scowled. "I'd hardly call once every two years, often."

"Actually–" he glanced at the clock "–I'm meeting my friend in an alehouse in Liverpool. I'd better go. Nice to see you, Aunty Rebecca."

What was that about? She studied Maria, whose eyes were watery. "Did you argue?"

"I didn't think so."

Alice shook her head. "She only asked if he'd come home and visit Dad. You heard the rest."

"He must still be upset at the way George has treated him over the years. He probably thinks it will get worse if you're not here."

Maria wiped a finger across her eyes. "Why can't they get along?"

"Maybe they will, but we can't force it."

"Actually, it's time I was going." Rebecca retrieved her handbag and stood up.

Nell glanced at the teapot. "Won't you have another cup of tea? It should be ready."

"No, thank you. I don't like to leave it too late getting back."

"Let me walk with you. Part of the way, at least." She looked at Alice. "Will you be all right for half an hour?"

She nodded. "I'll make a start on the tea."

Rebecca was waiting on the footpath as Nell pulled the door closed behind her. "I didn't want to say anything in front of Maria, but how are you really?"

Nell puffed out her cheeks as they started walking. "I presume you've heard from Thomas."

"The evening he left home. I expected you to follow him round."

Nell snorted. "I didn't want to be near him. Did he stay with you?"

"Only for the night."

"Do you know where he's gone?"

Rebecca shook her head. "He said he'd write to Hugh once he'd made up his mind, but we've not heard from him."

"I wouldn't be surprised if he's on a ship by now."

Rebecca's mouth fell open. "Aren't you bothered?"

"Did he tell you why he left?"

"No. He was too angry. He said it was better if he didn't see you for a while."

"I'd say the feeling's mutual." Nell turned her gaze to the footpath as Rebecca gasped. "Don't look at me like that. If Mr Grayson and Isobel had a falling-out, whose side would you be on?"

"Is that what happened? He argued with Elenor?"

"After a fashion, but if it was you, who would you support?"

"Well, it would depend who was in the wrong."

"So, there are circumstances where you'd let Mr Grayson send Isobel to the workhouse?"

"Of course not!" Rebecca lowered her voice. "What's Elenor done?"

"It's not what she's done, it's the way he reacted to it. He was horrible. If he doesn't like the way I've brought up my daughters, he needn't stay around."

"Oh, goodness. Is this to do with Ruth Pearse?"

"In a manner of speaking."

"You're not going to tell me, are you?"

"I can't. Not now. Is he likely to come back to your house?"

"I don't know. Hugh's not said anything."

Nell paused. "I doubt he'll visit during the daytime, so I'll call early next week. If you see him in the meantime, you can tell him not to bother coming home. I've enough on my plate with Maria." *Not to mention Elenor.*

CHAPTER TWENTY-FIVE

Alice lifted the wet clothes from the dolly tub and handed them to Nell and Elenor, who were waiting to feed them through the mangle.

"That's the last of them."

Nell shook the creases from one of James's shirts. "It's amazing how much difference an extra person makes. Still, it's only for another week."

Alice stepped to the other side of the washroom and folded a tablecloth. "Do you think we'll see him again after this trip?"

"If you'd asked me this time last week, I'd have said yes, but now I'm not so sure. He's been in a strange mood since he arrived."

"I'm glad you've noticed."

Elenor shuddered. "I don't like the way he keeps looking at me. It's as if he can sense something's wrong."

Nell sighed. "You've changed a lot since he last saw you, and it must be more noticeable to him than to those of us who are with you every day."

"I still don't like it." Elenor collected up a pile of washing and wandered into the yard where Nell followed with a bag of pegs.

"When are we going to tell everyone about the wedding?"

"What do you mean?" Elenor's cheeks coloured. "I wasn't planning on telling anyone."

"You can't keep it quiet. You'll be having the banns read soon and the family shouldn't find out from the vicar."

Elenor gave her a sideways glance. "I was hoping they wouldn't hear them. We're not getting married in St James's."

Nell stared at her. "Where've you booked then?"

"St Thomas's."

"You'll still need the banns read at St James's. You live in the parish."

"Not as far as the vicar's concerned. Will's arranged a house for us on Warwick Street, which is close to St Thomas's. That's the address we gave him."

Nell stopped, her hands holding a shirt in mid-air. "You're moving in with Mr Massey so you don't need the banns read at our church? Didn't the vicar say anything about you living together?"

"It's with a landlady, so we have separate rooms."

"Word's still bound to travel..."

Alice took the shirt from Nell. "What about Aunty Jane and Aunty Sarah? They go to St Thomas's."

Elenor groaned. "I'd forgotten about them."

Nell sighed. "If you'd wanted it kept secret, you should have applied for a licence. When are you having the first reading of the banns?"

"A week on Sunday."

"We'll have to start telling people then. They'll already wonder why it's so sudden."

"We can't tell them!"

"They'll find out soon enough once the baby's born."

Alice bit her lip. "Will we tell Mam?"

"Do we have any choice? Elenor will leave from here, and I'll have to put on some sort of spread for the wedding breakfast."

"Even if I'm showing?"

"We'll have to invite the family. And his."

"But what will we tell Aunty Maria?"

Nell paused. "I've already mentioned that you've met a young man you like, and that he's going to sea soon, which is why you've been so sullen. Why don't we say you want to be married before he leaves?"

Elenor gasped. "What did she say?"

"Only that she was pleased he was going away, and that it was the best place for him."

"Did you tell her we'd been walking out together?"

"No, but that doesn't mean you haven't been. We can say we didn't want her to worry. There'll be no need to mention the baby."

"And we say we want to be married before he goes away?" Elenor took a deep breath. "All right. When do we tell them?"

"I need to visit Aunty Rebecca this afternoon. Why don't I test it out on her? See what she has to say."

Elenor joined Nell on the walk to Sefton Park, but as Mr Massey came into view, she hesitated.

193

"I'll see you later."

Nell caught hold of her arm. "Don't be late and don't forget to tell Mr Massey what we're doing. The family will want to meet him before you're married."

"I won't." Elenor hadn't veered off the path when Mr Massey joined them. "Mrs Marsh."

"Good afternoon, Mr Massey."

"I'd like to apologise for the other evening. Tempers got a little frayed."

"It was hardly your fault. Well, the arguing wasn't."

"No, but I can understand Mr Marsh being upset. I'd like to apologise to him before the wedding."

Nell glanced at Elenor. "You've not told Mr Massey that Uncle Thomas has *gone away* for a while?"

"Gone away?" Mr Massey's forehead creased. "You just said he was never there."

Nell sighed. "I'm afraid he found it rather difficult to come to terms with the situation."

"I'm sorry."

"Yes, well ... we can't worry about it now. We've the baby to think about. That's all that matters."

He nodded. "I'll take care of it. I promise."

"I'll be happy if you do. Now, if you'll excuse me, I need to carry on to my sister's. I'll see you at home, Elenor."

Rebecca was stitching the hem of what looked like a new skirt when Nell arrived, and she took a seat while her sister fastened off the cotton.

"You've been busy."

"I need something to do and my old navy skirt's getting rather threadbare."

"How long does it take to make a skirt?"

Rebecca stood up and held the garment to her waist. "This has taken about a month, but I've been in no hurry."

Nell studied it. "It's very nice. Would you be able to make one for Elenor?"

"I suppose so, if you have the material."

"I don't yet, but I can go into Liverpool tomorrow."

"Is there an occasion, or is it an everyday skirt?"

Nell took a deep breath. "She's getting married."

"Married!" Rebecca's mouth fell open. "Who to? The young man I saw her with in the park?"

"His name's Mr William Massey."

"It's rather sudden, isn't it?"

"It is, but Mr Massey's going to sea, and they want to be married before he goes."

"Is that what Mr Marsh was so upset about?"

"He ... erm ... he doesn't know."

Rebecca cocked her head to one side. "What do you mean? Isn't that why he stormed around here last week?"

"No. He thought Elenor was too young to be walking out with anyone. Mr Massey hadn't proposed marriage at the time."

"And you're happy about it?"

"What can I do?"

"Stop her from seeing him! She's only seventeen. It's far too early to decide who she wants to spend the rest of her life with. I wish I'd taken longer before I married Hugh ... and I was twenty-three when I met him."

"I don't want to fall out with her. Besides, Mr Massey's nice enough."

"Have you told Maria?"

"Not yet. I know I should, but I keep putting it off."

"Have they set a date?"

"The sixteenth of September. It's a Monday."

"September! This year?"

Nell's cheeks flushed. "I told you, Mr Massey's going away..."

"Is she in the family way?"

"What makes you say that?"

"Because it's not normal to let your seventeen-year-old daughter get married at a month's notice. It would also explain why she needs a new skirt. In fact, is that why Mr Marsh was so angry he left home?"

Nell rubbed her hands over her face. "Promise you won't tell anyone? Not even Mr Grayson."

"So she is?"

Nell nodded. "I only found out a couple of weeks ago. She'd been so secretive..."

"So, who knows?"

"Alice, Edith and Leah."

"Why did you tell Mr Marsh?"

"We didn't." Nell shuddered. "We were talking in the backyard and he overheard us. I've never seen him so angry. That's why Edith and Leah know. They heard the argument that followed when he dragged Mr Massey to the house and insisted he marry Elenor. I thought he was going to beat Elenor at one point and even that he might start on me. That's when he left."

Rebecca gasped. "You thought he was going to hit you? That's not like him."

"You saw how angry he was. That's why I can't bear the thought of seeing him again. Not on top of everything else."

Rebecca shuddered. "I can't even imagine how Hugh would be if it was Isobel. I'm sure he'd kick her out."

"Thomas tried to do that with Elenor, but I said that if she went, I'd go, too. It probably didn't help his mood. He wrote the following day to say he couldn't live in the same house as her."

"But he may come back once she's married. I presume she'll move out."

"Mr Massey's arranged two rooms in a boarding house on Warwick Street for them. She's offered to go there now, but I'd rather she was at home. I wouldn't know how to explain her absence to Maria, for one thing."

"What a nightmare. Is she getting married soon enough to stop the scandal?"

Nell shook her head. "We think she's at least five months. She's not seen a doctor, but she's having to hide it."

"So, it's due before the end of the year?"

"I expect so. Please don't tell anyone."

"They won't hear anything from me. Good luck with Maria and Jane, though."

CHAPTER TWENTY-SIX

Nell studied the ingredients in front of her and scratched her head. It was a long time since she had made a pan of scouse by herself, and she didn't like to disturb Maria to check what she should be doing. *Alice usually does the meat while I peel the veg, so I'll do that first.* The butcher had diced the beef, and she tossed it into the melted dripping in the bottom of their largest pan and mixed it around. *That's a good start. Now the onions.*

Her eyes were watering by the time she'd diced them, and she wiped them on her apron as James joined her.

"Are you all right?"

"I will be in a minute once I've thrown these in here." She stirred them in before smiling at him. "I've never been good with onions."

"Where is everyone?"

"Alice and Elenor have taken the boys to the park and your mam's in the front room. Why?"

He shrugged. "The living room seems empty."

"You're used to your mam being there, that's why."

"You're right. Will you be able to go out for a walk when you've done that?"

"No, I can't leave her on her own, and I feel bad leaving Alice to do so much. She needs time with the boys. Georgie will be at school before you're here again."

"That's what I was hoping to talk to you about."

"What? Georgie?"

"No, coming home."

Her stomach flipped. "Why do I get the impression you don't want to see us again?"

"I do … some of you, at any rate, but I don't feel comfortable being here."

"Why not?"

He paced to the door and leaned against it. "I can't explain, but it doesn't feel like home any more."

"Is that a reason not to visit? Or is it an excuse?"

"Would you be upset if I didn't come again?"

She turned her back on him and placed a carrot on the chopping board. "I won't force you to do anything you don't want to. It's your conscience you'll have to live with."

"Dad won't miss me."

Nell chopped the carrots more viciously than she intended and moved on to the potatoes. "Maybe he won't, but he's not getting any younger."

"I doubt Billy and Vernon will, either."

"Who are you trying to convince? Me or you."

"I'm being realistic."

She turned round and waved the knife at him. "No, you're trying to justify not visiting again. The truth is, I'll miss you, so will Alice, and your nieces and nephews, some of whom you may never meet. But if we don't matter, then fine. Stay in Brazil. I've enough on my plate at the moment to be worrying about what you may or may not do in a couple of years' time."

He said nothing as she threw the chopped vegetables into the pan and reached for the cabbage leaves, which she set about attacking with the knife.

"For some reason, you've not been yourself on this visit. If you're going to be like this every time you're here, then perhaps you're as well not coming. We'll grieve for your passing when we grieve for your mam."

"I'm sorry. I didn't mean it to be like this, but you wouldn't understand…" He slipped out into the yard, and once she was alone, she lowered her head over the worktop. *I can't do this any more.* She wiped her eyes with the back of her hands. *Why does Maria have to leave us? When Elenor needs me, too. I'm the one everyone expects to be strong, but I'm not…*

She sobbed into her handkerchief and didn't hear the approaching footsteps until Mr Marsh turned her to face him.

"Come here." He wrapped his arms around her. "I'm sorry."

She wept into his chest, unable to speak.

"I didn't mean to upset you and I would never hurt you." He kissed the top of her head. "I believe Elenor's getting married."

She nodded, unable to trust her voice.

"At least she'll be able to hold her head up when it's born. Will she be moving out?"

Her voice squeaked when she finally spoke. "Yes."

"That's a relief. I don't want you associated with what she's been up to."

Nell pushed herself away. "Why aren't you at work?"

"That's what I'm here to tell you. I handed in my notice the other day so I can go back to sea. I finished in the office yesterday because I wanted to take a few days to sort myself out before I leave."

"Running away again?"

His eyes narrowed. "I told you the other night, I can't live in the same house as Elenor, so if you're determined to have her here, then you leave me no choice."

She stepped back to the pan and moved it to a cooler heat. "Are you going to Australia again?"

"No. New York. I didn't want to leave you for too long."

That's very thoughtful of you.

"I'll call each month and give you some housekeeping so you won't be short. I still love you, Nell, but this whole situation is intolerable. Perhaps once Elenor's gone, we can start again."

"You're not coming home?"

"Not if she's here."

Nell nodded. "When do you leave?"

"Next Monday."

"So you won't be here for the wedding, either."

"When is it?"

"The sixteenth of September."

"I'll be back around then, although whether I'd be comfortable being at the church..."

"I'll ask George to give her away then. He's been more like a dad to her than you, anyway."

"I'm sorry..." He stopped as the back door opened and James joined them.

"Mr Marsh, it's good to see you again." He offered him a hand. "Are you back from London for good?"

"London? Oh, yes. That was only a small assignment. I'm going back on the ships."

"Really!" James laughed. "Have you had enough of married life?"

"Not at all, but, well ... you know as well as I do, once a steward..."

"I do indeed. I hope Aunty Nell understands."

Nell added some water to the stew. "You know me. Never let it be said I stop people doing what they want."

James appeared to ignore her. "I'm about to go into Liverpool to meet a friend from Brazil. Would you care to join us? I've hardly seen you while I've been here."

"That's very kind, but I won't. I've arranged to meet Mr Grayson tonight."

"Ah, never mind. Maybe tomorrow..."

Nell didn't wait to hear the arrangements. "If you'll excuse me, I need to check on your mam."

She took a deep breath when she reached the hall and stopped to wipe her eyes. *Don't forget to smile.*

Maria tried to sit up when she went into the front room. "Have you been crying?"

"It's the onions from making the tea."

"I hope you're not lying. You look like you have the weight of the world on your shoulders. Won't you talk to me?"

"You've enough to do getting yourself better."

"I can still listen."

"And then lie there worrying once I've gone?"

"So, there is something wrong?"

Nell took a seat. "I'm worried about you. I hate you being like this."

"I'm not ready to go yet..."

"I'm glad." She paused at the knock on the door and Mr Marsh popped his head into the room.

"May I join you?"

"Mr Marsh, of course you may. Come in." Maria pushed herself up. "How was your trip to London?"

"Busy, but it's over now. How are you?"

"Not much change since I last saw you, but it's good to have you home. The house hasn't felt the same without you."

"Ah, well, I'm afraid you'll have to get used to it for a little while longer. I've decided to go back to sea..."

Maria spun round to face Nell. "Did you know about this?"

"About five minutes ago."

"So, you have been crying?"

"No, it was the onions. If Thomas wants to go away, then I won't stop him."

Maria pursed her lips as she turned back to Mr Marsh. "Would it have been too much to ask for you to stay in Liverpool? Nell's going to need you..."

"I-I'm only doing the New York route, so I'll be home every month..."

Nell put a hand on her sister's shoulder. "Don't worry about it. I have Alice and the girls."

"But you need someone to look after you..."

Mr Marsh studied the floor. "I'm sorry to disappoint you, but it's something I must do. I'm hoping it won't be for long."

Maria nodded. "I hope so, too. Now, would you help me into the other room and we can have a cup of tea?"

"I-I can help, but I need to go... I'm needed on the ship."

Maria's eyes narrowed. "You're going already? Nell's not known for half an hour."

"No, I arranged it when I was in London and wasn't able to tell her sooner." Mr Marsh gazed at Nell. "You don't mind, do you?"

"Not in the slightest." *Life will be easier without you.* She avoided his gaze as she helped Maria to her feet and led her to the hall. They hadn't reached the living room when the front door opened and Alice manoeuvred the pram inside.

"We timed that well."

"We?" Mr Marsh turned round as Elenor followed her in. They both froze when they saw each other.

Nell moved to Elenor's side. "Uncle Thomas was just leaving. He popped in to tell me he's going back to sea."

"Yes, that's right." He cleared his throat. "I'm sorry to leave so abruptly, but I'll see you next month."

Elenor's eyes bored into him, but she bit her tongue as he brushed past her. Nell followed him to the doorstep to wave him off but hovered by the door as Alice and Maria went ahead of them into the living room. Once they were alone, she closed the door and turned to Elenor. "I didn't know he was coming."

"At least he won't be back before the wedding. Did you tell him about it?"

"He'd already heard. From Mr Grayson, I presume."

Elenor gritted her teeth. "Make sure you let me know when he's between voyages. I never want to see him again."

CHAPTER TWENTY-SEVEN

James blew his nose with a large white handkerchief as he came out of the front room and gave Maria a wave.

"Bye, Mam." He didn't pause as he picked up his bag and stepped outside. "That's it, then."

Nell fixed his gaze. "If you don't plan on coming back, it will be the last time you see any of us."

"I'll be back, God willing, although I don't know when. I was being selfish the other day."

"Does that mean you left on good terms with your mam?"

"I tried." He gave a wry smile. "I even managed to stay calm when she told me for the thousandth time to find a nice young lady... That wasn't easy."

"I don't know why it always upsets you so much. Still, let's not argue. Have a safe trip."

He gave her a hug. "You look after yourself, especially now Mr Marsh won't be here all the time."

"I'll manage."

He turned to Alice and squeezed her shoulders. "You take care, too. Mam thinks the world of you. So do I."

"Thank you." Alice tried to smile but wiped her eyes as he set off towards Windsor Street. "We'll probably only see him when someone dies."

"I wouldn't even bank on that. I don't know what's happened to him, but he's not been the same since he settled in Brazil. Still, we've other things to worry about now. Like telling everyone about the wedding."

"Shouldn't Elenor do that?"

"If I leave it to her, they'll find out from Aunty Jane or Aunty Sarah, and I'd rather tell them than the other way around. I should probably call on Aunty Jane this afternoon and get it over with."

Nell let herself into Jane's boarding house and climbed to the first-floor landing where she knocked on one of the bedroom doors.

"Jane. Are you in there?"

"One minute."

Nell listened to the noise inside before the door opened. "Sorry about that, come in. Charlie was playing up."

Nell wandered to the cot in the corner of the room where Jane's young grandchild fought with a cloth rag. "Why's he here? Is Betty all right?"

"I've only got him for a few hours; she's worn out."

"Would you like to take him to the park? I presume that's his pram downstairs."

"It is and yes, I would. A sit-down in the fresh air while he runs around would be nice."

Nell bent over the cot and lifted Charlie out. "Come to Aunty Nell. Shall we go and find the ducks?"

The park was busy when they arrived, and Jane parked the pram beside the first empty bench they came across. "He's dozed off now, thank goodness. He's a handful when he's in one of his moods."

"Well, we can take him to the ducks when he wakes up. We'll be fine here, for now." Nell groaned as she sat down. "It's been a long day. James went back this morning."

Jane tutted. "Other than a quick visit last Thursday, I didn't see sight nor sound of him. Was he avoiding us?"

"Not you, specifically. He seemed to spend most of his time in Liverpool with this friend from Brazil. I felt so sorry for Maria. She'd wanted it to be special, but he wasn't interested in sitting and talking to her."

"How was he with George?"

Nell sighed. "They tolerated each other for Maria's sake, so there were no arguments, but I doubt he'll rush home if we find out George is ill."

"It's very sad. How are the girls getting on? Is Leah still enjoying work?"

"She is, and she enjoys having her own money. Elenor's been seeing Mr Massey, too."

"Is that the sailor?"

"He's an engineer, but yes. He goes away again in a few weeks, and they've decided they want to get married before he does."

"Married!"

Nell nodded. "She thinks it's the only way to guarantee he'll be back."

Jane studied her. "Are you sure that's the reason? I saw her last week, and she's put a bit of weight on."

Nell stared across the grass. "That's what she told me to

tell everyone. I thought I'd let you know because they'll be having the banns read at church soon, and I didn't want you to find out from the vicar."

"Does he live in the parish?"

"He has a room in a boarding house on Warwick Street."

Jane nodded. "So, she's in the family way?"

"I didn't say that."

"You didn't need to. Don't worry, your secret will be safe with me. You were very good with Betty when she came close to bringing shame on the family. What's Maria had to say about it?"

"I've not told her yet."

"Must you tell her?"

"How can I not?"

"If the family can keep news of her own illness from her, I'm sure they can keep this from her, too."

"She'll need to know before the day itself so we can have the wedding breakfast at home. Not that it will be a big do."

"Does he have much family?"

Nell sighed. "I've no idea. I want to invite him round to meet everyone before the wedding, which is another reason Maria will have to be told. George will need to meet him before he gives him Elenor's hand, too."

"George is doing it? Where's Mr Marsh?"

Nell bit her lip. "He's gone back to sea."

"Does he know about her condition?"

Nell nodded. "He's not happy."

"I'm not surprised. Still, George should take it all in his stride. He's very down-to-earth."

"I'm still nervous about telling him. Not that I can put it off for much longer. The wedding's less than a month off."

"She won't be able to hide it by then."

"Rebecca's making her a new skirt, which I hope will help, and she's getting married in St Thomas's so she won't need the banns read out at our church. The less the neighbours know, the better. Will you tell Betty for me? I'd like her to be there, if she can make it."

"She'll be there if Bert's mam can have Charlie for the day."

"That just leaves Sarah, then. Will you be seeing her this week?"

"I imagine so."

"Would you tell her for me? I don't want her hearing about it in church, but I can't face any questions from her."

"Leave it with me. I'll be the soul of discretion." Jane smiled. "At least our daughters are married and will give us grandchildren. I doubt any of hers will ever get married."

"There's time yet."

Jane shook her head. "Not the way she keeps an eye on them. They work at that table all hours of the day and never go out. I've no idea how they'll meet anyone. Still, she won't have to deal with any unexpected grandchildren."

"There's a lot to be said for it."

Alice was with Maria in the living room when she got home, and she poured Nell a cup of tea.

"How's Aunty Jane?"

"She was glad of the outing. She had Charlie, and he wears her out."

"Is Betty all right?"

"She's fine, just tired. Charlie seems to have more energy than the other two added together."

Alice nodded. "I can agree with that, especially now he's walking. She'll have her work cut out when this next one arrives."

Maria took a sip of tea. "It can't be long now, can it?"

"October, she thinks."

Maria tutted. "She needs to send Mr Crane to the alehouse more often."

"If only it was that easy." Nell smirked at Alice as she settled onto the settee, but Maria appeared not to notice.

"So Jane had no more news?"

"No, everything's quiet with her." She took a deep breath. "I have some news, though."

"That sounds serious."

It is. "Do you remember I told you the other week that Elenor had met a young man she was fond of...?"

"You said he was going to sea."

"He is, but they've decided they'd like to be married before he leaves."

"Married!" Maria grimaced as she straightened her back. "She's not twenty-one."

"Neither were you."

"That was different. Dad liked George, and he wanted to be sure the family had a breadwinner before he passed. You can't possibly agree to this..." Maria's mouth fell open. "... unless there's a reason."

Nell gritted her teeth. "She wants to be married and I don't want to fall out with her."

"Don't lie to me, Nell. The only reason you'd agree to her being married is if she's in the family way." When Nell said nothing, Maria continued. "She is, isn't she? I've been saying for years that you're far too soft with her, and this is how she repays you."

"It's not like that..."

"And what about this scoundrel going away to sea? You of all people should know it's not a good basis for a marriage. Does she want her children to grow up without seeing their dad?"

"I've told her, but she doesn't want to listen."

"Well, you need to speak to him and suggest he get a job locally. He can't leave a young girl like Elenor on her own for months at a time. She's not ready to run her own house let alone look after a child."

I'm aware of that. "He lives in a boarding house on Warwick Street and they'll move in there so she won't need to do much."

Maria sank back into her chair. "She'll never learn if she leaves it all to a landlady."

"They'll get a house when they can, and he'll be earning a decent wage if he's away."

Maria sat up again. "Where is she now?"

"She ... erm ... she was going to visit Ruth, I think."

"Well, tell her I want a word with her when she comes in." She wheezed as she reached for her cup.

"Please don't get yourself agitated. You've not got the energy any more. Let me deal with her."

"I would if I thought you'd do any good, but I know you. Why didn't you get Mr Marsh to speak to her?"

"She's not his daughter..."

Maria stared at her. "Has this got anything to do with him leaving?"

"Why would it?"

"It suddenly seems like a rather big coincidence."

Nell studied her hands. "He knows about it, but he'd already signed up to go to sea before I told him about the wedding."

Maria's eyes narrowed.

"He had."

"And what about the baby? Had he already decided to go before he found out about that?"

Nell's voice became a whisper. "No."

Maria sank back into her chair. "What's happening to this family? She wouldn't have done anything like that if I hadn't been ill."

Nell crouched beside Maria as her chest heaved. "This is why I don't tell you things. It takes too much out of you."

Maria gasped as the wheezing worsened. "I hope the shame doesn't kill me."

CHAPTER TWENTY-EIGHT

Edith and Leah shrieked with laughter as they arrived home from work, and Leah grinned at Nell as they joined her in the living room.

"Two days off work. It's good of Elenor to get married on a Monday..." Her face dropped. "What's the matter?"

Nell put a finger to her lips. "Keep the noise down. Aunty Maria isn't very well."

Leah glanced around. "Where is she?"

"In the front room. She's not been off the settee today."

"Shall we go and sit with her?"

"Alice is with her, but she's dozing at the moment. I suggest we have tea first."

Edith followed Nell into the kitchen. "Do you think the end is close?"

"I'm afraid so. I just hope we can get through Monday first."

"The wedding, you mean?"

Nell nodded. "I've spoken to Aunty Sarah and asked her to sit with her while we're at church, but it will be a sombre occasion for a marriage. Not that it was ever going to be a time of celebration."

"It's such a shame. Will we do anything for Elenor to mark the end of her being a spinster?"

"Mr Massey's coming for tea tonight so we can all meet him, and I've said I'll do her hair tomorrow. Aunty Rebecca's coming over with a new skirt for her, too, so she can try that on."

"It had better fit. She's no time to make any alterations if it doesn't."

"She's already had to alter it, so I'm hoping it will be fine." Nell paused as the front door closed. "That will be Elenor now."

Elenor's eyes scanned the room as she joined them. "What's wrong?"

"Aunty Maria's taken a turn for the worse."

"Will she be all right?"

"I don't know."

Elenor sank into a chair. "It's all my fault, isn't it? I shouldn't be getting married, should I? I shouldn't be like this, either." She gestured to her expanding belly. "This is what's done it."

"You can't say that. She was ill already." Nell looked at Edith and Leah. "Let this be a lesson to the two of you, though. This is what happens if you let a man touch you. Linking arms in the park has to be the limit until you're married."

Leah shuddered. "I won't be letting anyone touch me."

"Me neither." Edith sat beside Elenor. "You may not appreciate me saying this, but you've done us both a favour. I doubt we'd even talk about it otherwise."

Elenor gave a wry smile. "I'm glad I could help. What's for tea? I'm starving?"

"Sausage and mash."

"My favourite."

Nell straightened the tablecloth. "Is Mr Massey still joining us?"

"He is, but he called in at the alehouse first to introduce himself."

She grimaced. "That was brave of him."

"He said that's where men get to know each other best."

"That's clearly where Uncle Thomas went wrong. He didn't exactly hit it off with Uncle George the first time they met."

Elenor laughed. "That doesn't surprise me. Will's much more of a man than Uncle Thomas."

Nell winced. "That's harsh."

"It's true, though."

Edith nodded. "She's right. A man who enjoys serving other people and doing the cleaning isn't the same as someone working on the docks or doing a proper job on a ship."

"All right, there's no need to go on about it. Uncle Thomas has his good points."

Elenor smirked. "Like knowing when to go away and leave us alone, you mean?"

Mr Massey arrived at the house with Mr Wood, and he grinned at Nell as he hovered by the table.

"Thank you for inviting me, Mrs Marsh."

"You're going to be family soon, so it's about time we found out a bit about you. Was Mr Atkin following you?"

Mr Massey didn't have time to answer before the front door opened and George and Billy walked in.

"Evening, all." Billy took a seat at the table. "You didn't tell us Mr Massey was joining us."

Elenor's cheeks coloured. "We only arranged it the other day and I must have forgotten."

Billy laughed. "A likely story, but we're not that scary. Are you both ready for your big day?"

Elenor glanced at Mr Massey. "I am."

"And I am, too."

George looked over at him. "You go away soon, don't you?"

"Friday, although I'm thinking of staying in Liverpool when I've finished this trip. Being a married man and all that."

George tutted. "They all say that. Jack, Thomas ... I'll give you a year."

Mr Massey shook his head. "You've got me wrong. If I say I'm going to do something, then I do it."

Nell caught her breath. *Jack and Thomas. Both my husbands. Did I drive them away?* She stepped towards the hall. "Let me check on Maria and then I'll bring the tea through."

The room was dark when Nell went in. "How is she?"

"Asleep." Alice straightened the blanket as she stood up. I'll come and help with the tea."

"It's all done. I just need to get it served. I take it she won't want anything."

Alice shook her head. "She's ready to give up. We should

probably speak to the vicar in the morning about administering the last rites."

Nell closed her eyes. "To think we could have a marriage and a death on the same day."

"Don't." Alice took a deep breath. "Let's get this tea served."

George sat back as Nell put his plate on the table. "Where's Maria?"

"She's asleep."

His brow creased. "Has she moved from the front room today?"

"No. She's lost what little energy she had. She'd probably like you to sit with her once you've had your tea."

The smiles on the faces at the table disappeared, and by the time Nell and Alice returned with the last of the plates, the chatter had been replaced with silence. Only when there were nine clean plates did Nell collect them up and come back from the kitchen with a Victoria sandwich cake.

"I'm afraid my baking isn't up to the standard of my sister's, Mr Massey, but I hope it will do. Will you have a slice?"

"Yes, please. Any homemade food is a treat for me."

"Doesn't your landlady bake?"

"Oh, she does, and I don't mean her, but when you're on a ship, you don't get such refinements."

George grimaced. "I remember it well."

"I was always well fed before I signed up. Mam was a good cook, but she passed about eight years ago."

Nell handed him the plate. "You can't have been very old."

"Twelve. Thankfully, I've a sister, who took over the

running of the house. Had it not been for her, Dad would probably have scarpered."

"Is she much older than you?"

"She's younger. She was only nine, but Mam had started her early."

"That was fortunate. Will she be at the wedding?" *And will she be the same woman we saw at the docks?*

"I hope so. There's only the two of us now."

"I look forward to meeting her then." Nell turned to Elenor. "You'd better practise your cooking if Mr Massey's going to give up sailing."

"I know how to cook, I just don't do it very often."

"Well, with Aunty Maria being ill, now's your chance."

Billy dabbed at the crumbs on his plate with a finger. "You'll be living in Warwick Street, will you?"

"We will. It's a nice enough place, and the landlady keeps to herself."

Nell gazed into thin air. "I started my married life in a boarding house. On Windsor Street."

Elenor's head shot up. "I didn't know that."

"Well, no, you wouldn't."

"Was it nice having someone to look after you?"

Nell's smile slipped. "I've had someone looking after me my whole life, I just didn't realise it..."

Elenor's eyebrows drew together. "Is that why you and Aunty Maria live together now?"

"I missed her so much when I was on my own." She took Elenor's hand. "You can always come back here if you want to. Can't she, George? Especially while Mr Massey's not here."

"I daresay she can. We never turn one of our own away. The only ones who leave are those who go by choice."

Elenor's lip creased. "Thank you, but I need to learn to take care of myself."

Nell patted her hand. "I used to think like that, but if you need us, you know where we are."

CHAPTER TWENTY-NINE

There was a fine drizzle in the air when Nell drew back the bedroom drapes on Monday morning and she paused as she stared at the wet cobbles below. *That just about sums up today. Is there any chance it will get better?*

She trudged up the stairs to the girls' bedroom and knocked before letting herself in. Edith and Leah had already left, but Elenor lay in bed staring at the ceiling.

"Aren't you getting up today?"

"What if Aunty Maria passes while we're at church?"

Nell sat on the edge of the bed. "There's not much we can do about it."

"But we should be here with her."

"I'm hoping she'll hold on. We'll only be gone for an hour."

Tears rolled down the sides of Elenor's face. "I didn't want it to be like this. I always thought I'd have a happy wedding, with a special new dress and lots of happy guests..."

"Aunty Rebecca's done a good job with the skirt."

"It's not the same though, is it? It's a skirt I'll end up wearing most days until I lose weight again."

Nell stroked Elenor's hair. "These things happen for a reason, even if we don't know what that reason is. Now, put a smile on your face. You love Mr Massey, don't you?"

"Yes."

"Then that's something to be happy about. You'll love the baby when it arrives, too." Nell pulled back the bedclothes. "Come on. Let's have some breakfast and you can see Aunty Maria before we leave."

Edith and Leah were with Alice and George when they got downstairs, and Elenor took her seat as George studied her.

"Are you ready for today?"

"I am, but Aunty Maria should be with us."

"Aye, well, she'll be with us in spirit."

Elenor accepted the bread Alice offered her. "How is she today?"

"Quiet."

"I hope she's still with us when we get back."

"She'd like to see you before you go." Alice wiped the boys' hands.

"I'll go in when I'm dressed properly. What time's Aunty Sarah arriving?"

"About ten." Nell glanced at the clock. "You've plenty of time."

Leah pouted. "Why aren't we even bridesmaids?"

"Because it wouldn't be appropriate, not under the circumstances. We want the minimum fuss today. When it comes to your wedding, you can have as many bridesmaids as you like. Within reason."

"That won't be for years." She looked at Edith. "Haven't you met anyone yet?"

Nell gasped as Edith's face flushed. "Don't tell me you have?"

"Not exactly, but there's a man I've seen at work who's rather nice. He's having a suit made. Not that he'll have noticed me..."

"I'm glad he hasn't. One wedding a year is quite enough."

George studied Edith. "Do you keep in touch with your dad? You'll need him to give you away when the time comes."

She sighed. "Can't you do it? You seem to give everyone else away."

George chuckled. "I should start charging. I'd make a fortune."

Nell smiled at him. "You've certainly had plenty of practice. I worked out this will be your sixth time."

He shook his head. "A lifetime of memories. Rebecca was first, wasn't she?"

"She was. Then me, when I married Jack."

"Well, I hope Elenor's happier with her choice than either of you two."

Nell scowled. "I was perfectly happy with Jack."

"You were. I just pray that God has other plans for Elenor's young man."

Edith studied her. "Does that mean you're not happy with Uncle Thomas?"

"Oh ... I didn't mean it like that..."

"He has a habit of running off when he doesn't get his

own way." George smirked at Nell as she gasped. "You think I don't notice these things, but I store them away for when I need them." He tapped the side of his head. "Wait until I see him again…"

"Please. Don't make a scene."

"He married you for better or for worse. The least he should do is stand by you when you need him." He turned to Elenor. "Mr Massey would be as well to remember that, too. I'll give him what for if he treats you badly."

"I don't think he will…"

"See that he doesn't." He pushed himself up from the table. "I'm going to nip to the paper shop while I'm waiting. Don't spend all morning getting ready."

Rebecca's sewing had done a lot to disguise Elenor's growing figure, but Nell was grateful she'd given her a lace shawl to wrap around her shoulders. It was long enough to cover her bump, and with the large bouquet of flowers, Nell was satisfied that unless you knew she was carrying a child, there'd be no way of guessing. At least she hoped not.

The service was short with only two hymns, one at the start and one at the end, and once Alice and Mr Young had witnessed the signing of the register, the newlyweds climbed into the carriage that would take them home.

Rebecca sidled up to Nell as the carriage disappeared. "How are you feeling?"

"I've never been to such a sombre wedding. I hope it's not an omen for what she's got to look forward to."

"I half expected Mr Marsh to turn up. He must be due in Liverpool any day now."

Nell shrugged. "Who knows? I'm just grateful he didn't arrive here and create a scene. I've enough on my plate without worrying about him."

"Haven't you missed him?"

"There's been too much going on. If this is his way of punishing me for what happened, then it's not worked. He'll be the one who loses out in the long run." Nell indicated to the door. "Will you walk to the house with me? We don't have Maria preparing the food, and Sarah may not have had chance to do anything."

Rebecca nodded. "How was Maria this morning?"

"Not good. She's lost so much weight these last couple of weeks."

"She'd already lost a lot."

"I know. I only hope she's still with us when we get home."

"Have you arranged for the vicar to call?"

"Tomorrow at ten o'clock."

Rebecca sighed. "I'll be there."

There was no one by the front door when Nell and Rebecca arrived, and Nell hesitated as she opened the door.

"Is anyone home?"

Elenor opened the door to the front room. "We're in here. Aunty Maria wanted to meet Will."

Nell peered into the darkness. "How is she?"

"Alive." Elenor wandered back to the settee and Maria smiled when Nell and Rebecca joined her.

"Was it a nice service?"

"Yes, lovely."

Maria shook her head. "The first wedding I've missed." She took Elenor's hand. "I'm sorry."

"It's not your fault."

"No, but it's still annoying."

Nell checked the corner of the room behind her. "Where's Sarah?"

Elenor answered. "She went to the kitchen when we came in."

"We'll go and see her, then. We need to put the food out." Nell beckoned for Rebecca to follow her. "We'll be back later."

They found Sarah in the living room. "How's she been?"

"She was asleep most of the time, so I took the liberty to lay some of the food out for you."

"That's helpful, thank you."

Sarah sighed. "I can't help thinking this will be the last time I see her."

"We have the vicar calling in the morning if you'd like to join us. Ten o'clock."

"I'm not convinced she'll last that long." Sarah sighed. "I'll need to get my mourning dress out again. I'm wearing it far too often these days."

"We all are."

"Some of us wear it for the required length of time, not for a few weeks to show willing."

Nell took a deep breath. "Please don't criticise. Not today."

Rebecca studied the table. "Is this all you're putting out?"

Nell surveyed the spread. "It should do. There won't be many of us." She turned to the door as Jane joined them.

"Here you are. I waited for you at church until George told me you'd left. Thankfully, he offered to walk me here."

Nell creased her lip. "I'm sorry, I thought Betty would be with you. Is she not here?"

"No, she's been struggling these last few weeks, and her ankles are so swollen she decided against coming. She sends her apologies."

"That's a shame. Have you left her with Charlie?"

"I had no choice. I said I'd call this afternoon, but I want to see Maria before I go."

"I've arranged for the last rites to be read in the morning..."

"She's that bad?"

Nell nodded. "She's gone downhill very quickly."

"I'll be the eldest left once she's gone."

Sarah rolled her shoulders. "I think you'll find I'm older than you."

"I meant among the family. Me and my sisters. It brings it home to you."

"It certainly does." Nell paused as Billy stepped into the room ahead of a young woman.

"Aunty Nell, this is Miss Massey, Mr Massey's sister. She was on her own in church, so I offered to walk with her. Miss Massey, this is Aunty Nell, Elenor's mam."

Nell breathed a sigh of relief at the familiar young woman whose fair hair was attractively arranged in ringlets beneath an emerald green hat. "I'm sorry I didn't introduce myself in church. Things are a little overwhelming at the moment."

"So I heard. It must be quite an ordeal for you."

"The timing could have been better, but we'll manage."

Nell glanced around her. "I'm glad you could join us. Mr Massey said it was just you and him now your parents have passed."

"That's right. I'm hoping to be married myself next year, so I won't be on my own for long."

Mr Massey joined them from the front room. "Rachel! I thought I heard you." He put an arm around her shoulder. "You've met Mrs Marsh, I see."

"Yes, we've introduced ourselves." She flashed him a smile. "Congratulations. Who'd have thought you'd be a married man so soon?"

He laughed. "Not me, that's for sure..." He must have seen the look on Nell's face, "...but then, I didn't know I was going to meet Elenor."

"You must introduce us."

Nell cocked her head to one side. "Don't you live locally, Miss Massey?"

"I'm only in Liverpool, but this has all happened so quickly..."

"Well, yes..." Nell noticed the curiosity on Sarah's face and ushered them away. "Let me tell Elenor to join us and we can start the toasts."

Mr Massey stopped when they reached the hall. "Would it be possible to do that in the front room? I know Elenor would like her aunty to be involved."

"That's very thoughtful. Let me find out if she's up to it and then you can go in."

.   .   .

The guests didn't stay long, and Nell waved to Rebecca, who was the last to leave. *I hope Leah's wedding is a bit more cheerful when we get to it.*

She sighed as she went into the living room where Edith and Leah sat at the table.

"Are we all tidied up?"

Edith pulled out a chair for her. "We are. Come and sit down. You did Elenor proud, all things considered."

"I hope so. I'll go and sit with Aunty Maria when Alice comes out. I don't like leaving her on her own."

"I'll do that, if you like," Leah said. "I've not seen much of her today, and I'll be at work tomorrow."

"All right, we'll take it in turns. I've a feeling we won't need to do it for much longer."

CHAPTER THIRTY

The room was dark as Nell's eyes flickered open and she rubbed her neck as she sat up. *What time is it?*

She crept to the window and made a crack in the drapes. *Daylight. I must have been here all night.*

She stepped back to the chair beside Maria and checked her breathing. *She's still with us and looks so peaceful.* She squeezed Maria's hand as footsteps sounded on the stairs.

"It sounds like we have a visitor."

Alice pushed on the door but stopped when she saw Nell. "You were up early."

"I've not been to bed. I've a right crick in my neck, too."

"Oh, dear. How's Mam?"

"Still asleep. Why don't you sit with her while I put the kettle on?"

Nell shivered as she wandered through the empty living room to the kitchen. *Maria always had the fire going and a pot of tea made by the time I arrived in the morning. I'll miss that.*

The kettle was on the range when Edith and Leah joined her.

"I'll get the bread for you now. Did you both sleep well?"

Leah nodded. "It was strange not having Elenor with us."

"I'm sure she found it different, too. It's a big thing, getting married. The end of one life and the start of another. And then there'll be the baby..."

She paused as Alice called to her. "I'll be back in a minute." She hurried into the front room. "What's the matter?"

Alice leaned over Maria, tears rolling down her cheeks. "She's not breathing."

"She must be! I checked her no more than five minutes ago." She knelt beside Alice and placed a hand on Maria's forehead. "Maria. Can you hear me?" She shook her shoulder gently, but when there was no response, she sat back on her heels. "No. God bless her."

Alice buried her face in her hands. "I didn't even get time to tell her how much she meant to us all."

"You'd told her..."

"But I wanted to tell her again..."

Nell stood up and put her arms around her niece. "She's in a better place now. No more pain."

"I know." She sniffed as she wiped her eyes on the sleeves of her dress. "We need to tell Dad."

"You stay here. I'll do it."

George and Billy had arrived downstairs by the time Nell went into the living room, but with one look at Nell, George got to his feet and disappeared. Billy's mouth dropped open.

"Has she gone?"

Nell nodded. "Not five minutes ago." She wandered to the mantlepiece to stop the clock and put a cloth over the mirror as Billy followed George from the room. Once they were alone, she joined Edith, Leah and the boys at the table. Leah reached for her hand.

"Should we go in, too?"

"Give them a minute to be alone with her. Someone will need to tell Vernon, assuming he hasn't left for work already."

Edith got to her feet. "I'll go."

"Thank you. Someone needs to tell Elenor, too."

"I'll do that..." Leah stood up, but Nell caught hold of her arm.

"Break it to her gently."

"I will."

Once the girls had gone, Georgie and Freddie stared across the table as Nell wiped her eyes on her handkerchief.

"Why are you crying?" Georgie's eyes were wide.

"Granny's fallen asleep and we can't wake her up again."

"I can do it. She always tells me off..."

Nell shook her head. "Sit back down. You won't be able to disturb her this time."

Georgie's shoulders dropped. "May we have some more bread, then?"

Nell and Alice were wearing their mourning clothes when the vicar arrived several minutes before ten o'clock. His face was sombre as Nell opened the door to him.

"Am I too late?"

"I'm afraid so. She passed shortly before half past six this morning."

"I'm so sorry. May I offer my condolences?"

"Thank you. Mr Atkin is with her if you'd like to pay your respects."

Elenor joined her in the hall. "I don't feel right dressed like this when you're all in your mourning clothes. Should I wear an armband?"

"You'll be all right for today. Everyone else will be in the same boat when they arrive."

"I can only say that for today, but I don't have a mourning dress that fits me."

Nell sighed. "I'll get you one of mine before you leave. At least Leah can wear your old one."

Elenor wiped her eyes. "Aunty Maria was so disappointed with me..."

"Did she say that?"

"She didn't have to. She was trying to be kind when I introduced her to Will yesterday, but you could see it in her eyes."

"You can't think like that. She was proud of you in so many ways."

"I hope so..." Elenor had no time to finish her sentence before there was a knock on the front door and Rebecca let herself in.

"Oh, no."

Nell wiped her eyes. "She passed at half past six this morning."

Rebecca rummaged in her bag for her handkerchief. "I'd hoped to speak to her one last time, to thank her for all she did for us."

"I told her last night if it's any consolation." Nell blew her nose. "I wish I hadn't complained about her so much when she was alive. It seems so petty now, and she was only trying to protect us."

"We couldn't see it at the time..." Rebecca paused when Jane joined them.

"Don't tell me I'm too late?"

Nell nodded. "The vicar's with her, and George. We should wait until he tells us we can go in."

"Has the doctor been?"

"He came at about eight o'clock and confirmed the death. Cancer of the stomach."

"Such a terrible thing."

Nell ushered them into the living room where Billy, Vernon and Alice sat in silence round the table. "Take a seat and I'll make a pot of tea. Hopefully, the vicar will come and say a few words when he's finished with George..."

"Is Sarah joining us?"

"She should be..." Nell paused as the front door opened. "This will be her now." She walked to the hall but stopped in the doorway as Mr Marsh looked her up and down.

"Is that for Mrs Atkin?"

"It is. She passed at half past six this morning."

He put an arm around her. "I'm sorry."

"We all are. I wasn't expecting you today."

"I sent a letter. Didn't you get it?"

Nell glanced towards the mantlepiece. *It must be the one I didn't open.* "I've been busy. I must have missed it. How long are you here for?"

"Only until Friday." He stepped past Nell into the living room but hesitated when he saw Elenor. "Good morning, all."

Nell followed him in. "The vicar was coming to perform the last rites at ten o'clock, but we were too late."

"That's unfortunate." He took a seat by the fire as Nell hovered by the kitchen door.

"I'll make that tea. The kettle's boiled." She flinched as Elenor joined her.

"Let me help. I can't bear to be in the same room as him."

"It's a shame he came back today."

"It would have been worse if it was yesterday."

"I suppose so." Nell put the milk and sugar on the tea tray. "Take this through, and if you can, make sure he sees your wedding ring. It might stop him asking what's been going on."

Nell had a selection of cups and saucers out by the time George and the vicar reappeared. "Will you stay for tea, vicar?"

"No, thank you. I need to get on."

George took a seat at the table. "We've arranged the funeral for the day after tomorrow at ten o'clock."

The vicar glanced around the room. "My condolences for Mrs Atkin. If you'll bow your heads, I'll say a blessing for you at this difficult time."

Nell took a seat and lowered her head over her knees. *Rest in peace, Maria. I'll miss you.*

CHAPTER THIRTY-ONE

The air was warm as Nell walked beside Mr Marsh into Sefton Park, but she shivered as he looked down at her.

"You're quiet today."

"It's not the time for frivolous chat."

"You've known for months that Mrs Atkin wouldn't get any better."

"It doesn't make it any easier. Perhaps you'd be a little more understanding if you stayed around for long enough to care for someone."

"What's that supposed to mean?"

Nell raised an eyebrow to him. "Have you ever been with anyone when they've passed?"

"I've been at sea for most of my life."

"Running away."

"That's unfair."

"Is it?" She momentarily held his gaze but he looked away.

"You're well aware of what I think of Elenor's behaviour.

I couldn't be seen to condone it."

"It's not only Elenor. Your parents died without seeing you because you refused to make amends with them. No doubt your brothers and sisters will, too."

He sucked air through his teeth. "That was different."

"Not from where I'm standing. I'd better plan to be on my own when my time comes..."

"Is that what this is all about?"

"It wasn't, but it's a thought."

"Well, you shouldn't think that. I don't like leaving..." He sighed. "I love you, Elenor, but I didn't realise how hard it would be to take on three daughters..."

"Two of which, in your opinion, I've brought up badly." She stopped and glared at him when he stayed silent. "That's right, isn't it? In your head, this is all my fault?"

"No..."

"You're as good at lying as I am. The truth is, if you love me, you'll accept my daughters as they are. We come together."

"I've tried, but it's not easy..."

"Elenor isn't our responsibility any more, but in case you're worried, I've spoken to Edith and Leah about what happened. Neither would want to go through what she has ... and that's before she has the baby."

"Do you know when it's due?"

"Not exactly, because she wouldn't see a doctor until she was married, but she will once the funeral's over. It will be before the end of the year."

Mr Marsh huffed. "I've said I'll work on the ship until Christmas, so I'll find a new job then. I'd rather stay with you than go away."

"You've a funny way of showing it. I feel as if we're strangers..."

"I'm sorry. I'm hoping the new year will be a good time to start again."

And it will give me three months to get used to the idea.

The carriages for the funeral had arrived outside the house by half past nine the following morning, and Nell walked into the front room with George, Alice and Billy as the undertakers arrived to seal up the coffin.

"She looks lovely."

Alice wiped away a tear. "That was her favourite dress. Lilac always suited her. She should have worn it more often rather than saving it for best."

"You know what she was like."

George put a hand on Nell's shoulder. "There'll be a big hole in the family now."

"There will."

The undertakers gave them a minute's silence before they asked George for permission to fix the lid. As everyone left, Nell gazed out of the window. Six magnificent black horses stood outside, two pulling the hearse and four single horses harnessed to the carriages that would take the family to church.

"You're giving her a good send-off."

George nodded as he stood beside her. "I'd been saving. It doesn't come cheap."

"We've done a spread she'd be proud of, too. I'll put it out when we come back from church. Never let it be said we haven't done our best for her."

Mr Marsh was waiting with Mr Grayson when they returned to the back room and as they all walked from the house, Nell acknowledged a group of neighbours who'd gathered in the street to watch the proceedings. Several made ready to follow the procession as they left for church.

Nell and Mr Marsh joined the second carriage with the Graysons and Edith and Leah.

Edith wriggled onto the seat. "It's fancier than Mam's funeral. Dad only got one carriage for us. Not that there were as many as this."

Nell squeezed her hand as the carriage moved off. "It's sad that you've gone through this twice already."

Edith shrugged. "There's nothing you can do about it."

They made the rest of the journey in silence, and when they arrived at church many of the mourners were already seated. The funeral party processed slowly behind the coffin until it reached the front and Nell took her seat beside Mr Marsh. *This is it.*

The horses and carriages were waiting outside the church at the end of the service, and as they arrived home, Alice sighed.

"It was a lovely service. I just wish it hadn't been for Mam."

"I know. It was nice to see so many people there. She was more popular than she thought."

Alice smiled. "She'd have liked that. I suppose we'd better write to James tomorrow and tell him what's happened."

"I doubt he's back in Brazil yet. It's a shame he couldn't have stayed longer." Nell peered into the living room to check who had arrived. "There are not too many here yet. Shall we get this food out, and then we can speak to everyone when they arrive?"

Jane joined her at the table as she put out a plate of pork pies. "This looks lovely, Nell. I didn't know you had it in you."

"I didn't do it by myself. Alice did a lot. It was all a bit of a rush, to be honest."

"I'm sure. George wouldn't have thought of all the preparation needed when he set the date."

"I don't mind and at least it's done now. Have you got Betty with you?"

"Yes, she's around somewhere. You can't miss her."

"I noticed her in church. She mustn't have long now."

"Another few weeks. She'll be glad when it's over..."

Nell's stomach churned as Mr Marsh approached Elenor and Mr Massey on the other side of the room. "Will you excuse me?"

"...you got what you wanted, didn't you..." Mr Massey's voice was raised.

"Is everything all right?"

Mr Massey glowered at Mr Marsh. "It will be when he goes back to sea."

"What have you said?"

"Only that I was glad he'd done the right thing."

"You didn't need to say it with such a sneer on your face." Mr Massey took a step closer to him. "At least I'll be a father soon, which is more than can be said for you. I feel sorry for you..."

239

Nell held up a hand. "That's enough. We don't need a conversation like this today. Elenor, would you and Mr Massey like to get something to eat and go into the other room?"

Elenor glared at Mr Marsh. "With pleasure."

Nell waited for them to leave. "Are you sure that's all you said?"

"I don't want him getting his feet under the table."

Nell gasped. "He's family now, which is what you wanted. He's as much right to be here as you."

"Not when I'm paying the rent, he hasn't."

"We'll speak about this later, but not today." Nell turned and bumped into Betty, who was standing to her left. "I'm sorry, I didn't see you there."

"Don't worry, I'm getting in everyone's way at the moment. I know I've not been here long, but I've come to say I'm going. I'm afraid I'm exhausted. You did Aunty Maria proud."

"Thank you. I hope she'll be pleased if she's looking down on us. Will you be in if I visit in the next week or two, once Uncle Thomas has gone again?"

"I rarely go out these days. It's too much effort. Mam comes every weekday except Wednesday, if you'd like to come then."

"I may well do that." Nell gasped as Betty put a hand on her side and took a sharp intake of breath. "Are you all right?"

"Just the baby kicking. He seems to have more energy than any of the others. I'll be glad once he's out."

Nell smiled. "You should be careful what you wish for. If it's another one like Charlie, you'll be exhausted."

"I already am. I don't think it can get much worse."

CHAPTER THIRTY-TWO

Nell held Georgie's hand as Alice pushed Freddie in his pram along the road to Everton.

"It's been a long time since we walked up here together."

Alice sighed. "It is, but we'll have to leave early from now on. There's no one at home to make the tea any more."

"Perhaps we should come separately in future, so there's always one of us at home."

"We could, but it's nice having someone to walk with, especially now winter's approaching."

"We'll work something out." Nell exhaled as they rounded the corner of Betty's street. "It doesn't seem so far when you have company." She knocked on the door and they let themselves in, but Betty didn't stand up when she saw them.

"I'm glad you're here." Her smile was replaced by a grimace as she squirmed in her chair.

"Is the baby coming?" Alice put Freddie on the floor next to Charlie.

"Not yet. It's getting ready, though."

"May we get you anything?"

"A cup of tea would be nice. The kettle's boiled."

"I'll do it." Nell stepped into the kitchen. "Will you need the midwife?"

"Possibly, later. It's not supposed to be due yet, but the doctor may be wrong."

"Well, we're not leaving you here on your own. Is Mr Crane likely to come straight home tonight?"

"I think so."

"Good. I'll call and let your mam know, too."

Betty watched Nell as she returned with the tea tray. "I'll be fine now you're here. How's Elenor liking married life?"

"She's not had much time to find out. They were married on the Monday and Mr Massey left the day after the funeral. She reminds me of myself when I was first married. She thought she'd be grown up, but now she's in the boarding house, she's lonely. I see her more now than I did when she lived with us."

Betty nodded. "I remember it well, but at least Bert came home of an evening. Things will change once she has the baby. Will she be able to stay where she is once it's born?"

Nell's brow furrowed. "She hasn't said she can't, but she may not have asked. She's still trying to hide her growing girth, given she's only been married two weeks."

Alice stood up to pour the tea. "I'd have thought she'd have moved, anyway. Her landlady will realise she's not been married long when the baby's born, but if she goes somewhere else as a married woman, no one will question it."

"You're right. I'll tell her."

Betty accepted her tea from Alice. "Has she seen the doctor yet?"

"Yes, last week. He said it's due either late November or early December."

Betty grimaced. "That's not long off. Does that mean she'd known Mr Massey for longer than she let on?"

Nell took a deep breath. "I would say so, but I've not asked. There's no point going over it now and, to be honest, I'd rather not know."

Alice shook her head. "You're so different to Mam. She wouldn't have rested until she'd got the truth from us."

"It won't change anything, and I'd only upset myself, so..." Nell shrugged. "I just hope I never go through anything like this again." She stopped as Betty let out a groan. "That looked like more than a kick."

"It felt like more than a kick. Perhaps you should fetch the midwife."

Nell got to her feet. "What about Betsy? Does she need picking up from school?"

"No, she walks with her friends now."

"Good, right, I'll get the midwife. Where will I find her?"

The overcast sky made it feel later than it was as they set off for home, and Alice sat Georgie in the pram with his brother so they could walk faster.

"I didn't like leaving her."

"Me neither, but we couldn't stay, and she wasn't alone. I need to pop in and see Aunty Jane, too. She'll want to be there early in the morning."

"If you go there, I'll go home and get the tea started."

Nell nodded. "I won't be long."

Jane was in her communal living room when Nell arrived, but she hesitated when she'd opened the door.

"Oh, I'm sorry. Am I disturbing anything?"

Jane tutted as she stood up. "Not at all. This is Mr Bruce. He's recently moved in and wants to meet people." She ushered Nell out into the hall. "What are you doing here at this time of an evening?"

"Interrupting a cosy chat by the looks of it."

Jane tutted. "You're doing nothing of the sort. I'm being friendly."

"If you say so. Anyway, to answer your question, I'm on my way home from Betty's and wanted to tell you the midwife's with her. She thinks the baby will be born later this evening."

"Gracious. I wasn't expecting it so soon. Does she need me now?"

"No. Mr Crane should be home and a neighbour has Betsy."

Jane put a hand to her chest. "That's a relief; I'd rather not walk up there in the dark."

Nell cocked her head to one side. "You could ask your gentleman friend to escort you."

"I'll do no such thing." There was a glint in her eyes. "A gentleman should ask a lady to walk out, not the other way around. I'll go as soon as I can in the morning."

"Whatever you decide, let me know when we can visit."

The breakfast dishes were washed and put away when Elenor arrived the next morning. She stooped down to offer

Freddie one of his toy blocks.

"Are you doing anything exciting today?"

Nell put down her sweeping brush. "We're not sure yet. We think Betty had her baby last night, and we're debating whether to pay her a visit or wait to be invited."

"Shouldn't you wait?"

"Probably. Aunty Jane was going up there this morning, and I asked her to tell me the news. We just want to see it."

Elenor took a seat by the fire. "Are you excited about seeing my baby?"

"Of course I am. It's not how I'd hoped to be a granny, but once it's born, we'll love it."

Elenor smiled. "I'm glad. I don't want it being bullied for something I did."

Nell took the seat opposite. "Betty asked yesterday if you were going to stay in the house on Warwick Street. She said you'd be better moving so it will be easier to hide the dates of the wedding and the baby being born."

"I've not thought about it, but Will likes it where we are."

"He's not the one living there, and it's not his reputation at stake. When's he back?"

"The end of November."

"That's when the baby's due."

Elenor rolled her eyes. "I'm aware of that."

"I mean that it won't be a good time for you to move house. Are babies even allowed where you are?"

"Why wouldn't they be?"

"Because they cry a lot, and in houses full of men, it doesn't go down very well."

"I don't know, then. Do you think I should ask?"

"I would, but say you're asking for the future. You don't want to arouse any suspicion."

Elenor sighed. "I hope this is Will's last trip."

"He said it would be, didn't he?"

"He did, but I'm worried he'll change his mind. He said he'll earn more money if he stays at sea."

"And he will. He should be able to get a decent job at the docks, though." Nell studied Elenor as she leaned forward to help Freddie. "You can always move in here if you don't like being on your own."

"I don't know. Will's paid the rent until he comes home. He won't be pleased if I waste it."

"You could ask for it back."

Elenor gasped. "I couldn't do that."

"There's no harm in asking. I'll speak to the landlady with you if you like."

Elenor shook her head. "What about Uncle Thomas? Didn't you say he'd be staying at home next year?"

"I did, but you'll have had the baby by then. Even if you only stayed until the New Year, it may help you get used to being a mam."

"When's he due back?"

"Another couple of weeks. He'll probably only stay for four or five days, so you could move in when he goes again."

"Would you tell him?"

"Not if you don't want me to."

"And what about the others? Are you sure they wouldn't mind a baby crying?"

"We have Georgie and Freddie already, so one more won't make a difference."

Elenor nodded slowly. "I'll think about it."

CHAPTER THIRTY-THREE

Betty was cradling her young son when Nell and Elenor arrived the following week, but nothing she did could pacify his crying. Elenor stared at the child as Nell poured the tea.

"Has he been like this since he was born?"

Betty groaned. "It feels like it, but I don't know what to do with him. He won't feed, he cries when I pick him up, but it's worse if I put him down. I've winded him until my arms are ready to drop off..."

Nell took him from her. "Come to Aunty Nell." She rested him on her shoulder, bouncing gently on the spot. "There, there."

Elenor couldn't take her eyes from him. "Do they all cry this much?"

"Not at all." Betty sat back in her chair. "Betsy was a love. I hardly had a peep out of her. Charlie was more difficult, but nothing like this. I don't even remember what Albert was like, so he can't have been bad."

Nell changed shoulders as the baby screamed down her ear. "Has the doctor been?"

"He came yesterday and suggested he was probably hungry and that I should keep trying to feed him, but I'm so sore. Doctors don't understand..."

Elenor stood up and stroked his hand. "He's so tiny."

"It's because he was born early. We weren't expecting him for another couple of weeks."

Nell cradled the child in her arms. "He still seems smaller than you'd expect."

"I know, but what can I do if he won't feed?"

She offered the baby to Elenor. "Would you like to see if you can quieten him? It will be good practice."

Elenor grimaced as she took hold of the child. "I hope I don't have one that cries this much." She held him tightly as he nuzzled into her shoulder.

Betty smiled as he settled. "You can come again. You'll make a good mam if you carry on like that."

"I'm sure I was just fortunate. He must have been exhausted."

"He should have been." Betty stood up to take him from her. "Let me put him in his crib."

Nell held her breath as Betty lay the baby on his back, but relaxed when he remained settled. "That's a relief."

"It is, but I need to make the most of it." Betty passed Charlie a biscuit. "This should keep him quiet while I drink my tea."

Elenor perched on the edge of her chair. "Does it take a long time to learn what to do with them?"

"If you have your mam and Alice with you, you'll be fine."

Elenor's forehead creased. "What if I stay in the house on Warwick Street? They won't be with me all the time."

Nell looked at her. "Did the landlady say children can live with you?"

"I've not asked yet. I don't want to draw attention to it." She sighed. "I wish Will was here to tell me what to do."

"You won't be able to hide it until then."

"I can try." She stopped as a noise came from the crib. "Is he waking up again?"

Betty peered at her baby. "Oh, gracious. He's been sick. Not much, but it's green." She grimaced as Nell jumped up to check on him.

"That's not normal. I think you should get the doctor."

"I can't be wasting money..."

"It wouldn't be a waste. Feel his forehead. He's gone rather warm."

Elenor grabbed her cloak. "I'll fetch him. Where am I going?"

"Turn right, out of the front door, onto the main road and it's number one, four, five, on the left."

Nell leaned over the crib as Elenor disappeared. "Should I lift him out so you can clean the mess?"

"You'd better. I can't leave him there, but please try not to wake him."

Nell picked him up and rested his limp body on her shoulder. *This doesn't feel right.* "Has he been sick like that before?"

"No. He's not been sickly at all. He just cries."

"Perhaps he has an infection."

"I don't know what it is, but I hope the doctor has something he can give him." Betty worked quickly to change the sheet, and the child gave little more than a whimper as Nell lay him down again.

"He must have had an upset tummy. He seems more settled now."

"I hope that's all it is. I hate them being ill."

"Let him rest and hopefully he'll sleep it off."

They retook their seats but hadn't been settled long when Elenor returned with the doctor.

"What may I do for you?" He sucked air through his teeth as Betty explained. "I don't like the sound of that. You're sure he's not been taking any milk?"

"I can't say he's had none, but he doesn't suckle like the others did."

The doctor pressed down on the child's abdomen, causing him to let out a shrill cry.

"Not again." Betty's shoulders sagged, but as she peered into the crib, the noise quietened. "He's stopped."

"I'd say he's picked up an infection."

"Will he be all right?"

"It's difficult to tell. He's very warm, but that's a sign he's fighting it."

"What shall I do with him?"

"Keep him cool and give him nothing but boiled water until he's over the worst of it. It will help to flush his system out."

Betty's brow creased. "How do I do that?"

"Do you have a bottle with a teat?"

"No. I've never needed one."

Nell sat up straight. "We may have a spare one at home. I could get it to you tomorrow."

"I'll need it today. Let me see if any of the neighbours have one." She followed the doctor to the door before turning to Nell. "Will you wait with him while I'm gone? I won't be long."

Once they were alone, Charlie crawled to Elenor's legs and pulled himself up.

"There's a clever boy. Would you like another biscuit?"

When he nodded, Nell handed Elenor the plate. "You'll do well as a mam. They seem to like you."

"I'm still nervous."

"I don't know a woman who wasn't the first time round. It's all new, but you get used to it."

"I'm glad we live close to you. I wouldn't like to live as far away as Betty."

Nell smiled. "I'm relieved to hear it. It's bad enough walking up here to see Betty once every week or two." She checked her watch. "We need to go once she gets back."

"We can't leave her."

Nell checked the crib. "She should be all right now. The baby's settled. It must have been that bit of sick that was troubling him. We'll visit again once he's over it."

Alice had the tea ready when they arrived home, and she joined them in the living room.

"How was she?"

"She's fine, but the baby wasn't happy. We called the doctor out and he thinks he's got an infection."

"Poor thing. I feel guilty for socialising while we're in mourning, but I've said I'll go over tomorrow."

"I wouldn't say visiting family when there's a new baby is

really socialising. It wouldn't do any good if we couldn't call to help."

"That's my thinking, too, but Mam was a stickler for it."

"I'm sure she'd understand where Betty's concerned."

"I hope so." Alice looked at Elenor. "Did you have a hold of him?"

"I did." Elenor grimaced. "I can't believe I'll have one of my own in a couple of months."

"Neither can I. Still, you were very good with him." Nell smirked at Alice. "She managed to stop him crying."

Alice smiled. "You'll pick it up quickly enough. Has your mam spoken to you about moving back here?"

"She has, but I don't think I can if Uncle Thomas stays at home."

Alice turned to Nell. "Won't he forgive and forget once the baby's born?"

Nell shrugged. "He's not got a good track record. I won't let him stop Elenor living here, though, if she wants to, so he'll have to get used to the idea. Or go to sea again." She glanced over to the mantlepiece. "Is that a letter for me?"

"Oh, yes, I forgot. It came shortly after you went out."

"Mrs Robertson." She reached for the letter opener. "Hopefully, this means she's home for a few weeks and I can pay her a visit."

"Doesn't that count as a social call?"

Nell huffed. "I suppose it does ... but it's been nearly a month since your mam died, so by the time I visit, it will be fine. Let me see what she has to say."

Nell scanned the letter. "Splendid. That was her last trip of the year. I'll write to tell her about Maria and arrange to call next month."

Two days later, Nell's mouth fell open and tears welled in her eyes as Jane took a seat by the fire.

"When did this happen? I only saw Betty on Wednesday and the baby seemed settled when we left."

"He was, and he was better than he had been yesterday, but he deteriorated last night, and when she took him from his crib this morning, he was cold."

"The poor girl." Nell sank into the chair beside her sister. "Hasn't she been through enough?"

Jane shook her head. "It's so awful. She blames herself for not feeding him properly, but if he wouldn't suckle..."

Alice put an arm around Elenor's shoulders. "Don't look so worried. It doesn't mean it will happen to you."

Jane put her head in her hands. "That makes it worse. It should be those conceived out of wedlock that are taken, not legitimate children."

Elenor gasped. "You can't want my baby to die?"

"I didn't say that."

"But that's what you meant. I'm a married woman now."

"But you've a lot of explaining to do..." Jane stood up. "I should go. I need to see Sarah."

Nell closed her eyes as the front door slammed. *What a mess. To think Elenor wanted to be rid of her baby a few months ago, but now she could have a healthy baby while Betty doesn't.*

Elenor crouched down beside her. "Are you all right, Mam?"

Nell nodded. "I will be, but it's such a shock. And another funeral to go to."

"Will Uncle Thomas be back by then?"

"I doubt it. I'm not expecting him until the end of the week."

Elenor clutched Nell's hand. "I'd like to move back here once he's gone. I don't want to have a baby on my own."

"Then you shall. I don't care what he says."

Alice took the seat opposite. "What about Mr Massey? Will he be happy to live here once he's back?"

Elenor sighed. "Probably not, but I hope he'll understand. While the baby's small, at least."

Nell patted her hand. "As soon as Uncle Thomas goes away, we'll bring your clothes here, and by the time he's home again in November, you'll be in confinement, and we'll tell him you can't move."

"Will it get you into trouble?"

"Probably, but I'm used to it by now. I really do wonder why he ever married me."

CHAPTER THIRTY-FOUR

Nell took a deep breath as she stepped into the hall and hung her cloak next to that of her husband. *He's home then.*

Mr Marsh looked up from his newspaper as she wandered into the living room. "You decided to come home. I expected you to be waiting for me."

Nell swept past him to the kitchen. "Someone needs to do the shopping."

"I'd hoped Mrs Wood would have done it today. I wrote to tell you when I'd be arriving."

"I needed to visit Elenor, too."

"I really wish you wouldn't associate with her. You shouldn't be putting your reputation on the line."

Nell bit her lip as she slipped into the pantry. *Don't rise to the bait.* He was standing by the kitchen door when she stepped out again. "Did you have a pleasant trip?"

"Nice enough. We weren't full coming home, so we got the cleaning done."

"You'll be like that next month, too, with Christmas

being so close. Alice and I have a lot to do this year with Maria not being with us."

"It will be different, that's for sure. As will next year. I've told them December will be my last voyage."

"Oh. Right. When do you finish?"

"Probably the twenty-third, although it could be Christmas Eve before I'm back from the last trip."

"Have you sorted a job out for the New Year?"

"I'm hoping to do that before I leave on Tuesday."

"It doesn't give you a lot of time, with one day being Sunday."

"It will be enough." He watched as Nell put the kettle on the range. "Where's Mrs Wood? I expected one of you to be here."

"She's gone to Betty's. She had her baby a couple of weeks ago, a little boy, but unfortunately, he died last Friday. We only had the funeral on Wednesday."

"Oh, I'm sorry. I shouldn't have been so hasty..."

"I'm used to it."

He pursed his lips. "How is she?"

"About as good as you'd expect."

"Is that the second she's lost?"

"The second live baby. She's lost a couple shortly before they were due."

"I didn't realise."

"It's not exactly a conversation for the dinner table." Nell carried the tea tray through to the living room. "Have you eaten?"

"Some bread and jam would be welcome."

Nell nodded and returned to the kitchen. "Will you go into Liverpool this afternoon?"

"No. I thought we should take a walk. The weather's dry and we need to talk."

Nell rejoined him and handed him his bread. "Is there any point?"

His brow furrowed. "Why wouldn't there be?"

"Because I'm not prepared to turn my back on Elenor. If you can't accept that, then we don't have a future together."

"You'll do as you're told…"

Nell shook her head. "Not this time. Perhaps you should think about that while I get on with the cleaning."

The autumn leaves gleamed with a golden sheen as Nell walked into Sefton Park on Mr Marsh's arm, but her heart raced as he remained silent beside her. They were almost at the lake before he spoke.

"Do you know when the baby will be born?"

"It's most likely to be December."

He sucked air through his teeth. "Only three months after the marriage. Don't you feel any shame?"

Nell's cheeks coloured. "I'm disappointed, but why should I be ashamed?"

"Because a mother's supposed to be her daughter's moral guardian. The fact she's ended up like this reflects badly on you. Especially if you insist on being seen with her."

"If it's my fault, that's all the more reason to support her. I won't walk away."

"Is she living locally?"

"Yes, why?"

"She should have moved away. I don't know how she can show her face around here."

"Because she's frightened. She doesn't want to be on her own when this baby's born. Have you any idea how dangerous having a child is?"

"I know what your niece has been through..."

"No, you don't. You've no idea. I've not even told you half of what's happened to Betty, but at least she's still with us. Look at Mr Wood. He's only part of our family because his first wife died while she was giving birth to their baby. Sam lost his wife, too. It's a risk every woman faces, and I won't let Elenor go through it alone in another part of the city."

"She should have thought of that..."

Nell pulled her arm from his. "You really are the limit. What happened to the man I married?"

"I'm still here."

"No, you're not. You're so consumed by what you suppose to be Elenor's sin, you can't see how mean-spirited you're being." She sat down on the nearest bench and folded her arms across her chest as he hovered beside her. "If you can't live with what Elenor's done, then you may as well go back to sea and leave us alone."

After a second's hesitation, he sat down. "You don't mean that."

Her eyes were cold. "I managed by myself for ten years before we were married. If I need to do it again, I will."

"I don't want you to." He leaned forward, resting his elbows on his knees, and stared at his intertwined fingers. "Despite everything, I still want to be part of your life."

"Then you know what you need to do. Elenor's not likely to visit the house while you're here. She has no desire to see you any more than you wish to see her, but you'll have to face her sooner or later. Mr Massey, too, when he's back."

"I won't apologise for being angry. It's what any self-respecting father would do."

"You don't need to. Just accept what's gone before and be civil. That's all I ask."

He nodded. "Will she stay away from the neighbours? She shouldn't be drawing attention to herself."

"She'll be starting her confinement soon, so she won't be going anywhere."

"That's something." He took her hands. "I don't want anything bad to happen to her."

"I should hope you don't."

He hesitated. "Don't be angry with me. I miss you while I'm away and don't want to quarrel when I'm home."

"It's you who starts it. A little forgiveness and understanding wouldn't go amiss."

"No." He stood up and offered Nell a hand. "How's Mr Atkin been with Elenor?"

"George? He acts as if he hasn't noticed, even though I know he has. He's very loyal to the family, which is one of the reasons he's not always agreeable to newcomers. He expects everyone who marries into the family to put the family first."

Mr Marsh sneered. "I don't remember him being so forgiving to your nephew."

"They started their argument a long time ago. George has mellowed since then, but sadly James hasn't."

He pointed along the footpath. "Is that Mrs Read walking out with a suitor?"

Nell followed his gaze to see Jane on the arm of her new friend. "It is. They were sitting together in her shared lounge when I called the other week. She said she was only being friendly and didn't introduce us."

"Well, now's your chance. I think she's seen us."

Jane was coy as they approached. "Nell, Mr Marsh. I wasn't expecting to bump into you today."

Mr Marsh raised his hat. "I arrived back this morning, so we thought we'd make the most of the dry weather." He extended his hand to Jane's companion. "The name's Marsh. Pleased to meet you."

"Likewise. Mr Bruce." The short, grey-haired gentleman gave Nell a slight bow. "Am I right in thinking you're Mrs Read's sister."

"Yes, Mrs Marsh. It's nice to be introduced properly."

Jane huffed. "It didn't feel appropriate the other week. Mr Bruce had only just moved in."

Nell smiled. "I suspect you don't come from Liverpool with an accent like that."

He laughed. "No, I arrived from Belfast about a month ago, although I've heard I'm not the first to make the journey to Toxteth Park."

"No, indeed. My niece's husband, Mr Wood, came over several years ago."

"He's settled in by the sounds of it."

"I would say so. You'll find him in the alehouse on the corner of Windsor Street and Upper Warwick Street most evenings, if you'd like to introduce yourself."

"I may well do that. I've not ventured out far because Mrs Read has been very generous with her time."

"That's good of her." Nell bit her lip as she looked at Jane. "If you're going over to Betty's next week, I'll walk with you. If you don't mind."

Mr Marsh raised an eyebrow. "Why would she mind?"

"Oh ... no reason..."

Jane flicked her eyes to Nell. "I'll see you on the corner of Windsor Street at one o'clock on Wednesday, and we can talk on the way there."

CHAPTER THIRTY-FIVE

Elenor hung the last of her dresses in the wardrobe and sat down on the end of her bed.

"It's good to be home."

Nell sat beside her. "It's nice to have you back, and a relief I can keep an eye on you."

"It's annoying the landlady won't return the rent money we'd paid. Will won't be happy."

"It shouldn't matter. You won't need to pay anything here until he comes back, so it will all work out."

"I suppose so." Elenor looked around the room. "Where will he sleep? He can't stay in here."

"We'll work something out. The two of you will need a room of your own when the baby's born. Edith and Leah won't appreciate being woken in the middle of the night."

Elenor grimaced. "I don't like the sound of that, either."

"You'll get used to it. That's what being a mam is all about."

"I wish I'd known all this before I met Will."

Nell sighed. "So do I, but don't get all maudlin on me. You've a baby to prepare for, so let's get you into bed."

"Do you mind if Ruth comes to visit while I'm in confinement?"

"Is that wise? I don't want her upsetting you."

"Why would she do that? She's my friend."

"I get the impression you wouldn't be in this condition if it wasn't for her. She should have been chaperoning you, not turning a blind eye."

"That wasn't her fault."

Whose fault was it, then? Nell studied her. *Don't ask.* "Did you ever see her mam again after the accident at their house?"

Elenor shook her head. "She wanted to avoid me as much as I was avoiding her. Ruth said she was embarrassed she'd been drinking gin and hadn't realised I was there."

"Does she know about the baby?"

"No, Ruth wouldn't tell her in case she started asking questions about what *she* was doing."

Nell raised her eyes to the ceiling. "Thank goodness for small mercies. Is Ruth still seeing Mr Young?"

"He's away with Will, but she hopes to when he comes back. Not that she'll let him get close." Elenor's voice dropped. "I think I've been a lesson to everyone who knows me."

"I'm glad to hear it."

"So you'll let her visit?"

Nell nodded. "As long as you stay calm while she's here. If there's any noise, she'll have to go."

Elenor smiled. "We'll be quiet. Did you say you were walking up to Betty's this afternoon?"

"Yes, with Aunty Jane. Why?"

"Is she speaking to you after what happened the other week?"

Nell grimaced. "We'll see."

"I didn't mean to upset her."

"I know, but losing a child is hard. She wasn't her usual self."

"Will you tell her I'm sorry? And would you give Ruth a letter while you're out, so she knows she can visit?"

"I'll push it through the letterbox, but I'm not knocking. I've no desire to see her mam again, either."

Jane was waiting on the corner when Nell joined her, and she immediately started walking.

"I'd nearly given up on you."

"I'm sorry. I had a letter to deliver. Elenor asked me to tell you she's sorry about what happened last week, too."

"Apology accepted. I shouldn't have said what I did, either."

"It's not ideal whichever way you look at it. How's Betty been?"

"Not good, but you'll see for yourself. I wish the winter weather wasn't coming. It makes visiting even worse."

Nell followed Jane as she crossed to the other side of the road. "Does Mr Bruce work?"

"What's he got to do with it?"

"If you're walking out together, I wondered if he could escort you. It might make the walk better."

"We're not really walking out, certainly not in the dark.

Besides, we can spend any time together in the shared living room. It's usually free of an evening."

Nell sniggered. "That's very convenient."

"It's not like that. Not yet, anyway. We became friendly because of my time in Ireland, and we get along well."

"I was going to ask you about the Irish connection. He's not another Catholic, is he?"

"Would it matter if he was?"

"Not to me, but Thomas is of the opinion that any union between Protestants and Catholics is unforgivable."

"Does he know Patrick was a Catholic?"

"I mentioned it to him, and that's when I found out what he thought."

Jane sighed. "Well, for his information, Mr Bruce isn't, but it wouldn't matter at my age. Even if we were to marry, there'd be no children or in-laws to deal with."

"It's a benefit of growing old."

"Another is that you don't get swept off your feet so easily. There may not be any future in our friendship."

"I said that about Thomas, but now look at us. We've been married for over five years."

Jane studied her. "You're not the happy couple you used to be, though. And he's going away again. Is there something wrong?"

Nell sighed. "It's this business with Elenor. He's finding it hard to accept."

"It was a blessing Pat wasn't with us when Betty was in the same situation. He'd have taken his belt to her without a second thought."

"I shudder to think what Thomas would have done if I

hadn't been there when he found out, but seeing him as he was, made me question whether I was right to marry him."

"Really?"

Nell kept her eyes focussed on the footpath. "It turns out he isn't cut out to be a family man. I should have known given he was nearly forty when we married."

"Men rarely get involved with the children, whatever their age, except to discipline them."

"Unfortunately, Thomas wants to do a bit too much of that. The girls hate him for it."

"It's a fine line, especially for stepdads."

"It wouldn't affect you if you remarried. Betty has a husband, and the boys are men themselves."

"You'd still want them all to get along, though." Jane ushered Nell around the corner on to Betty's street. "I often tease, but the thought of walking out with someone makes me nervous after being on my own for so long, never mind being married."

"Why do you think it was nine years before I married Thomas? It's a big step when you can manage on your own."

"I know." Jane stopped before she opened the front door. "I've not mentioned Mr Bruce to Betty. It's not a good time under the circumstances."

Nell nodded. "Your secret will be safe with me."

Betty was at the table giving Charlie his dinner when they arrived, and Jane looked at the clock.

"You're late giving him that."

Betty shrugged. "I didn't realise the time. There's no rush, is there?"

"Only that the poor love will be starving. What have you been doing?"

"Not much."

Nell took off her cloak. "Let me make a fresh pot of tea. I'm guessing that one is cold." She studied Betty. "Have you eaten anything?"

"I'm not hungry."

Jane tutted. "What sort of talk is that? You need to eat to keep your strength up. You don't want the doctor recommending you go to the asylum again."

"Bert wouldn't let me go. He needs me here."

"Only if you're able to run the house and take care of the children. You're no good to him if you can't do that."

Betty sighed as she stood up. "I'll do it. I've had things on my mind."

Nell held up a hand as Jane followed her across the room. "Leave her. It's not two weeks since the baby passed."

"But she can't give in to the melancholy she had before. I can't have Charlie for days at a time."

The child banged his hands into the food Betty had left in his reach, and Nell made a grab for it. "Gracious, what a mess. I'll get a cloth."

Betty rested her head on the back of the chair and closed her eyes. "I hope Elenor doesn't suffer like I have. This must be God's way of punishing me for being with child before I was married."

Jane took the seat opposite her. "You can't say that. Plenty of other women suffer, and they won't all have been in the family way before they were married."

"I expect a lot were."

Nell returned from the kitchen and wiped Charlie's

hands. "Come on, that's no way to talk. I know you've not had things easy, but you've three lovely children. That's not a punishment."

"It should have been more, though. I feel for Bert, too. He's as upset as me, but he can't talk to anyone. He's been drinking far too much these last few weeks."

Jane took Charlie from his chair. "If you know what's good for you, you won't stop him. Let him drink enough that he falls asleep as soon as he gets home."

"He doesn't drink that much."

"Then have a bottle of brandy waiting on the table for him when he gets in. And make sure he has some. You don't want to go through this again."

CHAPTER THIRTY-SIX

M rs Robertson held out her arms in welcome as Nell joined her.

"You're here."

"I'm sorry for delaying the visit but with being in mourning..."

"It's perfectly understandable. I'm grateful you're here now. You sound as if you've had an awful time."

"I've had better."

Mrs Robertson nodded to the maid as she offered to bring a pot of tea. "I was sorry to hear about your sister."

"It was for the best in the end. I suspect she was in more pain than she liked to admit, and she had no energy. At least she was peaceful when the time came."

"Was your nephew home when she passed?"

"No, but he'd seen her about a month earlier. We've written to tell him, but not heard from him yet. I expect we'll get a letter before Christmas."

"Did they part on good terms?"

"I think so, but he was in such a strange mood while he

was here. With all of us, not just her. I don't know when he'll visit again. Not before George passes."

Mrs Robertson sighed. "I hope Violet doesn't leave us like that…"

"Girls are more likely to stay around. Mine are at any rate. Elenor was married in September, but she moved back in with us last month while she waits for the baby to be born. Thankfully, we're getting on a lot better than we ever did."

"So you've had some good news."

"That's about it. The wedding was the day before Maria died, so it was a sombre affair."

"How awful. Will there be a decent time between the marriage and the baby arriving?"

"Three months if we're lucky. She's quite frightened now."

Mrs Robertson sighed. "It's to be expected…"

"It's worse than usual because Betty had her baby at the beginning of October, but there was something wrong and he passed away less than a week later."

"Oh, my goodness." Mrs Robertson's hands flew to her mouth. "I'm so sorry. How is she?"

"Not well. We're quite worried about her."

"I'll write to her as soon as I get a chance. I imagine you'll be glad to see the end of this year."

"I certainly will, although it means Thomas will be home again."

"Haven't you seen him since I last spoke to you?"

"I have, but between now and the end of the year, he's stewarding on the New York route. He's got one more voyage after this one before he goes back to his old job in the White Star office."

"Have things settled down between him and Elenor?"

"They've not seen each other. She moved in after he left for his latest trip, and I've not told him yet."

"When's he due back?"

"Friday."

Mrs Robertson grimaced. "Do you think he'll be angry?"

"Probably, but she spends most of her days in bed, so he needn't see her. I'm more worried about how he'll respond to Mr Massey. He's due next week, too, but I'm praying it won't be until Thomas has gone again."

"You'll have a full house."

Nell creased the side of her mouth. "Not as full as it should be now Maria isn't with us..."

"It must be hard for you."

Nell paused as the maid arrived with the tea. "Alice and I can manage with the chores, but for all her faults, we miss having Maria there."

"You lived with her a long time."

"I did. It's strange how you take people for granted when they're there, yet once they're gone..." She sighed. "We hardly talk about her at home, either. I think everyone's worried they'll upset someone else."

"It's only natural, but you will in time. She's only been gone a couple of months."

"It feels like an age." Nell stood up and wandered to the window. "I'm sorry. I didn't mean to go all forlorn on you. It's just the most I've talked about her for weeks."

"There's no need to apologise. Come and help yourself to a piece of cake and tell me more about her."

. . .

The smell of meat pie cooking in the range hit Nell as she opened the front door, and she popped her head into the kitchen as soon as she'd taken off her cloak. Alice was mashing the potatoes.

"That was well-timed. Have you had a nice afternoon?"

Nell nodded. "I have, thank you. It makes a change to talk to someone who isn't so close to everything that's going on. You see things differently."

"What sort of things?"

She sighed. "Like missing your mam. It was nice to talk about her, and Mrs Robertson reminded me it's only been two months..."

"I know. Harry said the same thing to me the other night when I was upset."

"Uncle Thomas should be here to do that for me, but with the way things are..."

Alice put the lid back on the pan. "If you ever need to talk, I'm here, you know."

"I know, but I don't like upsetting you."

"Mam's never far from my thoughts..."

Nell paused as the front door closed and Leah and Edith joined them.

"Good evening." She stepped into the living room. "Did you see the men on your way here?"

"Not Uncle George, if that's what you mean." Leah giggled as Edith's cheeks coloured.

Nell put her hands on her hips. "What's going on?"

"Nothing." Edith glared at Leah. "She's being silly."

"You'll have to tell her sooner or later."

"Tell me what?" Nell looked between the two of them as Alice joined them. "You can't keep it to yourselves now."

Edith sighed. "All right, but it's nothing serious. It's the man I told you about, the one I'd seen at work having a suit made. He's asked if I'll walk out with him on Sunday."

"Oh." Nell took a breath. *Not you, too.* "Did you say yes?"

Leah giggled. "She did."

Alice gasped. "You can't go this Sunday. It's Stir-up Sunday. The first without Mam."

Nell put a hand to her head. "I'd completely forgotten. Can you change the day you meet him?"

Edith shook her head. "It's the only day he gets off work, and I won't see him again to tell him."

"Do you have an address where you can write to him?"

"No."

Alice sighed. "I suppose we can do it with the three of us, but I was hoping to make it a family event like Mam always did."

"And we will. The boys will be here, and I'm sure they'd like a stir."

"I suppose..." Alice returned to the kitchen as Nell ushered the girls to the table.

"Why don't you sit down and tell me more about your companion? What's his name?"

"Mr Lacy. He's recently moved to Liverpool to be a manager in one of the steelworks and needs a new suit."

Nell's shoulders relaxed. "It sounds like a good job. I look forward to meeting him when you're ready."

"That won't be for ages. I hardly know him myself."

"Still, when the time comes, don't be frightened–" Nell lowered her voice as she leaned in closer "–and please talk to me more than Elenor did ... if you need to."

"I can look after myself." Edith's smile faltered. "But I will. Thank you."

Nell turned to leave but stopped abruptly. "Uncle Thomas is home on Friday. How do we explain that you won't be staying in to help on Sunday?"

Edith grimaced. "Can't we send him out? I'm not meeting Mr Lacy until half past two, so I could wait until he's gone."

"The only problem is, if he goes out, he'll expect me to go with him."

Alice was close to tears as she reappeared. "You can't go out, too."

"I'll try not to, but..."

Leah interrupted. "Would we have time to do both? Edith won't be going out until two o'clock."

Alice wiped her eyes. "Not easily, but even if we could, it would take the fun out of it."

Nell placed a hand on Alice's arm. "Don't worry, I'll make sure I'm here. I don't want to leave you at a time like this."

CHAPTER THIRTY-SEVEN

Breakfast was over as Nell perched on the edge of Elenor's bed.

"How are you feeling?"

"Nervous. Must you tell him I'm here? He never comes onto this floor, anyway."

"I'll have to explain why I'm serving nine plates of food and bringing one upstairs."

"Then don't bring mine up at the same time. Keep it in the range until he goes out."

"I wish it was that simple, but he doesn't go out every night. He's not like Billy or Uncle George."

"Well, I wish he was. They don't seem concerned about me being here, or the baby."

Nell sighed. "I think they are, Uncle George especially, but he knows you're Mr Massey's responsibility now, so he won't say anything."

Elenor sat back with a pout. "Why does everyone blame me? It should be Will they're cross with."

Nell stroked Elenor's hair as she stood up. "We've had

this conversation, and you know very well why. Now lie there and relax. You shouldn't upset yourself when the baby could be on its way any day now."

"I'm not upsetting myself. It's him coming home that's doing it."

"I'll speak to him. Like you said, he never comes in here, so I'll try to keep it that way. I'll see you later."

Alice was putting a fresh pot of tea on the table when she went downstairs. "How is she?"

"Fretting. Not that I blame her. I'm just relieved Uncle Thomas will have left before Mr Massey arrives. It would be a lot harder to manage if they were both here."

"The day will come."

"As long as it's not before the baby's born."

Alice checked the clock. "Uncle Thomas should be here soon."

"Let me see if he's on his way." Nell sauntered to the window in the front room and groaned. "He's here now. Don't mention Elenor until he's settled in."

Alice raised her eyebrows. "I won't say a word." She disappeared into the backyard as Nell waited in the hall to greet her husband. She smiled as he opened the door.

"That was well-timed. We've just made a pot of tea."

"I'm usually prompt, but it's nice that you're here to welcome me this time." He leaned forward and kissed her forehead. "Has Mrs Wood gone to the shop today?"

"No, she's nipped outside to check on the boys. I did the shopping earlier this morning..."

He took his usual seat by the fire. "That's very considerate of you."

She bit her lip. "Did you have a good trip?"

"Not particularly. We had several new stewards who weren't up to the job, and then first class was almost empty on the way home, so I ended up in steerage."

"Oh, dear." *What's he been up to for them to send him downstairs?* "Still, you're home now. Would you like some bread and jam?"

"Please. How are things here? Has Elenor's baby arrived?"

"No, not yet."

He rested his head on the back of the chair. "I suppose every passing week makes it slightly easier to explain."

"Yes." Nell busied herself at the table with the bread. "Will you visit the White Star offices this afternoon to confirm you'll get your old job back?"

"No."

Nell turned to him. "No? Why not? When you spoke to them last time, your old boss told you he'd have something for you."

"I want a change."

She handed him his bread and jam. "What's brought this on? I thought you were happy about going back."

"Can't a man change his mind?"

Nell stepped backwards as he glared at her. "If you want to. I'm just surprised... What do you have in mind?"

"I'll try the Bohemian offices."

Nell's forehead creased. *He wants to turn down White Star to work for Bohemian?* "That's unusual."

"I've heard they pay more."

"Ah, that explains it." *I don't believe a word.* "Will you go into Liverpool this afternoon?"

"I have no choice. I leave again on Monday."

"Then I'll try not to be late with the dinner. If you'll excuse me, I'll start the peeling."

Mr Marsh's face was like thunder the following day when he arrived home from Liverpool, and Nell stood up from the table as he strode into the room.

"You were longer than I expected. Your dinner's in the range if you'd like to sit at the table."

He grunted but sat down without a word as Alice lifted Freddie from his chair.

"I was about to take the boys to the park. Will you excuse me?"

He stood up again as she left. "You may need an umbrella. It looks like rain."

Nell put a plate of liver and mashed potato in front of him. "Are you all sorted out now?"

"No."

"Oh. Where did you go?"

"The Bohemian and Bibby Lines, the Ellerman Line, Brocklebanks…"

"And none of them had a position for you?"

"Only if I want to start as a junior clerk." His knife almost cut the plate as he sliced a piece of liver.

"Did you go to White Star?"

"No."

Nell took a deep breath. *Leave him to calm down.* "Let me freshen up this pot of tea. I won't be a minute." She puffed out her cheeks as the kettle reboiled. *I can't mention Elenor while he's in a mood like this.* She hovered by the kitchen door until he laid his knife and fork on the plate. *Let's see if that helped.* She picked up the teapot and carried it to the table.

"Here we are. Would you like a piece of cake?"

"No, thank you." He stood up and moved to a chair by the fire. "I need to go out again as soon as I've had this."

"That's a shame. I'd hoped we could go to the park."

"We can do that tomorrow."

"I-I can't. It's Stir-up Sunday. Alice wants us all here."

"I'm sure it doesn't take four of you to make a Christmas pudding."

"But it's tradition."

"Aren't I more important than a silly tradition? I'm here for one more day, yet you can't make time for me."

"It's not that you're not important. Let me see if we can do both." *It should be all right if we don't go out too early.* "Where are you going this afternoon?"

"I've not decided yet."

Nell pursed her lips as she handed him his tea and sat in the chair opposite. "I can see you're upset. Would it help to talk about it?"

"I'm not upset. I'm angry."

"Did something happen on the voyage?"

"The voyage? No." He stared at her, his brow furrowed.

"With you being moved to steerage..."

"Nobody moved me. It was my decision. I offered to help rather than staying in first class twiddling my thumbs."

"Ah. I thought you must have fallen out with someone important on the ship."

"It's not White Star I'm angry with ... well, not only them."

Nell shook her head. "You're talking in riddles. Please tell me what's wrong."

"Mr Massey, that's what."

Nell's stomach lurched. "How can it be?"

"He was in the White Star reception area yesterday morning when I called, as bold as brass, enquiring about a job."

Nell's eyes widened. *He's in Liverpool but he's not been to see Elenor?*

"Did you hear me?"

"Yes, I'm sorry."

"How can I work at White Star if he'll be there?"

"Do you know for sure he's got a position? He's an engineer who's only worked on cargo ships, so he won't have the same experience as you."

"Judging by the smug grin on his face, he knew there was something for him. He even had the nerve to ask me when I was leaving. Not that I told him."

Nell stood up and wandered to the table. "You said you were going to put your differences aside. He's part of the family now, something you forced upon him."

"How can I be civil to him when he stops me from taking up my old job?"

"We all make mistakes, but he's made an honest woman of Elenor, and we're going to be seeing a lot more of him. Can't you learn to forgive?"

"He's brought shame on this family..."

"Thankfully, despite your best efforts, there are not many people who know about the baby. Elenor's done well to hide her condition and once it's born, she can go out without it for the first few months ... at least until people lose track of time."

"And what will she do with the baby? Is the landlady prepared to look after it?"

Oh, goodness. I walked into that. "N-no. I will."

"So you'll be round there more than you're here? There'll be no point me staying at home."

"I-it would only be during the day ... although..." *Here goes.* "...it would be easier if she lived here. Then Alice could help out, too."

"Here? With him? That's out of the question."

"Please. Think about it. Now Maria's gone, we have the room, and she needs help."

"That's not my problem."

Nell stood up. "Why do you have to spoil everything?"

"Me! I'm doing nothing of the sort. It's them."

"But you've jumped to conclusions and may have come up with the wrong answer. Again. Why don't you go back to the White Star office and ask about the job? Mr Massey may not have been successful."

His face remained stern. "If he was, I can't work with him."

Nell sighed. "It sounds to me like you're running out of options. Either you get your old job back in the office, or you stay as a steward. Which would you prefer?"

He stood up and marched to the hall. "I'll tell you what I want. I want to stay at home and work for White Star without seeing him or Elenor. Is that too much to ask?"

CHAPTER THIRTY-EIGHT

The church was cold and Nell shivered as the vicar gave the final blessing. Once he'd walked up the aisle and reached the door, she put the kneeler back in its place on the pew in front.

"Are we ready?"

"I am." Leah linked her arm as they stepped into the aisle. "Are you still going to Elenor's old house on the way home?"

Nell waited for George and Billy to go on ahead with Mr Wood. "Only if you all come with me and don't say a word about it in front of Uncle Thomas."

Alice nodded. "We can say we were talking if anyone asks why we're late."

Nell waited until the men had left the building then led the way outside. The wind whipped around her skirt and she held onto her hat. "It's to be hoped he's not gone to the alehouse himself."

Edith skipped to the side of Leah. "He may be at church."

"I'd be surprised. Men who spend most of their time at sea don't have a regular church. That's why Uncle Thomas rarely joins us." *And finds it so hard to forgive anyone.*

The front door of the house on Warwick Street was open when they arrived, and Nell stepped into the hall. "Is anyone home?"

The landlady appeared from the kitchen. "How may I help?"

"I don't know if you remember me, but my daughter lived here until about a month ago. Mrs Massey." Nell fixed a smile on her face.

"I remember you. You wanted the rent money back."

"Yes, but that's not why I'm here now. When she left, she gave you a letter to pass to Mr Massey when he came back. May I ask if you gave it to him?"

"I did, yesterday morning when he paid me another week's rent."

"More money." Nell gulped. "Didn't you tell him his wife had moved out before you charged him?"

"I did, but he wanted to stay, anyway. Perhaps he's realised married life isn't for him."

Nell gasped. "What did he say?"

"He didn't say anything, but it's a strange to-do if you ask me. If you want to know any more, you'll have to ask him yourself. He came in about ten minutes ago. First door on the second landing."

"Thank you. I will."

Alice and the girls waited in the hall as Nell climbed the stairs. She took a breath when she reached the top of the stairs before giving the door a short, sharp rap. Mr Massey opened it seconds later.

"I'm coming. Oh, Mrs Marsh." He took a step backwards and ran a hand over his neatly combed hair.

"Good afternoon, Mr Massey. I heard you were back in Liverpool but wanted to see for myself. It seemed strange that you were here but hadn't been to visit Elenor."

"Well, yes ... there's a reason."

Nell raised an eyebrow as he continued.

"I met your husband the day I arrived back, and he left me in no doubt that he didn't want to see me."

"He said that?"

"Didn't he tell you?"

"He told me he'd seen you, but not that you'd spoken. Did you know Elenor had left here when you saw him?"

"No, I'd not been back at that point. I wanted to find myself a job and surprise her, but when I read her letter, I realised I wouldn't be able to visit."

"Visit? She's expecting more than that. She's waiting for you to move in."

Mr Massey's mouth fell open. "How can I, when he's there?"

"He leaves again in the morning. Call any time after eight o'clock."

He smiled. "I will. I've been looking forward to seeing her."

"I'm glad." Nell turned at the sound of footsteps on the stairs. "It sounds like the visitor you were expecting is here. I'll see you tomorrow."

She passed Mr Young and, after exchanging pleasantries, continued to the hall, where Leah opened the front door.

"Where've you been? You were ages."

"I had to speak to him." Nell paused until the door closed behind them. "He met Uncle Thomas, and they had words."

"I didn't think Uncle Thomas knew Elenor was at our house."

"He doesn't. That was without him knowing. I hope he took himself off for a walk this morning."

Leah gasped. "What if he finds her while we're not there?"

Nell closed her eyes. "I don't even want to think about it."

The living room was empty when they got home and Nell headed for the stairs after she'd hung up her cloak.

At least he's not here. "Would you check the dinner while I speak to Elenor? She'll be wondering why we're late." She climbed to the second floor and knocked on the door. "It's only me."

Elenor sank into her pillow as Nell joined her. "Thank goodness you're back. I'd forgotten Uncle Thomas wouldn't have gone to church and went downstairs to use the privy."

"And he saw you?" Nell's stomach churned. "What did he say?"

"He wanted to know what I was doing here."

"Did you tell him you'd moved in?"

"I said I was here while Will was away."

"Was he upset?" Nell bit her lip as Elenor hesitated.

"He wasn't happy, but he didn't shout. He said he hoped I'd be going back to Warwick Street now Will's here. When I told him he wasn't due until next week, he said he'd seen him on Friday. Had he told you?"

Nell sat on the side of the bed. "He did, but only yesterday. I've been to Warwick Street to find out if it's true. That's why we're late."

"Was he there?"

"He was."

"So why hasn't he come here? I left him a letter..." Tears welled in Elenor's eyes as Nell held her hands.

"Don't cry. He told me about bumping into Uncle Thomas and said they'd had words, which is why he hadn't called."

Elenor sighed. "I don't blame him. I wish I wasn't here, either."

"Don't say that. Uncle Thomas will be gone tomorrow, so I told Mr Massey he could come around any time after eight in the morning."

"Did he say he would?"

Nell patted her hand. "He did. He said he'd been looking forward to seeing you."

The smile returned to Elenor's face. "Thank you."

"You're welcome. Now, I'd better go downstairs and help Alice with the dinner. I'll bring yours up as soon as I can."

Mr Marsh was still nowhere to be seen when she arrived in the living room and studied the table.

"Have we got everything?"

Edith brought in a loaf of bread. "I think so. We just need everyone here."

Nell popped her head into the kitchen where Alice was carving a large piece of ham. "Could we plate up Elenor's dinner first and I'll take it up to her before the others come in?"

"We can manage that. How is she?"

"Relieved there's a reason Mr Massey hadn't been round." She watched Alice spoon several potatoes and a pile of carrots onto the plate as the gravy came to a boil. "Excellent. I'll get this out of the way before..." Her heart skipped a beat as the front door closed. "I hope that's your dad." She waited for Alice to put the plate on a tray, but as she picked it up, Mr Marsh strode into the room.

"What are you doing with that?"

"I ... erm ..."

"When were you going to tell me Elenor was here?"

"I-I've not seen much of you..."

"You've seen me for long enough to mention a lodger."

"Y-you've not been in the best of moods, and I didn't want to upset you any more."

His eyes were cold. "That's very considerate of you. I expect you to take that walk this afternoon and explain precisely what's going on."

"I-I ... well..." She gestured to the tray. "Would you mind if I take this up? It's going cold."

He stood to one side as she scuttled past but caught hold of her arm. "I hope he's not up there with her."

"He's not. Apparently, you made it perfectly clear he wasn't welcome."

"Who told you that?"

"He did." She pulled her arm free and climbed the stairs to the first landing, where she paused for breath. *The sooner he goes again, the better.* She hadn't reached the second flight of stairs when Edith chased after her.

"I heard Uncle Thomas. Does that mean you'll be leaving Alice?"

"I don't want to, but what choice do I have? I'm hoping

we can start making the pudding as soon as possible so Alice won't be completely on her own."

"If you do go out, would you go to Princes Park? I'm meeting Mr Lacy in Sefton Park and I'd rather we didn't bump into Uncle Thomas. He's scary when he's in one of these moods."

"I'd rather he didn't see you as well. He needs to get used to Elenor being here before he has another young man to worry about."

Edith shook her head. "Why does he get like that? He's not my dad, not even my stepdad, so he shouldn't be bothered about me in the same way he is about Elenor."

Nell took a deep breath. *That's what you think.* "Maybe not, but while you live under this roof, he'll have something to say. He certainly won't want another incident like Elenor. I'd hoped that Leah would walk out with you this afternoon to act as your chaperone, but I daren't leave Alice on her own."

"Don't worry about me needing anyone, not on our first walk. I promise I won't let you down."

Nell gave a faint smile. "I know, but I suggest you watch out for us in Sefton Park, in case he insists on going there. He won't be very understanding if he sees the two of you together."

CHAPTER THIRTY-NINE

The leaves had long since fallen from the trees and the park was forlorn as Mr Marsh escorted Nell through the gates.

"I hate this time of year."

He glanced down at her. "I'd have thought you'd be looking forward to Christmas."

"I am, but I don't like the dark days. It won't be the same without Maria, either." *Or knowing I've not stirred the pudding for the first time ever.*

"You'll manage without her."

"It's not a matter of managing! We miss her. Hasn't it occurred to you?"

"Of course, but there are plenty of us at the house. It's not as if it was just you and her living together."

Nell gasped. "Would you say that if I was the one who'd passed?"

"Don't be silly."

"So why is it different for me with Maria when I've lived with her for most of my life?"

"It's a different sort of love."

It certainly is. She clenched her teeth. "It's the first Christmas without her, so it's bound to be hard for all of us. It will make us appreciate how much she put into making us happy, as well. At least we'll have a new baby to focus on and hopefully bring us some joy."

"Joy? I could think of many words to describe this baby, but that wouldn't be one of them."

Nell sighed. "I mean that Christmas will be different but having the baby will help fill the hole left by Maria."

"Does that mean you expect Elenor to join us for Christmas?"

"Of course I do. She'll be living with us until I'm happy she can manage with the baby by herself."

"What about *him*?"

"You mean her husband? Where do you think he'll be?"

"So they're both moving in? Why didn't you tell me before I arranged my new job? I'd have stayed away."

I wish you had. "You need to stop this nonsense. What's done is done, and it's time to move on."

He let out a loud groan. "We should rent our own house..."

"It wouldn't make any difference. Elenor's still my daughter, and this baby will be my first grandchild. It will arrive while you're away, so you need to be prepared for it when you come home."

Nell's heart pounded as he remained silent. *Change the subject.* "I'm glad you tried White Star again about the job. I didn't think an office-based role sounded right for Mr Massey."

"He'll still be part of the company."

"But you won't bump into him if he'll be working on the ships when they dock. I wish you could find something positive to dwell on."

"I don't feel like being positive."

Roll on tomorrow.

Mr Marsh's back suddenly straightened. "I know what will cheer me up. A visit to Mr Grayson. I've been so busy I've not had a chance to see him."

"B-but ... we're in the wrong park. It would take half an hour to walk over there."

He checked his watch. "We've time, and if we're fortunate, we'll meet them near the lake in Sefton Park." His grip was firm as he led Nell towards the nearest exit. "I don't know why I didn't think of it before."

"They won't be out today. Rebecca will be making her Christmas pudding like the rest of the women round here. It's what we do on the last Sunday before Advent."

"It doesn't take all afternoon."

"You don't know that. It's an occasion."

"They may still take a walk."

Along with Edith. Please, Lord, don't let him see her.

Sefton Park was even quieter than she expected, and as soon as they walked through the entrance, Nell began searching the surrounding faces. *Edith had her new hat on. With any luck, he won't recognise her, even if we see her.*

"Where is everyone?"

"I've told you. The women will be busy, so the men will either have stayed at home or be in the alehouse. You've missed out on so much real life with being away for so long."

"I was home for five years before this episode."

"Then you clearly took no notice of what was going on around you." She huffed as she studied those around them. "Haven't you seen Mr Grayson since last month?"

"No, the turnaround times have been too tight. If we want to check whether they're in the park, I suggest we head to the lake and walk around it in an anti-clockwise direction."

"We usually go the other way."

"Precisely, which means that if the Graysons are here, we'll bump into them. We'd be chasing them if we went the same way."

"We're wasting our time. Rebecca will have wanted to spend the afternoon with Isobel and Florrie talking about Christmas."

He whistled through his teeth. "All right, we'll walk up the path on the far side, and if we haven't met them by the time we get to the top end, we'll go to the house."

Their chosen route was almost empty as they hurried towards the furthest corner of the park, but Nell gasped when she saw a large yellow flower on the side of a wide-rimmed navy hat. *That's her. And him in his smart new suit.* She grimaced. *I hope that doesn't cause problems.*

Mr Marsh stopped as Nell pulled back on his arm. "What's the matter?"

"Just a bit of stomach ache. I'll be fine in a minute."

"Not again. You need to see the doctor if it carries on." He watched as she gripped the railings, but she looked past him, relieved to see Edith stop.

"It's nothing. We must have walked too far." *She's seen us ... but he wants to carry on walking. Why won't he listen to her?*

"You walk for miles when you go up to Everton."

"We're walking faster today ... and I wasn't expecting to come here." *Please hurry. I can't keep him here much longer.* Her shoulders relaxed as Mr Lacy relented and escorted Edith along a side path. *Thank goodness.* She released her grip on the railings and straightened up gingerly. "That's better. Shall we head straight to the Graysons' house? We're not going to meet them here."

Rebecca gasped as she opened the door to them ten minutes later. "What are you doing here?"

Mr Marsh raised his hat. "I wondered if Mr Grayson was at home. I've not seen him for a couple of months and I leave Liverpool again tomorrow."

"Well, yes, he's here, but I'm surprised you are." She held open the door, her forehead creased as Mr Marsh walked past her. "Haven't you made your pudding?"

Nell glared after her husband. "I had to leave Alice and Leah to do it. He didn't think it was necessary for us all to stay in."

Rebecca raised her eyebrows. "He'd have found out how important it was if Maria was still with us."

"He wasn't interested. I felt awful leaving them, too. Alice had wanted it to be special."

"Were Edith and Elenor helping?"

Nell lowered her voice. "I daren't encourage Elenor out of bed with the baby due, and Edith had to go out."

"Today?"

"She'd forgotten what day it was, and it was too late to change her arrangements."

"Poor Alice."

"I know, but the less said about it, the better, while he's around. I'll be happier tomorrow when he's gone again."

"Are you making a cup of tea?" Mr Grayson's voice rang into the hall.

"I'm coming."

Nell followed Rebecca into the living room. "I'm not sure we've time."

"Nonsense. Tea isn't until five."

"I can't leave Alice to do that, as well. She's enough on her plate."

"Mrs Atkin used to do most things by herself, so I'm sure the rest of you can. It's not often I get to sit down with Mr Grayson."

"Perhaps you could go to the alehouse later, instead."

"On the night before I go back to sea? I don't think so." He waited for Rebecca to disappear into the kitchen. "We have other things to do tonight."

Nell's cheeks burned, and she bent forward as her stomach griped again. *You may think that, but there's not a chance you're touching me while you're in one of these moods.*

CHAPTER FORTY

Nell carried her bucket to the front door but stopped when she saw a letter on the doormat. *I didn't hear the postman.* She picked it up and went into the living room where Alice was wiping the window.

"A letter from James."

Alice got down from her steps. "He'll know about Mam, then."

"I imagine so." She sliced open the top of the envelope. "Let's see. Yes, he got the letter, and sends condolences. He hopes we're all managing and even asks after your dad."

"That's not like him."

"No. I suppose grief changes things. He's back at work and seems to be enjoying himself." She shook her head. "It's as if he's forgotten about us."

"He won't have." Alice took the letter from Nell. "I still think he'll be home one day."

"We'll see. Are you ready for me to put the kettle on?"

"Yes, I'm done here."

Once it was on the range, Nell returned to the bucket in the hall but stopped when Elenor called.

"Mam!"

"I'm coming." She raced up the stairs to the first-floor bedroom Elenor now occupied with Mr Massey. She didn't pause for breath before barging in. "What is it?"

"Something feels different. My belly keeps going tight and hurting."

"When did it start?"

"Maybe an hour ago but it's getting stronger."

"All right, we've got time. When it happens again, take some deep breaths."

"How long will it go on for?"

"It's hard to tell. They may go away again, or it may mean the baby's on its way."

"How will I know?"

Nell sighed. "Either the pain will stop or it will get worse."

"Worse! It can't hurt any more."

"The baby has to come out."

"I don't like this." Elenor gasped as another sensation washed over her. "How does it even do that?"

Nell pinched the bridge of her nose. "Don't worry about that now. Focus on taking deep breaths instead. I need to tell the midwife what's happening, so she's ready."

"You can't leave me."

"It won't be for long, and you've time yet." *It will get a lot worse before the baby arrives.*

Alice had taken the kettle from the range by the time she went downstairs. "Do you have time to sit with Elenor? I think the baby's coming, so I'm going for the midwife."

"Of course I do. Let me check on the boys and I'll go straight up."

Nell escorted the midwife home and waited for her in the living room once she'd shown her upstairs. She raced to the door as soon as she heard footsteps on the stairs.

"How is she?"

"We've hours yet. It may even be tomorrow before it's born."

"Oh, gracious. She won't be happy about that."

"I'm afraid I can't do anything about it. It will be down to the Lord whether he grants her leniency."

"I'm sorry, I didn't mean to criticise."

"The real contractions haven't started, but once they do, we'll have a better idea of timing."

"They've not started!"

"They're building up to it. I'll call again this evening to see if anything's changed. Just keep an eye on her for now."

Nell showed her to the door, but her legs were heavy as she trudged up the stairs. *I hope the midwife told her what to expect.*

Elenor gritted her teeth and held her hands on her abdomen as Nell walked into the room. "It's not even started yet."

"No. The midwife said it could be a while."

Tears rolled down the sides of Elenor's face as she braced her body again. "I want it to be over now."

Nell ran a hand over her head. "Try to relax and take those deep breaths. They help. Trust me."

Once the tightening eased, she took hold of Nell's hand. "She told me what would happen."

"Try not to be frightened. We all have to go through it."

"You did this for me and Leah?"

"Of course. How else would you be here?"

"But it sounds horrible."

It's no better when you're going through it. "You'll forget about it once the baby's born and you hold it for the first time. It will be worth it."

Elenor's tears continued. "I didn't even want a baby. I only wanted Will to like me."

"And he does. I'll tell you what, why don't I move in here with you tonight, and Mr Massey can use my room? I won't sleep until the baby's born."

Elenor nodded. "I don't want to be on my own."

"And you won't be. Just be glad he's home and that you'll have your own little family very soon."

"I'll try."

Nell tapped her fingers on the windowsill in the front room as she waited for Mr Massey to arrive home from work. *Come on. It would be helpful if you were here before George and Billy.*

She was about to give up and go to the kitchen when she saw movement along the street. *That's him.* She hurried to the front door and pulled it open before he arrived.

"I'm glad you're here."

"Why? Is something wrong?"

"The baby's on its way. The midwife's with Elenor now."

"Really?"

Nell wasn't sure if it was excitement or fear on his face. "It won't be born yet, but it's not far off."

"Am I allowed to see her?"

"Oh, no, not until the baby arrives. It's best that way."

"How long will that be?"

"It's hard to say, but it could be overnight. I've been thinking that you'll need your sleep before you can go into work tomorrow, so use my room tonight. I won't sleep a wink until I know they're both safe."

"I-if you don't mind." He stepped away from the door as it opened and George and Billy let themselves in. "Evening."

George looked at Nell. "What's going on?"

"The baby's on its way…"

George grunted. "I wasn't expecting it so soon."

"No, it must be early." Nell followed him into the living room. "At least it will be over by Christmas. Remember when Alice was born…"

"Aye. The Christmas dinner was disrupted that year."

Billy took a seat by the fire. "It's as well Uncle Thomas isn't here."

"Why? What's he said?"

"Nothing, but it's hardly a secret he's not happy."

"None of us are happy." George stared at Mr Massey. "You should be thankful my late wife isn't here. If she had been, it would have killed her."

Mr Massey lowered his head. "I'm sorry. It was never my intention…"

"No, well, men like you should think on before you ruin people's lives. Have you told your friends why you were married so quickly?"

"A couple of them."

"Well, tell them all. Let it be a lesson to them."

Nell hovered by the door but scrambled up the stairs when she heard her name being shouted. "I'm coming."

The midwife was outside the bedroom door when she arrived. "There's no need to panic. I wanted to tell you the labour's progressing well, so we should be ready for the baby in a few hours."

Nell flinched as Elenor screeched. "Will she be all right for that long?"

"She'll be fine. She's a young girl with plenty of stamina."

Too young, if you ask me. "I hope so. I'm about to make a pot of tea. Would you like one?"

"Please. None for Mrs Massey, though. She needs to focus on what she's doing."

Elenor cried out again as Nell hurried back downstairs, but she paused in the doorway as seven pairs of eyes looked up at her.

"We've another couple of hours yet, so I'll get tea served and then we'll be ready."

The men had arrived home from the alehouse and gone to their beds when Nell crept up the stairs and knocked on Elenor's bedroom door.

"You'll have to wait…"

I've waited long enough. She pushed the door open a crack to see Elenor lying on the bed with the midwife crouched by her legs, a pair of large metal tongs in her hands.

Nell gulped. "What are you doing?"

The midwife jumped up, strands of her previously tidy hair hanging loosely around her face as she hurried to the door. "I could ask you the same thing. You shouldn't be here."

"But it's been hours. What are you doing with them?"

"Doing my job. The baby needs help…"

Nell's eyes widened. "With them!"

"It's perfectly normal."

Elenor's cries sounded weary as her body writhed on the bed.

"She's exhausted."

"Well, if you weren't wasting my time, I'd be getting on with the job."

"Do you need any help?"

"Have you done this before?"

"I've had children of my own."

"That's not the same."

"At least let me see her so she knows I'm here." Nell peered over the midwife's shoulder, but she moved to block her way.

"It won't make any difference. I've given her some laudanum to ease the pain."

"Won't that harm the baby?"

"Mrs Marsh. Do you want me to get this child out or not?"

"Yes, but…"

"Then let me get on." She slammed the door, causing Alice to appear from the room to Nell's right.

"What's the matter?"

"I've a feeling the baby won't come out."

"Oh, no." Alice's face paled. "It could be because she's not filled out yet. She's very slight."

"If the baby's early, it should be smaller."

301

"Is it really early?"

Tears welled in Nell's eyes. "I don't know. I don't know anything any more." She slid down the door until she was sitting on the floor. "I'm not going anywhere until I find out what's happening."

"You can't stay there all night. It's nearly midnight."

"I won't sleep wherever I am." Nell stared up at Alice. "What if she dies?"

"Don't say that."

"How can I not be worried?"

Alice sighed. "I don't know. I do know I need to get some sleep, though. I'm surprised the boys haven't woken, but either way, they'll have me up early in the morning. Try to get some rest."

"I will." She leaned against the door listening to Elenor's cries as Alice slipped into her bedroom. They were little more than whimpers, and as she closed her eyes, the scene not ten feet away filled her mind. *Please don't take her.*

She must have dozed, but her eyes flew open and she jumped to her feet as Elenor screamed. Without a second thought, she barged into the room. "What are you doing to her?"

"It's nearly here. The shoulders have moved, so one more push. I'll need some more towels and hot water. Now."

Nell's mouth fell open at the amount of blood, but the midwife raised her voice. "Mrs Marsh."

"Y-yes, sorry." She practically threw a stack of towels at the midwife before she raced to the kitchen. It was still dark when she arrived and her shaking hand struggled to light a gas lamp, but once it gave its familiar glow, she filled the kettle. *Don't take long to boil.*

After what felt like an age, she snatched it from the range and headed upstairs, but stopped halfway up when a baby cried. *It's here!* She wiped away some unexpected tears and ran into the room, where the midwife was wrapping it with a towel.

"Is everything all right?"

"I would say so. You have a granddaughter."

"A little girl." She put the kettle on the floor and gazed at the child in the midwife's arms. "What's the matter with her head? It's squashed."

"It was a struggle getting her out. Still, she's here now and it will straighten itself out."

Nell's eyes darted to the bed. "How's Elenor? Is she...?"

"She's sleeping. I gave her some more laudanum before the last push."

"So she doesn't know she's a mam?"

"I told her before she dozed off. She said the baby would be called Maria."

"Maria." Nell's tears overcame her as she took the child from the midwife. *So we'll have a Maria with us at Christmas, after all.*

CHAPTER FORTY-ONE

The wind rattled the windows as Elenor sat by the fire feeding the baby. Nell looked over at them from her seat at the table where she was peeling potatoes.

"She's taking it well now."

"Finally. I didn't imagine it would be so hard."

"I doubt you imagined it at all. None of us could have seen this a year ago."

"I know, but she's lovely. Especially now her head's straightened itself out."

"She is. And at least you're out of bed and walking easier than you were."

Elenor shook her head. "You know you said you forget the pain? I don't think I ever will. The day before I had her was probably the worst day of my life."

"You'll be glad of her, though, and it should be easier next time." Nell glanced at the clock. "You'd better hurry with that feed. Uncle Thomas could be home any time now and he won't be comfortable seeing you like that."

Alice appeared from the kitchen. "Shall I put the kettle on?"

"If you don't mind. Goodness knows what mood he'll be in when he arrives."

Elenor sat up straight and pulled the front of her dress across her chest. "She's had enough for now, anyway."

She hadn't finished buttoning herself up when the door opened and Mr Marsh strode into the living room.

"What's going on here?" He glared at Elenor as Nell stood up, wiping her hands on her apron.

"You're home. Did you have a good trip?"

"Pleasant enough." He didn't take his eyes off the child. "When was it born?"

"Three weeks ago."

"That was far too soon."

"Please don't make a fuss. This is your new granddaughter, Maria. You should be happy that her and Elenor are safe and well."

"Vernon already has a daughter called Maria."

Nell took a deep breath. "Elenor wanted to honour Maria by using the name again. Is that so wrong?"

"It's confusing."

"Well, given you hardly see Vernon's family, we can probably deal with it."

He took the seat opposite Elenor. "Must we have it in here?"

She pushed herself up. "I'll light the fire in the front room if you're going to be like that."

Nell caught hold of her arm. "You'll do no such thing."

"I'm not staying here with him."

Mr Marsh sneered at her. "Go into the other room if you like, but you're not wasting coal."

Elenor shrugged off Nell's hand. "My husband pays for us to be here, and he won't be happy if you banish us to a cold room."

"Stop this." Nell's voice silenced them both. "Elenor's not going anywhere. This is her home, and she's staying in this room with the rest of us."

Elenor glared at Mr Marsh before she placed Maria in the crib and hobbled to the back door. "I won't be long."

Nell placed her hands on her hips. "Have you forgotten it's Christmas Eve?"

Mr Marsh shifted in his seat. "I didn't expect to have an illegitimate child forced upon me as soon as I arrived."

"She's no such thing. She was born in wedlock and she's beautiful. I suggest you get used to her being here, because Alice and I have put a lot of effort into this Christmas, and I won't be happy if you spoil it."

"Is he living here, too?"

"Of course he is, they're a family. You had a lot to say when you thought he'd disappear without marrying her, so now he has, you should be glad he's here."

"I wanted them to be married so they could settle in their own house and leave us alone. I didn't plan on having my face rubbed in it every morning and evening."

"Well, I'm sorry to disappoint you. I expect they'll do that one day, but for now, if you can't be pleasant, I'd appreciate it if you'd hold your tongue."

Alice put the teapot on the table. "They've been very happy since they moved in and it's lovely seeing them with the baby. Even Mam would have had her heart melted."

Mr Marsh shifted in his seat. "Because it's women's stuff."

"It doesn't do any harm if men show some interest."

Mr Marsh harrumphed as Alice offered him a mince pie. "I'll do nothing of the sort."

Nell pushed the last of the stuffing into the turkey and reached for the string to tie it up.

"That should do for tonight. What time is it?"

Alice peered into the living room. "Ten o'clock. The men will be home soon, so we should tidy up before they arrive."

Edith joined them in the kitchen. "It's all tidy in here and the plates and cutlery are on the table for breakfast."

"And I've prepared the fire in the front room." Leah brushed a spot of dust from her skirt.

"Splendid." Nell shook her head. "I really don't know how Aunty Maria did it all by herself."

"I know." Alice sighed. "The more time goes on, the more I realise how much she did. At least there are four of us now, and by next year Elenor will be helping, too."

"If she's still here by then." Nell wiped her hands as Leah looked at her.

"Why wouldn't she be?"

"Her and Uncle Thomas haven't managed a civil word this afternoon, and did you notice how he was with Mr Massey over tea?"

Edith rolled her eyes. "You could hardly miss it, but when they're working, they'll only be together for breakfast and tea."

"It still makes me uneasy. Uncle George won't put up

with such nonsense, either. I'm hoping he'll speak to them both in the alehouse tonight."

"Bang their heads together more like." Alice emptied the water from the sink as Nell hung her apron on the back of the door.

"I'd like to do that myself. Not that I blame Mr Massey. He's trying to be civil."

Alice sighed. "If things haven't improved by the morning, I'll speak to Dad. If there's one person they'll listen to, it's him."

"It's a shame they take no notice of us..." Nell stopped as the front door closed. "That sounds like them."

Billy was the first to join them, a broad smile on his face. "Evening. Are you all done?"

"We are for now. How was your night?"

He sniggered. "Entertaining."

Nell's stomach churned. "Not because of Thomas, I hope."

George joined them with Mr Wood. "He brings it on himself. The pompous fool."

Oh, my. "What's he done now? In fact..." Nell checked the hall "...where is he? Didn't he walk home with you?"

"I told him not to bother coming back until he could hold a civil conversation with Will. He's done nothing but insult him all evening."

"I hope he wasn't indiscreet about the baby."

Billy grimaced. "Dad shut him up."

"Thank goodness."

"I had no choice. The whole alehouse would have known about it if I hadn't."

Nell groaned. "What's he playing at? He's the one who's

most embarrassed by it and yet he's the one who's done the most to tell everyone."

"He won't do it again."

Alice watched George as he hung his jacket on the back of a chair. "Where's Mr Massey? You've not left the two of them together?"

"They've got to sort out their own problems. I won't always be around to keep them apart. Right, I'm going to bed. We've a busy day tomorrow ... and I don't want to see that clown again today."

Edith grabbed Leah's hand. "We may as well go up, too. See you in the morning."

She pulled the door closed behind them as Billy took a seat by the fire. "Uncle Thomas isn't doing himself any favours. It's funny, though."

"For you, maybe. I'm the one who bears the brunt of it when he comes home."

"Then I'll sit with you until he arrives. Make sure he causes no more trouble."

"I was hoping to go to bed. Have you any idea how long they'll be?"

Billy shook his head. "No, but the place shuts at half past ten, so they shouldn't be long. Having said that, Will was buying two large rums when I left."

"Thomas doesn't drink rum."

Mr Wood chuckled. "That's what you think. Ooh ... is this them now?"

Alice opened the door to the hall. "Oh!"

"What's the matter?" Nell joined her as Mr Marsh stumbled into the wall.

"What are you looking at?"

"N-nothing. We just wondered who it was."

Mr Massey stepped into the house and closed the door. "It's both of us. On speaking terms, you'll be pleased to hear. Now, if you'll excuse me, I'd like to see my wife."

Mr Marsh held onto the doorknob as Mr Massey made his way upstairs. "I need to go to bed myself." He attempted to stand unaided but fell onto the wall as Nell reached for his arm.

"Let me help you."

"Are you coming to bed, too?"

"I'd better. You won't make it up the stairs without me."

Alice suppressed a grin. "It's time we were all asleep. It's almost Christmas Day."

CHAPTER FORTY-TWO

Nell woke the following morning to the sound of loud snoring from Mr Marsh's side of the bed.

What time is it? She held her pocket watch under the night light and flopped back onto the pillow. *Five o'clock. I may as well get up. I won't go back to sleep with that noise.* She sighed. *Maria would be preparing breakfast by now.*

The house was silent as she crept downstairs and the fire little more than embers. *I need to get that going.* She shivered as she lit the gas lamp but jumped backwards when she saw a pair of legs outstretched in front of the hearth.

"Billy!" She shook his shoulder until his eyes fluttered and he pushed himself up.

"What's up?"

"I thought you were dead. What are you doing down here?"

He rubbed a hand over his face. "I must have dozed off. Is there any chance of a cup of tea? My mouth's as dry as a bone."

"I've not put the kettle on yet, but I suspect you won't be

the only one like this. How much did you all drink last night?"

He shook his head but stopped abruptly with a groan. "More than usual, thanks to Will. He kept buying them, so we kept drinking them."

"Why did he do that?"

"He wanted to stop Uncle Thomas from being so uptight, but it took more drinks than he expected."

Nell sighed. *I don't know if it did the trick, but he was certainly less upright.* "So, you'll all have bad heads this morning? Your mam would've been furious."

Billy pushed himself up. "It may stop them shouting at each other. That's what you wanted, isn't it?" He wandered to the back door. "I'll take my tea upstairs when it's ready. I need to go to bed for a few hours before the fun and games start."

Elenor had joined her downstairs by the time the kettle boiled. "What are you doing up so early?"

Nell groaned. "They all came in from the alehouse worse for wear last night, and Uncle Thomas was snoring like an animal. I found Billy down here asleep."

Elenor rolled her eyes. "That explains a lot. I told Will that Uncle Thomas didn't drink much, and he seemed to take it as a challenge."

"Goodness knows what sort of day we're in for." She poured the boiling water into the teapot. "Billy's taking his upstairs, so once he's gone, we can have ten minutes before we start on breakfast."

"I hope Uncle Thomas isn't even angrier with Will."

"My guess is he'll be quite subdued. Just ask Mr Massey not to bait him."

"I doubt he'll be capable."

Nell raised an eyebrow. "He was the soberest of them all last night."

"Only because he's used to it. He woke me up when he arrived home, wanting some affection. I'd only just got Maria off to sleep, too."

Nell grimaced. "Perhaps they won't drink so much today, then."

"I wouldn't bank on it."

The breakfast buns were on the table and Alice was serving the scrambled eggs when Mr Marsh appeared in the living room and took his seat.

"Morning."

Nell pushed a cup of tea towards him. "Merry Christmas, don't you mean?"

"Oh, yes."

Mr Massey grinned at Billy. "How are you feeling, Mr Marsh?"

"I've felt better, thanks to you."

"We were getting to know each other. You seemed to be enjoying yourself, too. Once you loosened up a bit."

Mr Wood laughed. "He's suffering for it now."

"That's enough!" Mr Marsh raised his voice, but immediately lowered it. "I appreciate you trying to involve me, but I'd rather you didn't."

"Then put a smile on your face." George scowled as he accepted a plate of scrambled eggs from Alice. "Will was trying to cheer you up, and I won't have anyone being

313

miserable today. If Maria's looking down on us, God rest her soul, I want her to see us enjoying ourselves."

"And we will." Nell smirked at Mr Wood as she carried in more plates. "I've even remembered the mistletoe."

"I should hope so. What else do you have planned?"

"It will be pretty much the same as last year." *Without Maria.* "Church after breakfast, then home for dinner. Vernon and Lydia are joining us with the children."

"More children?" Mr Marsh groaned.

"Yes, and you should be pleased. They're what Christmas is all about."

"Where will we all sit?"

"We're having two sittings. We'll do presents once we've tidied up, but only for those who deserve them." She gave Mr Marsh a pointed stare. "Mr and Mrs Grayson and their daughters will join us for tea tonight."

George shifted in his chair. "What about Jane?"

"Not this year. She's going to Betty's for dinner with her new friend Mr Bruce."

George's forehead furrowed. "She told me he was nothing more than another lodger. What's he doing spending Christmas with them?"

"Erm, I think she feels sorry for him being on his own. Anyway, she's going to Sarah's tonight to be with her before the wedding tomorrow."

"Another wedding?" Mr Marsh looked up. "You've not mentioned it. Are we going?"

"We are, but with it being a second marriage for Sam, they want to keep it small."

Billy huffed. "That's nice."

"There are too many of us."

"We need to make the most of today, then." Billy checked his pocket watch as he helped himself to a bun. "We've another hour to get to church. Plenty of time to blow away any cobwebs from last night."

Nell placed a large trifle in the centre of the table and took a step back to admire the spread for the evening's festivities. *I think Maria would approve.*

Alice joined her with the bowl of punch. "That all looks nice."

"I'd say we've done ourselves proud." She turned to Edith and Leah. "We couldn't have done it without you, either."

Edith smiled. "We didn't do as much as you two. You should take the credit."

"It all helps."

Alice straightened the plates on the corner of the table. "We only need the Graysons now."

"I've been waiting for that all afternoon." Nell sighed. "Uncle Thomas hasn't been himself and I'm hoping Mr Grayson will put a smile on his face."

"At least there've been no arguments."

"They don't dare. Your dad would kick them out." Nell wandered into the hall as Rebecca let herself in. "It's only us."

"Merry Christmas." Nell grinned at her. "Have you had a nice day?"

Rebecca waited for her husband to go into the front room before ushering her daughters to the living room. "The usual. I'm hoping Mr Marsh will cheer him up."

"We were hoping the same of Mr Grayson. Thomas seems determined to be miserable."

"He's so like Hugh." Rebecca looked around. "Where's Elenor and the baby?"

"She slipped upstairs to feed her. It wasn't worth the trouble of trying to do it down here."

"Poor thing. She'll be freezing up there."

Nell lowered her voice. "I lit the fire for her. Just don't tell Thomas." She paused as Mr Wood appeared.

"They sent me to ask about drinks. Are any coming?"

"Yes, give us a minute. How are things in there?"

He grinned. "Interesting. You should join us."

"I'll come and ask what everyone wants to drink first." She followed Mr Wood into the front room, where the men had arranged themselves into small groups. Mr Marsh and Mr Grayson were huddled in one corner, while George was with Mr Massey in another, and Mr Wood joined Billy and Vernon in front of the fire.

"Aren't you all speaking to each other?"

George sat back in his chair. "We're having a change of company."

"As long as you've not fallen out."

"There's been nothing like that, has there, Will?" George winked at Mr Massey.

"No, we're all on good terms here. Even Mr Marsh almost raised a smile."

"I was pleased to see my friend."

Mr Grayson leaned forward and pointed at Mr Massey. "You'd do well to remember your manners. Mr Atkin won't always be around to protect you."

"But I'm here tonight, and I'll remind you that there'll be no arguments over the festive period."

Nell held up a hand. "Before there's any trouble, may I ask what you'd like to drink?"

With requests for two glasses of punch and five ales, she went back to the living room. "The truce is still holding, but I suggest we start the party games as soon as possible. Everyone needs the distraction. Oh!" She stopped as the front door opened. *This could be the biggest one of all.* She stepped into the hall. "Jane. I wasn't expecting you. And Mr Bruce."

He removed his hat. "Merry Christmas. I'm sorry to intrude, but Mrs Read insisted we call..."

"Of course I did. I'm here every Christmas, and it didn't seem right to miss out this year. Especially now Maria isn't with us." There was a twinkle in her eye. "Have you put up the mistletoe? We won't get any at Sarah's..."

George appeared in the hall, a sheepish grin on his face. "Merry Christmas. Nell said you weren't joining us today."

"I wasn't supposed to be, but it wouldn't be Christmas without calling. I'll stay for a drink, too, if Nell's offering."

George beamed at her. "Will you join us in here? Nell and Alice may have provided the mistletoe, but so far the ladies haven't been in."

"You know me." She linked George's arm. "Lead the way ... *to the mistletoe.*" She pretended to whisper the last few words, but Mr Bruce hesitated as Jane left him in the hall.

"Please go in, Mr Bruce ... and don't mind my sister. She's only teasing. Would you prefer punch or a glass of ale?"

"Ale for me, please. And a punch for Mrs Read."

Nell grinned. "I already know her order. I'll join you in a moment."

Nell rounded up the rest of the ladies. "The distraction's arrived."

Rebecca chuckled. "We heard. I don't understand why she's brought Mr Bruce with her, though."

Nell shook her head as she poured the drinks. "She'll have her reasons. Shall we go?"

One branch of mistletoe was already missing its berries by the time Nell carried in the drinks, and Jane took the punch from her. "Here you are. I was beginning to think I'd have to collect all the berries myself."

"You needn't worry about that." Mr Wood jumped up and held the mistletoe over Alice's head before planting a kiss on her lips. "There we are. It feels like Christmas now."

CHAPTER FORTY-THREE

Six months later

E lenor took a seat at the table and sat baby Maria on her knee.

"Let's see how she manages this." She buttered a piece of crust and handed it to her daughter.

Nell joined them. "Hopefully, she'll sleep better for you tonight."

"I'm used to managing on a few hours a night now. I'll rub some brandy on her gums like you suggested."

Nell smiled. "I don't know what I'd have done without it when you were little. At least she won't need much."

"I hope not." She picked up the bread Maria had dropped. "I think she likes it."

"She'll like the firm crust. It will give her something to bite on."

"How long will she be like this?"

Nell grimaced. "It will come and go, but it could last for a few years."

Elenor huffed. "It's a good job she's worth it." She kissed the blond curls on her daughter's head as the front door opened. "Who've we got here?" She looked up as Leah came in from work and sat beside her to hold the baby's hand.

"Have you been a good girl today?"

"Not bad." Elenor wiped Maria's hands. "Would you like her while we wait for everyone else?"

"Of course." Leah lifted Maria onto her knee as Alice carried the teapot to the table.

"Where's Edith?"

"She won't be long."

Nell stared at her. "Why, where is she?"

"She wanted to walk home with Mr Lacy."

"Straight from work? Unchaperoned."

Leah grinned. "It's getting serious."

"All the more reason for you to stay with them."

Elenor's forehead creased. "Has Uncle Thomas met him yet?"

"No. Neither's Uncle George. Edith keeps putting it off."

Leah gave the baby another piece of bread. "She won't be able to for much longer."

Nell's head shot up. "Why not?"

"Don't look so worried. I mean it wouldn't be normal, if things are getting serious. Besides, there's no reason for them not to like him."

"That counts for nothing with Uncle Thomas."

The front door opened again, and George, Billy and Mr Massey joined them.

"Evening, all." Billy was the first to the table. "We saw Edith outside with her young man. Is he coming for tea?"

"No." Nell's stomach flipped. "Where were they?"

"On the corner of Windsor Street."

"Where Uncle Thomas would see them?"

"He would if they stay there."

George took his seat. "I thought you said he had a position at the steelworks."

"He does."

"Wearing a suit?"

Before Nell could answer, Mr Wood arrived.

"Ah, I'm not the last. Where's Mr Marsh?"

Alice took his jacket from him. "We don't know. Did you see Edith outside?"

"Not near the house, but I didn't walk the usual way tonight. Why?"

"Billy saw her on the corner of Windsor Street, so I wondered if she was still there."

"Would you like me to go and find her?"

Nell shook her head. "No, she'll be fine. She was with Mr Lacy."

"So, why are you worried?"

"We're not, we're curious." She paused as the door opened again and seconds later, Mr Marsh arrived with Edith close behind. "Did you bump into each other?"

Mr Marsh wore a broad grin as he took his seat. "We did, and Edith introduced me to Mr Lacy. I believe you've already met him."

"Only when he's called to pick Edith up. He seems nice."

"I thought so, too. Very well-mannered."

Nell didn't miss the glare he shot at Mr Massey. "I'm glad you like him. Now, let me serve the tea."

It was almost half past six by the time Nell cleared the dinner plates and brought in a jam sponge pudding.

"Are we all having a piece?"

"Erm, not for me." Edith left the table. "Mr Lacy's picking me up shortly."

"He's keen."

Edith stepped to the mirror over the fire. "We're taking a walk tonight and want to make the most of the light evening."

"It should stay nice for you." Nell looked at Leah. "Are you going with them?"

"Don't I always? May I have my pudding first?"

Nell handed her a bowl but hadn't finished serving everyone when there was a knock on the front door. "Will this be him? He's early."

"I expect so." Edith darted to the door but returned a minute later on Mr Lacy's arm. "Everyone, I'd like to introduce Mr Ernest Lacy. Ernest, this is Uncle George."

George ran his eyes over him. "You don't look like someone from the steelworks. Not in a suit like that."

Mr Lacy extended a hand. "I'm a manager."

George opened his mouth, but Mr Wood's arm cut across him. "Harry Wood. Pleased to meet you."

"Likewise." He offered his hand to Billy and Mr Massey, finishing with Mr Marsh.

"Won't you take a seat?" Mr Marsh nodded to Edith's empty chair.

"No, thank you. I'd like to make my announcement first."

"Then don't let me stop you." Mr Marsh grinned as Mr Lacy took Edith's hands.

"Earlier this evening, I asked Edith to be my wife, and I'm delighted to say that not only did she accept, Mr Marsh has agreed to the marriage."

George spun round, with a grunt. "It's not his place..."

He was interrupted when Alice jumped to her feet, a grin splitting her face. "How wonderful. Have you chosen a date?"

"The first of October."

Her smile slipped. "That's not long off."

"We didn't want to wait any longer."

Why not? Nell's heart pounded as she studied Edith's girth but became distracted as Leah bounced on her chair.

"She wants me to be a bridesmaid!"

Edith tutted. "Alice and Elenor, too."

"Really?" Elenor's eyes lit up as Nell struggled for breath.

She knew before me, too. It serves me right. Why would she tell her aunty first?

"Aren't you pleased, Aunty Nell?" The excitement faded from Edith's eyes.

"Yes, of course. I wish you'd told me so Mr Lacy could have joined us for tea."

He nodded at her. "That's very kind of you, but there'll be time for that. I wanted to make the announcement now so you can all bear witness to our pledge." He took out a small box and placed it on the table as he reached for Edith's left hand. He raised it to his lips before he slid a ring onto her third finger.

Edith's eyes filled with tears as she gazed at the ring. "It's beautiful." She held out her hand for everyone to see the single diamond set in an elaborate gold setting.

Mr Marsh got to his feet and grasped Mr Lacy's hand. "Congratulations, young man. This calls for a toast." He turned to Nell. "Do we have any sherry or brandy?"

"I think I can find some. Will someone help me with the glasses?"

Alice followed her to the pantry. "Are you all right?"

"I'm fine. Just being silly."

"Don't you like him?"

"It's not that..."

"So why are you glum?"

Nell shrugged. "It was the way he asked Uncle Thomas for Edith's hand, when it isn't his to give."

Alice gave a crooked smile. "He was never going to ask you. That's not how it works."

"I know, but why ask Uncle Thomas? It would be more appropriate to ask her other dad. Even your dad noticed."

Alice grimaced. "I must admit he wasn't happy. She probably made the best choice asking Uncle Thomas. He wasn't going to say no."

No, he wasn't. "She still should have asked her other dad. I think I'll mention it to her..."

"Are you two coming?" Mr Wood's voice boomed from the living room.

"Yes, one moment." Nell hurried back with the bottles. "Sorry about that. They were hidden at the back."

Alice followed with a tray of glasses. "Here we are. Is it brandy for the men and sherry for us?"

When she got a nod of agreement, Nell picked up the

sherry bottle, but looked at Leah before she poured the fifth glass. "Will you have one?"

"May I?"

Nell glanced at George, but Mr Marsh interrupted. "She's far too young."

Nell pursed her lips. "A small glass won't hurt, and it's a special occasion." She passed around the drinks as Mr Marsh stood up and raised his glass.

"To Edith and Mr Lacy. May they have many happy and fruitful years ahead of them."

Nell raised her glass to repeat the toast. *As long as she's not fruitful this year, I'll be happy.*

CHAPTER FORTY-FOUR

Edith fastened off a piece of thread and pushed the needle into the pin cushion before she stood up to shake out the pale blue dress she'd been working on.

"There. What do you think?"

Nell studied it. "It's coming on."

"It's more than that." Leah straightened out the skirt. "It's gorgeous. If I ever get married, will you make a dress for me?"

Nell tutted. "Poor Aunty Rebecca will be out of a job."

"I don't mean her to be, but Edith is so clever. All I can do is serve afternoon teas."

Edith studied the waistband. "It's not hard if you put some effort into it. I've been sewing since I left school. I liked it when Mam showed me how to sew, so it made sense to carry on."

Elenor sighed. "I was never very good at anything. I hated school and couldn't wait to leave."

Nell nodded. "I remember the trouble I had getting you there. Not that you were as bad if Alice took you."

"I hated you going away, that's why. I thought that if I went to school, you'd be gone when I came back."

"And yet you didn't speak to me when I was at home."

Elenor sighed. "I hoped that if you saw me upset, it would stop you going."

"I stayed at home for over a year between ships, but it made no difference."

Leah gave Elenor a sideways glance. "I was always pleased to see you."

"You were. And it was lovely. I didn't mean to upset Elenor, though." She smiled at Alice. "Hopefully, you won't have the same problems with Georgie. Is he ready for school on Monday?"

"He seems to be. Whether he'll be so keen once he's been going for a week, I'm not so sure."

"You've not long to find out." Nell glanced at the clock. "It's time we were going to bed. We've church in the morning, and Elenor needs her sleep before Maria wakes her up again."

Leah sighed. "If children are so difficult, why do we keep having them?"

Nell grimaced. "The world would be in a sorry state if we didn't. Besides, if we want a husband to keep a roof over our heads, we don't have a lot of choice."

"Why can't we do that ourselves? You used to work, and me and Edith do, too." She grinned at Edith. "We could get a room of our own if we wanted."

Edith grimaced. "Not once I'm married."

"I didn't mean that. I meant you needn't get married if you don't want to."

"I do want to. You'll meet someone when you're older who you want to spend the rest of your life with."

Nell nodded. "I've told her, but she doesn't want to listen."

Leah huffed. "I don't want to be forced to have children I don't want. I'm happy with Maria."

"You're only sixteen, but in another five years, you'll change your mind. Now bed. We need to be up in the morning."

Nell and Alice washed and dried the last of the plates after Sunday dinner, before Nell hung the drying cloth over the range and stepped into the living room. Mr Marsh was reading the newspaper in his usual seat by the fire.

"Are you ready to go?"

He folded the paper up. "I am if you are. I've arranged to meet the Graysons in Sefton Park so we can visit the new Palm House. We'd like to see it."

"I thought you might." *And my company clearly isn't good enough.* "I'd hoped to speak to you about the wedding while we're out. We'll have to talk on the way."

He wrapped her summer cape around her shoulders. "What is there to discuss? Everything's under control."

"It is, but I'm bothered about Edith's dad." She stepped onto the footpath and waited for Mr Marsh to join her. "Shortly after she announced her engagement, I spoke to her about asking his permission, but she said she doesn't want to see him again. The thing is, I worry that he should be the one giving her away."

"Instead of me?"

"Well, yes. As far as she's concerned, you're only her uncle. If her dad's still alive..."

"I suppose you're right, although I was looking forward to it. It might be the only chance I get."

"There's still Leah."

"She'll expect Mr Atkin to give her away, like he did for Elenor."

"Not necessarily. You were hardly on the best of terms with Elenor when she got married, so George was a natural choice. You get on much better with Leah."

"And will continue to, as long as she doesn't go down the same path as Elenor."

"I doubt she will, but that's not for now. What do you think about me writing to Edith's dad?"

Mr Marsh stared straight ahead. "I'd say you're asking for trouble. You've kept your secret from Edith for all these years. What will you do if he says anything?"

"He wouldn't."

"You don't know that. Give him a few glasses of ale and a tot or two of brandy at the wedding breakfast, and you don't know what he'll say."

"So, you don't think I should tell him?"

"Not unless Edith wants you to. It's not as if he's her real dad."

"I still worry that someone will ask why he's not there."

"Say he isn't well. It shouldn't be difficult for someone with your experience of bending the truth."

Nell took a deep breath. *Don't let him upset you.* "I could."

"Are many coming to the wedding?"

"Only immediate family and a few friends from our side so we can accommodate Mr Lacy's family. There are rather a lot of them."

"We'll have to do Edith proud. I don't want them looking down their noses at us."

"Why would they do that?"

"You've met Mr Lacy. He's a thoroughly respectable young man with a job in management. His father doesn't work for a living either, which suggests they have money. We can't disappoint them. Should we have the wedding breakfast in a tea room ... or even the Adelphi?"

"Don't be silly. It would cost a fortune. Besides, if we do it for Edith, we'd have to do it for Leah, so be careful."

"Only if she married the right calibre of gentleman. It might be a lesson to her. She could have an embarrassment of a wedding like Elenor, or an impressive one like Edith, depending on who she chooses to marry ... and the size of her waist."

"That's unfair. When you set your heart on someone, you can't do much about it."

"We need to prompt her to make the right decision, then."

Nell sighed but bit her tongue as Rebecca and Mr Grayson came into view. "There they are. They have a seat, too."

"They were obviously early. Would you like to sit with Mrs Grayson while I visit the Palm House with Mr Grayson?"

"Aren't we all going?"

"Judging by the crowds, it's going to be busy. I'll go with

Mr Grayson to see what it's like, and we can go another day when it's quieter."

"Are you trying to get away from us?"

"Not at all, but it will probably be crowded and not suitable for women."

As you like. I'll come one afternoon with Alice or Elenor instead.

Once they'd exchanged greetings, Nell took a seat with Rebecca.

"Do you know what they're up to?"

Rebecca watched them go. "I've no idea, but they seem keen to be without us."

"They do. Not that I'm sorry. We can't talk the same with them around."

"What's troubling you?"

"Edith. I asked Thomas if he thought I should write to her dad to tell him about the wedding and give him the chance to walk her down the aisle?"

"What did he say?"

"That I shouldn't."

"I must admit, I agree with him."

"What if the guests want to know where he is?"

"Is that what's bothering you?"

Nell nodded. "Sarah, especially. You know what she's like."

"I wouldn't worry about her. Tell her he's ill."

"Thomas said that. Perhaps I will."

Rebecca studied her. "Now Edith's settled with you, why don't you tell her the truth?"

"T-the truth?" Nell gasped. "I can't do that. What if she hates me for what I did?"

"Don't you think she'll understand if you explain about baby Jack dying?"

"She may, but I wouldn't blame her if she didn't, given how unhappy she was living with Jack's brother."

"She liked her mam, though, and she wouldn't be a tailoress if she'd lived with you."

Nell grinned. "That's true."

"So, it may not be so bad telling her, and it would get it out into the open."

Nell shook her head. "I couldn't. What if I frighten her away? She won't need me or Thomas once she's married, so she could disappear."

"And you wouldn't like that?"

"Of course not. She's my daughter."

"Do what Mr Marsh suggests, then, and say nothing."

CHAPTER FORTY-FIVE

Nell wiped the dining table after breakfast as Elenor took Maria upstairs.

"Will you start making the beds while you're up there and I'll join you when I'm done down here?"

Elenor nodded. "I can do that. Don't be long."

"I won't. Alice should be back from school in a minute." She hadn't finished talking when the front door opened and Alice bounced Freddie's pram into the hall.

"Was Georgie all right when he got to school?"

"He was once he saw his friends. Not that they're allowed to talk in the class. I think that's what he doesn't like."

"He'll get used to it soon enough." Nell leaned over the pram and lifted Freddie out. "And then it will be your turn." She set him on the floor as Alice went into the living room.

"Where's Elenor?"

"She's taken Maria upstairs. Why?"

"I've got some news." A sparkle appeared in Alice's eyes

as she shut the door. "Please don't say anything, but I think I'm in the family way again."

"Oh, Alice, that's wonderful." Nell's face broke into a grin. "Have you seen Dr Randall?"

"Not yet, but I've been counting the days. I told myself that if I got to forty days without ... you know ... then it would be a good sign."

"And today's the fortieth day?"

"It is. I'm so excited. I don't want to say anything until I've had it confirmed, but I had to tell someone." Her smiled dropped. "It will be my first baby without Mam being here, though. It takes away some of the excitement."

Nell put a hand on her shoulder. "I know it's not the same, but I'll be here for you. When's it due?"

"April, I think, but I need to check." Her face brightened again. "I should be thankful I'll get into a normal-sized dress for Edith's wedding. If I'm to be her witness and bridesmaid, I need to be trim..."

"Which reminds me, we need to get a move on with the dresses. We've only got a month."

"Edith has it all under control. She's not put her needle and thread down for weeks other than to sleep and eat."

"She's always busy. I don't know what she'll do when she has to give up work."

"She's not planning to." Alice hesitated as Nell stared at her. "We were talking the other day, and she said there's no reason she can't carry on sewing at home."

"As long as Mr Lacy's happy for his wife to work. Mr Grayson wouldn't let Aunty Rebecca carry on once they were married."

Alice smirked. "Mr Lacy and Mr Grayson are rather different. I doubt Edith will have a problem."

Are you sure? "I hope you're right. At least if they move in here, me and Leah will stand up for her."

"She seems confident they will. She's persuaded Mr Lacy she doesn't want to be at home on her own after the wedding."

"That's nice to know." *Although it would have been nicer if she'd told me herself.* "We'll need to reorganise the bedrooms again."

"We'll manage. I hated it when I moved out, so it will be worth it."

Edith had a spring in her step when she and Leah arrived home that evening, and Nell looked up from the magazine she was reading.

"Have you had a good day?"

"A worthwhile one. I was talking to a customer in the shop, and when I told her I was about to be married, she said she'd start bringing all her tailoring to me at home."

"That's good. Does she have much?"

"Enough."

"You need to be careful your boss doesn't find out you're taking his customers. He won't be pleased."

"He was out. That was why we could talk. He doesn't allow it when he's there."

"You should still be careful. You've another four weeks to go."

Edith shook her head. "I'm not worried. The worst he

can do is get rid of me, but I'm leaving, anyway. I'll just start working here sooner than planned."

"You've got it all worked out then."

"I have ... ooh, I forgot to tell you. I took your advice, after all."

Nell's forehead creased. "Which advice?"

"About contacting Dad."

Nell's stomach flipped. "You said you wanted nothing more to do with him."

"I didn't, but when I thought about it, I decided I shouldn't exclude him. Even though he did it grudgingly, he put a roof over my head for nearly sixteen years. I'd like to see my brothers, too."

Nell's mouth was dry. "Would you like me to write to him?"

"There's no need. I did it yesterday."

"And you've posted it?"

"Of course. Why wouldn't I?"

"No reason. I ... erm ... I was just checking." Nell bit her lip as Edith skipped to a small pile of letters on the dresser. "Are these more acceptances for the wedding?"

"Most of them. There's one couple who can't come, but it's from Mr Lacy's side of the family."

Edith flicked through the replies. "If I remember rightly, they're an elderly aunt and uncle. It's a long way, coming from Yorkshire, so they probably don't want to make the journey."

"That's a shame."

"It is, but there are plenty coming. Thirty-two so far, if I've added them up properly."

"Are we expecting many more replies?"

"I don't remember off the top of my head, but I'll check my list later. Have you remembered Mr Lacy's joining us for tea?"

"I have. He should be here soon."

Edith was still sorting through the acceptances when there was a knock on the door. "This will be him." She raced to the hall, but when everything went quiet, Nell followed her.

"Is everything all right?"

Edith stepped backwards. "Yes, why wouldn't it be?" She made a point of hanging Mr Lacy's coat up carefully.

"No reason, but Uncle George will be home soon, so you'd be as well keeping the hall free."

"Ah, yes." Edith ushered Mr Lacy towards the living room where he gave a slight bow.

"Good evening, Mrs Marsh."

"Mr Lacy, please, take a seat. You didn't go to the alehouse with the others?"

He smiled at Edith. "I didn't want to be late and waste time we could be spending together."

Edith lowered her eyes. "You say the nicest things."

"Because it's true." He gazed at her before turning to Nell. "I prefer the coffee shops in town when I socialise. There's more stimulating conversation."

"That's nice." Nell raised an eyebrow at Alice as she headed for the kitchen. *It's a lot more expensive too, I shouldn't wonder.*

George and Billy had joined them by the time she carried the teapot to the table.

"Are the others not with you?"

"They're coming. Thomas was doing his best not to run

when he saw us ahead of him." George grinned at Billy. "He thinks Mr Lacy's more refined than the rest of us. Fool."

Nell took a step backwards, but George appeared unrepentant.

"Do you live locally, Mr Lacy?"

Mr Lacy cleared his throat. "I've taken some rooms in a house on Parliament Street. They're rather nice."

"Some rooms? How many of you are there?"

Mr Lacy's brow furrowed. "I'm on my own."

"Then why do you need more than one?"

Confusion crossed his face. "Isn't that obvious? The least a man requires is a drawing room, dining room and bedroom. You have all that here."

"Between nine of us. Not each..."

Mr Marsh gasped for breath as he barged into the room. "Sorry I'm late. I couldn't get away earlier."

George glanced over to him. "Don't worry. We didn't miss you."

"Mr Marsh." Mr Lacy stood up and extended his hand. "It's good to see you again. I hope I've not taken your seat."

"Not at all. Make yourself at home. You're still moving in here after the wedding?"

"As long as I'm welcome."

"Certainly, you are. I'm looking forward to it. We don't want Edith on her own all day, either."

George groaned. "Will you sit down and stop being such a bootlicker?"

Mr Marsh glared at him. "Excuse me!"

"You heard. It's my name on the rent book and I'll say who stays or goes, not you."

"You can't turn Mr Lacy away..."

"I can and I will if he causes any trouble. We're all workers here, and management are not welcome. He needs to show why we should make an exception."

Mr Lacy's face reddened. "I meant no offence, sir. I only want what's best for Edith."

"We all do, which is why I'll give you the benefit of the doubt, but don't come over all high and mighty, or you'll be shown the door."

CHAPTER FORTY-SIX

Nell's heart raced as she stared at the letter she'd picked up from the doormat. *He's addressed it to me.* Her hands trembled as she pushed it into the pocket of the apron. *I can't open it until Alice goes out.* She glanced at the clock. *Four o'clock. Another three-quarters of an hour.*

Alice was by the fire finishing her tea when Nell wandered into the living room. "Who's the letter for?"

"Letter?"

"The one you went to pick up?"

"Oh, that. Only another reply for the wedding."

"I thought Edith said last night she'd had them all."

"She must have miscounted." Nell reached into her pocket and slipped it under the letters on the dresser when Alice returned to her magazine.

"How many do we need to cater for?"

"I-I think Edith said forty-three."

"Can't the latecomers make it?"

"Erm, no." *I hope not, anyway.*

"They've left it late to tell us. Half the food's ready, and we'll have to do the rest in the next couple of days."

"There's always someone. Now, let me see to the tea. Everyone will be home before we know it." Nell unwrapped the minced beef she'd bought that morning and dropped it into a pan before moving it over the heat. *Why would he write to me and not Edith? I hope it doesn't mean he's coming. No, he'd tell Edith that. More likely, he'll want me to tell her he can't come. I hope I'm right.*

"Is something burning out there?" Alice was by the kitchen door before Nell realised she'd spoken.

"Oh, gracious." Nell pulled the pan from the heat and turned over the meat that was still in a lump. "It's not much. I can scrape that bit off."

"Are you all right? You've gone very pale."

"I'm just cross I did this." She flicked the burnt meat onto the waste paper. "I obviously wasn't paying attention."

"What were you doing, then?"

"I must have been thinking about the wedding. It's going to take over our lives for the next few days."

"It's times like this we really miss Mam. She'd know what to do."

She'd be someone to talk to, too. "We'll manage between us. Let me try again with this. You'll need to be going to school shortly."

Alice beamed at her. "There's no need tonight. Elenor said she'd pick Georgie up on her way home from Ruth's."

"Oh." A lead weight settled in Nell's stomach. "You should have said."

"It doesn't matter, does it?"

"No..."

341

Alice took the wooden spoon from Nell. "Are you going to stir this? You'll be burning the rest of it in a minute."

"I'm sorry. Actually, I need to nip out to the privy. Would you watch it until I come back?" She didn't wait for an answer before she disappeared into the yard. *Of all the days.*

Once in the toilet, Nell leaned her back on the door and retrieved the letter.

Dear Nell

I don't know if she told you, but Edith wrote to tell me she's about to be married.

You clearly haven't told her I'm not her dad, and she asked if I'd walk her down the aisle.

I've not yet replied, but I don't think it's my place to give her away. I also think it's time she knew the truth.

I told her brothers that she's their cousin, not their sister, and they accepted it well enough.

Now she's come of age, I imagine she would, too.

I'm sorry for the lateness of the letter, but I struggled to know what to say. If I don't hear from you by return, I'll write and tell her that Jack was her dad and that she should be proud to name him on her marriage certificate. It should make things easier for you not having to lie.

Yours sincerely

David

Nell put a hand to her mouth as an acrid taste rose to the back of her throat. *He told her brothers! Why didn't I keep my mouth shut?* Tears stung her eyes. *He's not said if they're coming to the wedding, either. What if they talk to her?* She reread the letter. *He'll expect a reply by tomorrow, which means it needs to be in the post by five o'clock.* She checked her watch. *That's less than half an hour. Why did Alice choose today not to go to school?*

Her niece was still by the range when she returned to the kitchen, but Nell didn't stop on her way to the living room. She grabbed the writing set from the dresser and dipped the pen in the ink. *It will have to be short...*

Dear David

> *I got your letter.*
> *PLEASE DON'T WRITE TO EDITH.*
> *I'll explain to her why you can't be at the wedding.*
> *I'm sorry she contacted you. Rest assured, it won't happen again.*
> *Yours sincerely*
> *Nell*

That will do. She stuffed the letter into an envelope and rummaged for a stamp. *Where is it? I know I had a spare one.* Perspiration covered her forehead as she double-checked all the compartments. *There it is.*

She didn't go back to the kitchen as she shouted to Alice. "I'm nipping to the post box. I won't be long." *Why did he give me so little time to reply? He never did have Jack's brains.*

The footpath was busy with women walking to school, and Nell weaved around each group until she reached Windsor Street, where she scurried across the road. Her pace slowed as she walked against the tide of those going the other way. *For goodness' sake. Can't children walk home from school by themselves any more?*

The post box was on Upper Parliament Street and her

lungs burned as she moved onto the road and hurried past those walking the other way. Her pace didn't slow until she reached the street corner, but her heart sank. *Where is everyone? There are usually dozens heading towards it to post their letters.*

She broke into a run for the last ten yards, but as the letter clanged on the bottom of the post box, she dropped her head onto its red top. *All that rushing for nothing. It sounds empty. Please Lord, let it have been a quiet day.*

Her mouth was dry as she made the reverse of the journey down Windsor Street, and she only lifted her head when Elenor waved from the corner of Upper Hill Street.

"What are you doing here? I thought you were having an afternoon in."

"I was, but I needed to write a letter and get it in the post."

"You left it a bit late. The post will be long gone."

It wasn't my fault. "I didn't realise the time."

Elenor rolled her eyes. "Some things never change."

CHAPTER FORTY-SEVEN

Alice and Elenor stood in the girls' bedroom wearing their bridesmaid dresses, while Edith straightened out the skirts. She stepped back and folded her arms.

"I'm pleased with them."

"I should think you are. They're lovely." Nell moved from her place by the door. "It's a shame Leah had to work today. Does her dress fit as well as these?"

"It does. She tried it on last night, and I don't need to do anything more to it."

"And what about your dress? Has anyone helped you with that?"

"I did that at the same time with Leah and Alice."

Alice nodded. "It was perfect. She's so clever."

Edith shrugged. "It's a big day. I want it to be right."

"It will be lovely." *I just wish you'd involve me more.* "Why don't you get out of those dresses and hang them up while I make some tea?"

Elenor reached for the button on the back of her neck. "I

need to see to Maria, before I come down, so leave mine in the pot."

"Will do."

The kettle was close to boiling and the tea tray was set when the letterbox rattled. *What's this?* She moved the kettle from the range and headed to the hall but stopped when Edith bounced down the stairs and picked up the letter.

"It's from Dad. I was beginning to think he was ignoring me."

Nell's stomach churned. *Didn't he get my letter?* "Why would he do that?"

"He's a strange man." She sat down at the table. "Is the tea ready?"

"Erm..." Nell hovered beside Edith. "Nearly. I'm waiting for the kettle to boil."

Alice walked to the kitchen. "It won't boil very fast when it's not on the heat."

"I-I took it off when I went to the hall. It was almost ready." Nell didn't take her eyes off the envelope as Edith sliced open the top. "Is this the first time you've heard from him since you left home?"

Edith cocked her head to one side. "He sent a Christmas card that first year, but nothing since. Not that I should complain. I've not kept in touch with him, either."

"What does he say? Is he coming to the wedding?"

Edith unfolded the paper but said nothing as her face paled.

"What's the matter?" Nell's voice squeaked.

"This."

Nell's hands shook as Edith passed her the single sheet of paper.

...it's time you were told that I'm not your dad ... ask Aunty Nell, if that's what you call her. She'll tell you the truth...

Stars danced in front of Nell's eyes, and she dropped into the nearest chair.

"What does he mean?"

"I... I..."

"Is everything all right?" Alice put the tea tray on the table as Edith answered.

"Dad's not my dad."

Alice's forehead creased. "What do you mean?"

"Look." She took the letter from Nell and handed it to Alice.

"Aunty Nell?"

Nell pinched the bridge of her nose. "Will you give me a minute? I need to collect my thoughts."

"What about my thoughts?" Edith gasped. "Dad's just told me he's not my dad. You need to tell me what's going on."

"All right." Nell blinked back her tears. "The thing is..." she took a deep breath "...when they were young, your mam and dad weren't blessed with a child. After several years, your mam became so distressed she chose to adopt one. And that was you."

Edith sat back in her chair. "So Mam wasn't my mam either?"

"No."

"Who am I, then?" She stared at Nell. "I felt sure I belonged here..."

"And you do." Nell bit her lip. "It wasn't a lie that your dad was my late husband's brother."

"But you can't be my aunty if Dad wasn't my dad."

"No. I'm not your aunty." Nell's voice was a whisper as Alice took a seat.

"Do you know who her real mam was?"

I could say no...

"Dad's letter says you'll tell me the truth..."

Alice kept her gaze on her. "Aunty Nell."

Nell glanced at Edith. "All right. When your mam couldn't have a child, there was someone close to her who was struggling to take care of her baby. You. The woman was suffering from serious melancholy and she agreed to let your mam bring you up." She held Edith's gaze. "They both thought they were doing the best for you."

"Why wasn't I given back to my real mam when she was better? She did get better, didn't she?"

"She did, but by then she was expecting another child and you were settled. We decided it would be best if you stayed where you were."

"But Dad didn't want me."

Nell raised her hands. "I know nothing of that, I thought he did, but your mam would have been heartbroken if we'd taken you from her. You were the child she'd always wanted, and she loved you very much."

"But she had my brothers."

"Not until later."

The three of them fell silent until Alice looked at Nell. "You said *we*."

"I'm sorry?"

"You said '*if we'd taken you from her*'. Were you involved in the decision?"

"Yes."

Edith wiped her eyes. "But what about my real mam? Was she asked?"

Nell swallowed hard. "Yes, she was."

"So you know who she is?"

Nell nodded.

"Then you have to tell me."

Nell closed her eyes as she fought for breath. "I am."

"You." Edith gaped at her, her mouth open. "Why didn't you tell me?"

"How could I? You'd just lost your mam. It was enough for you to deal with."

"But that was years ago. You could have told me once I was over it."

"You'd settled in by then and were happy. I didn't want to upset you..."

Elenor appeared at the door. "Did you say Edith's my sister?"

The silence was as good as an answer, and Nell lowered her eyes. "I'm sorry. I'm not proud of what I did, but I couldn't take care of you."

Elenor shook her head. "So, you were in the family way before you got married, too?"

"No! It wasn't like that." Nell jumped to her feet but sat down again as her head swam. "Your dad is Edith's dad, and we'd been married two years before she was born. He was away at sea at the time and I struggled..."

"You had Aunty Maria."

"Only after Edith had gone."

Alice stared at Nell. "Did Mam know?"

"She did. And Aunty Rebecca. No one else. Not until Edith came here and Uncle Thomas guessed."

Edith wiped the tears from her cheeks. "How?"

"Haven't you noticed how much like Leah you are? And me? And how we all get so easily bored..."

Edith sighed. "I suppose I should be happy that you're my family, but it doesn't seem real. Why did you give me away when you kept Elenor and Leah? Did I do something wrong?"

"No! It was my fault."

"My life would have been so different if you'd kept me."

"So would mine." Elenor sat down. "I'd have had a big sister to turn to when Mam left us."

"I'm sorry." Nell reached for her handkerchief.

"Why didn't you even visit? I'd never heard of you until Mam passed."

Nell sighed. "Once you were settled, your mam didn't want me to see you. She thought that if I did, I'd want you back again..."

"Do you think you would have?"

Say yes. "Probably. I've certainly enjoyed you being here these last six years and wish I'd known you better. I realise now that what I did was wrong."

Edith squeezed Alice and Elenor's hands. "I don't know what to say. This is the day before my wedding, the most special day of my life, but none of it seems important now."

Alice stood up and reached for the teapot. "Of course it is. This time tomorrow, you'll be Mrs Ernest Lacy and you'll be starting a new life."

"But we'll be living here. How can I do that now?"

Nell's eyebrows drew together. "What do you mean?"

"Do we carry on the charade of me calling you Aunty Nell, or do we tell everyone the truth?"

"I haven't thought of it. Your dad's letter caught me as much by surprise as you."

"We have to tell Leah, don't we?" Elenor looked around the table. "She should have been here today."

Nell held Edith's gaze. "What do you want to do?"

"Other than tell Leah, I don't know. I wish I was seeing Ernest tonight so I could ask him."

"Why don't we keep it to ourselves for now and you can talk to him after the wedding? There's no point upsetting the plans for tomorrow."

Edith nodded. "Very well, but I won't be able to call you Aunty Nell again."

CHAPTER FORTY-EIGHT

Nell took her seat at the front of church and smiled at Mrs Robertson as she surveyed the congregation. *I'm so pleased she could join us. Violet, too.* She gave a discreet wave to Rebecca and Jane, who were in the pew behind her. *It's a decent turnout.*

She turned to the back of the church as the organ struck up the opening notes of the "Bridal Chorus". Edith's pale blue dress with its flattering bustle and short train set off her slim waist, and Nell sighed as she approached the front. *She looks lovely. Jack would have been so proud of her.*

She made her way slowly down the aisle on Mr Marsh's arm, and Nell smiled at Leah as she followed behind with Elenor and Alice. *At least she's happy.*

Once Edith stood with Mr Lacy, Leah took the seat beside Nell.

"This is so exciting. Much better than Elenor's wedding. I don't know why Edith's so serious."

Nell put a finger to her lips. *I should have told her what's going on.* She looked along the pew to Alice, who was on the far side of Elenor. They both wore solemn expressions as the vicar gave the opening welcome. *Maybe not.*

The hymns were long and the sermon longer, and it was nearly an hour later before Edith walked towards the back of church on Mr Lacy's arm. They made a handsome couple with him in a new suit, his fair hair and complexion a contrast to Edith's olive skin and dark features. Nell followed behind with Mr Marsh and the rest of the bridal party, but once they reached the door, she stopped and stepped to one side.

"A penny for your thoughts?"

She flinched as Rebecca crept up beside her. "Oh, it's you."

"That's nice."

"I didn't mean that, just that I can relax."

"What do you mean?"

"I can't say much now, suffice to say..." Nell glanced over both shoulders "...Edith knows I'm her mam."

"No!"

"Shh! I'll tell you about it when we're alone, but if you're wondering why she doesn't look very happy, that's why." She pulled the confetti from her bag. "Do you have yours? I need to give this to Leah."

Rebecca held a small amount in her hand. "I've already given mine to Isobel and Florrie."

"I'd better go, then."

"I'll come with you."

A smile had appeared on Edith's face by the time the guests threw the confetti, and she gazed up at her husband as he escorted her to their carriage. Nell watched until the coachman closed the door.

"I suspect they'll take the long route home. She'll want to talk to him."

"Has Mr Marsh arranged a carriage for you?"

"He has, but I'll be with Alice and the girls. There'll be room for you if you want to help with the food. I'm sure Mr Grayson will be happy with Thomas's company."

Rebecca rolled her eyes. "Happier than he is with mine. Let me tell him." She'd no sooner left than Mrs Robertson moved to Nell's side.

"That was a lovely service. Thank you for inviting us."

"You're most welcome. Seeing that you couldn't be at my wedding, this is the next best thing." Nell looked at the young girl with them. "Good afternoon, Violet. I can't believe how you've grown."

Violet lowered her eyelids as her mother spoke.

"I could say that about your girls. They were still young children when we met."

"We've known each other a long time, which is all the more reason I'm delighted to see you here. I hope you won't mind our humble house. It's not up to the standards of yours."

"I've already told you, it doesn't matter. You'd have been in our position if your husband hadn't been in an accident. And I in yours, had I had the misfortune to lose mine."

"That's very true. Still, I hope you can see beyond the size of the rooms." Nell paused as a carriage pulled up outside the church. "This will be for me and the bridesmaids. Will you excuse me? I need to get home to serve out the food. I'll speak to you later."

She beckoned to Rebecca as she walked down the steps towards Alice, Elenor and Leah. "Are we ready to go?"

Alice nodded. "We are, although we'll have time before Edith gets to the house." She dropped her voice to a whisper. "She asked Mr Lacy if they could take a drive around the park on the way."

"Will she tell him?"

"Yes. She's been putting on a brave face, but she feels rather lost at the moment. I hope he can cheer her up."

"So do I."

Nell admired the spread of food as she laid the last plate of cakes on the table.

"That looks nice."

She smiled at Rebecca. "It does, thanks to everyone. Alice and I couldn't have done it without you. I hope there's enough."

"There'll be plenty. I'm surprised Edith isn't here yet, though. Is this to do with the news?"

"I'm afraid so. She only found out last night and she's not taken it in yet."

"What made you tell her?"

"It wasn't out of choice, believe me, but..."

Jane strode into the room with Betty behind her. "Oh, Nell, you've done yourself proud."

"Thank you. We just need the bride and groom now." Nell glanced over Jane's shoulder. "Where's your friend, Mr Bruce?"

"Oh, I didn't bring him." She lowered her voice. "I don't think George likes to see us together."

Nell raised an eyebrow. "Has he said something?"

"Not exactly, but I can tell. He was disappointed that he wasn't the one to give Edith away, too."

"He told you that?"

"In a manner of speaking."

"I didn't know he confided in you."

"Oh, yes." Jane smirked as she straightened her shoulders. "We've been close over the years..."

Betty tutted. "Not that close, and Mr Bruce is still around, so don't go starting rumours."

"As if..." Jane paused as murmurs of Edith and Mr Lacy arriving reached them. "You'd better go and welcome them."

"And find Thomas, while I'm at it."

Most of the guests were outside waiting for the carriage when Nell got to the door, and she spotted Mr Marsh away to her right with Mr Grayson. She was about to join them when the carriage pulled up and the coachman opened the door. Mr Lacy climbed out first and turned to help Edith down the steps.

She's been crying again. Why did David tell her the day before her wedding? She sighed. *Why didn't I tell her when she first arrived? I'm no better than him.*

Edith's smile seemed forced as she walked towards the house. "I've told him."

"I thought you might."

"He'd like to tell everyone else."

The blood drained from Nell's face. "What? When?"

"Now. Once we come in. I don't want to live a lie any more."

"But..." Nell struggled to breathe. "I-I've not told Uncle Thomas you know. Or Leah. A-and I've the food to see to... Would you give me time?"

Mr Lacy put an arm around his bride. "The sooner people know, the better, but as you've asked, I'll announce it during the speeches instead."

"Very well. Thank you." Nell held onto the door frame as she stepped onto the footpath. "Welcome home. I hope you'll be happy here."

Mr Lacy bowed. "I'm sure we will be. For now." He bent down to pick Edith up. "Let me carry you over the threshold."

What does that mean?

As soon as they'd disappeared, Nell invited the guests to follow them. Mrs Robertson stopped by her side on her way in. "She looks lovely."

"She does. She made her dress, and the bridesmaid dresses, herself."

Mrs Robertson sighed. "I wish I could do that."

"Me, too. I don't know where she gets it from."

"Her mother must have taught her well."

Nell bit her lip. *Do I tell her? Not here.* "Would you mind excusing me for a moment? I need to speak to Thomas."

Nell acknowledged Mr Grayson as she joined them. "Good afternoon. I wonder if I might have a word with Thomas before we go into the house. It's rather important."

Mr Marsh huffed. "What could be so important today?"

"Please, if we could have a moment, I'll explain."

He nodded to Mr Grayson. "We'll speak again later." He ushered Nell to one side. "What is it?"

She took a deep breath. "It's Edith. Did you notice how unsettled she was today?"

"I assumed she was nervous about the wedding."

357

"It was more than that. She had a letter yesterday from her dad. Or at least the man she thought was her dad."

Mr Marsh's back straightened. "Go on."

"He told her he wasn't her father and that she should ask me to tell her the truth."

"Did you?"

"I had no choice. Unfortunately, she didn't take it well."

"She's upset you're her mam?"

"Upset that I'd lied to her for all these years."

He stared over her head down the street. "Why did you need to tell me now?"

Nell let out a deep sigh. "She told Mr Lacy after the ceremony, which is why they were late arriving here. He's decided it shouldn't be a secret and plans to make an announcement when he gives his speech."

Mr Marsh's eyes bulged as his face reddened. "He can't do that."

"I'm not sure we can stop him."

"You may not be able to, but I can. Who does he think he is...?" He pushed past her. "Keep everyone out of the backyard."

Nell chased after him. "Don't do anything stupid."

He'd already grabbed Mr Lacy's arm before Nell caught up with him, but she stopped as they went through the back door. *Please don't make a scene.* She stayed by the kitchen door but watched through the window as Mr Marsh's face grew redder.

"What's going on?" Alice peered into the yard. "Mr Lacy should be with Edith to welcome the guests."

"And he will be. Uncle Thomas wanted a quick word...."

"I'd say it's more than a word."

Nell shuddered as the two of them squared up to each other. "Mr Lacy wants to tell everyone about the *news*, and Uncle Thomas is furious. I hope it doesn't spoil the wedding."

"It's a bit late for that. Have you seen Edith?"

Nell peered into the living room. "No. Where is she?"

"Upstairs with Elenor and Leah. Crying."

Nell closed her eyes. "Has she told Leah?"

"She was about to."

I hope Leah doesn't hate me for it. She was jolted from her place by the door when Mr Marsh pushed it open. "Careful."

"I'm sorry." His face was stern as he shut the door behind him. "He won't say anything. Not today."

Thank goodness. "Where is he now?"

"He needed a minute to himself but asked if I could arrange for Edith to be in the kitchen when he gets back."

Alice turned to leave. "I'll fetch her. She may need a few minutes, too."

Nell waited until they were alone. "What did you say to him?"

"I pointed out how *uncomfortable* it would be for them to live here if he disgraced you in such a public way."

"Thank you. I suppose we'll have to tell the family once the wedding breakfast is over."

"Not necessarily. I'll be having another word with him tomorrow to see what this is all about."

CHAPTER FORTY-NINE

The tea room was almost empty when Nell pushed open the door and Leah saw her immediately.

"Mam! What are you doing here? On your own, too."

"I wanted to talk to you. Will the manageress let you join me for a pot of tea?"

Leah glanced around. "I doubt it. We're getting ready for dinnertime."

"Please, will you ask?"

She gave a brief nod. "Give me a minute."

It was five minutes later before she returned carrying a tea tray. "Shall we sit in the corner?"

Nell pulled out a chair as Leah set the tray on the table and sat opposite her.

"Is this about Edith?"

"It is. I want to apologise for not telling you sooner. It wasn't intentional."

"I heard you didn't tell anyone. Not even her."

Nell sighed. "It's a difficult thing to admit. I'm not proud of what I did. I wanted you to know that."

"Why did you do it, then?"

"You've seen how hard it is for Elenor to look after Maria, and she has me and Alice to help. When I had Edith, I had no one, and I was already grieving for a son I'd lost. I couldn't do it."

"You'd lost a child as well? Edith didn't mention that."

"I didn't tell her. She was unsettled enough as it was. I'll tell her once things calm down."

"If they ever do. She's very upset that you gave her away but kept me and Elenor."

"I did what I thought was best for her. I hope she'll forgive me one day."

Leah picked up the teapot and poured out two cups. "Is that all you wanted to say?"

Nell studied her. "I wanted to make sure you weren't angry with me. I'd hate it if we fell out."

Leah smiled. "I'd never do that. What would I do without you?"

"Have a less complicated life."

"Then it would be boring." Her face became serious. "I've been thinking about how little I know about you. Why have you never told us we had a brother? And why did you go away to sea?"

"They're not the sort of things people talk about."

"Will you tell me one day?" She glanced over at the counter. "Not now, though. I've been here long enough."

Nell nodded. "One day. When you're a bit older."

Leah was the first to arrive home that evening and Nell placed the last of the cutlery on the table.

"Are you on your own?"

"I am. Everyone must have forgotten I don't have Edith to walk with any more." She peered into the kitchen. "Where is she?"

"She went to Windsor Street to meet Mr Lacy. I'm surprised you didn't see her."

"I took the cut-through." Leah paused. "She told me this morning that Mr Lacy wants to tell the rest of the family the news tonight."

Nell's stomach fluttered. "Was she still upset?"

"She's putting on a brave face, but yes. I'd say so. Where's Elenor?"

"She's taken Maria to bed. She won't be long."

"Is she seeing to the boys, too?"

"No, they're in the backyard with Alice. They'll be coming in shortly."

Leah took a seat at the table. "Children really change your life, don't they?"

"They do, but it's usually worth it."

"Only usually?"

Nell's eyes drifted to the floor. "Sometimes they can break your heart, but it's not their fault. Now, let's not be serious. We need this table set before everyone comes in." She disappeared into the kitchen as the front door opened and George and Billy joined them.

"Evening, all." Billy took his seat at the table opposite Leah. "Where is everyone?"

"Edith's gone to meet Mr Lacy, but I don't know where Uncle Thomas or Mr Wood are."

George huffed as he sat down. "We're not getting into the

habit of waiting. If they can't be here for six o'clock, we start without them."

The front door clicked again. "This may be them now." Nell popped her head into the hall. "Oh, it's you."

"That's not a very nice welcome." Mr Marsh hung his hat on a hook as Nell pulled the living room door closed behind her.

"I didn't mean to be rude. I thought it might be Edith and Mr Lacy. Leah said he wants to make his announcement tonight."

Mr Marsh sucked air through his teeth. "I thought I'd changed his mind."

"It doesn't sound like it."

He held her gaze. "Are you up to this?"

"I think so. I've tried to prepare myself."

"Very well." He strode up the hall but hadn't gone into the living room when Mr Lacy opened the door for Edith. Mr Marsh's eyes narrowed. "You're going ahead with it, then?"

Mr Lacy hung up his hat. "We've been through this. There should be no more lies. Edith wants everyone to know the truth."

"Are you sure it's Edith?"

Mr Lacy's lip curled. "We need to clear the air."

"I didn't mean for it to get unpleasant." Edith caught hold of his arm as he took her cloak, but he shook her hand away.

"You're the innocent party in all this. People need to know the truth." He escorted Edith to the living room. "Good evening." He held out a chair for her before taking the seat beside Billy.

"You're late." George scowled at him.

"Edith and I needed to talk."

"That's no reason to keep everyone waiting. We'll be starting without you if you make a habit of it."

"We're not likely to do it on a regular basis, but we have something to tell you this evening."

George studied the two of them. "Get on with it, then. My stomach thinks I'm not getting fed."

Nell carried two plates of fried kidneys to the table. "Can't it wait until we've eaten? Mr Wood should be home by then, too."

"I'd like to get it off my chest now." Mr Lacy didn't look at her. "You may have noticed that since the day before our wedding, Edith has been rather subdued." He didn't pause for breath. "That's because she found out that the people she called mam and dad for as long as she can remember were no such thing. Her actual parents were Aunty Nell and her late husband."

George hadn't waited to start his tea but turned to Nell with a forkful of mashed potato halfway to his mouth. "She's yours?"

Nell nodded. "You were away at the time ... shortly after baby Jack died."

George's brow furrowed. "I remember Maria saying you'd had a bout of melancholy. Was that it?"

"It was. I couldn't deal with being a mam again, but Jack's sister-in-law offered to bring her up for me... She was desperate for a child..."

"So, she had a good home?"

Nell looked at Edith. "I think so."

"From what I've heard, it wasn't as good as it would have been here." Mr Lacy sneered at her.

"Y-you don't know that. She told me she was happy enough..."

"That's enough." George banged a hand on the table as he glared at Mr Lacy. "You've not been in the family a week, yet you seem to want to upset those of us who have made it what it is. Why?"

Mr Lacy stood up. "My wife's been distressed, and she wanted everyone to be told the truth."

"Was it her? Or was it you hoping to punish Mrs Marsh?"

Mr Lacy glared at him but said nothing.

"Exactly. Now sit down, eat your tea, and be glad we tolerate you."

Edith and the girls had gone upstairs, and Alice was seeing to Freddie as the light from the fire faded. *I should put some more coal on, not that I can be bothered. What time is it?* Her eyes hadn't focussed on the clock when the front door opened. *Someone's home early.* She sat up straight as George joined her.

"I wasn't expecting you yet."

"I wanted a quick word before you went to bed." He took the chair opposite and studied her. "It must have been quite a shock when Edith turned up here."

"More than that. I was terrified Thomas would find out and call our wedding off."

George pursed his lips. "Why did you tell her the truth now?"

"I had no choice. She'd written to her dad to ask if he'd walk her down the aisle, and he decided it was time she knew."

"Was that the first Thomas heard of it?"

"No, I told him shortly after she came here. Or rather confirmed what he suspected."

"And he's been all right with you this week?"

"He's been very protective, actually."

"I'm glad to hear it. Was Jack her father?"

"Oh, yes ... and we were married. He was home for her baptism, which was when we spoke to his brother- and sister-in-law about taking care of her."

"Mr Lacy upset you, though, I could tell. Would you like me to ask him to leave?"

"No. If he leaves, he'll take Edith with him and I might never see her again. I'm hoping that if she stays, she'll get used to me being her mam. There are no more secrets now."

"Very well." George stood up. "Out of interest, did Maria know?"

"She did. Her and Rebecca."

"How did she react?"

"Like a mother. They both agreed that giving her up made sense. I was in no fit state to look after myself, let alone a child."

He shook his head. "I never would have thought Maria would have given her blessing. Perhaps I didn't know her so well after all."

CHAPTER FIFTY

Nell picked up her granddaughter from the rug by the hearth and sat down with her on her knee.

"Come and give Granny a birthday cuddle." She gave Maria a squeeze as Elenor arrived with a large cake that she placed in the centre of the table. "To think, this time last year, I didn't know if you were going to survive."

Elenor shuddered. "I didn't either. I don't want to go through that ever again."

"It should be easier next time, and you've filled out this year, which will help. If you started with another one now, you'd be the ripe old age of nineteen when it's due."

"I'd rather not think about it." She handed Maria a biscuit as Alice came in from the backyard and rubbed her hands by the fire. "It's chilly out there."

"It's been cold all week. More like January than December." Nell paused. "Was that the letterbox? The postman's late if it was."

"I'll go." Alice strode to the hall but returned with a smile on her face. "It's from James."

"I was thinking about him the other day. We've not heard from him for months. What's he got to say?"

Alice stood in front of the fire as she opened the envelope. "Well, he's not very considerate. The first thing he mentions is that the weather is a lovely eighty degrees Fahrenheit. Can you even imagine it?"

Nell shivered. "Not on a day like today. In fact, not at all. It doesn't even get that hot here in the summer. Does he say anything about coming home?"

Alice read the other three sides of writing. "Not that I can see. He wishes us all Merry Christmas and has asked for a reminder of who lives with us now. He says he's lost track."

Nell laughed. "I'm not surprised. We should tell him he needs to come home. He hasn't met Mr Massey yet, let alone Mr Lacy."

"I'm not sure he even knows Mr Lacy exists and he won't know the latest news about Edith…"

"No." Nell bit her lip. "There's no need to tell him, either."

Leah shivered as she came home from work and stood by the fire in the back room. "My, it's cold out there."

Edith joined them. "It's not so warm in the front room. My fingers are numb. I'll have to start sitting in here."

"You're more than welcome." Nell watched Edith as she took a seat at the table. "Are you all right? You've been very quiet today."

"Just hungry. Is tea ready?"

"Nearly." Elenor paused as the wind whistled through the living room door and Billy joined them.

"Evening, all."

"Are you on your own?"

"The others are coming, but I didn't want to hang about..." He rubbed his hands together. "I'll have a cup of tea while I wait if there's one going."

"It's on its way." Nell poured some milk into a cup as the door blew open again and George joined them.

He sniffed in the air. "My, that pan of scouse smells good. The others had better be quick."

"I'll give them five minutes and then serve it out."

They were all waiting at the table when Mr Lacy finally arrived, and Nell closed the door and put some cushions along the bottom. "That should keep the draught out."

George glared at Mr Lacy, but he ignored him as he cleared his throat.

"Before we eat, I've an announcement to make."

George groaned. "As if being late home wasn't enough..."

Nell looked between him and Edith. "Is this why you've been quiet?" *It's too soon for her to be in the family way...*

"It's Ernest's news, really."

"It's rather exciting, too." He pushed out his chest as he stood with his hands behind his back. "I've got myself a new job. I'll be earning twice as much money as I do now."

Billy stared at him. "How've you managed that?"

"It's a promotion. A more senior job managing the riffraff."

George pushed himself up, his nostrils flared, but Nell put a hand on his shoulder.

"That's nice."

"Nice! He's got a nerve..."

"Isn't a man allowed to improve his lot in life?"

"Of course you are, but it's not for everyone." Mr Marsh smirked as he glanced towards George. "Is it with immediate effect?"

"No. It's not with the same company, so I won't start until the New Year."

Mr Marsh cocked his head to one side. "You already work for the largest steel firm in Liverpool. I wouldn't expect you to get more money by going to a smaller company."

"I'm not. I'm moving to a bigger company, in the home of steel, no less!"

Mr Marsh's face fell. "Sheffield?"

"Exactly. You can't get the best jobs in steelmaking if you work in Liverpool."

"But ... you can't leave."

"I'm sorry, Mr Marsh, but it's time to move on. I'm more settled in Yorkshire, anyway."

"But Sheffield's such a long way away." Nell's voice squeaked.

"And more difficult to get to from here." George studied Mr Lacy. "Did you deliberately set out to upset Mrs Marsh?"

"Not at all. I gave Edith the choice of whether to stay here or not. Something she's not been given before."

Nell grabbed George's arm as he jumped to his feet, his fist clenched.

"Please don't do anything rash. We can't stop Mr Lacy from taking a better job."

"I've no intention of stopping him. I've had more than enough of him and his pompous attitude. The sooner he goes, the better."

Nell sighed. *I just wish he wasn't taking Edith with him.*

Nell was the last in the living room, but she looked up from her magazine when the cushions behind the door moved and Edith joined her.

"I thought you'd gone to bed."

"I rarely go to sleep until Ernest comes in, and I wanted to talk to you."

"Is there much to say?"

"I want you to know it was Ernest's idea to move."

"I have no doubt of that. He said he'd spoken to you about it, though."

"He did, but I couldn't really refuse. It's such a good opportunity for him..."

"So, there wasn't much choice?"

She shook her head. "Not if I want to keep him happy."

"I understand."

Edith sighed. "I didn't mean to upset you. You've been very kind to me since I came here. More than I could have hoped." She gazed into the fire. "I remember when I first arrived, I was jealous of Elenor and Leah for having you as a mam. You seemed so different." She lifted her gaze to Nell's. "Why wasn't I happy, when I found out you were mine, too?"

"It was a big shock, especially coming when it did. I don't blame you."

"It was me who spoiled it, though. If I hadn't been so silly, Ernest wouldn't have behaved as he did. I'm sorry."

"So am I. I should never have let you find out as you did." Nell watched as Edith continued to stare into the fire. "May I keep in touch with you when you've gone?"

Edith looked up with a smile. "Of course, by letter at least, and I'll visit when I can."

"I'd like that. And please let me know when you make me a granny. It seems strange to think I could have a grandchild I won't see."

"There's no need to worry about that at the moment."

"I'm not worried. Not in the way I was with Elenor, anyway, but I'd like to know if you have any children."

"And you will."

Nell nodded. "When will you leave?"

"We've not decided yet. We need to find somewhere to live, so it may be straight after Christmas. Boxing Day, perhaps. It will be up to Ernest."

"It would be nice if you could stay for Christmas. It may well be our last one together."

CHAPTER FIFTY-ONE

A lice was by the fire, her knitting needles clicking loudly as Nell picked up a letter from the doormat. "It's from Edith."

"What does she have to say?"

Nell took it from the envelope. "Let's see. Oh, that's good. She's got several new clients for her business since she last wrote."

"I hope that helps her settle in."

"She says it has. She's busy most days now, and she's started meeting new people."

"I'm glad. Mr Lacy took her away with no thought..." Alice paused as she struggled to breathe.

"Are you all right?"

"Not really. My chest and throat hurt, and I'm far too hot for this time of the year."

"You should be in bed."

"I don't have time for a proper confinement."

"I don't mean that. If you've picked up a chill, you need to look after yourself."

Alice glanced at the clock. "I'll have an early night. I need to pick Georgie up from school soon."

"You'll do no such thing. I'll go, but not before I put you to bed. Elenor will watch Freddie."

"I need to get this finished." Alice held up the baby jacket she was knitting.

"You can take it upstairs. Now, come along. I don't have a lot of time if I'm going to school." She helped Alice from her chair and followed her to the bedroom. "Where's your nightdress?"

Alice reached under her pillow. "I can manage."

"Maybe you can, but it doesn't mean I won't help. It's cooler up here, which won't do you any harm."

"I hope you're right. I'd rather not take a tonic."

"You'll do as you're told. Imagine your mam being here listening to you."

Alice smiled. "It's because she's not that I keep trying to get away with it."

"Well, don't forget, she was my sister, and I'm here to take over from her. Now, get yourself into bed and I'll pop outside and tell Elenor where you are before I go to school. I won't be long."

Once Nell had left the school gates, Georgie ran ahead of her, but as she approached the corner of Windsor Street, she met Leah coming from the opposite direction.

Leah waved as she crossed the road. "What are you doing here?"

"Alice isn't well, so I've sent her to bed."

"Is the baby on its way?"

374

"Not yet. I think she's picked up a chill. A few days in bed and she'll be right as rain."

Leah waved to Georgie as he stopped to wait for them. "I wonder if he'll have a brother or sister."

"I've a feeling Alice would like a girl this time. Not that she's said as much, it's just a few things I've picked up on."

"That makes a change. Uncle Vernon and Aunty Lydia want another boy after three girls."

"Let's hope they both get what they want, then."

"And that Edith has a baby soon. She told me she'd like one."

"I'm sure she does, but she's time yet. She's only been married four months." Nell paused. "We had a letter from her earlier. She seems to have settled more in Sheffield."

"That's good. I can't wait to visit her in the summer. If Mr Lacy lets us stay with them."

"Us?"

"Me and Elenor."

"Are you sure she'll go? She won't want to take Maria so far."

"You could mind her. You left me at that age."

Nell rolled her eyes. "And didn't hear the end of it, but yes, I could. She'll have to decide if she wants to leave her. And if Mr Massey will let her go."

Leah huffed. "I hate the way we have to ask permission to do anything."

"It's just the way it is. You'll get used to it."

The house was empty when they arrived home, and Nell hurried to the dresser once she'd taken off her cloak, to retrieve the cutlery. "We'd better get this table laid. Everyone will be home soon."

"I'll do it. Is tea ready?"

"There's a meat and potato pie warming through."

Leah smiled. "I didn't use to think you could cook, because Aunty Maria always did everything."

"She enjoyed doing it and I was happy to let her. She taught me a lot of what she knew, though."

"I should take more notice in case I get married and we don't move in here."

"There's time for that..." She paused as the front door opened. "Who's this home early?" She peered into the living room as George appeared. "Is everything all right?"

"I'll be fine."

"Which means you're not now?"

"I've overdone it today, that's all."

Nell studied him as he sat by the fire. "How did you get home so quickly?"

"I took a carriage."

Nell's brow creased. "Then there must be something wrong. You don't waste money like that if there isn't. Have you considered getting an easier job? You're not as young as you used to be."

"I still need to work. Nobody gives you money for doing nothing."

"But you could do something less strenuous. You don't need to bring in as much now we have three other men in the house earning."

"I'll get over it."

Nell put a hand on his forehead. "You're burning up. Alice is the same, and she's gone to bed. That would be the best place for you, too."

George glared at her. "I said I'm fine. Stop fussing."

"I'm only trying to help." Nell checked the table as Elenor sat the children along the back wall. "Leah, will you finish here? I'll go and see if Alice wants anything to eat before everyone comes in."

Alice was dozing when she went in, but her body jerked and she opened her eyes as Nell stood by the bottom of the bed.

"How are you feeling?"

"I've felt better. This baby is so active, though. It's just woken me up."

"It must be because you're so warm and it's not used to it. Hopefully, it will tire soon. Would you like anything to eat?"

Alice shook her head. "A cup of tea will be enough, and would you ask Harry to come up when he gets home?"

"I'll get him to bring your tea." Nell wandered to the door. "Shall I bring the boys?"

"I've not got the energy. Tell them I'll see them at bedtime."

Mr Wood was in the hall as Nell walked down the stairs and he gave her his usual smile. "Good evening, Mrs Marsh."

"Good evening. Alice has been a bit under the weather this afternoon, so she's gone to bed."

"Is she all right?"

"She will be. She asked if you'd take a cup of tea up to her. If you wait a moment, I'll pour it for you."

He followed her into the living room but stopped when he saw George. "You're home early."

"I overdid it at work, so I took a carriage home."

Mr Wood whistled through his teeth. "You can't do that too often."

"And I won't. I shouldn't try to keep up with these young men any more."

Mr Wood grinned. "I can't manage that, let alone you." He picked up the cup and saucer Nell pushed towards him. "Let me take this to Alice and I'll be back."

Nell stood beside George. "How's your appetite? Same as usual?"

He hesitated. "Not so much tonight."

"Now I know you're ill. I hope you're not planning on going out later."

"If I want to go out..."

"I know, you'll go."

"Mrs Marsh..." Mr Wood's voice bellowed down the stairs. "Come quickly."

Nell yelped before she headed to the Woods' bedroom. "What is it?"

Alice gasped. "The baby. It's coming."

Nell stood at the foot of the bed. "It's too early."

"It kicked, and it's started things off. Everything's wet..."

Mr Wood looked from one to the other as he edged towards the door. "I'll leave you to it."

"No, wait!" Nell followed him. "You need to fetch the midwife. She only lives in the next road. Number twenty-six. And ask her to hurry because we think it's on its way."

He didn't hang around and was out of the front door before Nell returned to Alice.

"What happened?"

Tears filled Alice's eyes. "I don't know. The baby was kicking and as I turned over, the waters started."

Nell placed a hand on her forehead. "You're still hot. Let me get some cold water and wipe your face."

Nell acknowledged Billy and Mr Marsh when she reached the living room but darted straight through to the kitchen where Elenor and Leah were serving the tea. Elenor stopped what she was doing.

"What's going on?"

"It's Alice. The baby's on its way."

"It's not due yet."

"I know, but it's coming, anyway." She filled a jug with cold water. "I need to take this upstairs. Will one of you put the kettle on? The midwife will want some hot water when she arrives."

Nell was on the stairs when Mr Wood returned. "She's on her way."

"We may need Dr Randall, too. I'd say Alice and George have both got a chill, and if it doesn't clear up, they'll need a tonic."

"I'm not having a doctor..." George's voice boomed through the house.

Nell tutted. "It's for your own good. And for Alice."

"There's nothing up with me that a good night's sleep won't fix."

Nell shook her head at Mr Wood. "Will you show the midwife up when she gets here?"

"As long as I don't need to come in."

"Just tell her which door to knock on."

Alice was groaning on the bed when Nell returned.

"What hurts?"

"All of me."

Nell filled up the basin on the dresser and soaked a cloth

in the freezing water. "Here, this may help."

Alice flinched as she placed it on her forehead, but relaxed into the pillows. "Why did the two things have to happen at the same time?"

"It wouldn't surprise me if it was the fever that started it..."

Her sentence was cut off when the midwife opened the bedroom door. "What's going on in here?"

Tears spilled from Alice's eyes. "It's the baby..."

"It's not due for another two and a half months."

"But it kicked..."

Nell stepped back to the door. "There are towels on the dressing table if you need them. Would you like some hot water?"

The midwife nodded. "Please. Leave it outside the door when it's ready."

"I will. I won't be long."

The dishes had been tidied, and the men had left for the alehouse, when Nell heard a baby crying. "Has she had it?"

Elenor's forehead creased. "That was a lot quicker than me."

"That's not always a good sign." She hurried up the stairs and waited for the midwife to open the door after she knocked.

"Is the baby all right?"

"I delivered her safely if that's what you mean, but I've not seen one so small. I doubt she'll be able to feed properly."

"A little girl?" A smile crossed Nell's lips. "May I see

her?" She crept towards the bed where Alice sat propped against some pillows with a tiny bundle on her chest.

"My goodness, the size of her!"

Tears welled in Alice's eyes. "She's so small. How can she possibly survive?"

"We'll give her all the help we can, that's how. Have you tried feeding her?"

"Not yet. She's too sleepy and I'm exhausted."

The midwife wiped her hands. "I'd say the fever broke while she was pushing, so if she can get some sleep, she should feel better."

"That's a relief, but will you help her with the feeding before you go?"

"Don't I always?"

"Yes, I'm sorry." Nell stroked the baby's cheek. "What will you call her?"

Alice rested her head on the pillows. "I haven't even thought about it. I would have called her Maria after Mam, but we already have a Maria living with us, so it will get confusing."

"How about calling her Mary? It's similar enough, but a little different."

"Yes, I like that. If Harry's happy, I'll announce it later."

CHAPTER FIFTY-TWO

Betty sat by the fire, Alice's tiny daughter cupped in her hands. "I've never seen a baby so small."

From the chair next to her, Alice leaned over. "She's grown a little, too. We weighed her yesterday, and she's nearly three pounds now."

"That's still no weight."

"It's an improvement on two pounds four ounces. We've been drizzling tiny spoonfuls of milk into her mouth around the clock and it must be working."

Jane sighed as she stood behind them. "There doesn't seem to be any end to the way these children test us." She squeezed Betty's shoulder. "I hope this one you're carrying gives you an easier time."

"I hope so, too. I wouldn't be able to feed it so regularly."

Alice took the baby from Betty and reached for the milk. "I don't mind too much. Aunty Nell and Elenor help me, and at least she's alive."

Betty sighed. "I was never that fortunate when mine were early."

"No." Jane retook her seat. "At least Elenor's got the hang of being a mam."

Nell smiled. "She has. Little Maria's doing well."

"Is there any sign of her having another one?"

Nell shook her head. "Not that she's told me. She was just unfortunate to be caught when she was. Either that or it was punishment for what she did. Still, we seem to have got over it."

Alice smirked. "Uncle Thomas is even civil with Mr Massey when the mood takes him."

Jane looked over at Alice. "How's your dad now? Is he over the chill he had?"

"You mean the chill that turned into a chest infection because of his stubbornness? He is, thank goodness. He's back at work now."

Nell huffed. "I'm not sure that's anything to be pleased about. I worry about him doing such a physical job at his age."

Jane studied her. "How old will he be?"

"I've not worked it out, but let me think. He was about five or six years older than Maria and she was thirteen years older than me. I'll be fifty next year, so he must be in his late sixties."

Jane nodded. "That sounds about right; I think he's about ten years older than me. He won't be as strong as he used to be."

"You can't tell him, though. He'll be working until he drops at this rate."

"I'll see if I can talk some sense into him."

"What about Mr Bruce? Won't he mind?"

"It doesn't matter if he does. It's a friendship that's run its course, and I don't want to see George kill himself by working too hard. I'm sure Maria would have had something to say about it."

Alice creased the side of her lip. "I'm not sure Dad would have taken any notice. You know what he's like."

Alice showed Jane and Betty to the door as Nell dripped milk into Mary's mouth. "There's a good girl." She stopped as milk dribbled from the corner of her mouth. "Oops, did I give you too much? I'm sorry."

"Is there a problem?"

"Nothing I can't manage." Nell wiped the baby's face with a cloth. "She just didn't want as much as I gave her."

Alice's forehead creased. "She did that with me this morning."

Elenor joined them from the kitchen. "She did it yesterday, too, but I thought it was me being careless."

"Maybe we're giving her too much."

Alice didn't seem convinced. "If she does it again, will you tell me? I don't want her to stop taking it."

Nell offered the child to Alice. "Would you like to do it and I'll finish the tea? It might reassure you."

"I would, thank you." She handled her daughter like a china doll. "Come to Mammy. We'll make you big and strong."

Nell watched as Mary took a small teaspoon of milk. "There, she liked that. They always know when they're with their mam."

"As long as I don't have to do it all the time. I'll be exhausted."

"We'll still be here, and Elenor will take care of the boys, won't you?"

"Of course. Speaking of which, I need to go for Georgie."

Alice watched Elenor as she left. "I don't know what I'd have done if I'd had Mary when we were in Wales. Edith couldn't have helped in the way you both have. Not if she wanted to keep her job, anyway."

"Don't worry about things that never happened. Just be glad Mr Wood agreed to move back when he did."

Nell hadn't reached the kitchen when the front door closed. "Is this Elenor? What's she forgotten?" She popped her head into the hall as George hung his cap on a hook. "Have you taken a carriage home again?"

"I mustn't be over that chest infection yet. It's been hard work today."

"Come and sit down, then. Do you want a cup of tea while we wait for the others?"

"If there's one going."

"Let me freshen the pot up."

Alice sighed as he took his seat. "Why won't you consider a different job? You know we're all worried about you."

"I'll be fine. I've done this sort of work for the last fifty-odd years."

"Exactly." Nell came back to the living room. "Fifty years is a long time. It would be different if you were the only breadwinner, but you're not. Even Jane's worried."

"Really?" A smile flitted across his lips. "I thought she was more bothered about that companion who follows her everywhere."

"Well, she's not. You've looked after all of us for nearly as long as we can remember. It's time we looked after you. Especially if you won't do it yourself."

Alice gazed down at her daughter as more milk dribbled from her mouth. "I want her to grow up with a granddad. It will be bad enough that she'll never know Mam."

George sighed as Nell handed him his tea. "All right, I'll think about it."

Billy and Mr Massey were the first down the following morning, and Nell poured them both a cup of tea and pushed one to Billy.

"Isn't your dad with you?"

"He was still in bed when I came down. It wouldn't surprise me if he doesn't go in today."

"It must be serious, then. Was he all right in the alehouse last night?"

He paused before taking a bite from his bread. "He was quite subdued, now I think about it."

"And irritable." Mr Massey added. "Mr Marsh said something to him, and he nearly bit his head off."

Well done, Thomas. "Billy, will you nip up and see him before you leave? Ask if he'd like me to take anything up for him."

"I'll go now while this tea cools down." He crossed paths with Alice as he headed for the stairs.

"Good morning." Nell's forehead creased. "Didn't you want to bring Mary with you?"

"She was asleep and looked so peaceful, I didn't like to disturb her."

"Bless her. We need to keep up with the milk, though."

"I know. I've only come for a cup of tea and I'll take it upstairs."

Billy bounded down the last of the stairs and rejoined them. "You can make that two cups of tea. Dad says he's very achy, so he's not going in."

"I hope it's not that infection come back. We don't want anything spreading round the house."

Billy shook his head. "He's worn out, that's all."

"I hope you're right." Nell pulled two cups and saucers towards her and added an inch of milk to each. "Let me get these poured and I'll take him one up."

George was lying on his back when Nell went in, and he turned his head to face her. "You'll need to help me sit up. My back's seized up."

She put the cup and saucer down. "You should have asked Billy. You're too heavy for me."

"I don't want him seeing me like this ... and you're not to tell him. Here, give me your arm."

He pulled himself up and waited for Nell to straighten his pillows.

"I want you to see the doctor if you're no better when you've had this."

"I'll be fine." He studied the tea she placed on his lap. "Some bread and jam wouldn't go amiss."

She tutted. "You could have told Billy. You're on the top floor, remember?"

"Sorry!"

"I should hope so." She smiled as he grinned at her. "Give me five minutes." She made her way to the first-floor landing and put her head in Alice's room. "I'm getting your dad some bread and jam. Would you like any?"

Alice shook her head but said nothing.

"What's the matter?"

"She won't take any milk. Even if I try to open her mouth with the spoon, she doesn't want it."

"Let me try." Nell pushed together the edges of her lips to open them. "How's that?"

Alice spooned a drop of milk into her open mouth, but after a second, the baby coughed, and it dribbled down her chin. "What's wrong with her?"

"Let me." Nell took Mary from her and held her on her chest. "Come on, little girl. You wake up for us." She ran a finger down her back, but the child didn't move. "Shall I send Elenor for the doctor?"

Alice took her daughter back. "Please. I don't like her being like this."

George had made his way downstairs by the time the doctor knocked on the door and he glared at Nell as Elenor showed him in.

"Is he here for me?"

Nell rolled her eyes. "No, he's not. Mary's not feeding."

The doctor gave a polite cough. "Is Mrs Wood upstairs?"

"Yes, let me show you." Nell led the way up the first flight of stairs. "Alice, the doctor's here."

Alice looked up as they went in. "Thank goodness you're here. I was beginning to think you weren't coming."

"I had a couple of patients to see before I got here. What seems to be the problem?"

"She's not taking any milk. We've been trying for over an hour."

Nell nodded. "She didn't take it properly yesterday, either."

"Let me see." The doctor lay Mary on the bed. "Her breathing's very weak. And her muscle tone." He placed two fingers on her chest. "Her pulse is almost nonexistent."

Alice had tears in her eyes. "What does that mean?"

He scratched his head. "I'm afraid there's nothing I can do for her. If it's any consolation, I'm surprised she's lasted for as long as she has. You've done your best."

"So what do we do? We can't leave her to die!"

The doctor picked Mary up and passed her to Alice. "Just hold her. It won't be long, probably minutes rather than hours. I'm sorry."

CHAPTER FIFTY-THREE

The morning was still dark when George took his seat at the breakfast table and he groaned as Nell arrived to pour him a cup of tea.

"What's the matter with you?"

"I'm feeling my age, that's what."

"It's better than the alternative." Alice scowled. "What's up with you?"

"That bed, for one. I'm sure it's getting worse. My back's sore every morning when I get up."

Billy tutted. "Do as you're told and get a different job, then. Working in those cramped conditions and bending over all day won't help."

"And earn a pittance?"

"It doesn't matter. If you work in the alehouse, you save as much as you lose in wages by getting free ale."

Mr Massey winked at him. "And you won't need an excuse to be down there every night."

Billy laughed. "He doesn't, anyway."

"All right, enough of your jokes." George helped himself

to some bread. "For your information, I spoke to the landlord last night and he may have something for me. He'll tell me later."

Nell took her seat. "I'm glad to hear it. It would be nice to see you looking cheerful for a change."

"I don't know what you mean."

She raised an eyebrow at him. "Oh, yes, you do. Now, we haven't forgotten it's your birthday, so as a treat, you can decide what you'd like for tea. Any ideas?"

"A birthday tea?" He suddenly found his smile. "Anything I like?"

"Within reason."

"All right, if you can get some mutton, how about making a Lancashire hotpot?"

Nell nodded. "I can do that. It shouldn't be too expensive. With a pie crust over the top?"

"Of course. It's only half done, otherwise."

"I'd better be quick going to the shops, then. It will need a lot of cooking."

Elenor looked up from giving Maria her breakfast. "At least we can get it in the range before we go out and it will be done when we get home."

Mr Marsh stared at Nell. "Where are you going?"

"Elenor's seeing Ruth, and Alice and I are meeting Rebecca in the park. We're all itching to get out of the house now the weather's picked up."

George's eyes registered interest. "Does Jane join you on these trips?"

"Sometimes, but I'm not expecting her today. Why?"

"You could invite her for tea if she's nothing better to do."

"I'll call round on the way to the shop, if you like, and ask her." She smirked as George shifted in his seat.

"Don't go to any trouble..."

"Very well. If we meet her, I'll ask."

Alice held Freddie's hand as they crossed the road to Sefton Park, but once they were inside, she let him run on ahead. Nell smiled as she watched him.

"It's nice that he plays on his own. Many children don't know how to do that."

"He likes it when Georgie's at school. When they're together, Georgie's always the boss."

"That's what older brothers do. I remember Uncle Tom being a terrible bully with us ... not with your mam but with the rest of us."

Alice cocked her head to one side. "James wasn't like that with me. Or the others, for that matter. I doubt Mam would have let them."

"No. She always liked things fair."

"I would have been like that with Mary." Alice wiped her eyes. "I miss her terribly."

"You wouldn't be human if you didn't."

"I know. At least it gives me some idea of what Betty's gone through over the years."

"It's not the sort of thing you want to find out. I'm just relieved she's had no problems so far with the one that's on its way."

Alice shook her head. "I wouldn't wish it on anyone."

Nell waved when Rebecca appeared on the footpath

ahead. "She must have left home early to be meeting us here."

"We're not late, are we?"

Nell took out her watch. "No."

Rebecca grinned as she reached them. "Are you wondering what time I left home?"

"We were checking we weren't late."

"You're not, but I've some news I couldn't wait to tell you."

Nell's face brightened. "That sounds exciting. What?"

Rebecca didn't pause for breath. "We're moving house!"

"Really! Where to?" Nell's grin was almost as broad as Rebecca's.

"We don't have a house yet, but we're coming back to Toxteth Park."

"That's wonderful. What's brought this on?"

"I can't be sure, but I suspect Mr Marsh has something to do with it."

"Thomas? Why?"

"Him and Hugh have been as thick as thieves lately. Hugh must have decided it would be better if we moved closer."

"It's about time, too. Will you get any say in where you move to?"

"I doubt it, but if you spot anywhere nice while you're out, mention it to Mr Marsh. I may get through to him that way."

Nell grinned. "I'll start walking the streets to see what's available. Nothing too far away."

Rebecca's grin remained fixed. "May we do that now

instead of going round the park? I'm so excited about finding somewhere. I've already started packing."

"When will you move?"

"As soon as we find a house."

Nell turned on her heel. "What are we waiting for, then?"

Nell's feet throbbed by the time they got home, but the smell of Lancashire hotpot distracted her as she hung up her coat.

"I hope they're all home early tonight. I don't want to wait too long for that. It smells lovely."

Alice put a hand to her mouth. "We didn't invite Aunty Jane."

"We didn't see her."

"I know, but Dad will be disappointed."

"He won't be..." Nell paused as the living room door opened and Elenor sidled up to her. "Aunty Jane's here. She said Uncle George invited her for tea."

"I had a feeling he would." She grinned at Alice. "He wasn't going to leave it to chance." Nell fixed her smile as she walked into the room. "Jane! I'm glad George saw you. I was going to invite you myself if you'd been in the park."

"Oh, I am relieved. I thought he'd spoken out of turn and you wouldn't have enough. It smells too nice to be turned away from."

Alice took a seat at the table with Jane. "When did you speak to him?"

"He called this morning on his way to work."

"You live in the opposite direction!"

"So I do. Maybe that was why he was in a carriage."

"Again!" Nell looked at Alice. "Didn't he go out with Billy this morning?"

"Now I think about it, he said he needed the privy and left about five minutes later."

"He can't carry on doing that..."

Jane tutted. "Leave him alone. He can take a carriage if he wants to."

"Then why keep it secret?" Nell put her hands on her hips. "I'll be having words with him."

Alice grimaced. "Not when it's his birthday tea."

"No, you're right. I hope he comes straight home and doesn't go to the alehouse..."

Jane rolled her eyes. "The poor man. You're worse than Maria."

Nell gasped. "I am not..." She paused as the front door opened and peered into the hall as Mr Marsh hung up his coat. "Are you on your own?"

"Mr Atkin said he wouldn't be long."

Nell's forehead creased. "When did you see him?"

"Five minutes ago, in the alehouse. He was with Billy and Mr Wood."

"I knew it! This tea will be ruined. I may as well take it out of the range." She headed across the living room but stopped and turned back to Mr Marsh.

"What were you doing in there?"

"Meeting Mr Grayson."

"What was he doing over here?"

"He's moving to Toxteth Park and wanted my advice on some houses."

"That was quick."

"Not really. He's been planning it for weeks."

"Then why has Rebecca only just found out? In fact, why have I, when you've known for so long?"

"It's not for me to share his news." Mr Marsh smiled at Jane. "Good evening, Mrs Read. Are you joining us for tea?"

"I am, thank you."

"Mr Atkin will be pleased. I think we can take his word that he won't be late, then..." He took his seat by the fire. "I presume you've seen Mrs Grayson this afternoon."

"We have. She's very excited about moving. We saw a nice house on Upper Warwick Street while we were out..."

"Mr Grayson's already made a decision. I expect he'll tell his wife this evening."

"Oh. Well, I hope she likes it."

"She should be delighted. Mr Atkin was in a good mood when I left him, too."

"Celebrating his birthday?"

"No. He's got his old job back at the alehouse and starts next week."

"That's wonderful." Nell smiled at Alice. "By the time you take out the money for his ale and carriages he's taken to using, he probably won't bring home any less than he is now."

CHAPTER FIFTY-FOUR

The late summer sun was sinking behind the houses as Nell and Rebecca walked home from Princes Park. Nell glanced up at the cloudless sky.

"We'd better make the most of the nice days. In another month, they'll be gone."

"It's not like you to be so down."

"I'm just saying we should enjoy the weather while it lasts. I'm hoping it will help George's chest, too. How he caught another infection in the middle of August, I don't know."

"Is he no better?"

"He's getting worse, and his cough's terrible."

"Isn't that good to clear his airways?"

"He'll be coughing his lungs out at this rate."

"Well, I hope he's better soon. Send him my best wishes and tell him I'll call next week." Rebecca stopped as they reached her front door, and stared up at the two-storey house. "I still can't believe we live here."

"You waited a long time for it."

"I did. It's a shame Hugh chose the cheapest place he could find, but I can put up with it now we're closer."

Nell smiled. "He was never going to pay more than he needed to. Will I see you on Sunday?"

"I imagine so. Hugh's likely to have arranged something with Mr Marsh. Not that he's told me what."

"Perish the thought. I've a feeling we'll see Jane, too. She called in to see George the other evening, and she's exhausted with calling at Betty's and looking after Charlie now the new baby's here. Mr Crane will be at home on Sunday, so she's having the day off."

Rebecca studied her. "Her and George seem rather friendly since Maria passed. You don't think...?"

"No. Not at all. They enjoy each other's company, but it doesn't go beyond that."

Rebecca raised an eyebrow. "I'll take your word for it."

The walk from Rebecca's took a little over ten minutes, and Alice was coming down the stairs when Nell arrived home.

"What are you doing up there?"

She sighed. "Dad's taken a turn for the worse, so I insisted he went to bed. He's exhausted with this cough and he's struggling to breathe."

"Have you called the doctor?"

"He won't let me. He said he'll get more benefit buying a bottle of brandy."

Nell tutted. "I'll have a word with him. Is everything else all right?"

"Tea's nearly ready and Elenor's outside with the

children, if that's what you mean. You can take Dad's tea up if you like. See how he is yourself?"

"I will. If I can make one journey instead of two, it will be even better."

"Give me a minute."

Once the tray was ready, Nell walked slowly up the stairs and paused outside the bedroom door to catch her breath. She knocked before she let herself in, stopping to adjust her eyes to the darkness of the room. "How are you?"

"I've felt better."

Nell put the tray on the end of the bed and pulled the drapes back from the window. "There, you can see what you're eating now. Oh..." She stopped where she was, her mouth open. "You look awful."

"Thanks."

"You know what I mean. You're burning up." She put a hand on his clammy forehead, but he knocked it away.

"I'm freezing."

"Does anything hurt?"

"Everything. Especially when I breathe."

Nell shook her head. "Then why won't you let us call the doctor? Even if you had some laudanum, it would help you sleep."

"Brandy will do that."

"You won't wake up again if you have too much and Jane said she'd call tomorrow. You want to be better by then."

George sighed. "All right. If you must."

"It's for the best. Now, try to eat something while I go and get him."

She hurried back to the living room and smiled at Alice. "He said I can fetch the doctor."

"That's a relief. Will you go now?"

"I may as well. I won't be long."

The doctor's was a short walk from the house, but when she arrived, the only person at home was the housekeeper.

"I'm afraid Dr Randall's out and I don't know when he'll be back."

Nell sighed. "Will he be able to call later?"

The woman shrugged. "He hasn't told me his plans. If you leave your details, I'll make sure he calls either later this evening or tomorrow morning."

"As soon as he can, please. My brother-in-law's very poorly."

Nell strolled home, hoping to meet the doctor, but when there was no sign of him, she quickened her pace. Mr Marsh looked up as she went in.

"I thought you'd gone for the doctor."

"I had, but he's already on a visit. He'll call later or in the morning."

Alice sighed. "It's Dad's own fault. He should have let me get him earlier."

Billy reached for a piece of bread. "Why do you bother asking? When he's this ill, you should just do it."

"It's all right for you, but I need permission. I don't want to upset him."

"He doesn't know what's good for him at the moment."

Mr Wood laughed. "I'll tell you what's wrong. He hasn't had any ale for the last four days. The alehouse will be saving a fortune."

Alice glared at her husband. "It's no laughing matter."

"I'm only trying to lighten the mood."

"It doesn't need lightening."

Nell followed Alice as she stomped to the kitchen. "Don't be cross with him. He only wants to help."

"But he doesn't realise how ill Dad is." Alice reached for her handkerchief as tears spilled from her eyes. "I've never seen him like this before. He didn't even try to eat his dinner."

Nell pulled Alice into an embrace, but she continued to sob.

"I don't want him to die. It's not two years since Mam passed, and we've already lost Mary this year."

"He's not going anywhere. He's had a bad chest before and always pulls through."

Alice nodded. "You're right, I'm being silly. I don't know why I'm so tearful."

Nell raised an eyebrow at her. "I imagine being in the family way doesn't help. It does strange things to you."

"I can't even do that any more." She squeezed her eyes tight. "When I went to bed last night..." She gasped to control her sob. "It's gone."

"Oh, Alice, I'm sorry. Why didn't you say anything?"

"How could I when Dad's so ill?"

"Because this is just as important. I'm not surprised you're tearful. Don't be so hard on yourself."

Alice inhaled deeply. "I'll try not to be."

"Come on. Let's get tea served so we can get everyone out. We'll talk then."

"Thank you. I miss Mam so much at times like this."

"Well, you've got me. I'll never replace her, but if you need to talk, I'll always be here."

. . .

Billy was downstairs early the following morning, but he didn't sit down.

"We need to find out where the doctor's got to. Dad really isn't well."

"What's up with him?"

"What's right? He doesn't know whether he's hot or cold, he can't breathe because of the pain in his chest, his heart's racing..."

"I'll go." Nell dashed to the hall but hadn't fixed her hat before there was a knock on the front door. She snatched it open.

"Dr Randall, thank goodness. I was about to come and get you." She ushered him inside. "He's on the top floor. I'll show you up. He's really not well..."

"How long's he been ill?"

"Since Thursday of last week. He didn't even go to church on Sunday, and he took to his bed yesterday." Nell led the way, not pausing for breath before she pushed open the bedroom door. "George, the doctor's here."

They were met by silence, followed by a deep cough.

"You'd better go in."

The doctor closed the door behind him, but Nell stayed on the landing, keeping an ear close to the door. She hadn't been there long when Alice joined her. "Have you heard anything of interest?"

"Nothing except a lot of coughing and groaning."

Alice closed her eyes. "I hope he can do something."

"At the very least, he'll be able to stop the pain when your dad breathes. That will be a relief and he may sleep."

"It will, but I don't like him not eating. Food's usually the last thing he gives up."

"He's tough. If anyone can pull through, he can."

They stayed with their ears to the door until the doctor pulled it open and they both jumped backwards onto the landing. He gave a loud harrumph.

"Are you ladies the only ones in the house?"

Alice nodded. "Our husbands have gone to work."

"I'd better speak to you, then. Shall we go downstairs?"

Nell and Alice stood near the fire as the doctor stayed by the door.

"It would appear that Mr Atkin has developed pneumonia. It's spread throughout his lungs, but I've done as much for him as I can."

Alice's eyes widened. "Will he get better?"

"It's difficult to say. I've applied a mustard plaster to his chest. It's a paste that will need washing off in about half an hour. I've also placed drops of chloroform on his hand for him to inhale. Don't wash that off. I've given him a dose of laudanum, too, to help him sleep. I'll call again this afternoon to check on him."

Nell's shoulders slumped. "I knew we should have called you earlier."

"If it's any consolation, it wouldn't have made much difference." He glanced at the clock. "If you'll excuse me, I need to get on. I'll let myself out."

Alice flopped into a chair as the front door closed. "I don't believe him. Dad wouldn't have got worse if he'd called yesterday."

Nell took the seat opposite. "We don't know that, and your dad didn't want him..."

"He makes me so angry sometimes..."

Elenor paused by the door as she arrived home from taking Georgie to school. "What's the matter?"

"Uncle George is very ill."

"We already knew that."

"The doctor says it's serious..."

Elenor's face dropped as she took a seat by Alice. "I'm sorry."

"So am I. I'm not ready for this. He was right as rain this time last week..."

Nell gave a faint smile. "And he might be again by this time next week. Let's not write him off yet."

"You're right." Alice pushed herself up. "We'd better get the place tidied up and start dinner before we wash off that mustard paste. We'll see how he is then."

Nell knocked on the bedroom door as Alice held a fresh pitcher of water for the bowl on the washstand.

"George, are you awake? We've come to wipe that paste off." When there was no answer, she pushed on the door, but caught her breath as the chloroform vapours stuck in her throat. "My goodness. That should clear his chest."

Alice followed her into the room and poured the water into the bowl. "I hope so." She opened the drapes as Nell leaned over George. "Are you awake?" When she got no reply, she rolled down the sheets to reveal the mustard colouring on George's chest. "Perhaps we can take it off without waking him. I'll try to be gentle."

"You should be fine if the laudanum's doing its job."

"That's a point. Do you have the cloth?" Nell pushed

back the wisps of greying ginger hair from George's forehead as Alice soaked the cloth in water. "Oh, my..."

"What's the matter?"

"That's not right." Tears stung Nell's eyes as she moved her hand close to George's nose and mouth. "He's not breathing."

"Not..." Alice pushed Nell out of the way as she shook George's shoulders. "Dad. Wake up."

His head bounced on the pillow until Nell pulled her away. "Alice, stop. He's gone."

"But he can't be. The doctor's coming back... And Aunty Jane..." Tears rolled down Alice's cheeks. "He can't..."

Nell rested a hand on her shoulder before walking to the window to re-close the drapes. *The end of an era.* "He was like a dad to me, too."

"We've so many people to tell."

"All in good time. We need to get him cleaned up first and wait for the doctor."

Alice bowed her head over the bed. "He'll be with Mam again. I pray they rest in peace."

CHAPTER FIFTY-FIVE

18 months later

The winter had been harsh, but with the daffodils flowering in the park, and her granddaughter running on ahead, Nell smiled at Mr Marsh.

"Look at her." She nodded towards Maria. "It's nice to see someone without a care in the world."

Mr Marsh scowled. "It won't last long. I'll give her until she starts school. Why have you brought her out with us? Couldn't Elenor have her?"

"I told you, I'm giving Elenor a bit of peace. She's just had a baby, and it's hard having a toddler at the same time. Babies are so much easier to settle when they're on their own."

"At least there was no scandal with this new one. I'm still not comfortable being seen with Maria."

"That's all down to you. She's nearly two and a half now, and we've moved on. You're the only one who brings it up."

"Because I don't like it, especially when we take her to church like we did this morning. We should be thankful Edith didn't let us down."

Nell sighed. "That's not necessarily a good thing. She should have produced by now. If she's not careful, she'll end up with the shame of being childless. I don't know which is worse."

"I do." Mr Marsh glared at her, but Nell rolled her eyes.

"As a woman, there is no greater punishment from God than not having a child. Try seeing it from our point of view for a change."

Nell bent down to Maria as the child ran back to them. "There's a good girl. Shall we go and see the ducks?"

Maria nodded. "Yes." She toddled off, stopping occasionally to check Nell was following.

"It's Rebecca I feel sorry for. Isobel's twenty-three and isn't showing any interest in men, let alone having a family."

"That's no age."

"Maybe not, but Rebecca's the only one of us without a grandchild, yet she was the one who wanted one the most. I suppose her time will come."

"Could she step into Mrs Atkin's shoes? She has seven grandchildren now, unless Vernon's wife has had another one I've missed."

Nell groaned. "She hasn't, and no, she couldn't. Being a granny's a very personal thing."

"I'm sure Mrs Read would share some of hers. How many does she have?"

"Only four, but it could be another two this year."

"Two?"

Nell tutted. "Don't you ever listen? Betty's expecting again and Matthew's wife is due to have their first in the next few weeks."

"There you go, then. Enough to share with Mrs Grayson."

Nell shook her head as they arrived at the lake. *Ignore him.* "There are not many people out today. It's still too cold."

"Bracing, the word is, and it's good for the lungs. Shall we sit down?"

"I need to help Maria with the bread first. She can't do it herself yet."

Mr Marsh's face dropped.

"I'll sit with you when we're finished." *He's like a child.*

"I'll wait here for you."

It didn't take Maria long to throw her bread into the water, and Nell shivered as she returned to the seat.

"She's happy watching them for now. We shouldn't stay for too long, though."

Mr Marsh nodded. "I'll be quick then. I wanted to ask you what you thought of the conversation we had last night about moving house?"

"I don't know why we need to. We're managing for money where we are and it's nice having more space."

"If Mr Massey wants to move Elenor and the children out, it will change things."

Nell's shoulders slumped. "I'm hoping to change his mind. They've no *need* to go, and you and him get on well enough now."

"I wouldn't say that, but I'll admit it's tolerable."

Nell looked up at him. "What do you think?"

"That it would be nice if we had a house of our own. We've been married nearly ten years and yet we've never lived alone."

"We have our own room, and I like having Alice and Elenor for company when you're at work."

"But Elenor wouldn't be there."

"Alice would. Besides, if we move, we'll have Leah with us, so we wouldn't be alone."

"She'll be married soon enough..."

Nell stared across the lake. *He's right.* "She's still only nineteen, so I hope she'll be with us for another few years."

"She's certainly lasted longer than Elenor."

"What's that supposed to mean? Elenor's still with us."

"She may be in the house, but she'd had a child and had been married for two years by the time she was Leah's age." He paused as they watched Maria chasing the ducks that climbed from the water. "Even if Leah comes with us, we'd be on our own more than we are now."

"But I'd be on my own all day and so would Alice. Men don't understand how lonely it gets at home."

"So, you don't like the idea?"

"Not really." She squeezed his hand. "Would it be so bad if we stayed where we are with Alice's family and Billy?"

"That would mean only three of us would be paying the rent for a four-bedroomed house. If you want my opinion, it's too extravagant."

"Couldn't we try it, though?"

He let out a deep sigh. "I'll think about it."

. . .

Elenor was feeding her baby son, Harold, when they arrived home, and Mr Marsh quickly excused himself and disappeared into the backyard.

Nell grinned as he left. "He'll never get used to seeing you do that, even though there's nothing to see."

"I should do it more often if it gets him out of the way." Elenor moved the baby onto her shoulder. "You were home sooner than I expected."

"It's cold out there, so we didn't sit for long."

"My saw the ducks." Maria grinned at her mother.

"Did they like the bread?"

"Yes. I had some, too."

Elenor looked at Nell. "It was stale."

"It was only a piece. I stopped her when I noticed." Nell took Harold from Elenor as she fastened the front of her dress and stood up.

"Alice put the kettle on before she went outside. I don't know where she's got to.

"I'll make a pot of tea, then. Is Leah still out?"

"She is. She was going to Sefton Park with her friends."

Nell shuddered. "She'll be cold when she comes in. I'd better get the fire stoked up. Are the others at the alehouse?"

"What do you think? I told Will to be home for half past four. Hopefully, he was listening."

Nell peered into the kitchen as the back door opened and Alice joined them. "There you are."

"Sorry I took so long. Uncle Thomas was asking what I thought of us all moving house."

Nell sighed. "I was going to ask the same thing." She looked at Elenor. "Why does Mr Massey want to move all of a sudden?"

"He's been talking about it for months. Ever since he knew I was expecting Harold. He said that he earns a decent wage and so we should have our own house."

"Did you tell him it's nice to have help with the children?"

"I didn't want to upset him. He's so excited and we won't go far."

"It gets lonely in the house by yourself all day."

"I could still come here, couldn't I?"

"If we're still here. Uncle Thomas thinks we should have our own house, too. He says it would be extravagant to stay here."

"Where would you go?"

Nell shrugged. "We didn't get that far, but it would be local."

Alice took a seat. "We couldn't leave Billy on his own."

Nell's eyes narrowed. "He'd stay with you, wouldn't he?"

"I'd hope so, but it would be up to Harry. If everyone else is getting their own houses…"

Nell groaned. "We all need to tell them we'd rather stay as we are. It's not as if they're here that much. We're the ones who'll be on our own if we move."

"We could try." Alice paused as the front door opened. "I hope this isn't them. I'd better get the tea ready."

"And I need to get him in his cot." Elenor took Harold from Nell. "I won't be long." She hurried to the hall but stopped before she reached the stairs. "Oh, it's you."

"Who did you think it was?" Leah's voice rang around the living room.

"I thought it might be Will. I'm just taking Harold upstairs."

Nell smiled as Leah joined her. "We're expecting everyone home anytime."

"I'm hoping it's too early yet, because I want a word with you."

"That sounds serious."

"It might be." Leah perched on the edge of a chair and took a deep breath. "My friend Miss Clark introduced me to a young man this afternoon. He's a friend of one of her brothers, so I've already seen him a few times, but her brother told Miss Clark that he likes me."

Nell's stomach flipped. *Here we go again.* "Has he asked you to walk out with him?"

"He has, but I wanted to see what you said first. After everything that happened with Elenor, I don't want to cause trouble for you and Uncle Thomas."

"I'm pleased to hear it."

Leah tried to smile. "I wondered if you'd be happy for Miss Clark to chaperone us."

"How can I be when we've never met? I don't know if I can trust her. Ruth Pearse wasn't exactly reliable with Elenor."

"She's better than her."

"I should hope so. Have you made any arrangements with this gentleman? What's his name?"

"Mr Breton, and we didn't make any firm arrangements other than I'd see him and tell him my answer next Sunday."

"Perhaps I should come and meet him then, and Miss Clark."

Leah grimaced. "You usually take a walk with Uncle Thomas on Sundays, and I'd rather you didn't bring him with you for that first meeting."

"I don't know what else to suggest, then. I expect Mr Breton will be at work all week, and it's too dark to go out at night."

Leah sighed. "Please, will you trust me to meet him with my friends on Sunday, then? They won't leave me, and I promise I won't do anything I shouldn't. If I find I like him, I'll invite him for tea."

Nell's heart raced. *She'll be fine. She saw the trouble Elenor caused.* "Very well. Don't mention it to Uncle Thomas, though. Not yet. I'll tell him when the time's right."

CHAPTER FIFTY-SIX

Nell was in the kitchen when Leah arrived home from her now regular Sunday outing with Mr Breton.

"How was the walk?"

"Wonderful." Her eyes sparkled. "He's such a gentleman and says he's looking forward to meeting you."

"I'd like to meet him too, but I don't know when we'll find a suitable time. It's a problem with you working every day."

"Even if I didn't work, he does, so it wouldn't help anything."

Nell sighed. "I know you've only been seeing him for a few weeks, but do you ever meet him after work to walk home?"

"I wouldn't dare, in case Uncle Thomas saw us. Why?"

Nell studied her. "I've not walked up to Betty's recently, but I'm hoping to go soon. If I came to the tea room on my way home, would Mr Breton be able to meet us there?"

"I don't see why not. Shall I ask him next Sunday?"

"Yes, do that and I'll speak to Aunty Jane about the best

day to visit Betty. I'll make sure Uncle Thomas isn't going to be around, too."

Mr Massey was the first home from the alehouse and he had a broad grin across his face when Maria toddled towards him. Elenor watched as he picked his daughter up and gave her a hug.

"You're happy."

"I've found the perfect house!"

Nell turned her gasp into a cough. "I'm sorry. I had something in my throat. Where is it?"

"Grinshill Street, just off High Park Street."

Elenor tried to smile. "That's near where Aunty Rebecca lives. And it's close to Princes Park. May I see it?"

"You can do more than that. You can start packing your bags. It's ours."

Elenor's eyes widened. "Already?"

"When you see something you want, you don't hang around." He winked at Elenor causing her to blush, but Nell's brow furrowed.

"Have you seen it?"

"I have. A bloke in the alehouse told me about it so we nipped out this afternoon."

Elenor looked at Nell. "What will you do with this house if we move out?"

She shrugged. "Wait to see what Uncle Thomas, Mr Wood and Billy have to say. They'll be the ones who need to find the extra money."

Mr Massey gave Nell a crooked smile. "I'm sorry, Mrs Marsh, but I thought you'd be pleased I want to support my family. I'm sure Mr Marsh will be glad to see the back of us."

"Maybe he will, but I'll miss you all. I don't want to move the rest of us, either."

"You could stay here and take in a lodger or two."

Nell grimaced. "My husband won't be keen on that idea."

Mr Massey grinned. "He may surprise you."

Surprise me. You'd have to pick me up off the floor. "Somehow, I doubt it. Are you staying here until teatime?"

"I am. We need to start collecting up our personal property. I've arranged a carriage for Friday evening."

"As soon as that?"

"There's no point waiting. Now–" he took Harold from Elenor and passed him to Nell "–would you mind watching him while we sort ourselves out?"

Nell held her grandson on her shoulder as they disappeared up the stairs, then wandered to the kitchen.

"Did you hear that?"

Alice nodded. "I did, but there didn't seem any point interrupting."

"No." Nell gazed back into the living room. "I expect we'll all be packing up soon."

"Where will we go, though? A lot of houses won't be big enough for all of us."

"We may not be able to move together."

Alice sighed. "Mam would have hated it."

"I'm not so keen on the idea myself. Goodness knows what Uncle Thomas will say."

"You won't have long to wait."

Nell put Harold into his crib and was setting the table when Mr Marsh arrived home and took his seat by the fire.

"Have you had a good afternoon?"

"Pleasant enough. What about you? How was Mrs Grayson?"

"She's fine. We were saying that we need to get out more now the weather's improving, so I thought I'd walk up to Betty's one day next week."

"Have you seen Mrs Robertson lately?"

"I saw her last week, but she's going to South Africa a week on Tuesday, so she won't be here for a couple of months. Violet's a young woman now and they enjoy travelling together. What a way for her to meet an eligible bachelor..."

"It's good for them, less than ideal for you." He studied her. "Are you busy?"

"What? Now?"

"Can you sit with me?"

"Erm, yes, I suppose so. The tea's ready." Nell's eyebrows drew together as she took a seat. "What is it?"

"All this talk of moving house has had me thinking. I miss going to sea, and I miss you when I go on my own, but–" his gaze met hers "–how would you like to go to sea together?"

"To work?"

"Why not? The girls don't need you any more, so we could get positions on the same ship."

Go away again...

"What do you think?"

"I-I don't know. It hadn't even crossed my mind."

"Give it some thought, then. We could travel the world.

417

Not quite in the way the Robertsons do, but the next best thing."

"We couldn't go far." Her heart raced. "The girls may have grown up, but they still need me. Especially Elenor now she has the children."

"You can't let them rule your life."

"And they don't, but ... I-I need to be here in case Leah meets a young man. We don't want any more ... *accidents*."

"She's much more sensible than Elenor ever was, and she'd have Mrs Wood."

"Even so..."

"Putting that aside, I've been looking into it, and not all ships require the segregation of married couples. I'm sure we could get a post on one of those that doesn't." A twinkle appeared in his eyes. "It would be good for us."

"I'll think about it." Nell gave a sigh of relief when the front door opened and Billy and Mr Wood joined them.

"Is that all of you?"

Billy scanned the room. "Is Will not home?"

"He's upstairs with Elenor."

He grinned at Mr Wood. "He's keen."

"That's enough." Nell shot him a glance. "He has some news for us once we're at the table. Take your seats and I'll tell them you're here."

Nell wondered if Elenor had been crying when she came back downstairs, but Mr Massey still wore his broad smile as Billy leaned forward across the table.

"What's this news, then?"

"I've found us a house." He took Elenor's hand. "We move out on Friday."

"Friday!" There was a gasp around the table and Billy

looked to Mr Marsh before turning back to Mr Massey. "Why the rush?"

"Why wait? The house was available, so I paid a week's rent from Friday."

"And what about us? How are we supposed to find the extra money at such short notice?"

"It needn't be for long. You can always find a boarder or two. You'd get at least four into our room if you changed the beds."

Mr Marsh got to his feet. "I've no intention of letting lodgers into my house when my wife is here on her own. Not to mention Leah. She's at a very vulnerable age."

"Then don't. It was only a suggestion for if you're struggling."

"You've done this on purpose, to make life difficult." Mr Marsh leaned over the table, but Nell pulled him back.

"Let's not argue. It's done now. We can decide what to do later."

Billy finished his bread. "I'd take in a few boarders."

Mr Marsh huffed. "What about your sister? Would you be happy for her to be on her own with them?"

"We could insist on married couples only. That would solve the problem."

"No!" The room fell silent as Mr Marsh glanced at everyone around the table until his eyes settled on Nell. "Are you going to serve this tea? I need to go out."

"Y-yes, of course." She hesitated once she'd stood up. "May we talk about this later when we've had time to think?"

Mr Marsh sat down. "There's nothing to think about. For once, I actually agree with Mr Massey. It's time we all had our own houses instead of living in each other's pockets. I'll look for something for you, me and Leah."

"What about us?" Billy gaped at Mr Wood.

"We'll have to find somewhere smaller, I suppose."

"We could take some lodgers if it's just us. It would earn us a few extra shillings."

Alice stared at her brother. "And who's going to do all the extra work?"

Billy's forehead creased. "You are. Why?"

"Don't you think I'll have enough to do if I'm on my own...?"

"Stop!" Mr Marsh picked up his knife and fork as Nell disappeared into the kitchen. "Sort yourselves out later, but I'll start looking for somewhere immediately after tea."

CHAPTER FIFTY-SEVEN

Leah was about to turn the sign on the door to closed, when Nell arrived at the tea room, and she stepped back to let her in.

"I've been looking out for you."

"I'm sorry I'm late. Charlie fell over in the street, so I sat with the baby while Betty dealt with him."

"Was he all right?"

"Eventually, but he banged his head, so he was screaming, as you can imagine."

"He's always been a handful. I'd hate to have a child like that."

"I'm afraid you don't get to choose. Poor Betty's worn out with him, especially now she's in the family way again."

Leah creased her cheek as she locked the door. "You'd think she had enough children. Why doesn't she stop?"

If only it were that simple.

Leah shuddered. "I won't be having that many."

"Things may be different when the time comes. All I ask is that you wait until you're married."

"I'll wait years if I can."

Nell smirked. "It's to be hoped it's not serious with Mr Breton, then. I take it he hasn't arrived."

"No. He shouldn't be long, though." She peered through the door again. "Let me give the manageress the keys, and we can go out the back door to wait for him."

They hadn't been outside for more than a minute when Leah bounced on her toes. "He's here." She turned to Nell. "I hope you like him."

"He can't be all bad if he likes you."

Mr Breton waved to them as he approached. "You must be Mrs Marsh."

Nell nodded. "Mr Breton. It's nice to meet you."

"Likewise." He winked at Leah as she gazed up at him, her large brown eyes sparkling. "And you're a sight for sore eyes. Have you had a busy day?"

"It's gone slowly, waiting for you."

Nell coughed to interrupt. "Shall we start walking? I don't want to arouse any suspicions at home by being late." She walked between them as they headed through town. "What is it you do for a living, Mr Breton?"

"I'm a gas fitter, like my dad and two of my brothers."

"You must be busy, then."

"I am. We're fitting out a row of new shops at the moment."

"All of you?"

"My younger brother's still working his apprenticeship, but yes, we're all together."

"How nice. As long as you get along with each other."

"Oh, we do. Mam sees to that. Arguments aren't allowed."

"That sounds like a good idea. Leah said you're a friend of one of Miss Clark's brothers."

"I am, we were at school together and usually go to the park on a Sunday. That was when I saw Miss Riley." He peered around Nell to grin at Leah. "We're always with our own groups of friends, though."

"So I believe. I presume Leah's told you she's only nineteen? You don't look much older."

"We worked out there's six months between us. I'll be twenty in October."

"That's still young to be walking out together. You know I'll expect you to have a chaperone while you're together?"

"I wouldn't expect anything less. Nor would my mam. That's why we always stay with our friends when we see each other."

Nell turned to Leah. "Have you met Mrs Breton?"

'Not yet, but I will soon."

Mr Breton nodded. "She keeps asking when you're coming for tea."

"I know, but I need to be able to explain to Uncle Thomas why I'm not at our house for tea, and I'm not ready to tell him yet."

"Will you tell him now your mam knows?"

Nell grimaced. "I wouldn't just yet. Get to know each other better first, to make sure you're ready."

Mr Breton frowned. "Is it something I've done?"

"You've asked Leah to walk out with you. He's very protective."

"Ah. I'll try to be on my best behaviour then. I don't want him to dislike me before he gets to know me."

Mr Breton walked them down Windsor Street, but Nell

stopped when they reached the corner with Upper Hill Street.

"This will be far enough for now." She smiled at Mr Breton. "I'd rather you weren't around when my husband arrives home."

"I quite understand." He gazed at Leah. "May I see you again on Sunday?"

She glanced at Nell, who nodded. "Yes. The same time and place as usual?"

He grinned. "I'll look forward to it. Well, it was good to meet you, Mrs Marsh."

"And you." Nell stood with Leah on the corner as he continued on his way.

"Does he live locally?"

Leah didn't take her eyes off him. "I don't know exactly, but somewhere further down Windsor Street."

"He seems like a nice young man."

Leah beamed at her as she took Nell's arm. "I'm so glad you think so. I've been worried about you meeting him all day."

"You really like him, don't you?"

Leah blushed. "I remember you told me once that you know you're in love if your heart rate quickens or skips a beat when you see someone. That's how I feel."

"Isn't it a little soon to be talking about love? He's the first man to pay you any attention, and that can have a similar effect. I suggest you get to know each other better before you get too serious about him."

"I will. I just can't stop thinking about him. I hope he feels the same about me."

. . .

Nell sighed as she hung up her cloak and walked into the living room with Leah close behind.

"What's the matter?"

"I hate the house being empty."

"Me too. I miss Maria running for a hug when I come home."

"This is the worst time to come home, too, when Alice has gone to pick Georgie up from school. I need to aim to be in before half past four so her and Freddie are at home."

"It won't be much longer before he starts school, too."

"Don't say that." Nell went into the kitchen and put the kettle on the range as Leah took a seat by the fire.

"I wonder if Elenor feels the same. Did you go round this morning?"

"No, I've not been since yesterday. She seems settled enough, and she has the children to keep her busy."

"I never thought I'd miss her as much as I do. We were never close when she lived here."

"You probably miss the children, too. It's only going to be worse if we move out of here and we don't even have Georgie and Freddie."

Leah sighed as Nell joined her in the living room. "Does Uncle Thomas still want to move house?"

"Who knows? His latest idea is that he wants us both to go back to stewarding so we can travel together."

Leah gasped. "You can't do that! What about me?"

"We wouldn't leave you on your own. We'd make sure Alice or Elenor would have you ... not that I'm keen on the idea."

Leah's eyes welled up. "I don't want you to go..."

"Then I'll tell him. He thinks you and Elenor don't need me any more..."

"Well, he's wrong. You've seen how Alice has been since Aunty Maria passed. I don't want to be like that, even though you'd still be alive."

"I don't want to leave you either, but once I tell him, he's bound to start looking for a new house more seriously."

"So we could be moving out of here quite soon...?" She stopped as the front door opened and Georgie and Freddie burst into the room. She gave Georgie a hug. "Go and wash your hands, then you can have some bread."

Freddie wiped his down the front of his jumper. "Mine are clean."

"They still need washing."

Alice smiled as they charged up the stairs. "I'm sorry I'm late, I got talking. Did you read the letter from James?"

Nell turned to the fireplace. "No, I missed it. What does he have to say?"

"Much the same as usual, to be honest. Reports on the weather and how he's enjoying himself."

"No hint that he might come home?"

"He mentions it but doesn't say when."

Nell scanned the two-page letter. "They're getting shorter too, as if he's nothing to say any more. I thought he'd visit once your dad passed, but I was clearly wrong."

"Why don't we ask him to visit? We've left it to him to decide for long enough, but it clearly isn't working. There've been a lot of changes since he was last here, too. We should write him a full report of what's happening and ask when we'll see him again."

426

Nell nodded. "Perhaps he thinks we don't want to see him because we've not mentioned it. Let's get this tea out of the way and once the others go to the alehouse, we can write a letter between us."

CHAPTER FIFTY-EIGHT

Nell stood with Alice and Leah in the centre of the living room as Mr Marsh carried the last of the boxes to the waiting carriage. She wiped a tear from her eye.

"This really is the end of an era. Last time we moved, we were all excited about getting a bigger house and being together, but this is different."

"We're leaving Mam and Dad's memories here, too." Alice wiped her own eyes as Nell put a hand on her shoulder.

"Don't start me off again. At least we won't be far from each other. I'll be round for a cup of tea every afternoon after you've dropped Georgie at school."

Alice sniffed. "I'll invite Elenor, too. We won't let something like this keep us apart."

Mr Marsh interrupted as he strode back into the room. "Are you coming? It will be dark soon."

"I am, but it's a big moment for us."

"It is for me, too." He puffed out his chest. "I'll be head of the house for the first time."

"So you've said." There was weariness in Nell's voice as she bent down to kiss Georgie and Freddie. "I'll see you both soon." She straightened up and flung her arms around Alice's neck. "I'll see you round tomorrow."

The carriage ride to their new house took less than two minutes, but it felt as if she'd stepped back in time when she climbed onto the footpath. *It's smaller than Merlin Street. Is this Mr Grayson's doing...?*

Leah seemed not to notice and linked Nell's arm. "There shouldn't be much cleaning to do."

"You always manage to find the positive. Shall we go in? We've got the fires to light and beds to make before we do anything else."

"We need to inspect the place first and see what we've got."

That won't take long. Nell stepped into the hall and pushed open the door to the small front room. Cold air met her, causing her to shudder. "I don't know when the fire was last on in here. Look at the mould down there." She pointed to the wall that ran beneath the window and into the corners. "It's black. We'll need to give it a good airing tomorrow."

"The furniture's decent, though. I hope the chairs in the living room are comfortable." Leah led the way but sighed as she studied the hearth. "There are only two armchairs."

"We'll manage. Uncle Thomas goes out most evenings. I'm more worried about sitting here on my own when you're both at work."

"You'll have plenty of visitors."

"I hope so."

Mr Marsh arrived with a box of items for the pantry. "Shall I put this straight in the kitchen?"

"Please. We could do with the bed linen and towels next, so we can get the beds made."

"They'll all be here in the next ten minutes. I'm meeting Mr Grayson in our new local in half an hour, so I don't want to dally."

It's all right for some. You tell us we're moving and we do all the work... She sighed. "Let's see what upstairs is like."

Leah went first but stopped on the landing, staring between the doors. "Only two bedrooms?"

"Uncle Thomas didn't want to risk having any visitors or lodgers."

"I don't know why he's so worried. Half the people I know have a lodger."

"It's how he is." Nell went into the front bedroom. "At least this is a decent size. Only one window, though."

"It's enough. It will keep the draught down in the winter."

Why can't I be as cheerful? "I hope your room's nice." Nell wandered to the back room. "It's a good size. You should be all right in here."

"It will be nicer when my quilt's on the bed."

"Let's get the fires made up and then we'll come and do it."

Mr Marsh was ready to leave by the time Nell stood up from lighting the fire in the living room. "We won't need that on for much longer. It's almost summer."

"We need to take the chill off the place."

He leaned forward to kiss her forehead. "It will soon feel like home. I'll see you later."

She waited for the front door to close before she joined Leah upstairs. She'd already made her bed and some of her personal effects were dotted around the room.

"That's better."

"It is. I might give it a wash down on Sunday, but it will have to do for now."

"You can come and help me with my room, then." They started by turning the mattress, and once the bottom sheet was on the bed, Nell broke the silence.

"It will be further for you to walk home from work. Does Mr Breton ever walk with you?"

"Sometimes, but only when his dad's there to chaperone us."

Nell smiled. "He really is considerate. Now you've met his mam and dad, I wonder if it's time we invited him for tea so he can meet Uncle Thomas."

Leah paused as she smoothed down the sheet. "Do you think that's a good idea?"

Nell shrugged. "It's as good a time as any. Uncle Thomas is in a good mood about being head of the house and would probably be delighted to show off his achievement to someone."

"Wasn't he disappointed when you said you didn't want to go to sea?"

"He was, but he's over it now. Having the house helps."

Leah took a deep breath. "All right then. When would you suggest?"

"One Sunday, after you've been for your walk. We usually go out too, which always improves his mood."

"When do you think? A week on Sunday?"

"Why not? That way, we can be less secretive."

"As long as he likes him."

The following afternoon, Nell walked round to Alice's new house on Dombey Street and studied the façade. *She has the extra bedroom window and the bay downstairs. Why couldn't we have one like this?* She knocked on the door and let herself in, stopping when Freddie ran towards her, clapping his hands.

"Aunty Nell."

"I told you I'd see you. Is Mammy in the kitchen?"

He pointed. "In there."

Alice was cleaning the table as Nell's eyes swept around the room.

"It's bigger than ours. I thought it would be."

"We have two wages coming in."

"I'm sure Uncle Thomas could have afforded something like this if he'd wanted to. Our house is so small."

Alice straightened up. "Are you all sorted out?"

"I've unpacked the boxes, if that's what you mean. I'm sure I could have cleaned it better, but I hate it."

"You'll get used to it. Any house around here would be small compared to Upper Hill Street. Let me put the kettle on and I'll show you around."

As soon as Alice returned, Freddie clambered up the stairs. "This is my room." He bounded into the front bedroom. "And my bed." He pointed to a double bed under the window. "I sleep by the wall and Georgie is on this side to stop me falling out."

"That's good of him. I hope *he* doesn't fall out."

Freddie giggled. "He won't. He's eight now."

Nell studied the larger bed on the opposite wall. "You've plenty of room."

"We have." Alice walked into the smaller bedroom next door. "This is Billy's room."

Nell's forehead creased. "Why's he chosen the smallest room in the house?"

Alice laughed. "He's more than happy to have a room to himself after all these years. He doesn't want to share any more and wasn't taking any chances. Besides, he wants to rent out the bigger room." She walked to the back bedroom. "This is the one that's empty."

Nell sighed. "This would have been big enough for us."

"I thought that. I'm going to invite Edith to stay before we rent it out. Whether she'll come is another matter."

"It would be nice if she did, but I know Mr Lacy always finds a reason for her not to visit. It seems like years since we last saw her."

"I was going to write as soon as I had the house sorted out. Why don't you write too, so she knows we've not forgotten about her?"

"I will, although the way I feel about the house on Dorrit Street, I'll be asking if I can go and stay with her."

CHAPTER FIFTY-NINE

The sun had been pleasant while Nell strolled around the park with Mr Marsh, but she shivered as they approached the house.

"You will be nice to Mr Breton, won't you?"

"It depends on what I think of him."

"Leah's very taken with him, and that's the most important thing."

"I'm afraid I disagree. She's far too young to know what's good for her. She shouldn't be interested in young men, and I won't have you encouraging her."

"I'd rather her talk to me about it than go behind my back. She asked if she could walk out with him, and they always have a chaperone when they're together. It's more than Elenor did."

"The less said about her, the better, but it doesn't make what Leah's doing acceptable."

"Please, have a heart. Just because you went to sea at that age, doesn't mean it's the right thing for everyone."

"I'm not saying it is, but this suitor must be right for her."

"That should be her decision, not yours."

"You should be more concerned about your daughter's future than worrying about how she feels."

Nell sighed as Mr Marsh held the door open for her. *I hope Mr Breton's on his best behaviour.* "They'll be here shortly. At least the tea's ready." *I'll lay it out now, and put the kettle on, so I don't need to leave them on their own for any longer than I need to.*

Nell had just placed a plate of sandwiches on the table when the front door opened. "They're here." She stood up straight, her heart pounding. "Aren't you going to stand up...? Oh, Mr Breton, how nice to see you." She coughed to clear the squeak in her voice. "This is my husband. Mr Marsh."

Mr Breton extended his hand as Mr Marsh stood up. "It's nice to meet you, sir."

Mr Marsh ignored it and nodded to the chair opposite. "Take a seat. And you." He stared at Leah.

"Y-yes..." She grabbed a chair from the table and positioned it next to Mr Breton's. Nell pulled up her own chair.

"Did you go to Sefton Park?"

Leah let Mr Breton answer. "Yes. It was busy, too. The sunshine must have brought everyone out."

Nell smiled. "It was in Princes Park, too."

"Were you with your friends?" Mr Marsh's eyes narrowed as he stared at Mr Breton.

"Yes, sir. At all times. I heard about the incident with your other daughter, and we're keen not to repeat it."

Mr Marsh glared at Leah. "You told a stranger something as personal and private as that?"

435

Nell interrupted. "He's hardly a stranger, not to Leah, and it's as well to be cautious..."

"That sort of information is not for sharing." He returned his gaze to Mr Breton. "If word gets out..."

Mr Breton held up his hands. "You can trust me to keep it to myself, sir. I hope you'll believe me."

"How can I when I've never met you before? If I hear any whispers..."

"Please, Uncle Thomas, don't be angry. I only told him because I want to do what's right."

There was a pause as Mr Marsh eyed them both, his eyes settling on Mr Breton. "Very well. What is it you do for a living?"

"I'm a gas fitter."

"You've finished your apprenticeship?"

"Yes, sir. Earlier this year. I work with my dad now. We're doing some new shops in Liverpool."

"A good steady income, then?"

"I can't complain."

Nell heard the kettle boiling. "This tea will be ready as soon as I pour the water into the teapot. Would you like to take your seats at the table?" She indicated for Leah to stay with the men as she disappeared into the kitchen. *I wish Thomas would relax. Mr Breton's trying his best.*

Nell fixed a smile on her face as she carried the teapot to the table, and she offered Mr Breton a sandwich as the conversation switched to his family.

"I have four brothers and three sisters. The girls are all older than the boys and I'm the second oldest boy."

Leah gasped. "Your mam must have been busy. Even my cousin Betty doesn't have that many."

Mr Breton shrugged. "She always managed. It probably helped that by the time my younger brothers were born, the girls were old enough to help. Dad was the one who worked all hours to keep a roof over our heads."

Nell nodded. "I'm sure he did. It's hard when you've a big family and there's only one breadwinner. My brother was the same with his family..."

Mr Marsh cut across her as he helped himself to another sandwich. "Where is it you live? I imagine it must be a bit of a squeeze."

"Oh, it is. We're in a house like this on Sussex Street. Do you know it?"

Nell thought her heart had stopped. *Sussex Street. He can't be.*

Mr Marsh cocked his head to one side. "Remind me where it is."

"Further up Windsor Street, on the other side of Upper Warwick Street."

The significance suddenly registered. "The Catholic area?"

"It's not all Catholic, but that's how outsiders describe it."

Nell held her breath as Mr Marsh formed his next question.

"Are you one of them?"

Mr Breton stammered as Mr Marsh glowered at him. "A-actually, yes..."

The colour that drained from Leah's face seemed to find its way to Mr Marsh's as he turned scarlet. "And you dare to come and sit at *my* table and eat my food?" He was on his feet, pointing to the door. "Get out. Now."

Mr Breton stood up. "I-I didn't mean to upset you." He made to leave, but Leah grabbed his arm.

"No. Don't go."

Mr Marsh flashed a hand across her face. "Don't touch him."

Mr Breton put an arm around her as she rubbed her cheek, but Mr Marsh pulled him away.

"I'm the head of this house and I said out."

"No." Leah's eyes were wild. "He's not going without me..."

"You'll stay where you are..."

Mr Breton reached out a hand to her. "Let me go now and I'll see you soon..."

"You'll do no such thing. I don't want you seeing each other again. Do you understand?"

"You can't stop us." Leah scrambled to get close to Mr Breton, but Mr Marsh dragged him away.

"While you live under this roof, you'll do as I say. Now..." He pushed Mr Breton into the hall before following him. "Out!"

"No..." Leah tried to follow them, but Mr Marsh locked the front door and pushed her back to the table where Nell stood open-mouthed.

"I don't believe what I've just seen."

"She had no right bringing a Catholic into this house."

"She lives here."

"And I'm the head of this house, so she does as I say."

Nell stared at him as he retook his seat at the table. "You really think that's what being the head of the house is all about? I've never felt so ashamed in my life."

"That explains a lot. You've had far worse things to be ashamed of. I'm only protecting her."

"It's *you* she needs protecting from."

Tears rolled down Leah's cheeks as she huddled behind Nell. "Mr Breton wouldn't hurt me. Not like you, you brute. He loves me..."

"Love! You're nineteen years old. You can't possibly know what love is. Now get up to your room."

"I'm going." She snatched at the door and fled upstairs, before slamming her bedroom door.

Nell pinched the bridge of her nose before collecting up the dirty dishes. "I'll get these washed." Tears stung her eyes as she leaned against the sink. *Of all the things. I never even thought to check...*

"This teapot will need freshening up." Mr Marsh spoke as if it was a routine afternoon.

"Let me reboil the kettle." Nell took a deep breath. "Are you going out tonight?" *Please say yes.*

"How can I? I won't have that fellow coming back, and I can't trust you not to let him in."

"There's no chance of that after the way you behaved, and I don't blame him."

"Well, I'm not having Leah going out looking for him, either."

She stepped back into the living room. "What will you do? Keep her locked in the house for the rest of her life?"

"Don't be silly. She'll have calmed down by tomorrow and we can talk some sense into her."

"*She'll* have calmed down! You're the one who lost his temper."

"What do you expect? It's quite unforgivable for Protestants to marry Catholics."

"They're only walking out together. There's been no talk of marriage."

"And we need to keep it that way. You can't let these things run unchecked."

"If you hadn't overreacted, we could have talked about it sensibly. Now, the only thing she'll want to do is to see him again. Haven't you learned anything about jumping to conclusions?" She pulled open the door.

"Where are you going?"

"To see Leah."

"What about the tea?"

She glared at him. *You can do it yourself.* "I'm going upstairs first." Her heart pounded as she knocked on Leah's door. *I hope she doesn't blame me.* "May I come in?" When she got no response, she pushed on the door and found Leah lying on her bed, her face buried in her pillow.

She sat on the edge of the bed and stroked Leah's hair. "I'm sorry for what happened."

"He can't stop me from seeing him."

"While you live here..."

"Then I won't stay. Alice would let me move in with her. Or Elenor. She knows how horrible he is."

"You'd leave?"

"What else can I do? I won't stop seeing him. I love him."

"You need to think about it, though. You'll make life difficult for yourself if you marry a Catholic. Did you know about it before we had tea?"

"I told him not to mention it, but he's too honest."

"We'd have found out sooner or later."

Leah rolled over to look at her. "Why does it matter? He's still a kind, considerate man."

"Perhaps you should talk to Aunty Jane. She spent years in Ireland because she married a Catholic. She's told me it wasn't easy, and Aunty Maria never really forgave her."

"It's stupid…"

"Maybe it is, but if you ever have children together, it will cause no end of arguments."

"I don't care about that."

"Well, you should." Nell rubbed her back before she stood up. "I need to go downstairs, but we'll talk about this tomorrow. And please trust me. I only want what's best for you."

CHAPTER SIXTY

Nell swept the last of the ashes from the hearth and tipped them into her bucket before she carried them to the ash pit in the yard. *That will do. If he doesn't like it, he can do it himself.* She took off her apron and threw it over the back of a chair. *It can stay there. Nobody's here to notice.*

The sun was pleasant as she walked around to Alice's house, and she gave a brief knock before she let herself in. "It's only me."

Alice met her in the hallway. "You're early. I've only just got home from school."

"I'm fed up of being in that house on my own. I wish I could move in here with Leah and leave Uncle Thomas to it."

"Are things not improving?"

She shook her head. "I doubt they will until he stops being so harsh with her."

"He still won't let her move here to be with us?"

"No, he says he needs to keep an eye on her."

"Poor thing. Has she seen Mr Breton?"

"I can't be certain, but I doubt it. Uncle Thomas is still escorting her to and from work, and if we go out for a walk, he makes her come with us." Nell took a seat and put her head in her hands. "I wish there was something I could do."

"Did she talk to Aunty Jane like you suggested?"

"She's not interested in hearing reason. All she wants is acceptance of their relationship." Nell leaned back in her chair. "It's times like this I'm glad your mam isn't here."

"She'll be turning in her grave if she knows what's going on."

"What should I do?"

"In what way?"

"How do I sort out this mess? I'm trapped between the two of them."

"Who do you think's right?"

"I can see both sides..."

"But if you had to choose? Would you be prepared to see Leah settle down with this Mr Breton, or would you rather split them up to please Uncle Thomas?"

She groaned. "Why did he have to be a Catholic? Do you think he'd change for her?"

Alice grimaced. "I doubt it. If anything, he'd expect her to turn."

"He'd want their children to be brought up Catholic, too." She puffed out her cheeks. "I'd struggle to agree to that myself."

"So, you'd side with Uncle Thomas?"

"Not if it meant Leah hated me... I need to tell Uncle Thomas that we have to accept that Leah and Mr Breton want to be together, and we'll deal with each problem as and when it arises."

"Why don't you talk to her again?"

"Because he's always there..." She paused as the front door opened and Maria toddled into the room.

"Granny!"

A smile flitted across Nell's lips as she scooped up the child. "Where's Mammy?"

"I'm here, and I thought *I* was early."

Nell shook her head. "Alice may need to do dinner for us at this rate. I hate that house." *And the company.*

"How are things with Leah and Uncle Thomas?"

"Worse, if anything, because they're both digging their heels in."

Elenor took a seat. "I'd leave my job if I had to walk there and back with him. When he fell out with me, I couldn't bear being in the same room as him, let alone being with him all the time."

"She's better at work than being stuck in the house all day. It would drive her mad not being able to go out."

"The fact he makes her walk with you on a Sunday afternoon is even worse. Tell her to come to our house instead, to give her a break?"

"What about you going out with Mr Massey?"

"He won't mind, and I can go out whenever I want. One afternoon won't matter."

"Thank you. I'll suggest it, but I don't know what Uncle Thomas will think. He doesn't exactly trust you."

"What harm would it do letting her sit with me for a couple of hours? I'll have a word with him myself if he insists on being a fool..."

Nell held up a hand. "That's enough. He is my husband."

"More's the pity."

Alice stood up and headed for the kitchen. "Will you ask Uncle Thomas before you mention it to Leah? You don't want to raise her hopes only for him to upset her again."

"He couldn't upset her any more. They were arguing again last night, and he told her she was wasting her time even thinking of him, because there were no circumstances where he'd ever agree to their marriage."

Elenor raised an eyebrow. "What did she say?"

"She took herself off to bed and I've not seen her since."

"Why don't you visit her at the tea room, then? He won't be able to interrupt you there."

"She's busy when she's working."

"Mam! That's nothing but an excuse. Do you want to help her or not?" Elenor stood up and paced the floor. "You have to find a way to stop this. I'm sure she'd make time for you if that was why you were there."

Alice nodded. "It's got to be worth a try."

Nell stood at the door of the tea room and took a deep breath. Leah was waiting on a table at the far side of the room, and she waited for her to walk back to the counter before going in.

"Mam!" Leah's face lit up when she saw her. "What are you doing here?"

"I've come for afternoon tea ... and to talk to you. We don't get the chance at home any more."

Her face dropped. "No."

"Will you be able to take a break?"

She looked around the crowded tables. "It won't be easy

when we're this busy. It usually quietens down in the next half hour. Would you like your tea first and we'll talk later?"

"I would. Do you have a table for me?"

"There's a quiet one in the far corner behind a potted palm. It will make it easier for me to have a few words, too."

"Lead the way. I don't want much to eat, just enough to keep me going until you can join me."

Nell had eaten her cake and was on her third cup of tea by the time Leah arrived and took a seat.

"I've only got five minutes, but it's better than nothing. What did you want to speak to me about?"

Nell studied her. "Everything, really. I miss not having our chats."

"You know who's to blame for that."

"And I'm not here to defend him. How are you feeling?"

"Terrible."

"Have you been in touch with Mr Breton?"

"How can I?"

"He's not called in here?"

Leah said nothing as she studied the tablecloth.

"Don't look so worried. I won't scold you. How is he?"

Leah's shoulders dropped. "He's been so nice. He said it was all his fault for mentioning it after I'd told him not to."

"He wasn't to know how Uncle Thomas would react. I'm just embarrassed about what happened."

"He knows that. I've told him how nice you are."

Nell smiled. "Do you have any idea what you'll do?"

"Not really. I only see him for a few minutes at a time when he calls in on his way home for dinner. I need Uncle Thomas to get bored of escorting me, so Mr Breton can walk me home. I deliberately don't speak a word to Uncle Thomas."

"Elenor was asking after you this morning and said that you can sit with her for a couple of hours rather than going to the park with us on Sunday."

"That's kind of her. Will he let me?"

"We can only ask. He's cross that I'm not speaking to him at the moment, so if I suggest it would improve our relationship..."

"You'd do that?"

"We can't carry on as we are. And neither can you. I'll ask and see what he says."

Leah glanced over at the counter. "I need to go but thank you. I don't know what I'd do without you."

CHAPTER SIXTY-ONE

The roses were in full bloom as Nell walked through Sefton Park on Mr Marsh's arm and she took a deep breath as they passed a border of yellow flowers.

"Don't they smell wonderful?"

"Nearly as nice as the rosewater you wear."

Nell smiled. "It always reminds me of summer. I'm not surprised Betty named her new baby after them. A summer baby with a summer name. She looks like a rose, too, with her lovely red cheeks."

"And she's healthy."

Nell grinned. "She is. It seems the curse has finally moved on from her. She's had two now with no problems. I hope it lasts."

"It would be more prudent for her to stop producing them. Five healthy children should be enough for anyone."

"I'm sure she'd love to. It's Mr Crane who should be told." Nell paused as Mr Marsh's back stiffened.

"There's no need to be vulgar."

"I'm sorry." *But it's true.* "Are you expecting to meet Mr Grayson this afternoon?"

"I hope so, but we've not made any arrangements. I've not seen him all week."

"Don't you think all this with Leah has gone on for long enough? You've no need to stay in every night."

"Not until she's over him."

"How will you know when she is? She's not likely to tell you."

"She'll stop moping around the house for one, and she might engage in some conversation on the way to and from work."

"Has it occurred to you she's miserable because she can't go out? She hasn't even seen her friends."

"If I let her out, she'll meet him again. It's not worth the risk."

"She won't meet anyone new if you keep her locked up. Do you want her to be a spinster for the rest of her life?"

"It won't come to that. He'll find someone else before long and when he does, I'll relax the rules."

"Are you checking up on him?"

"Not exactly, but we walk home down Windsor Street and he always used to visit the park. I'm hoping to see him with another woman on his arm."

"But that's..." Nell let her voice trail off. *That's horrible.* "You mean you want Leah to find out like that?"

"It's what she needs. It will shake her out of her melancholy."

"Stopping this nonsense will do that..."

His smile was more like a sneer. "We've been over this. I'm doing it for her own good. I've been gracious enough to let her sit with Elenor on a Sunday, which is more than generous under the circumstances. Shall we leave it at that?"

Do I have a choice? She sighed as Mr Marsh ushered her to a seat.

"That was fortunate."

Nell looked around. "There's no sign of the Graysons."

"We're early today. I don't know why you were in such a rush."

"I didn't think I was. Still, it's a nice day to watch the world go by." *Come on, Rebecca, where are you?*

They hadn't been seated long when Nell pointed away to her left. "There's Isobel and Florrie. What are they doing here?"

"Meeting their old friends, I imagine."

"I wonder if Rebecca's with them. Let me go and ask." She didn't wait for a reply and she waved as she hurried towards them. "Isobel. Florrie."

"Aunty Nell."

She smiled. "I was sitting by the lake with Mr Marsh and spotted you. Are your mam and dad with you?"

Florrie sighed. "Not today. Mam has a headache."

"That's a shame. Is she all right?"

"She will be. She went for a lie-down."

"Well, tell her I hope she feels better soon and I'll call tomorrow. Did your dad come out?"

Isobel shrugged. "We've no idea."

"Oh well, if he's in the park, I'm sure we'll bump into him. Enjoy your afternoon."

Mr Marsh looked up when she returned. "Are they here?"

"I don't know about Mr Grayson, but Rebecca's not well,

so she's gone for a lie- down."

He tutted. "That's annoying. I'd hoped to talk to him."

"I'm sure Rebecca's sorry she's inconvenienced you."

"What?" He stood up. "We should carry on walking in case he's sitting down."

"Can't he come and find us?"

"That's not very considerate." He offered her his arm as they continued clockwise around the lake.

"Did you want to talk to Mr Grayson about anything in particular?"

"To apologise for not being in the alehouse again this week. We'd hoped this nonsense with Leah would have passed by now, but I need to report that she's more stubborn than I'd imagined."

Stubborn! That goes to show what you know. Nell shook her head but stopped abruptly and turned to face the way they'd come. *Elenor! What's she doing here?*

Mr Marsh looked down at her. "What's the matter?"

"My ... erm ... my gloves. I must have left them on the bench."

"Which ones? I don't remember you wearing any."

"The beige ones. They're skin-coloured so you may not have noticed them."

"We'd better go back then. Why did you take them off?"

"M-my hands were too warm."

"Aren't they meant to keep them cool?"

Will you stop asking so many questions? "You always said I was never normal..."

When they reached the bench, three women had taken their place and Nell approached on her own. "I'm sorry to disturb you, but did I leave a pair of gloves here? I can't find them anywhere."

A younger woman with flowers decorating her summer hat answered. "I've not seen them. What colour were they?"

Nell explained what she'd lost and once they'd all searched the surrounding area, she backed away.

"Never mind, I must have dropped them somewhere else. Have a nice afternoon."

She shook her head as she walked back to Mr Marsh. "I must be mistaken. I could have sworn I put them on."

"That's annoying. We'll have missed Mr Grayson with all that messing about. We may as well go home and you can check there."

"Already?" The pitch of Nell's voice was too high. "It's not four o'clock yet. Perhaps we could walk the long way around the lake. We may meet him coming the other way."

"Very well." He offered her his arm as he spoke of some tedious issue at work.

Where's she gone? Her eyes scanned every face multiple times as they headed towards the entrance. *I hope she's on her way home.*

Nell knocked on Elenor's front door, but paused before she let herself in. Mr Marsh stared at her.

"What are you waiting for?"

"Nothing. Why?"

"You usually go straight in."

"I'm going now. You distracted me."

Elenor and Leah sat on opposite sides of the fireplace

with Maria and Harold playing on the floor between them as Nell hesitated by the door.

"Have you enjoyed this afternoon?"

"Yes, it's been good." Leah looked down at her niece and nephew as she stood up. "We didn't realise the time."

Nell bent down to the children. "Granny can't stay today, but she'll see you tomorrow."

Maria waved to her but burst into tears as Harold knocked over the tower she'd been building. "Mammy!"

Nell grimaced. "I'm sorry. We'll leave you to it."

Elenor rolled her eyes. "See you tomorrow."

Mr Marsh strode on ahead as they walked down High Park Street but stopped outside Rebecca's house. "I'm going to check if Mr Grayson's home. You can wait there."

"Can't we come in to see Rebecca?"

"If she's not well, she won't want any visitors."

How would you know? "Shall we carry on without you...?"

"No. I need to keep an eye on *her*." He glared at Leah. "I won't be long."

Leah sighed. "I don't even have a name now."

"Take no notice of him. How was this afternoon?"

"I've already told you..."

"Are you sure? I saw Elenor and Mr Wood in Sefton Park with the children." Nell studied Leah as her face turned crimson.

"Did Uncle Thomas see them?"

"Thankfully not, but may I assume Mr Breton paid you a visit?"

The colour deepened on Leah's cheeks. "Yes."

"How did he know you'd be here?"

"I told him when he called at the tea room."

"When exactly? You've been coming here for the last month."

"A few weeks ago."

"So this isn't the first time you've seen him here?"

"No." Leah's eyes remained fixed on the ground.

"And there was me thinking it was Elenor who'd cheered you up."

"She has ... but she's not the only reason."

Nell bit her lip as she turned away. "I could swing for her. She's no right to leave you on your own. I hope you behaved yourself."

"She doesn't leave us for long..."

"What if the neighbours saw him? All those who stay at home on a Sunday use their front rooms."

"Nobody will have seen him. He comes in through the back door."

"You still shouldn't be alone in the house."

Leah lifted her eyes to Nell's. "We love each other, Mam. We don't want to be apart."

"That doesn't alter the fact that neither of you has come of age. Uncle Thomas has told you in no uncertain terms that he won't give his permission for a marriage. Can't you wait until you're twenty-one, then you needn't involve him?"

Leah's voice was little more than a whisper. "We don't want to. We're hoping to change his mind."

Nell raised an eyebrow. "And how will you do that?"

Leah stared straight ahead. "We'll find a way ... somehow."

CHAPTER SIXTY-TWO

The postman was about to push a letter through Alice's letterbox but stopped and handed it to Nell when she arrived.

"Sorry for the delay. It went to the wrong address. You need to let your acquaintances know you've moved."

"We must have missed one..." She studied the envelope. "Ah, it's from my nephew in Brazil. It takes time to get a message out there. He'll know for next time." She waved the letter in the air. "Thank you."

She called to Alice as she took her cloak off.

"In the kitchen." Alice smiled as she joined her in the living room. "The kettle's on. What have you got there?"

"A letter from James, but never mind that. How was Freddie at school this morning?"

Alice's eyes watered. "He was fine. It's me who wasn't. It was strange coming home on my own."

"That's why I'm here every afternoon. We should never have moved."

"I keep thinking that. Not that it will do any good.

"Let's see what James has to say then, see if he can cheer us up." Nell reached for the letter opener. "The postman said it had gone to Upper Hill Street, which is why it's taken so long."

"I thought he was ignoring us."

"So did I. Do you want to open it?"

"You do it while I make the tea."

Nell pulled the letter from the envelope. "He didn't write it until July, which is another reason it's late."

"It still must have been weeks in Upper Hill Street." Alice carried the tray to the table. "What's he got to say?"

"He's sorry for the delay in writing, but him and a few friends have been to America during their time off!"

"America! So he had time to travel but chose not to come here?"

Nell sighed. "It sounds like it. He says one of the men working with them comes from a place called ... Virginia, I think that says ... and so they travelled with him and stayed with his family."

"Does that mean we can expect a group of them to turn up here when he comes home? If he ever does."

"Who knows? He says he was pleased to get our invitation and that he'll visit next year."

"That's very generous of him." Alice's shoulders slumped. "It feels as if everyone's ignoring us at the moment. Even Edith doesn't want to come."

Nell raised an eyebrow. "You've heard from her?"

"I got a letter yesterday. I'm surprised you didn't. She said Mr Lacy's too busy, and she'd rather not travel on her own."

"That doesn't sound like her."

"No. Would you say it's Mr Lacy who won't let her come?"

"Almost certainly." Nell smiled as Elenor joined them. "I'm sick and tired of men telling us what we can and can't do."

Elenor put Harold on the floor. "Is Uncle Thomas no better with Leah?"

"He's getting worse, if that's possible. Last night, she asked politely if she could have the writing set so she could write to her friend Miss Clark. At first he refused, but after they'd had words, he relented on the condition that he read any letter she sent."

Elenor gasped. "He can't do that. I hope she didn't bother."

"She didn't."

"Why do you let him treat her like that?"

"What can I do? We have to live with him."

"No, you don't. There's a spare room here you could use. Why don't you leave him?"

Nell picked Harold up from the floor and sat him on her knee. "Billy wants to let it out to boarders and I don't have the money."

"I'm sure he'd let you stay for a week or two. He can't be desperate because he's got nobody in yet."

Alice blew out her cheeks. "He was waiting for Edith to visit, but I had a letter from her yesterday to say she's not coming."

"She's not?" Elenor's forehead creased. "She was really excited about seeing everyone again. Especially the children."

"Mr Lacy's changed her mind."

Elenor paced across the room. "What's got into everyone? Will wouldn't dare treat me like that, and I doubt Mr Breton would with Leah. If she's ever allowed to see him." She stared at Nell. "You need to do something, Mam. Tell Uncle Thomas that unless he stops this nonsense, you're leaving him. I'm sure Billy would put you up, and you can always take a job in town if you want to pay your way. You've done it before."

"I-I'm not a young girl any more."

"That's no reason not to stand up for yourself. You wouldn't have let anyone treat you like that before you married him."

"Being married changes the relationship. I'm not Nell Riley any more, I'm Mrs Thomas Marsh. I'm already more independent than most women, but this would be a step too far. Whoever heard of women leaving their husbands...?"

"It shouldn't stop you from standing up for Leah. She can come and live with me..."

"He won't let her. That was her first thought."

"Then we need to sneak her out."

"No."

Elenor gasped. "What do you mean, no? Don't you want her to be happy?"

"Of course I do, but not like that." When Elenor glared at her, she looked over to Alice. "Do you remember years ago, when I did the same thing for Miss Ellis? We helped her escape from her parents' house in the middle of the night so she could marry Mr Cavendish..."

Alice sighed. "I do."

"It was terrifying. The worst part was that the man Miss Ellis was running away from came after her. All the way to

Surrey. Had Mr Cavendish and ... *his friend* ... not been with her, she wouldn't have made it down there." She turned back to Elenor. "How long do you think Leah would last at your house before Uncle Thomas came after her? He'd be there as soon as he realised she was missing. And do you think he'd treat her kindly when he found her? It's all very well having these grand ideas, but they have consequences."

The room fell silent until Maria tried to pull Harold from Nell's knee and Elenor stood up to separate them.

"There must be something we can do. We can't sit back and let him carry on as he is."

"Do you think I haven't tried? The thing that usually works is being submissive and letting him think he's the one who makes all the decisions. That's how I got him to agree to letting her visit you on a Sunday afternoon, but there are limits to how long I can play the dutiful wife."

Elenor shook her head and handed Maria her doll. "If Miss Ellis's escape only worked because her husband-to-be was helping her, then we need to get Mr Breton involved. Could Leah move in with his family? Uncle Thomas wouldn't go round there with all the men in the family. If he even knows where he lives."

"Encourage her to live in Sussex Street?" Nell's mouth fell open as she gaped at Alice. "Your mam would turn in her grave."

Alice bit her lip. "She would, but Mam's not here. Leah is."

Elenor cocked her head to one side. "Do you want to help? Or are *you* bothered about Mr Breton being a Catholic, too?"

Nell shifted in her chair as Elenor watched her. "I'm not

as concerned as Uncle Thomas, but ... well, it would cause her no end of problems if they get married, especially if they have children. Ask Aunty Jane..."

"Aunty Jane still married Mr Read, and the children grew up fine."

"It wasn't without heartache, though."

"Life isn't without heartache, but if you want something badly enough, isn't it worth fighting for?"

"She's only known him for six months. Isn't that too soon to take such a big step?"

Elenor glared at her. "I'm sorry, Mam, but I'd say you're part of the problem. Imagine how you'd have felt in Leah's situation."

Nell paused. *If Maria had told me I couldn't do something... She did tell me ... and look what happened...* Her eyes flicked between Alice and Elenor. "What would you think if she married a Catholic?"

Alice stared at her hands. "It's difficult for me, having Harry to consider."

Elenor scowled at her. "You can't let him dictate what Leah does."

"I know, but he left Ireland because of the Catholics, so I don't know how he'll react to this." Alice huffed. "If you want my opinion, the more you try to keep them apart, the more desperate they'll be to see each other. Do you remember when Mam didn't want me to walk out with Harry...?"

Nell nodded. "I thought she was being unreasonable."

"And I left home for nearly a month. Nothing was going to keep us apart. If Leah feels the same, you won't stop her. You'll push her away."

"Uncle Thomas won't change his mind."

"Maybe in time?"

Nell shook her head. "No. If I support Leah, and she ends up marrying Mr Breton, it will be the end of our marriage."

Elenor looked down at her. "I suspect you've known that for a while, which is why you've done nothing, but you need to decide whose side you're on. She may seem calm, but I'll tell you now, Leah won't put up with the current situation for much longer."

CHAPTER SIXTY-THREE

The leaves were already changing colour on the trees, but Nell barely noticed the yellows and browns as she strolled around the park with Rebecca.

"Has Mr Grayson said anything about Thomas staying at home every evening?"

"He grumbles about it, especially because his friendship with Mr Marsh was the main reason we moved back to Toxteth, but he doesn't blame him for what he's doing. He says he should be firmer with Leah and put an end to the nonsense."

Nell's eyes widened. "What else would he have him do?"

Rebecca took a moment's pause. "He wrote to him the other day and suggested he send her away..."

"Where to?"

"He didn't say, but the only reason I know is because he asked me where Edith had moved to."

"Sheffield! She can't go there. It's miles away and I never see Edith..."

"That may have only been one option. It was a long letter, and I heard him muttering about the asylum, too."

"She's not going there." Nell spoke through gritted teeth. "That would be the final straw."

"How will you stop him?"

Tears welled in Nell's eyes. "I don't know, but I won't let him take my daughter from me. What right does he have? He's not even her father."

"I presume you don't need me to answer that."

"No." Nell held Rebecca's gaze. "How would you feel if Isobel or Florrie wanted to marry a Catholic? Would you forbid it?"

"I wouldn't have to. Hugh would. He's worse than Mr Marsh."

"So, what would you do? Abandon your marriage for the sake of your daughter?"

Rebecca gasped. "Is that the choice?"

"What other options are there?"

"Is leaving Mr Marsh really an option? I wanted to leave Hugh once, if you remember, but George talked me out of it. Everything he said about me not being able to support myself made sense, and I didn't have the courage to leave."

"So you'd stay with him?"

"Yes ... well, probably ... it's difficult to say when you've not been in that situation."

"Would you be happy to never see Isobel or Florrie again? Or your grandchildren?"

"Of course not."

"But Mr Grayson would forbid it if he's worse than Thomas."

Rebecca shook her head. "What a nightmare. I'll have to pray they both find good Protestants."

"I don't have that option."

Rebecca studied her. "You've always been pluckier than me. Do what you think is right and don't worry about anyone else."

The tea room was busy the following afternoon and Nell stood at the window watching Leah at work. *The smile's gone. So has her bounce. I've let Thomas do this to her.* She wiped her eyes before letting herself in. *Not any more.*

"Mam. I didn't expect you. Is everything all right?"

"No, it isn't. We need to talk."

"Is there much to say?"

"Yes. May I speak to the manageress? I'd like to ask her if you can join me for afternoon tea."

Leah looked round. "We're busy."

"You're also miserable, and I want to help. Please."

Leah wandered to the counter and introduced Nell to the woman at the till.

"Good afternoon." Nell cleared her throat. "I realise it's irregular, but would you be able to spare Miss Riley for half an hour? I'd like to buy her afternoon tea."

"I don't..." The woman's face was stern as she started to speak, but Nell interrupted.

"Please. I wouldn't ask if it wasn't important." Nell held her breath as the woman scanned the room.

"Twenty minutes. No longer."

Nell exhaled. "Thank you. You're very kind."

"Yes, thank you." Leah slipped behind the counter. "You find a seat while I get the tray. The same as last time?"

"Please."

A table in the window was being cleared and Nell waited for the waitress to take away the dishes before she sat down. The street outside was busy with people rushing to get out of the rain, and with the plants behind her, she felt quite invisible. She was watching a woman with a young child when Leah arrived with the tray.

"Here you are. Two scones with jam and some Victoria sandwich cake."

"That looks nice." Nell checked her watch. "I hope the twenty minutes only starts now."

"It will. She's not as bad as she pretends to be." Leah helped herself to a scone. "What did you want to see me about?"

"First, I want to apologise for not standing up for you."

"You've tried."

"Not enough. I shouldn't let Uncle Thomas treat you like he does. I presume you're still seeing Mr Breton at Elenor's house."

She nodded. "It's the only thing keeping me going."

"Do his mam and dad know what's going on?"

"They know I'm a Protestant."

"What do they think about Mr Breton walking out with you?"

"They're not happy."

"So even if Uncle Thomas relented and let you see Mr Breton, would his family try to stop you?"

Tears welled in her eyes. "They might."

Nell sighed. "I'm sorry."

465

"It's not your fault."

"No, but I should have warned you sooner that you can't walk out with just anyone."

"Why does it matter? It doesn't to me or Larry."

Larry. "It matters to a lot of people. I've mentioned it before, but have you seriously considered waiting? That extra year would make a difference, and if you still want to get married once you've come of age, no one could stop you."

"That's over a year off. We don't want to be apart for that long, and who'd make sure we didn't see each other in the meantime? Isn't that what all this chaperoning's about?"

Nell sighed. "I suppose so, but I'm struggling for other ideas."

Leah played with the spoon on her saucer. "I'm not sure I should tell you this, but we've spoken of eloping."

Nell nearly choked on her scone. "To Scotland?"

"There's a place called Gretna Green. Lots of couples go there if their families won't let them marry."

"You'd do that?"

"We've not decided. We could save for the train fare easily enough, but we don't know what we'd do once we were married. Or if we'd be able to come back to Liverpool."

Nell blinked away her tears. "Don't do that. We'll find a better way, and if you do get married, I'm sure Billy would let you live with them."

"What about Mr Wood? I heard he doesn't think Protestants and Catholics should marry."

"He wouldn't turn you away if Mr Breton pays some rent, but he wants you to understand the problems you'll face if you're together. Uncle Thomas will only be the first of many."

"What about you? Would you be angry with me?"

"No. I want you to be happy, and if that means you being with Mr Breton, then I'll be happy, too."

"You're the best, Mam." Leah's familiar grin returned, but quickly dropped again. "What about you and Uncle Thomas? He'll be furious if he knows you've encouraged me."

"Let me worry about that." She took a slice of Victoria sandwich cake. "Something else I wanted to ask. What number Sussex Street do the Bretons live?"

"Twenty-nine. Why?"

"I wondered about calling on his mam."

Leah shook her head. "I wouldn't. She's very devout and the one who's most upset about me."

"What about his dad? You said he chaperoned you."

"He did until he found out. Now, he's not terribly pleased, so I doubt he'd help."

"Then I don't know what to suggest."

"Even knowing you're not mad with me makes me feel better. I'll have to hope something turns up."

The house was cold as Nell let herself in and she threw some coal onto the fire and stoked it until the flame grew in the grate. Satisfied it was lit, she went to hang up her cloak but paused when the letterbox rattled. *It's from Edith. For Thomas. Is this about sending Leah away?*

She placed the letter on the mantelpiece and stared at it. *Dare I open it? Then what would I do? Confront him? No. Throw it on the fire and pretend I hadn't seen it? What if Edith says Leah can't go to stay? He'll need to know about that. Or would he? A lack of a reply may be enough.* Her heart raced as she picked it up again. *I can't leave it there. He's not sending my daughter anywhere.*

She slid the letter opener under the flap of the envelope and flicked it sideways. *There's no going back now.* Her hands trembled as she unfolded the single sheet of paper.

Dear Uncle Thomas

I'm sorry for the delay in replying, but I've been at a loss for what to say.

Why is it so wrong for Leah to walk out with a Catholic? It may not be the done thing, but if he's a nice man who treats her well, isn't that better than a Protestant who doesn't?

When I lived with my other mam and dad, several Catholic families lived near us and they were all nice.

I can't offer Leah a home here, because sending her away wouldn't be in her best interests. She'll only grow to resent you and it wouldn't be fair on her mam, either.

I hope you understand.

Yours sincerely

Edith.

She stood up to him! I couldn't have put it better myself. He needs to see this ... but I've opened it. A shiver ran through her. *How do I explain that?* She folded it and carefully returned it to the envelope. *I could say I thought it was for me. Or open it as soon as he comes in and make him think I'm keen to hear from Edith. Yes. I'll do that.*

. . .

Half a dozen kidneys and a pan of potatoes were cooking on the range when Mr Marsh and Leah arrived home, but Nell was waiting by the fire with the letter and letter opener in her hands.

"There's a letter here for you from Edith." Her hands shook as she made the motion of opening the letter. "Why would she be writing to you?"

He snatched the envelope from her. "That's private business."

"With Edith?"

"I had a question for her. Now if you'll excuse me, I'll read this in private."

Leah looked at Nell as he stormed into the front room. "What's that about?"

She turned to stoke the fire. "I've no idea."

CHAPTER SIXTY-FOUR

Thick grey clouds drained the colour from the streets and Nell hurried to Alice's house, hoping to beat the rain. Maria ran to the door to meet her when she arrived.

"Granny!"

"Good afternoon." She hugged her granddaughter and ushered her into the living room, where Elenor was already by the fire. "You're early today."

"Harold had me up for half the night. His back teeth are coming through, and so when the first sign of daylight appeared, I decided I might as well get up and start the cleaning."

Nell bent down to pick him up. "Poor love. I thought his cheeks were red. Rub some brandy on his gums tonight."

Elenor giggled. "I'll be giving him a glass of the stuff. Will wasn't pleased about being woken up, so he won't stop me."

"It shouldn't be for long." Nell set him down on the floor and took a seat. "I've got some news. I had a letter from Edith yesterday."

Alice wandered from the kitchen with the tea tray. "I only heard from her last week. What did she have to say?"

"Not much about what she's doing, but she was replying to a letter I sent her a couple of weeks ago asking why she'd written to Uncle Thomas."

Elenor's forehead creased. "Edith wrote to Uncle Thomas? You didn't tell us."

"I wanted to find out why first."

"Didn't you open the letter?"

Nell avoided her gaze. "You can't open your husband's mail."

"I would have."

Alice took the seat beside Elenor. "What did Edith say?"

"She told me he'd written to her to ask if he could send Leah to Sheffield to live with them."

Alice's back straightened. "Is she in the family way?"

"Don't be daft. She hardly sees Mr Breton, and even if she did, after what happened with Elenor, she's determined not to do the same. No. Uncle Thomas has got it in his head that if she doesn't live around here, she won't bump into Mr Breton, and he can start going out again in the evening."

Elenor's nostrils flared. "He'd send her away so he can go out with Mr Grayson?" She stared at Nell. "Why on earth did you marry him? Couldn't you see what he was like?"

"He wasn't like this then. How was I to know he'd struggle with having a family?"

"So when's she leaving?"

"She's not!" Nell grinned as Elenor's mouth fell open. "Edith told him he had no business sending her away just because Mr Breton's Catholic and that she wanted no part in his plan."

"She did! Oh, well done, Edith. The rest of us need to learn to stand up to him like that."

"It's easier when you don't have to live with someone." She looked across at them. "Not that it stopped me trying last night. I told him about the letter and asked when he was going to tell me he was sending *my* daughter away."

"What did he say?"

"I got the usual nonsense that it was all for her own good, and that he wouldn't have done anything without speaking to me, but I didn't believe a word. I said that if he carried on like this, he'd force me to choose between him and Leah."

Elenor's face lit up. "I bet he didn't like that."

"No. He came over all sanctimonious and started preaching about why Protestants and Catholics should never marry. That was the final straw." She took a deep breath. "I told him I didn't recognise him any more, and if he wouldn't let Leah walk out with Mr Breton, then he wouldn't have me as his wife. Not in the sense that I'd be living with him, anyway."

Alice gasped. "You said that!"

Nell nodded. "It was one of the hardest things I've ever done..."

"What did he say?"

"Nothing." Nell's posture slumped. "After all that, he just got up and walked out. I presume he went to the alehouse. I've not spoken to him since."

"What about breakfast?"

"He sat at the table in silence and left before Leah came downstairs."

Elenor clapped her hands together. "Oh, Mam. I knew you could do it. I bet Leah's delighted."

"She was pleased he wasn't around to walk her to work, but furious he wants to send her away. I hope she doesn't do anything rash."

"Like what?"

"I don't know. She really was angry with him when I showed her Edith's letter. I'll have to try and calm her down later."

The pan of scouse she'd made before she went out was simmering on the range when she got home, but as the clock struck half past five, the familiar feeling of nausea settled over her. *Goodness knows how they'll be tonight.* She took a seat by the fire, but when the hands of the clock showed little sign of moving, she stood up. *A tot of brandy might do the trick. It's good for an upset stomach.*

She poured herself a good measure and retook her seat. *Only two minutes later than when I stood up.* She took a large gulp of the amber liquid and sat up straight as it burned on its way down. *That will either kill me or cure me.* She closed her eyes and rested her head on the back of the chair. *It might take another mouthful.*

She'd nearly emptied the glass when the front door crashed against the wall in the hall and Mr Marsh stormed in.

"Where is she?"

"Who?"

"Who do you think? Leah."

She got to her feet. "I assumed she'd be with you."

"Well, she's not. Apparently, she handed in her notice this morning and left."

"You've chased her away..." Stars danced in front of Nell's eyes. "This is all your fault. If you hadn't been so strict with her..."

"My fault! You're the one who's supposed to teach her the rights and wrongs of life. I'm trying to correct her behaviour before it's too late."

"What do you know about young women? You've no idea how they think. You bluster about telling them what you want them to do..."

"Until they get a husband, they're my responsibility, and I won't have Leah bringing disgrace on the family..."

"She'll do nothing of the sort." Her legs were like jelly as she stumbled to the door. "I don't know where she is, but I hope it's a long way from you, and that she's happy." She grabbed her cloak but didn't stop to fasten it. "You can serve your own dinner ... if your conscience is clear enough to eat anything."

She had no thought for where she was going, but five minutes later, she was outside the house on Dombey Street. She let herself in without knocking and stepped into the living room, hesitating as all eyes turned to her.

"Aunty Nell." Alice stood up. "What are you doing here?"

"Leah's gone." She ran a hand across her face to wipe her tears. "Is she here?"

Alice shook her head. "No, we've not seen her."

"I didn't think you would have, but I didn't know where else to go. She wouldn't go to Elenor's either, because it would be the first place Uncle Thomas would look."

Billy got up from the table. "Come and sit down." He

wrapped an arm around her shoulders. "Would you like some tea?"

She shook her head. "I couldn't eat a thing."

"A cup of tea then? With extra sugar." He nodded to Alice. "There must be other places she could go."

"I don't know where half her friends live."

Alice retook her seat. "Elenor might, and if you can find Miss Clark, she may know the rest."

"I don't even have her address."

"Then we'll start by asking the friends we do have addresses for."

Nell took a deep breath. "You're right. I need to stop and think. I'm so cross with Uncle Thomas. If it wasn't for him, none of this would have happened."

Mr Wood reached for another slice of bread. "All this for a Catholic."

Alice glared at him. "That's enough."

"I'm just saying. If she insists on seeing him, this will only be the start of the trouble for them."

"Don't think I haven't tried to warn her, but she's adamant they want to be together."

"Could she be at his place?"

Nell fumbled for her handkerchief. "I doubt it. His family aren't happy, either. I hope she's all right. She's never been on her own before." She wiped her eyes. "I want her home."

"Of course you do." Alice ran a hand over Georgie's head. "I'd be worried sick if anything happened to him, never mind a daughter."

"I don't know what to do next. Or what to say when I see

Uncle Thomas again." Her hands trembled. "I walked out on him and told him to serve his own tea."

Billy nudged Mr Wood. "Perhaps we should pay him a visit in his *new local*. I expect Mr Grayson will be giving him some words of advice..."

"Causing trouble, you mean. He won't be happy until everyone's as miserable as him."

Nell groaned. "What a mess."

"It's nothing we can't sort out." Billy patted her hand. "It's a shame we don't still live in the same house. It would never have got to this."

Alice sighed. "There wasn't much we could do about it."

"I didn't say there was, but we never used to have problems like this." He looked at Mr Wood. "Why don't we finish tea and once Aunty Nell's ready, we'll walk her home?"

She put a hand to her chest. "I can't go back!"

"Won't you want to be there in case Leah turns up? We'll speak to Uncle Thomas if he's there, and if not, we'll go and find him."

Nell squeezed back her tears. "She won't turn up, and I can't face being on my own with him."

Alice took Nell's hand. "Let Aunty Nell stay here and I'll make up the bed in the back room. You two can still go to the house."

"Will you call at Elenor's, too? See if either of them have been there?"

Mr Wood nodded. "What about this Mr Breton? It might still be worth calling on him."

Nell sighed. "I doubt it, but there would be no harm checking. It's twenty-nine Sussex Street."

CHAPTER SIXTY-FIVE

Nell peered out of the window in Alice's front room, the sour taste in the back of her mouth lingering despite her latest cup of tea. Alice let herself in after delivering the boys to school.

"I presume there's no sign of her."

She shook her head. "It wouldn't surprise me if she isn't halfway to Scotland by now. They'd already talked about it..."

"She might not be. Mr Breton was still at home when Billy and Harry called last night."

"That was last night, and he may have lied about not knowing where she was. What if they'd planned to leave on the early morning train...?"

"Come on." Alice put an arm around her shoulder. "You're letting your imagination run away with you."

"What else can I do?"

"You can come into the other room. It's warmer in there. Staring out of the window isn't helping."

"I shouldn't have told her Uncle Thomas wanted to send her away. That's what this is all about..."

"Stop blaming yourself. It's not your fault."

Nell let Alice lead her into the living room and settle her in a chair.

"Let me put the kettle on. Elenor said she'd be here this morning."

Before Alice had come back from the kitchen, the front door opened and Maria ran into the living room.

"We're here."

Nell forced a smile. "Good morning."

"We saw Aunty Leah."

"What?" Nell jumped to her feet as Elenor joined them.

"She called this morning once Will had left for work."

Nell peered into the hall. "Where is she? Didn't she come with you?"

"She wanted me to check you weren't cross with her."

"Of course I'm not. I'm worried sick. Where's she been?"

"She wouldn't say, but she said she's fine and doesn't want you to worry."

"But what will she do for money ... and clothes ...?"

"She'll be all right. Let her be for now. She's upset about Uncle Thomas."

"Aren't we all?"

"How's he been with you?"

"I've not seen him. I stayed here last night."

Elenor's eyes widened. "You've left him?"

"Not really. I'll need to go back at some point, but I've not decided when. Has she seen Mr Breton?"

Elenor nodded. "She waited for him on his way home from work and he took her to his house."

"Did she stay there?"

Elenor shrugged. "She wouldn't tell me."

"No, you said." Nell huffed. "Should I go and speak to his mam? Find out what's going on?"

"I wouldn't. Leah said she'd be in touch. Give her time and you'll see her soon enough."

Nell took a breath. "If you see her again, please tell her to make it sooner rather than later. If it carries on much longer, it will be the death of me."

Alice was washing up when Nell carried the last of the dinner dishes to the kitchen.

"Will you walk to school with me when we've done this? It will do you good to get out, and we can call at your house if you want to pick anything up."

"I may as well while Uncle Thomas isn't there."

"You'll need to speak to him, eventually."

Nell leaned back against the counter. "I know and I should get it over and done with, but I don't know what to say."

"Would you go back to him if he got over the problem with Leah?"

She sighed. "Maybe if I had to. I often wonder what I ever saw in him. I think it was for security and to have a companion as I got older. It's not much to build a marriage on, is it?"

"There are women who've married for less."

"More fool them. We should be able to go out and make our own living without people sneering at us. Even once we're married. It would save a lot of misery."

"You know that will never happen, so you need to make a choice. Go back to being a wife, or live the life of a widow, even though your husband only lives around the corner."

Nell shook her head. "He wouldn't stay where he is if I left. He'd go to sea."

"You think so?"

"I'd put money on it. It's what he always does when we have a serious argument and he'll never change. He may have gone already."

"So soon?"

"No. Probably not. Anyway–" she checked the clock "–we'd better get these boys back to school."

The house was cold when Nell opened the front door and let Alice inside.

"Go into the back room if you like while I nip upstairs to get some clothes." She hadn't made it to the third step when Alice called her back.

"What is it?"

Alice nodded to a chair by the fire, where Mr Marsh sat wearing his coat. "I'll wait in the front room."

"Elenor."

"Why aren't you at work?"

He stood up. "I wanted to talk to you. Where've you been?"

"I didn't want to come home. You frighten me when you're in one of your moods."

"Frighten?" There was confusion in his eyes. "You should know I'd never hurt you."

"But you shout, and I've seen what you've done to Leah."

"I didn't mean to, but she made me angry…"

"Which is why I don't trust you." She studied him. "You're not the man I married. That man would have done anything for me."

"I only want what's best for you."

"No." Nell's eyes narrowed. "You want to do what's best for *you*. You want the perfect family, but unfortunately, we're not good enough."

"Is that wrong?"

"It is when the people involved don't agree with you."

He edged towards her. "I want you to come home."

She took a step backwards. "What about Leah?"

"Have you seen her?"

"I don't know where she is."

"I'm sorry. I didn't want that to happen."

"Perhaps you should have stopped to think."

He reached for her hand. "Please, if you come home, we can sort something out."

"That's not good enough." She stared at him. "You need to give Leah her life back. If I agree to come home, will you allow her to move in with Alice?"

"But she'd…"

"She'd do as she wants. No restrictions, except the obvious. If she wanted to walk out with Mr Breton, the only stipulation would be that they'd have a chaperone. It may be that when they can meet each other freely, they drift apart. All you've done is push them together."

He nodded. "If it brings you home, I'll listen to you more often … and I promise I won't hurt you. If we're fortunate, they'll lose interest in each other."

"Very well. I'll come home once Leah's settled in with Alice."

"That could be weeks."

Nell shrugged. "That's not my fault."

"I'll help you look for her..."

"No! You've done enough damage. Leave her to me and give us time to get over this. If you cause any more problems, I can't promise I won't leave again, and next time it will be for good."

CHAPTER SIXTY-SIX

Nell stepped back and admired the walls and floor of the front room. She'd worked solidly since she'd returned home, trying to turn the house into somewhere she wanted to live. It almost felt ready for Christmas. *If we do Christmas here. Now Leah's living with Alice it would make more sense for us to go there. Another change...*

She wandered to the kitchen and threw the dirty water into the yard. *Right, tea.* She lifted two bacon chops from the pantry and placed them next to the range but stepped back to the living room when the front door opened. *Who on earth's this?* She only waited a moment before Leah joined her.

"It smells like you've been busy in here."

She grinned at her. "I decided to give the place a good clean, now I'm staying. What are you doing here?"

"I thought I'd come and see you."

"Have you seen the time? Uncle Thomas will be here in about half an hour."

"I won't stay, but I've something to tell you and I didn't want to say anything in front of Alice."

"Would you like to come home?"

Leah chuckled. "Not unless Uncle Thomas goes to sea and doesn't come back."

"That's a shame. What is it, then?"

Leah's cheeks coloured as she searched for the right words. "I-I hope you won't be cross with me, but Mr Breton's asked me to marry him ... and I've said yes."

"Marry?" Nell's mouth fell open. "Will you wait until you're twenty-one? You know Uncle Thomas won't agree to it."

The smile disappeared from Leah's lips. "We think he will."

"What do you mean?"

"You'd better sit down." Leah pulled out a chair from the table and sat in the one opposite.

"What have you done?"

"There was only one way he'd agree to us being married, so we had no choice." She took a deep breath. "I'm in the family way."

"Oh, my..." Nell swayed on her chair until Leah caught hold of her arm.

"Are you all right?"

"No. No, I'm not." Her breathing was shallow as she struggled to focus. "Are you sure?"

"I've spoken to Elenor, and she says I am..."

"After everything we've said... How far gone are you?"

"We think about three or four months."

"Oh, Leah, what have you done?"

"Uncle Thomas made us do it."

Nell gasped. "Did you do it on purpose?"

"We had no choice. If he'd let us walk out together like a normal couple..."

"That's not an excuse for *ruining* yourself." Nell pressed her fingers into her temples. "I can't believe you've been so stupid."

"I'm sorry, Mam. Please don't be angry with me."

"How are you going to tell him...?"

"I thought you might..."

Nell jumped back in her chair. "I'm not telling him."

"Please, Mam."

"No. Absolutely not. You were the one foolish enough to get yourself into this mess, so you and Mr Breton can tell him ... and you'd better do it soon. I don't want another wedding where we're hiding the proof of what you've been up to." Nell's eyes narrowed. "Did Elenor have anything to do with it?"

"Don't blame her. All she did was talk about how Uncle Thomas forced her to marry Mr Massey and I thought it would help persuade him about me and Larry..."

"I'll kill her..."

"It's not her fault."

"Not her fault!" Nell spluttered. "She left the two of you alone in the house for hours at a time on a Sunday. A Sunday!"

"But you knew..."

"And I trusted you! After what happened with her, it didn't occur to me for a second that you'd deliberately do the same thing."

Tears welled in Leah's eyes. "All I want is to be with Larry."

"It was no reason for you to bring shame on this family

again. What will people think? I've two daughters and you've both *fallen* before you've walked down the aisle."

"Nobody need know."

"Of course they will, unless you lock yourself in the house or go and stay with Edith. When's it due?"

"Early May."

"So if you get married any later than January, you'll be showing. Oh, Leah. Why did you do this? You realise I'll be homeless if I stand by you?"

"No, you won't." Leah fell to the floor by Nell's legs. "As long as I have a roof over my head, so will you. I've already spoken to Larry and we won't leave you on your own."

"But Uncle Thomas..."

"I'm sorry, really I am." Her sobs grew louder. "Please don't be cross with me... I love him..."

Nell clung to her daughter, unable to stop her tears. "He'd better be worth it."

"He is, I promise. And we'll sort something out."

They held each other until the clock sounded for half past five and Leah pulled away, wiping her eyes on the backs of her hands. "I'd better go. I don't want to be here when Uncle Thomas gets home. I'll see you tomorrow." She gave Nell a final squeeze and raced to the door.

She hadn't been gone five minutes when Mr Marsh arrived home and Nell scurried to the kitchen before he took his seat by the fire.

"You've been busy. I can smell the disinfectant."

"I'm afraid it made me late with the tea. I didn't notice the time."

He chuckled. "Some things never change. Not to worry. Did you get those stubborn stains from the wall?"

"I did." She took the frying pan from its hook on the wall but fumbled as she sensed his eyes on her.

"Is everything all right? You don't look happy."

"I'll be fine. I'm worried about Leah, that's all."

He sighed. "The sooner she's finished with that Catholic, the better. Have you seen her today?"

"She ... erm ... she popped in this afternoon. I suggested she might want to visit while you're here. The pair of you need to make up before Christmas." She put the chops in the frying pan.

"How was she? Any remorse?"

"Not that I noticed. I called at Alice's, too. Elenor was there with Maria and Harold. They're growing up quickly. Can you believe Maria's nearly four?"

He straightened his newspaper. "That wasn't one of the happiest times of our lives."

"No, but it turned out all right in the end, didn't it?"

"I suppose so. As they say, time's a great healer."

Let's hope it heals a lot quicker this time round.

Alice was alone the following morning when Nell arrived and she joined her in the kitchen.

"I'm sorry I'm early. I couldn't wait until this afternoon."

"It's all right. I was expecting you." Alice filled up the milk jug and set it on the tea tray.

"Where's Leah?"

"She wanted to see Elenor."

"Couldn't she wait for her to come here?"

"Apparently not. She told you her news, I believe."

Nell studied her. "You know, too?"

"She told me last night after Harry and Billy had gone out."

"After she'd seen me, then." Nell shook her head. "I just don't know what to do."

"You didn't tell Uncle Thomas?"

"I did not." Nell shuddered. "I told her yesterday it's not my place."

"She doesn't want to tell him, either."

"She has no choice if she wants his permission for the wedding."

"She said she needs moral support."

"Then she can take Mr Breton with her." Nell huffed. "He won't have even asked Uncle Thomas for her hand in marriage..." She paused as the front door closed and Elenor let herself in.

"Are you on your own?"

"No, I'm here." Leah followed her in. "Are you still cross with me?"

"I'm mad at both of you." She glared at Elenor. "What were you thinking, encouraging her?"

"I was trying to help her stand up to a bully."

"There are better ways to do it than by bringing an innocent new life into the world."

"Not with him." Elenor stood with her hands on her hips. "He would never agree to them getting married, so it needed something like this."

"She could have waited another year."

Alice carried the teapot to the table. "Calm down, everyone. The fact of the matter is, we are where we are. Leah needs to be married as soon as possible, and someone needs to tell Uncle Thomas."

Nell glared at Leah. "I've told her, she's telling him. I'm not getting involved."

"What about the wedding?" Alice looked at Leah. "Have you spoken to the vicar at St Thomas's?"

Leah's cheeks flushed. "Larry wants to be married at St Patrick's."

"The Catholic church?" Nell gasped. "No. That's a step too far. They'd force you to turn."

Alice took a breath as she sat with Leah. "Have you told him that's not an option?"

"The whole marriage isn't an option, according to Uncle Thomas, so what difference does it make which church we're married in?"

"What difference...?" Nell struggled to breathe. "How can you say that? And does the priest know you're in the family way? You'd have to go to confession and tell him before he married you..."

"Larry said you don't need to tell him everything."

"You'll have no choice. It's November already, which, at best, is only two months before people start noticing. Even if you want to turn, it won't happen overnight. The priest will need to speak to you about becoming a Catholic..."

Leah's face was pale. "So it will delay the marriage?"

"I would say so. By quite a while, too."

"Larry didn't mention that."

"Probably because they're more than happy to have converts." Nell stared at her. "Now do you see some of the problems? I wasn't making it up."

"Would he need to convert to the Church of England if we want to be married in St Thomas's?"

"It will be up to the vicar."

"There's always the register office." Elenor took a step back as Nell glared at her. "There is. They don't mind what religion you are."

Leah bowed her head. "I wanted a big wedding, like Edith..."

"You should have thought of that. This marriage will be as sparse as we can make it. Not that I want you married in that godless place."

"So you'd rather they weren't married at all?" Elenor gasped.

"No." Nell's eyes rested on Leah as she sobbed into Alice's shoulder. "Not now there's a baby..." *What an ordeal. And this is before we tell Thomas.* "We have to come up with something."

"And Uncle Thomas needs to know he caused this." Elenor was the only one not crying. "I hope he's happy with himself when he finds out."

Alice lifted her head from Leah's and looked at Nell. "It's Stir-up Sunday next week. Why don't we make the puddings at your house and tell him together? It will give Leah time to speak to the vicar, too."

Nell was numb as she leaned her head against the back of the chair. "There's no way of sugarcoating it. He'll be furious. Will you get the spare bed ready in Leah's room? I've a feeling I'll be needing it."

CHAPTER SIXTY-SEVEN

Nell's cheeks were sore from forcing her smile, but she let it drop as Jane joined her in the queue for the back of church.

"That's not a very warm welcome."

"I'm sorry. I'm feeling a bit under the weather and I've had enough of the pretence."

"Nothing serious, I hope."

Far too serious. "Just a bit of a cold."

"Well, I hope you're better for Advent next week. You'll need to get busy. Are you doing your pudding this afternoon?"

"I am. Alice and the girls are joining me."

"That's nice. I'm going over to Betty's, but it may not be for much longer."

"Why? What's happening?"

Jane beamed at her. "Our John's doing so well at work that he's going to rent a house of his own and move me in with him."

"You're moving! How exciting." Nell grinned. "You won't have any excuse not to help out at celebrations now."

Jane rolled her shoulders. "It was always a perfectly reasonable excuse…"

"Where will you move? Closer to Betty?"

"No, we want to stay around here. He saw a place he liked on Elwy Street the other day, so I'm hoping he'll secure it soon."

"That's between Elenor and Rebecca. That will be handy."

"That's what I thought. Not far from where we are now, either, so I'll still get to see my friends."

"What about Mr Bruce? Does he still warrant any consideration?"

Jane shook her head. "No. It was only ever a passing friendship. I doubt I'll see much of him when I move."

"It's probably for the best." *I wish I'd kept Thomas as nothing more than a friend.*

"I think so." Jane sighed. "What will you do for Christmas now you've all split up?"

"We're going to Alice's. She has the biggest house, and she likes to do things the way Maria did."

Jane nodded. "I'll say that for Maria. She knew how to do a good Christmas. If Alice can do the same, I'm sure you'll have a wonderful time. I'll be at Betty's for dinner, but we'll see after that." She shook hands with the vicar and waved to Nell as she left. "I'll be in touch."

Mr Marsh came up behind Nell as Jane left. "She was in a good mood."

"She's moving out of the boarding house. John's renting somewhere for the two of them."

"I'm not surprised she's happy, then."

"No, she deserves it after living there for all those years. I couldn't have done it."

"You could if it was your only option."

"That's true." They set off along the church path. "Have you remembered Alice and the girls are coming round this afternoon for Stir-up Sunday?"

"I have, and I'll be out of your way. I'm meeting Mr Grayson in Princes Park so he can leave Mrs Grayson and her daughters to do their pudding. We'll probably call in at the alehouse once it gets dark, to make sure everyone's gone before I get home."

"Oh. I-I'd hoped you'd be home while they're still there. Leah would like to speak to you."

"She would?" He raised an eyebrow.

"Yes, well, with it being nearly Christmas it would be nice if we could all get along."

He sighed. "Very well."

"Don't be like that."

"I just can't get past her walking out with Mr Breton. I hope your idea of them drifting apart happens sooner rather than later."

Nell bit her lip. "Couldn't you accept them as they are? Leah's not a bad girl."

"It's not her I have the problem with."

"No." *It's not her I have a problem with, either.*

The puddings had been made, wrapped and were ready for the steamer when Nell glanced at the clock. "We'd better get this table tidied. He'll be home any time."

493

Alice carried her pudding to the hall. "Are you putting yours on now?"

"No. I want to be able to take it with me, if I need to."

Leah put her hands on her stomach. "I feel sick."

"You should have thought of that before you came up with your bright idea."

Elenor bent down to tidy the children's toys. "Why didn't you ask Mr Breton to join you? He should be the one protecting you."

"After the way Uncle Thomas was with him? I don't think so. It would have made things worse." Leah shuddered. "I hoped that you'd stand up for me."

"Of course I will. He can't do anything to me now."

He can to me. Nell carried the last of the dishes to the kitchen, but a knot settled in her stomach as the front door closed. *This is it.*

"Good evening, Uncle Thomas." Alice's voice was upbeat. "Did you have a pleasant afternoon?"

"Very nice, thank you. Are you finished here?"

"Nearly. We'll be tidied up soon enough. Aunty Nell's in the kitchen."

I'd better show my face. She smiled as she joined them. "The weather stayed fine for you."

"It did. The park wasn't too busy, either." He sneered at Leah. "To what do I owe this pleasure?"

Leah's hands shook as she reached for the back of the nearest chair. "I-I've something to tell you."

"Are you ready to apologise?"

She looked across to Nell. "N-no. I-I wanted to tell you that L-Larry, Mr Breton, has asked me to marry him ... and I've said yes."

Mr Marsh's mouth opened and closed several times. "Marry? That's out of the question."

"Y-yes, but ... you see..."

Nell thought Leah was about to collapse and moved to her side to hold her up.

"I-I'm in the family way ... a-and the baby will need a dad."

The room fell silent as the colour drained from Mr Marsh's face. "A baby... You trollop!" He turned to Nell. "And you knew?"

"I-I've not known for long."

"Didn't I tell you they had to be kept apart?" The colour returned to his face until it burned red. "This would never have happened if we'd kept her here."

"That's where you're wrong." Elenor straightened her shoulders. "It happened because you refused to let her out even to see her friends. If you hadn't been so unreasonable, they'd be walking out together like any normal couple."

"How dare you...?"

"I dare because it's the truth."

"You don't know that."

"S-she does." Leah refound her voice. "W-we're going to be together, whether you liked it or not."

"If you think I'll give my permission for an inappropriate marriage, then you're mistaken..."

Elenor interrupted. "So, you'd rather have an illegitimate grandchild than let her marry Mr Breton?"

"The child can be got rid of as soon as it's born ... a husband can't be..."

Elenor gasped. "Get rid?"

"I meant put it up for adoption. Let someone else take care of it."

Nell glared at him. "After everything that happened with Edith, you expect me to put my grandchild through the same thing?"

"It was conceived out of wedlock."

"I don't care." Her voice rose as she left Leah with Alice. "How can you be so heartless?"

"I only want what's best for everyone."

"No, you don't." She stamped her foot. "If you want the best for Leah, you'd agree to the wedding and welcome Mr Breton and their child into the family. You're more interested in what people think of you. Especially Mr Grayson. Is he the one who's wound you up over all this?"

"He doesn't need to. I care about the reputation of this family."

"And I care about the people who are important to me. If you can't accept Leah as she is, then it's time we went our separate ways. For good."

"Separate... For good?" His forehead creased. "You're my wife. You can't leave because you disagree with me."

"It never stops you from running off to sea."

"That's different."

"And you've always said I'm different, so now you'll find out how much."

"You promised to love, honour and obey me, and I forbid you from leaving."

"You try keeping me in this house against my will and you'll never see me again."

"Mr Grayson advised me to tell you I have the law on my side."

"And I have my family. It's a shame you never understood how important they are."

Mr Marsh's eyes flicked to each of them but rested on Alice when she spoke.

"Leah and Aunty Nell are welcome at our house for as long as they want. Billy would never turn them away."

"You may think you've got it all sorted out, but don't expect my blessing or cooperation. I will not allow *her* to marry a Catholic..." He marched to the door but stopped and glared at Nell. "I won't be home until late and I expect you to be here. We're going to talk."

You can expect all you like. "We'll talk once you've calmed down, and not when you've been in the alehouse all evening with Mr Grayson. In the meantime, I'll be with Alice. Write to me when you're ready."

Nell's legs were shaking as Mr Marsh slammed the front door and Elenor led her to a chair as Leah darted to the kitchen with Alice following close behind.

"I'm proud of you, Mam. You did the right thing."

"Are you sure...?" She paused as Leah vomited into the kitchen sink.

"Yes. He needed telling. How could he even think of giving Leah's baby away when it has a mam and dad who'll love it? All for his stupid principles."

"I don't know."

"You'll be better off without him. Will and Mr Breton won't let you starve, and Billy will always look after you."

Nell wiped her eyes as Alice and Leah returned. "We were supposed to grow old together and keep each other company."

Elenor sat with her. "You don't need his company when you have us."

Why did I think I did? "I suppose it was a nice idea while it lasted."

Alice sat at the table. "I made the spare bed up for you. I presume you won't be waiting here for him."

"There's not a chance."

"What will we do, though?" Leah's cheeks were wet with tears. "He still won't give us permission to be married."

Nell sighed. *Will he change his mind if I stay with him? It may be our only option.* "Let me see what he has to say when he calms down."

CHAPTER SIXTY-EIGHT

The leaves had long since left the trees and there were no signs of life in the empty flower borders as Mr Marsh offered Nell his arm. His letter confirming he was ready to talk had been brief, and Nell's reply shorter, but they were both in Princes Park the following Sunday, at the appointed time.

Nell glanced over her shoulder to check Alice and Mr Wood were behind them, but they were so discreet Mr Marsh failed to notice.

"How've you been managing?"

He sniffed the air. "It's not ideal, but Mr and Mrs Grayson have been very generous. I've eaten with them each day."

"So I heard."

"How about you? Have you been comfortable with the Woods and Mr Atkin?"

"I like having company in the house again. I missed it."

"Is Leah still with you?"

"Yes." *Why wouldn't she be?*

"And she's still determined to ruin her life?"

"If you mean, is she still determined to marry Mr Breton and have a family of her own, then yes?"

"You know I can't live with that."

"You've made it perfectly clear."

"Have they made any arrangements for the marriage?"

"They're waiting for your permission before they book anything, but they're having trouble. The vicar at St Thomas's won't marry them, and the one at St John's wants to interview them before he decides."

"Quite right, too. The church shouldn't permit mixed marriages. That would stop them in their tracks."

"There are two other options. The priest at St Patrick's will marry them if Leah agrees to convert..."

"She can't do that!" Mr Marsh stopped in his tracks as his face flashed red.

"It will be the price she has to pay if she wants a church wedding. The priest has suggested he may be more lenient on the age, too, so they wouldn't need your permission."

"He'd override my authority?"

"There's a chance..."

"He should be ashamed of himself, taking advantage like that. That's Catholics for you."

"You can't blame them if our churches are so intolerant..."

"I'd hardly call it intolerance." He paused, his brow furrowed. "What's the other option? You said there were two."

"The register office."

A smile crept across his lips. "A nondescript office away from prying eyes. It sounds the perfect place to stop her being married in a Catholic church, although I doubt it qualifies as a proper wedding."

"Of course it does. They wouldn't be able to conduct services otherwise."

"So, if they married there, there'd be no fancy service or walking down the aisle?"

"I've not been to the place, but I wouldn't think so. It would be as low-key as we could make it assuming we had your permission."

"You know that even if I agreed, I couldn't come to the service."

"You wouldn't give her away?"

"To a Catholic when she's clearly with child?" He snorted. "I'm sorry to disappoint you. No. I'm afraid my time as a family man is over."

"Will you go back to sea?"

"It's for the best." He held her gaze. "We had a few good years, and I'll remember them with fondness, but we're better off apart."

Nell nodded. "I presume you'll let go of the house on Dorrit Street?"

"You don't want to stay there?"

Nell shuddered. "No, thank you. I've hated it since the day we moved in. I'll be glad to see the back of it."

"If you move your belongings out by Friday, I'll tell the landlord. On the rare occasions I'm in Liverpool, I'll stay in a boarding house. Perhaps we could take the occasional walk when I'm here."

"As long as Leah's married by then."

He gave her a wry smile. "Even now there's a catch. If it

makes you happy, I'll sign any relevant paperwork from the register office giving my permission. Nowhere else."

"Thank you."

He stared into the distance. "All this is on the condition that nobody outside the family finds out what's going on."

"What do you mean?"

"You're still my wife and I promised to love and cherish you till death us do part. And I will." His eyes were moist as he gazed at her. "I'd like to continue the illusion that we're living as man and wife. I'll be away at sea for most of the year, which isn't uncommon for men around here, so it shouldn't be difficult to keep up the lie. I'll still give you your housekeeping, too, so we're not abusing Mr Atkin's hospitality."

"Thank you. I can't deny it won't come in handy. How do we explain you staying in the boarding house?"

"I doubt anyone will notice, but if they do, we'll tell them it's due to lack of space in Dombey Street and we'd like some privacy when I'm here."

Nell's eyes widened. "You expect me to stay with you?"

He looked down at her. "Wouldn't that be nice? Unfortunately, I know it would upset you, so we'll only be seen there if it's necessary."

He's thought of everything. "When do you leave?"

"Thursday. Only to New York, though, so if Leah needs any papers signing, I'll do them when I'm back."

"You're away over Christmas?"

"There's no point rushing back to Liverpool. The ship's staying in New York for a week, then we'll start bringing the holidaymakers home." He stopped and took her hands. "To think we could have been there together and left all this behind..."

Mr Marsh walked Nell back to Dombey Street and bid her farewell at the door. She didn't wait for him to disappear before she went inside. She was still in the hall when Alice followed her inside.

"That seemed to go well from where we were watching... Oh, Aunty Nell, what's the matter?"

She wiped her eyes. "It's nothing. I'm just being silly." She blew her nose as Mr Wood shut the front door.

"Was it something he said?"

"In a manner of speaking, but not anything nasty. He was so nice..." Tears continued to run down her face. "Why does he always make me feel guilty?"

Mr Wood shook his head. "I'll never understand women. Why are you crying if he was being nice?"

Alice batted him on the arm. "Be off with you."

"I'm going!"

Alice leaned against the wall as the boys followed their dad into the living room. "Are you all right?"

"I will be. He's going back to sea."

"You said he would. Will you miss him?"

"In some ways. Not the arguments, though." She stopped as Leah joined them.

"What did he say? Will he give his permission for the wedding?"

"He will, on condition it's at the register office. Being married at St Patrick's would be too much."

Her smile was weak. "Thank you. It's more than I could have hoped for."

"You need to set a date. He's going to sea on Thursday, but he'll sign any papers when he's back from New York around the middle of January. The sooner we get it done, the better."

"I'll ask Larry to call in tomorrow and find out what we need to do."

"Ask him to try for a date in the third week of January. I doubt many people get married there, so there shouldn't be much of a wait."

Leah sighed. "I'm sad I won't get a big wedding like Edith."

Nell squeezed her shoulder. "If you love Mr Breton, it won't matter."

CHAPTER SIXTY-NINE

Nell sat up straight in the wooden chair opposite a closed mahogany door. Alice, Elenor and Edith sat to her left on one side of the corridor, while Mr Wood, Mr Massey and Mr Lacy sat facing them. The groom's family were further down the corridor. *What a strange way to get married.*

The polished wooden floors did nothing to stop the sound of footsteps echoing around the corridor as Leah arrived on Billy's arm. Her smile brightened her entire face, and Nell hoped it would distract people from her rotund midriff that was insufficiently hidden beneath the silver-grey dress Rebecca had made for her. Nell was on her feet before they reached her.

"We've not gone in yet."

Billy checked his watch. "It's all right. We're a few minutes early."

"But Mr Breton will see her."

Leah rested a hand on Nell's arm. "Stop worrying. It doesn't matter so much here."

"Well, it should. It's not right." She turned as the office door opened and a couple, followed by several guests, filed out.

"We should be next."

Once the last of the previous guests had departed, a man in a dark suit stood in the doorway.

"The marriage of Breton and Riley, please."

Nell hovered nearby as the groom's family filed past her and when given her cue, she followed them into the small wood-panelled room and took a seat on the front row. *It's a good job we didn't invite everyone, they wouldn't have fit.*

The registrar stood adjacent to her facing the door and as soon as everyone was seated, Billy led Leah into the room where they took the few steps needed to reach Mr Breton.

No music, no flowers, no laughter... Certainly no champagne. Not that it would ever have been as grand as Ollie's marriage, whoever she'd married.

The registrar cleared his throat before reading from his service sheet. Fifteen minutes later, he pronounced them man and wife.

Is that it? As quick as that... Why was there such a long wait for a date if they can marry three couples in an hour?

Once Leah and Mr Breton had signed the register, Nell turned to Alice, who was on her left.

"We'll be home early at this rate."

"I must admit, Mam wouldn't have liked it. Not even a hymn..."

"No, she wouldn't, but I suppose the world is changing..."

An usher interrupted her when he indicated to the door. "If you wouldn't mind leaving quickly, there's another service in five minutes."

"Yes, of course." Nell waited for the other guests to leave and followed Mr and Mrs Breton from the room. Once they were back in the corridor, Mr Breton turned to her.

"Mrs Marsh."

Nell smiled. "Good morning. It's nice to meet you."

"I'd hoped to meet your husband and find out why he allowed his daughter to disgrace herself..."

"I'm afraid he's away at the moment. He's a ship's steward..."

"That explains a lot. No discipline around the home. Her and Larry should be in confession every day from now until the child is born."

"Erm ... Leah won't be turning..."

Mr Breton glared down at her. "She'll do what her husband tells her and be glad to pay some penance."

Nell took a breath. "Is that why you insisted they move in next door to you? So you can tell your son how to treat his wife?"

Mrs Breton tittered. "Oh, Larry won't need telling, he knows how to behave. No, we wanted them next door so we can be sure the child gets a good Catholic upbringing. I'm sure you understand your daughter will need help as far as that's concerned."

Nell gawked at them. *That's what you think.* "If you'll excuse me, I need to get back to the house. I'm expecting guests."

Mrs Breton lifted her nose in the air. "I'm afraid we won't be able to stay for long."

"Never mind, I'm sure we'll manage without you."

. . .

Betty and Jane were waiting for them at the house and had the food laid out on the table. Nell ran an eye over it.

"Thank you for helping."

Betty grinned. "It's the least we could do. It's a lot easier than looking after Charlie and two toddlers. I felt guilty leaving them with Betsy, but she was adamant she could manage."

"Make the most of it, then."

"Oh, we will." Jane's eyes settled on Leah as she spoke to the guests. "Was it a nice service?"

"It was different. Similar to a church service, but no mention of God, no prayers, no hymns."

"How can that even be legal if they don't mention God?"

Nell shrugged. "Don't ask me, but apparently it is. You were fortunate you were married in church."

"Or unfortunate, depending on how you look at it. It was the incident in church with Maria that hastened my move to Ireland." Jane continued to watch Leah. "Does she know what she's let herself in for?"

"I don't think so, but there was no talking to her."

"What about the children? How will they bring them up?"

"That's a battle for another day. I met Mrs Breton at the wedding, and she seems to think they'll be brought up Catholic. She's going to be in for a shock."

"When's she due?"

Nell's mouth fell open.

"Don't act so surprised. She keeps resting a hand on her belly."

"Please, not a word. Not everyone's as observant as you."

"You can trust me. I'd say she's still a little while left."

"Until May."

"Not as long as you'd have liked, then..." Jane stopped when Sarah arrived.

"I'm sorry I'm late. I didn't expect the bride and groom to be here yet."

Nell sighed. "That's what you get for being married in a register office. There's no fuss."

"A bit like the wedding breakfast. You've not invited many."

"No, well, we wanted to keep it low-key. Under the circumstances. Mixed marriages aren't for everyone."

"I see Mr Marsh couldn't even make it. Whoever heard of the bride's father not being at her wedding?"

"He's not her father, Jack was, and it was one of those things with his roster. We couldn't get the availability of the register office to coincide with his shore leave."

"It's strange to me that he's gone back to sea at all."

Nell glared at her. *Do you ever stop?* "He enjoys the work, that's why."

"Tom would never have left me like that."

"He was in the alehouse all the time, that's why." Nell rolled her eyes at Jane but took a step backwards as Edith walked past. "Will you excuse me?" She caught hold of Edith's arm as she approached the kitchen. "I've not had chance to tell you, but I'm so glad you're here. Leah is, too."

"She told me. I'm sorry I've not visited sooner. Ernest's always busy."

"I'd often hoped it was because you were in the family way and couldn't travel..."

"I'm afraid not. I've not given up hope yet, though. How've you been?"

"It's been an interesting few months, but we've got through them."

"Are you sure? Elenor told me about Uncle Thomas."

Nell sighed. "It was for the best. If I'm being honest, I should never have married him. I like my independence too much."

"I know what you mean, but we need someone to keep a roof over our heads and we don't all have a Billy."

Nell cocked her head to one side. "Are you having trouble with Mr Lacy?"

"Not really, but he likes to make all the decisions and, well, I suppose I'm more like you than I'd care to admit."

"You know where we are if you ever need us."

"I do, thank you." Edith glanced around. "I'm looking for Vernon and Lydia. Have you seen them?"

"Are they even here yet? I know Lydia was struggling to find someone to have the younger children."

"It wouldn't usually stop Vernon from joining us. Perhaps he's late because you didn't invite him to the marriage service. I heard he was put out that Billy and Alice were there and he wasn't."

"I heard that, too, but you saw the size of the room they were married in. If we'd invited everyone we wanted, they'd have been standing in the corridor."

Edith laughed. "I'll tell him if he's still sulking." She nodded to Rebecca, who was heading towards them. "I'll speak to you later."

"How was it then?" Rebecca's eyes shone.

"As good as can be expected. Is Mr Grayson with you?"

"When his friend's not here? What do you think?"

Nell snickered. "That's why you're so cheery, then. What about the girls?"

"They're here somewhere, with Elenor and the children." Rebecca sighed. "To think I was the one who wanted to be a granny the most and yet neither of them are showing any interest. It serves me right for wishing my life away."

"Nonsense. Florrie's still only twenty. In an ideal world, Leah wouldn't be getting married today. I'm sure you wouldn't swap."

Rebecca shuddered. "I wouldn't. I doubt I'd get rid of Hugh as easily as you did with Mr Marsh, either."

"I'd say that's a certainty. I'm sure we could find room for you here, though, if you ever needed it."

"As much as Hugh annoys me, I hope that isn't necessary."

"As long as he doesn't take you away from Toxteth again."

"I don't think he'd dare, but if you could hint occasionally that Mr Marsh may settle down again, it wouldn't do any harm."

"There's not a chance of that. Thomas may catch wind of it..." Nell chuckled but stepped to one side as Alice joined them.

"It's nice to see you enjoying yourselves."

"It's relief that we've got her married and she's happy." She looked over to the table. "I didn't even get a sherry. Would you both like one?"

"Before we do, I want to show you this." Alice waved an envelope in the air. "The postman's just brought it."

Nell gasped. "From James. He couldn't have known about today when he wrote. What does he say?"

Alice bounced on the spot. "He's coming home! He should be leaving Brazil in the next week and he'll be here in May."

"That's wonderful. Let me get those sherries." She handed out two glasses before she picked up her own and raised it in the air. "To James. Let's hope it's not another five years before he visits again."

The three of them clicked their glasses. "To James."

Rebecca took a sip of hers. "Has he really not been home since Maria passed?"

"No. We had hoped we'd see more of him once George had gone, but..." She shrugged. "We can't dwell on that now. He'll be here soon enough."

The food had long since gone by the time Nell waved off Jane and Rebecca and she returned to the living room and flopped into a chair opposite Alice.

"That went better than I expected."

"It was lovely. Leah was quite overwhelmed when Billy read out the cards."

"I've not seen much of her since. Where is she now?"

"In the front room with Mr Breton."

"I'd have thought they'd want to go back to their own house now they can. Not that I'm happy about her living on Sussex Street."

"She was telling me earlier in the week that they won't stay there long. It's only to keep Mrs Breton quiet."

Nell shook her head. "She still thinks it will be easy. Your mam would be apoplectic."

"Uncle Thomas won't be too pleased when he finds out, either."

"I won't be telling him." She glanced around the room. "Did Edith go with Elenor?"

"She did, but she said she'd be round in the morning for a cup of tea."

Nell rested her head on the back of the chair. "They're all lovely girls, despite ... you know. I wish Jack was here to see them."

"He'll be looking down on them." Alice smiled as Leah and Mr Breton joined them. "Have you had a nice day?"

"It's been the best." She grinned at Nell. "Thank you, Mam. It wouldn't have happened without you."

Tears welled in Nell's eyes. "If you have a daughter of your own, you'll understand that you'll do anything for her."

"We hope we do. We've decided that if we have a little girl, we're going to name her Nellie after you. I can see her already..."

EPILOGUE

Twelve years later
12th April, 1912

T he front room of their house on Upper Warwick Street was one of Nell's favourite places to sit in the afternoon. The road was wide enough to see the sky above the houses opposite, and until about four o'clock, clouds permitting, sunlight filled the room. The weather had been kind today, but now the sun had disappeared, it was time to move.

She struggled to push herself up and dropped back into her seat as Leah joined her. "Have you had a nice doze?"

"I've done nothing of the sort. I read Alice's letter and was watching the world go by while I thought about my reply. I was glad to read she has Edith's boy staying with her again."

"We should suggest she brings him to visit. Was that going to be part of your reply?"

"I hadn't got to that bit. I was wondering if Mr Lacy would let her." Nell's eyes narrowed. "It's been too long since I saw him. Mr Lacy has no right to keep him from us."

"Sadly, he does, and that's the problem. At least Alice is in Sheffield now, so she'll tell him about us. She's got the photographs we sent her, too."

Nell smiled. "He'll like that. It's about time they sent one of him."

"Alice has promised she will." Leah offered her an arm. "Now you've finished daydreaming, are you coming into the other room? Larry and Billy will be home soon."

"What about the girls? Have you called them in?"

"You can't have been watching the world that closely! I sent Nellie out to get them. Didn't you notice her passing the window?"

"I didn't realise she was going for the others." She let Leah help her from her seat. "She's been a good help to you while she's been off school. You'll miss her when she goes back."

"It's only for another term, then she'll be here all the time. She helped me make the tea tonight, so I hope you like it."

Nell patted her hand. "I always do."

The walk to the living room was slow and Nell paused for breath as she reached her chair by the fire. "This confounded heart. I never used to struggle like that."

"You do very well. Now, sit there and I'll pour you a cup of tea."

She'd just got comfortable when the front door opened and Billy arrived.

"Evening, Aunty Nell."

"Good evening. Are you on your own?"

"Larry won't be a minute. He met the girls in the street, and they slowed him down." He unrolled a newspaper he'd brought in under his arm. "It will give me time to show you this. One of the lads in work bought it yesterday, and I asked if I could have it once he was finished with it."

"What is it?"

"Give me a minute." He turned through the pages until he found the one he wanted. "This." He folded it in half and pointed to a large photograph of a passenger liner. "What do you think of that? White Star's new ship."

"Gracious me. The *Titanic*! I've heard you talk about it but look at the size of it. Four funnels, too."

"It will keep the firemen busy."

"It certainly will. They'll be hot shovelling all that coal, too. I only went down to the hull of my ships a few times, but I couldn't stay there for more than ten minutes. There are no sails on the *Titanic* either, so it will rely on the furnaces."

"I hope they pay them well then."

Nell studied the other photographs. "Have you seen this? How glamorous to have a café like that on a ship. It's better than the tea rooms around here. It's a shame Uncle Thomas didn't live to see it. He would have loved it."

"There's more, too." Billy took the paper from her and turned to another page before handing it back.

She scanned the text. "One thousand four hundred passengers. Good grief. How many stewards and stewardesses must they need?" She returned to the page of pictures. "How I'd love to go on board."

"Are you sure? Read this." He flicked back to the text. "It nearly had an accident when it was leaving Southampton."

"My, my. The pull from the ship was too strong for the ships docked nearby. She shook her head. "They won't let that happen again. Not that it would have happened at all if it had sailed from Liverpool. I don't know what they were thinking, sending it to Southampton."

"Either way, I'm glad it didn't sail thirty years ago when you were at sea. Mam was always worried sick about you as it was, without something like that happening."

"She never did herself any good worrying." She looked up as her granddaughters joined her and Nellie peered at the newspaper.

"What are you doing?"

She flicked back to the photographs and turned the page to show them. "Granny used to work on a ship like that. Not as big, we only had one funnel, but we used to sail all the way to America."

The middle child, Alice, gasped. "You worked on a ship?"

"It was a long time ago. Your mam was only little, like Leah is now." She ran a hand over her youngest granddaughter's hair.

"I wouldn't like Mam to go away."

"No. Your Aunty Elenor never liked it, either. I must write and tell her to keep an eye out for the pictures." *She may be interested after all this time.* Nell lifted her head to Billy. "Thank you for bringing this. May I keep it, or do you need to give it back?"

"It's all yours."

A smile brightened her face. "Tell your friend he's very kind. I'd like to spend longer reading about it. It's brought back so many memories..."

"Before you hide it away, may I see?" Larry leaned over and took the newspaper from her. "Gracious. What a shame it didn't come to Liverpool."

"Maybe it will once it's back from New York. I'm sure everyone around here would love to see it." Nell looked up at Billy. "If it does come here, will you take me to see it?"

"Of course, I will. Anything for you, Aunty Nell."

AUTHOR'S NOTE AND ACKNOWLEDGEMENTS

So, there we have it! I hope you enjoyed the story.

The storylines in this book were not originally part of my plans when I started the series, but when I looked more closely at the dates of birth of Nell's grandchildren in relation to when Elenor and Leah were married, I realised they needed to be included.

I remember within my lifetime, having a child outside wedlock often brought disgrace to the family, so I imagine that one hundred and twenty years ago, it would have been one of the worst things a daughter could do. For Nell to have both daughters six months pregnant at the times of their marriages seemed incredible and must have put a terrible strain on the family.

As told in the book, Elenor's first baby was born five months after her seventeenth birthday, so she would have only been sixteen when she became pregnant. To get an idea of what that would have been like in the late Victorian-era, I read some true-life accounts from the time. It appears that many mothers as well as fathers had little sympathy with their daughters. The social and economic values of the time encouraged the ostracism of women to make them an example to other women. Many were forced to leave their homes in disgrace and move to an area where they were not known. Keeping a roof over their heads became impossible unless they were taken in by someone they knew, as any employment would have been terminated as soon as the pregnancy became obvious. To add to their shame, they may have been forced to turn to mother and baby sanctuaries. Things didn't get any easier once the baby was born, and many would give their children away (sometimes to baby farmers) so they could find work and regain their reputation as virtuous women. On top of everything else, they may never have been accepted at home again.

In the story, I mentioned some pills Elenor read about in the newspaper. They were essentially herbal abortifacients that were sold by chemists to desperate women. They were not only used by single women but often by married women who felt they couldn't manage with any more children. There are also stories of women forcing their daughters to take them if they found out they were expecting an illegitimate child in the hope of sparing the shame on the family. The text Nell read from the newspaper advertising these tablets ("Banner's patent female pills... Reliable to bring about all that is required.") was taken directly from an 1895 English newspaper. The language was coded so women understood the meaning, while it meant nothing to men.

All the above is why, in the book, Mr Marsh's reaction to Elenor's news was so hostile. As a man who, I presume, had little previous interaction with children, certainly not teenage girls, it would have been difficult for him to accept. If he ever did.

The situation may have been bad for Elenor, but I decided it was probably worse for Leah. She was twenty at the time the baby was born, but this wouldn't have made much difference to the notion that she was a 'fallen woman'. The thing that in all likelihood made it worse was that the father of the child was Catholic. I hint in the series about the sectarian troubles in Liverpool, and these were very real. The troubles started in Ireland and as they became more hostile, many Irish emigrated to Liverpool, bringing their beliefs with them. Again, in my lifetime, I remember there was a distinct divide in Liverpool based on these religious views.

Did it really cause the breakup of Nell and Thomas's marriage?

I don't know for certain whether Leah's marriage led to Nell and Thomas going their separate ways, but in the 1901 census, shortly after the end of the main story, Nell was recorded as a visitor to Dombey Street, staying with Billy, Alice and her family, and Leah, Larry and their baby daughter. Mr Marsh is not with her. By the 1911 census, she was still with Leah and her family, and Billy, but by then she lived with them, rather than being a visitor. She was also a widow.

I know from the census in 1891 that, following his marriage to Nell, Thomas took a job as a clerk, but after that, I can find no records for him. Most crucially, I can't find a death certificate. I wondered if that meant he died abroad, possibly while he was at sea. This was the thought process I followed in the book and made me suggest that unlike most women of the time, Nell did actually leave him – or he left her.

Was Nell to blame?

As Nell had two daughters considered 'fallen women', as well as [potentially] an estranged husband, it made me wonder if any of it resulted from Nell's absence while Elenor and Leah were growing up. Perhaps the characters of Maria and Mr Marsh were right when they said that she was too lax with them. Was it because she felt guilty about leaving them, or was it just a lack of discipline because Jack wasn't there and Nell didn't marry soon enough to give them a father figure until it was too late? Was it because she remarried but Mr Marsh treated the girls badly enough for them to want to leave?

Whatever the reason, I'll never know, but I'm sure accusations about her being a bad mother must have been hurled at her.

Despite that, I believe she stayed very close to Leah. Throughout the series, I suggested Leah was her favoured daughter. This was because Nell was visiting Leah in 1901 and living with her in 1911. In addition, when Nell died, she made Leah an executor to her will. Did this show the closeness of their relationship?

Elenor, on the other hand, was different. I portrayed her as more difficult because I knew that by the end of the book she had moved away from Liverpool to a place called Preston, which is about forty miles to the north. She was also not an executor to her mother's will. Was this a sign of a rift between them? I wondered if the distance could have been a factor, but I suspect not. The other person named as executor was Alice, but by 1911 she had also moved away, and lived in Sheffield, a place less accessible to Liverpool than Preston.

What happened to everyone else?

As I mentioned in the back of the last book, I know very little about Edith's life. I only found three documents for her. The first was her baptism record that showed she was the eldest daughter of Nell and Jack. The second was the census record of 1891 where she had moved to Wales with Alice and Mr Wood, and the last was her marriage certificate. There is no mention of her on any census after 1891, and no baptism certificates for any children. As hinted at in the book, however, in 1911, a child with the same surname as Edith and her husband is recorded as a visitor with Alice. Was this Edith's son? And was it the only child she gave birth to? Did she survive the birth? I can't say with any certainty, and so I left the end of her story rather ambiguous.

Betty continued to spend most of her life pregnant and by the time of the 1911 census, she had six living children and four others who had died. How terribly sad that must have been.

As far as Maria's sons are concerned, Vernon remained in Toxteth, and by 1911 had eight living children.

Billy stayed single and was the head of the house when Nell and Leah lived with him in 1911.

I don't know what happened to James. It's true that he worked as a steward on ships to Brazil, but once he'd taken that role, there are no further records for him. For the purposes of the story, I decided he stayed in Brazil, although I can't confirm that.

Finally, Nell...

I'm sure it won't come as a surprise that Nell never got to see the *Titanic*. Three days after the epilogue, where she read the news of its launch, the ship hit an iceberg on its way to New York and sank. Not that she would have seen it even if it had come back to the UK. Six weeks after the end of the book, she died at home, with Leah at her side. She was buried in a family grave with Maria and George.

In answer to Nell's question in the epilogue about the number of stewards and stewardesses on the Titanic, I found some detailed reports that say there were 272 stewards and 20 stewardesses (including one matron). That's obviously a lot more women than Nell was used to working with, but it still means that less than 10 per cent of the stewarding staff were women.

If you'd like to know more about life in Victorian-era England, including women's rights, and baby farming, you can visit my website here:

https://www.valmcbeath.com/victorian-era-england-1837-1901/

Thanks...

As ever, thanks, must go to my husband Stuart and friend Rachel for their feedback on the early drafts of the books. I'd also like to thank my editor, Susan Cunningham, for her excellent work and my team of advanced readers for final comments before the book was published.

Finally, thank you to you for reading! None of this would have been possible without your support.

Best wishes

Val

WHAT NEXT?

At the time of writing, I don't have any plans for another family saga, but if you haven't yet read them, you may like the books in The *Ambition and Destiny* Series.

Set in and around Birmingham and Handsworth (UK), this series is a compelling story of one family's trials, tragedies and triumphs as they seek their fortune in Victorian-era England. For more information, visit my website here:

https://www.valmcbeath.com/books/the-ambition-destiny-series/

Alternatively, if you like murder mysteries, you may enjoy *Eliza Thomson Investigates*, a Miss Marple-style murder mystery series set in Edwardian-era England and featuring a woman sleuth with attitude. Further details can be found here:

https://www.valmcbeath.com/books/eliza-thomson-investigates/

Both series have FREE introductory novellas. If you'd like to get your copies, visit: **www.vlmcbeath.com**

If you're signed up to my newsletter, you'll be the first to hear when I have a new project. If not, you can sign up here:

https://www.subscribepage.com/fsorganictdd

ALSO BY VL MCBEATH

The *Windsor Street Family Saga*

The full series:

Part 1: *The Sailor's Promise*

(*an introductory novella*)

Part 2: *The Wife's Dilemma*

Part 3: *The Stewardess's Journey*

Part 4: *The Captain's Order*

Part 5: *The Companion's Secret*

Part 6: *The Mother's Confession*

Part 7: *The Daughter's Defiance*

The *Ambition & Destiny* Series

The full series:

Short Story Prequel: *Condemned by Fate*

Part 1: *Hooks & Eyes*

Part 2: *Less Than Equals*

Part 3: *When Time Runs Out*

Part 4: *Only One Winner*

Part 5: *Different World*

A standalone novel: *The Young Widow*

Eliza Thomson Investigates

A Deadly Tonic (A Novella)

Murder in Moreton

Death of an Honourable Gent

Dying for a Garden Party

A Scottish Fling

The Palace Murder

Death by the Sea

A Christmas Murder

To find out more about visit VL McBeath's website at:

https://www.valmcbeath.com/

ABOUT THE AUTHOR

Val started researching her family tree back in 2008. At that time, she had no idea what she would find or where it would lead. By 2010, she had discovered a story so compelling she was inspired to turn it into a novel.

This first foray into writing turned into The *Ambition & Destiny* Series. A story of the trials, tragedies, and triumphs of some of her ancestors as they sought their fortune in Victorian-era England.

By the time the series was complete, Val had developed a taste for writing and turned her hand to writing Agatha Christie style mysteries. These novels form part of the *Eliza Thomson Investigates* series and currently consists of five standalone books and two novella's.

Although writing the mysteries was great fun, the pull of researching other branches of the family was strong and Val continued to look for other stories worth telling.

Back in 2018, she discovered a previously unknown fact about one of her great, great grandmothers, Nell. *The Windsor Street Family Saga* is a fictitious account of that discovery. Further details of all series can be found on Val's website at: www.vlmcbeath.com.

Prior to writing, Val trained as a scientist and has worked in the pharmaceutical industry for many years. In 2012, she set up her own consultancy business, and currently splits her time between business and writing.

Born and raised in Liverpool (UK), Val now lives in Cheshire with her husband, Stuart. She has two daughters, the younger of which, Sarah, now helps with the publishing side of the business.

In addition to family history, her interests include rock music and Liverpool Football Club.

FOLLOW ME

at:

Website:

https://valmcbeath.com

Facebook:

https://www.facebook.com/VLMcBeath

BookBub:

https://www.bookbub.com/authors/vl-mcbeath

Printed in Great Britain
by Amazon

32791739R00310